I0564079

More books available by Alice Coldbreath:

The Vawdrey Brothers Series:
Book 1: Her Baseborn Bridegroom
Book 2: His Forsaken Bride
Book 3: An Ill-Made Match

The Brides of Karadok Series:
Book 1: Wed By Proxy
Book 2: The Unlovely Bride
Book 3: The Consolation Prize
Book 4: Her Bridegroom, Bought and Paid For
Book 5: An Inconvenient Vow
Book 6: The Favourite

The Victorian Prizefighter Series:
Book 1: A Bride for the Prizefighter
Book 2: A Substitute Wife for the Prizefighter
Book 3: A Contracted Spouse for the Prizefighter

I would like to dedicate this book to Marliese. Thank you for encouraging me and always looking forward to the next book!

~ Alice

1

No sooner had Theodora shut the door to their dressing room behind them than she turned excitedly to her sister. "Who *are* they? Did you see them? You must have, for it was the only full box in the house."

Henrietta cast aside her shepherdess crook and bouquet of roses. "Heaven only knows," she answered wearily. "I am just glad that Matthew was not here to see the scant respect they showed our craft. They talked all the way through the second act. Help me out of this, will you?" She turned her back pointedly.

Hurrying to her sister's side, Theo started unlacing Hetty out of her elaborate shepherdess costume. "One of them was smoking," she rambled on, unabated. "Did you notice? Yet no one sent Vincent up to sort them out," she said, naming their formidable doorman. "They must be backers or sponsors or something of that nature or Felix would surely have had them thrown out on their ears."

Her sister scoffed. "More than likely Felix did not send Vincent up for fear of starting a brawl," she said dryly. "They were *not* respectable folk, for all they are dressed up in their Sunday best. A couple of them had broken noses to rival Vincent's own."

Theo was just reflecting this was likely true, for there had been a disreputable air about the group, though they clearly had money in their pockets. A certain brashness you could not mistake. A knock on the door interrupted her ruminations. "It's Lil," she said, recognizing the pattern and flinging open the door before Henrietta could object. For some reason, her sister did not approve of the older actress of late, whereas Theo adored her.

"Did you see them? In the grand circle?" Lil demanded as she shut the door behind her. Off stage the powder and paint she

1

loaded onto her face made her look every minute of her fifty or so years. Under the stage lights, however, she could still pass for considerably younger, maybe thirty on a good day.

"We did," Theo confirmed as Henrietta whisked away tight-lipped to the back of the room. "Do you know who they are, Lil?"

"Lord love you, 'course I do! That's what I've come to tell you." Lil glanced around as though checking for eavesdroppers, despite the fact the sisters had never had their own personal dresser.

Theo started untying the blue silk sash at her waist.

"Don't undress yet, ducky," Lil said, staying her hand. "Your brother's about to send for you if I'm not mistaken."

"Really? But Hetty has already started changing—"

"I am not meeting anyone off stage rigged out in this hideous costume," her sister cut in smoothly. "I don't care if it's the Prince of Wales himself."

Lil snorted. "No such luck. Bet your brother would love to stick a 'royal' in front of the theater's name."

"Not just Felix," Theo admitted. "I would love that too. Hetty and I own shares as much as Felix. Just imagine, The Royal Parthenon." She glanced across at her sister. "It has a ring to it, you will admit."

Henrietta shrugged a pale shoulder as she stepped out of her hooped skirts. Not for the first time, Theo reflected that her sister showed but a scant interest in the family business these days. Her head seemed filled only with thoughts of the honorable Matthew Hillingdon, her current admirer. Theo frowned. In her estimation, her sister could surely prioritize both her suitor and the theater at the same time. One was her livelihood after all.

"Have you ever heard of The Eagle and Sun concert rooms in Shoreditch?" Lil continued, leaning a hip against their dressing table.

2

"Shoreditch?" Hetty repeated with a curl of her lip. "Certainly not."

Lil sniffed. "They perform to a packed house from Thursday to Sunday, two shows a day, matinee and evening performance."

"A full house? At each performance?" Theo asked, startled. They had not had such a thing at The Parthenon in years.

"S'right," Lil affirmed with a nod of her head. "I know someone what knows someone who's on his books. Says he runs a neat operation and no mistake. Started out eighteen months ago with a supper and song outfit. Nine months later he had his own premises. Now he's looking for a theater."

A knock on the door interrupted them, just as Theo fastened the last of her sister's pearl buttons. Vincent's rather large, broad face poked around the door. "Miss Henrietta, Miss Theodora, yer bruvver wants to see you both in the auditorium," he growled, his eyes flying to Henrietta first as they always did before lowering respectfully.

"What about me, Vinnie love?" Lil piped up.

"He never mentioned you, Lil."

Lil's shoulders drooped a moment before she squared them bravely. "I reckon I'll come along and all," she announced, and the four of them duly trooped out of the dressing room and along the winding corridors until they came out into the auditorium.

Theo glanced about with her usual pride at the sumptuous décor of The Parthenon's pillars, frescoes, and fancy moldings. In the subdued gaslight you could not see that the velvet curtains were looking worn, and the gilt paint needed more than just a touch-up.

Theo's heart swelled as it always did. Peg Woffington, the famous Irish actress, had appeared on stage on this very site. True, it had been an earlier incarnation of the theater they stood in today, one that had burned down in the eighteenth century,

3

but all the same, such facts added to The Parthenon's rich history.

"Ah, here they are," she heard her brother comment before he threw a quick frown her way. She glanced down at her silk breeches and frilly shirt. Sometimes Felix could be surprisingly stuffy. "Mr. Dabney, allow me to introduce you to my sisters, Henrietta and Theodora Fields," he said, ignoring Lil's presence altogether. Theo looked over the large male stood next to her brother with interest. He was not looking at her, of course, but at Henrietta.

Theo did not resent this. Henrietta was so very lovely that people were usually much struck on their first meeting with her, and often second and third. Instead of resenting his keen appreciation of her sister's looks, Theo took the opportunity to size Dabney up.

His suit must have been custom made for him, she decided, for his shoulders and chest were far broader than the average gentleman, and he was tall too, at least six foot two, and towered above Felix and almost everyone else milling about.

He was good looking, extremely good looking, with hazel eyes, black brows, and full lips. These features distracted you from noticing a certain coarseness which, on second examination, prevented him from any claim to classical good looks. His neck was too thick, his face too tanned, and his lazy smile too crooked for conventional tastes. On top of this, his nose had clearly been broken at some point.

Felix cleared his throat. "Mr. Clem Dabney has recently joined the ranks of our profession, opening a little concert room establishment," he said patronizingly, and Theo saw at once that her brother did not like Dabney and felt uneasy in his company. By the flicker in Clem Dabney's eye, Theo deduced he also had not appreciated Felix's insinuation that he was a mere novice to the business, but he looked affability itself as he gave a lazy grin and removed the cigar from his mouth.

4

"I'm charmed, ladies," he said, extending his hand to Henrietta and gazing intently at her sister as she murmured back some greeting, eyes demurely lowered.

Theo cleared her throat. "I am also happy to make your acquaintance, Mr. Dabney," she said loudly, for it was clear he had forgotten all about her. He turned to her at once and shook her hand, though his eyes skated over her, clearly dismissing her in almost the same instant as undeserving of his notice.

Theo almost rolled her eyes. "And this is our colleague, Mrs. Lillian Longdon," she said pointedly, for clearly, her brother had no intention of introducing Lil. Clem threw the older woman the most cursory of glances before nodding his head. "She played the shepherdess Amaryllis," Theo added. "How did you find our little play?"

Dabney's eyebrows rose a moment as though her persistence surprised him. "Quite honestly? A little highbrow for me," he admitted. "I confess I'm a simple man with simple tastes. Magic fountains and satyrs are a bit beyond my ken."

One of the pretty ladies in his company tittered and another shoved playfully at his arm in mock reproach. "Go on with you!" she tutted. "You are ungallant to Miss Fields," she cooed and shot a challenging look at Henrietta, who was smoothing her skirts and not paying either of them the slightest attention.

Theo deduced the beauty must be an established actress already in Dabney's outfit. Likely she was keen to prove her own superiority to a perceived rival. Theo thought it telling that Dabney had not bothered to introduce the pretty blonde who was clearly disappointed that Henrietta would not be baited.

Instead, her sister sent the actress an absent smile, so sweet and pitying that Theo almost applauded, for she could see how it set the other's teeth on edge. She tried not to take it personally that her own presence they barely acknowledged.

"It is a pastoral tragicomedy," Felix responded rather stiffly. "Such features are staples of the genre."

5

Clem shrugged and spread his hands wide. "I'm sure they are, and I meant no offense, Mr. Fields," he answered smoothly, and Theo almost snorted, for she could tell Mr. Dabney was not remotely abashed by his "confession." Indeed, the way he delivered it sounded almost like a brag. Clearly, he had no shame admitting he was culturally a philistine.

"I am sure you know your business," Dabney concluded and cast an unhurried eye over the rows and rows of empty seats. Theo saw her brother flush and wondered where Dabney had learned to give such offense in such a guileless manner.

Wherever it might have been, there was an air of brash assurance about Clem Dabney that stuck in your craw. His tweed suit was a shade too loud, though the cut was good. The pattern was too bold to be genteel and the colors jarring. He made little attempt, she thought, to pass for a gentleman born and bred.

Dabney's tie pin, in the shape of a large glittering horseshoe, was decidedly vulgar, and she found herself wondering about his background. He must be getting on for thirty. How had he wound up running a supper and song outfit? His background was surely not theatrical.

"Big handsome brute, ain't he?" Lil murmured in her ear as the conversation drifted away from them. Clem had reclaimed Henrietta's attention once again, and Felix was attempting politely to extricate himself from the pretty blonde actress who had managed to wangle her introduction after all.

Theo shrugged. "He is not quite as brutish as Vincent," she pointed out.

"Vincent! I should say not! He's a sight prettier than Vincent, my dear, and from what I hear," Lil leered, "a good deal more successful with the ladies. Quite the lady-killer is Mr. Dabney by all accounts."

"I'm afraid he does not tickle my fancy," Theo murmured, and Lil let out a chuckle.

6

"Go on with you," she said slyly, poking Theo in the side.

"He doesn't," Theo insisted, thinking instead of Harold Allsop's sensitive profile as he bent over his piano keys. Harold had such a noble brow.

"You'll catch cold thinking of that musician of yours," Lil commented sadly, and Theo felt herself turn red at the accuracy with which her friend read her thoughts.

"Who said I am thinking of Mr. Allsop?" she asked, pulling absently on the ribbons of her shirt.

"You're always thinking of him, more's the pity," Lil sighed. "No, don't bother denying it," Lil said, cutting her off as Theo opened her mouth. "Lord, I've known this past year you're sweet on him, but he's a lost cause, my dear, and you need to wake up to the fact."

"We are just friends!" Theo hissed, glancing about to make sure no one was paying them any heed. Fat chance of that, she realized wryly, seeing how Mr. Dabney had her sister cornered and Felix was attempting to pry pink tinted talons from his coat sleeve. "I had better go and rescue Hetty."

Lil nodded, and Theo sailed across to her sister's side. To her surprise, instead of looking grateful for her intervention, Hetty gave a guilty start and hurried to tuck what looked like a small business card into her sleeve.

"As I said, Mr. Dabney," her sister said aloud, "we are not looking to join another company. In fact, I will soon be leaving the stage on the event of my marriage, and I doubt you can interest anyone else from my brother's ensemble to abandon The Parthenon for your own repertoire."

Marriage? Theo gave a start. She had not realized things were quite so advanced along with Hillingdon's courtship. Had a date been named?

"A pity," Dabney responded smoothly. Too smoothly. Theo looked from one to the other with the oddest feeling they were covering up the true nature of their conversation. For one

7

wild moment she even considered that Henrietta might have agreed to jump ship for Dabney's music hall outfit. *Ridiculous*. That was even less likely than Hetty falling victim to Dabney's dubious charms.

"*I* am not retiring," she stated boldly, but her announcement was met with pointed silence.

Clem Dabney cleared his throat. "I am afraid no one else here caught my eye," he had the nerve to respond blandly after an awkward pause.

Theo met his hazel gaze head on and felt a jolt of annoyance down her spine. The man was insufferably rude. "Really?" she heard herself ask, and she was pleased to hear her voice sounded calm and collected instead of mortally offended.

"Lily Longdon's voice is very fine indeed," she pointed out with perfect truth. "She is quite the finest soprano in London. If you did not recognize that then I am afraid that I cannot think very highly of your discernment or judgment in this business, Mr. Dabney."

That did earn his full attention, though he looked dubious. "I have heard several claimants to that particular title, present company included," he said, his eyes flickering briefly for a moment to Henrietta.

"My sister has a pretty voice," Theo acknowledged coolly. "But it has neither the purity nor the training of Mrs. Longdon's."

Henrietta smiled graciously. "I have never claimed it did. I am a conventional creature and will retire from the boards as soon as I am married."

Dabney acknowledged this with a shrug. "A shame," he said. "As I'm sure you're aware, it's not always the greatest singer that draws the biggest crowd."

He was talking about looks, of course. At fifty-three, no amount of powder and paint could disguise the fact Lil was long past the first flush of youth. Always, Theo thought with faint bitterness, it came down to attractiveness with women.

Her gaze traveled over Mr. Dabney's shoulder to look at his motley company of players. A rotund gentleman in a straining waistcoat was laughing uproariously at something a thin, bewildered-looking man was whispering in his ear. A comedic double act, she deduced.

Next to them a wizened little man was fanning a deck of cards and muttering under his breath; a magician if Theo was not mistaken. They would all continue to command a high fee so long as their talent remained, but the same was not true with female performers.

"I was never the greatest boxer," Clem Dabney continued in his mellow, pleasant voice. "But I could always draw a crowd."

"I expect they all wanted to see you punched in the face," Theo answered thoughtfully. "I know I would."

"Theo!" Her sister was horrified.

"Oh dear, did I say that out loud?" Theo asked, pulling a face. "*Do* forgive me, Mr. Dabney. And after you have been so excessively polite too." Her tone was wry, and she saw his eyes narrow, though he laughed after a moment, showing strong white teeth.

"Are you really addressed by a boy's name generally, or only when you are in costume?" he asked, turning fully toward her for the first time. His light eyes raked over her appraisingly once more, as though only just deciding she deserved a second look.

To her surprise, his eyes lingered on her legs longer than was entirely seemly, and for a moment, Theo felt self-conscious about the fact she was still dressed in knee breeches. Ah well, in for a penny, in for a pound. At least she wasn't knock-kneed. "My name is Theodora," she answered shortly. "Only my family and intimates call me Theo."

9

"Really?" His light eyes held her own, a faint smile on his lips. "I believe I shall call you Dora."

It was such a gross impertinence that, in the moment, she could think of no reply. Later, of course, she could think of a dozen. It was always the way. *As you shall have no occasion to address me with such informality, I imagine the point to be a moot one, Mr. Dabney.* That would have been perfect. Uttered in a dry tone, of course, or perhaps with the utmost indifference. She kicked herself afterward whenever she thought of it. At the time though, she just turned rather pink and inclined her head.

Mercifully, they were interrupted by the pouting blonde actress who had clearly made no headway with Felix. Hetty slipped her hand through Theo's arm, and they beat a hasty retreat.

"You need to have a care around that one, Theo," her sister had remarked disapprovingly as they made their way back to their dressing room. "I've never seen you like that before, vying for a man's attention."

"What do you mean, *vying*?" Theo felt stung. "He annoyed me that's all!" But she had a horrible feeling that Hetty was right. People overlooked her all the time, but for some reason, Dabney's doing so had been insupportable.

She followed Hetty inside their dressing room and shut the door behind them. "Let me tell you," she rallied, "if you found my behavior wanting, then the feeling was mutual! When were you planning on telling me of your plans to quit the stage? Fancy telling a stranger like Dabney before your own sister!"

Henrietta turned toward her, pulling on her gloves. "I have not had the opportunity of late to confide in you, Theo. Every time I turn around you are whispering in corners with the likes of Lillian Longdon." She pronounced the words with distaste.

"What have you got against Lil?" Theo demanded. "She has always been very kind to us. When we started out in the business, she kept a careful eye out for us, and if memory serves, we were very grateful for the fact."

"I have nothing against her," Henrietta interrupted crisply, "but even you will admit, Theo, that she is—" Her lips formed a moue of distaste.

"What?" asked Theo, plunking her hands on her hips. "She is what, Hetty?"

Hetty lifted her chin. "That she is *vulgar* and not desirable company for a respectable woman."

Theo almost reeled. "Oh, is that what you are now?" she asked when she could once more catch her breath. "A respectable woman? Simply by associating with the likes of Sir Matthew Hillingdon?"

Hetty turned red. "I have always been respectable!" she snapped. "Our parents were musicians, and if they had not died, we would *never* have been put on the stage to earn a living!"

Theo nodded slowly. "I see. So now you're ashamed of the life Uncle provided for us instead of slinging us into the nearest orphanage."

"Of course not!" Hetty spluttered. "Uncle Barnabus did the best he could, but there is no denying that our lives would have been very different if not for that carriage accident. Uncle was Mama's younger brother and the black sheep of the family. They could never have imagined that he would be the one that raised the three of us."

Theo frowned. "What are you saying?" she asked quietly. "They *did* die, and we *were* raised in this life."

"I'm saying that it's not too late for things to revert to how they should have been," her sister concluded steadily. "Uncle is gone now too," she said with a sort of quiet finality that Theo found disturbing.

"This theater is his legacy and lives on," Theo pointed out. "*We* are his legacy. He raised us. You can't just rewrite our

11

history because it does not suit your current notions of respectability."

Henrietta rolled her eyes. "I am not the one acting deluded, sister," she said dryly as she lifted her bonnet from its stand and set it atop her glossy curls. "Felix and I are quite in agreement on this matter at least."

Oh, they were, were they? "What does that mean?"

"Do not force me to say it," her sister responded. "I do not wish to be cruel."

A cold feeling settled in the pit of Theo's stomach. "No, say it," she insisted, though her lips felt a little numb. "Clearly you and Felix have left me out of some important family decisions of late. Why should I be the only one left in the dark?"

Hetty regarded her gravely as she tied her bonnet ribbons. "I know you love it," she said abruptly, "the theater I mean, and how much you have thrown your body and soul into it over the years. Out of the three of us you probably love it best of all. But you are *not*…not an actress, Theo," she said pityingly. "Not really. Uncle put us on the stage when we were mere children, and we have long outgrown the role of *Babes in the Wood*. Neither of us are cut out for all this in the long term."

Her sister crossed the room quickly and took her coat down off its peg. She drew in a deep breath before turning to face Theo once more, her features sternly set. "If it were not for me, The Turtle Doves would never have lasted past our adolescence, Theo. Think about it and be honest with yourself for once. The admirers, the accolades, the flowers, they were all for me, not you. I do not mean to be unkind." Henrietta averted her eyes as though it cost her something to say the words out loud.

"You are my only sister and very dear to me. But you need to be realistic about the future that faces you now. You are six and twenty, not some overgrown schoolgirl. The time for

12

foolish dreams is over." She paused with her hand on the doorknob. "Felix wants what is best for you, and so do I," she added in a softer voice. "We are your family, and we love you. In time, you will realize the steps we are taking are for your own good."

"What steps?" Theo asked hoarsely, but her sister was already through the door. A swish of wide skirts and the sound of the door closing behind her told her that her sister had already gone and left her behind.

2

If you had asked her afterward, Theo could not have said how long she had sat there in the draughty dressing room. At some point, she had sunk down onto a hard wooden chair, and slowly she became aware of the fact that she was shivering. Her flimsy stage costume offered little by way of protection against the cold.

With stiff fingers, she removed first the billowing shirt, hanging it carefully on the rail beside her sister's hooped skirts, then added the blue silk sash and the silk breeches beside it. Luckily, she needed no help with the donning of her own garments, for Theo favored the aesthetic style and wore her gowns unencumbered with rigid corsetry and stiff petticoats.

Instead, her russet-red gown was shaped with pleats and smocking, so much more comfortable than the structured gowns of fashionable women. Her dark hair was already tidied into a tightly pinned bun, so she simply skewered a few more pins into it and twisted a string of red beads around her neck. That completed her uncomplicated toilette, and she was just reaching for her hat and coat when she heard the brisk knock on the door.

"Theo?" It was Felix. "I've been waiting an age for you! Are you dressed?"

"I'm just coming." She turned down the lamp and swung the door open, joining him in the gloom of the corridor.

"I thought to go home together as we have a few things to discuss," her brother said, clearing his throat.

"Oh, I did not realize. I took my time as I thought you might still be entertaining your guests," Theo lied, shutting the door behind her.

"Guests!" Felix's lip curled. "Dabney's nothing but a damned opportunist! Fellow runs a music hall establishment in Shoreditch and has the unmitigated gall to cast covetous eyes over The Parthenon!"

14

Theo watched her brother's indignant expression. "He means to expand his company?" she asked with interest. "And buy into a theater?" She knew exactly the type of low whistle her friend Albert would have emitted at this news. Dabney *must* be doing well.

"Uncultured swine!" Felix exploded. "Did you hear what he said about John Fletcher?" Her brother was clearly outraged.

Theo didn't think Dabney had said one word about the playwright, though he had not seemed terribly keen on the play. "He was very complimentary about Hetty," she murmured instead.

"Pah!" Felix scoffed. "He probably wants her to kick up her skirts at his filthy music hall."

Theo's eyes widened. "Do you think so?" she asked aloud. Privately she reflected it was *her* legs Dabney had taken a good look at, not Hetty's. "I thought the cancan was a feature of the Parisian dance hall rather than the British music hall."

Felix cleared his throat, as though realizing their conversation had strayed into inappropriate waters. "I—er—I have no idea if the fellow actually has French dancers in his employ. I would not put it past him though," he added darkly.

Theo nodded. "And he wanted to buy into *our* theater?" she asked, half aghast, half thrilled. Just think of the customers he could bring their way, she thought. Not the stuffy barristers and solicitors that Felix courted, but people from *all* walks of life.

"The cheek of it!" Felix brooded until they emerged into a gray afternoon in February. It was not busy on the corner of Oxendon that Sunday afternoon, but there was always a bustle of some sort in a London street. To Theo's surprise, Felix's arm shot out to hail a passing hansom cab. Theo's eyebrows rose at this extravagance. Usually, she was expected to navigate the twenty-minute walk to the tall, gloomy townhouse their uncle had bought on becoming their guardian.

15

He held out a hand to help her up the step, and Theo sank into the seat with a sigh.

"I wanted to talk to you," Felix announced without preamble as soon as he dropped into the seat next to her. He rapped the roof with his cane and shouted, "Juniper Row!"

The cab lurched off, and Theo felt a sudden impulse to ward off her brother's little talk. She could already tell from Hetty's words earlier that it would not bode well for her. "I think Hillingdon must have collected Hetty from the theater again today," she said, patting the shallow pockets of her coat.

"What are you doing?" Felix asked irritably.

"Looking for a handkerchief," she admitted.

"Really that coat… It's not fit to be seen in," he replied, eyeing the garment she had worn in the winter for the past three years.

"What is wrong with it?"

"Why is it so shapeless?" he asked tetchily. "I can't tell if it's a cape or *what* it is."

"It's a paletot," she told him. "I like it because it has pockets, even if they are not deep enough. You do not know the struggle," she told him darkly, "of finding a woman's outdoor coat which has pockets."

Felix's eyes had traveled up now to her disreputable woolen felt bonnet, and he gave a slight shudder. Theo felt on slightly less certain ground here, as she knew the bonnet was in a rather sorry state. Still, it kept her ears warm, and that was all that counted, in her opinion, during the winter months. Both her siblings were fashionable dressers, whereas Theo adhered to the principles of comfort and practicality.

When her search proved fruitless, her brother sighed and passed her his own clean handkerchief. Theo accepted it, giving her nose a good blow. Doubtfully, she offered it back, and when he declined with a pained look, she tucked it gratefully into her sleeve.

"Theo," he started again, "we must talk. It is long overdue, but with one thing and another…" His words trailed off and she eyed him uneasily.

"Talk about what?"

"Your future."

Theo felt a wave of alarm break over her. She sat up straighter. "Yes?"

"Clearly, you have decided against the more conventional avenues open to you," he said uneasily, his eyes darting all around the carriage rather than settling on her. She supposed acting was still considered unconventional for women, but as Felix himself was in the theatrical business, she thought it absurd of him to take so narrow a view.

"We need to face facts, however uncomfortable they might sit with us," her brother said heavily. "Henrietta has told me her plans, and though it might be considered unfortunate for The Parthenon, I understand her viewpoint of course."

Oh, he was talking about *marriage*, Theo realized belatedly. Marriage was the conventional avenue open to women. She opened her mouth, but he held up a hand to forestall her.

"I must ask you now to do something unselfish," he said portentously. "Something which will allow me to focus solely on the future success of our business. Something which puts the theater first."

Theo was puzzled, but she nodded anyway. The Parthenon was always first and foremost in her thoughts. "I love the theater, you know that—" she started, but he did not let her get any further.

"By offering me your assistance in the only way which materially helps me," he insisted loudly.

Theo looked at his tense face. "And how is that precisely?" she asked, her brow furrowed. For the life of her, she could not see where this was going.

17

He took a deep breath. "I need you to pick up the running of the house," he said flatly.

Theo's mouth dropped open. "The house?" she squeaked.

He nodded. "I've given Mrs. Cherwell her notice. I need you to pick up the reins there, Theo. Meals, housekeeping, cleaning." He waved a hand around. "Ordering coal and beef and tea and all the other millions of tasks traditionally associated with your sex."

The house? Theo could not even find words, and after a heavy pause, Felix finally met her stunned gaze head on. "You're not...meant for the stage, Theo," he said solemnly. "On some level, you must see that. You and Hetty have not been The Turtle Doves for years. It ran its course. The act is finished. Over. There's no room for me to insert my sisters into future plays. You need to be brave and realize where you will be best disposed to help in this family."

"Best disposed?" Theo echoed. "I know nothing about running houses! No more than you!"

"Then you must learn. I am persuaded such things come easier to women."

Theo spluttered. "I have no inclination to learn domestic tasks! Uncle certainly never expected that I should, and I think you take too much on yourself to give Mrs. Cherwell her notice before consulting the rest of us!"

Felix drew himself up. "Take too much on myself?" he repeated coldly. "I am the head of this family now, my girl, and you had best adjust your ideas accordingly! Uncle Barnabus is dead," he said curtly. "We all miss him, but this ship needs to be steered on a new course. Currently, we are headed for *disaster*."

"Finally, something we agree upon!"

He ignored her interruption. "We can ill afford Mrs. Cherwell's wage in light of how things have been going with ticket sales. I have consulted with my—our—partner," he

18

corrected himself quickly, "and he agrees with me. Wholeheartedly."

Theo inhaled sharply. "Harold *agrees*?" That was a blow. The fourth partner in their business and the man she…admired more than any other agreed her rightful place was in the kitchen? She was reeling.

Felix nodded. "Without you and Hetty drawing a wage, that will free up some money too," he said, unconsciously revealing that she was also to be an unpaid drudge. When words failed her, he awkwardly patted her shoulder. "I know it is not…the stuff of dreams, old girl," he said with determined cheer, "but we are not all destined to be stars. Some of us must eke out an existence on the stage of life. Your contribution will still be appreciated, and you will *always* have a place at my table."

Theo's chest heaved. The house belonged to the three Fields siblings, not just Felix. Harold lodged there in the attic, but he owned no part of the house. Before she could give utterance to the words that burned on her tongue, their arrival home rendered speech unnecessary. She would not have been able to find words in that moment, not even for a hundred pounds.

She was all alone, she realized bleakly. Betrayed by first her sister, and then by her brother. Even Harold had backstabbed her, she thought despairingly. Harold, who lent her his books and let her have first glance at his compositions. Her eyes welled up. Never again would she admire the sensitive turn of his countenance!

They had conspired together against her and decided she was unfit for the life she adored, the life she had grown up in. They had plotted to ensure she would never again grace the stage she had always considered her true home, more than this tall, narrow house on Juniper Row would *ever* be!

19

Well, they would be sorry, she vowed as she followed her brother up the path to the front steps. To add insult to injury, Felix had the nerve to look relieved, as though he had successfully navigated some ordeal and come out of the other side of it unscathed. He cared not a jot that he had thrust a knife through her bosom and done his level best to kill her dreams stone dead!

A domestic drudge, she seethed as the front door swung open and they walked into the gloomy passageway, wiping their feet on the mat. What did she know about planning meals and seeing the lamps were kept trimmed? She knew even less about scrubbing front steps and polishing floorboards, she thought, her spirits sinking by the minute.

Mrs. Cherwell had always had a woman come in twice a week to do the rough work, a Mrs. Hubble. Had Felix dismissed her too? Theo would not demean herself by asking. In fact, she would not speak again to Felix this evening, she vowed, *or* Hetty or even Harold. Shedding her bonnet and coat, she hurried upstairs to her solitary bedroom and threw herself down on her bed to bury her face in her pillow.

Well, she would have no consideration of their feelings in the future, that was all! She owed them no loyalty, she thought fiercely. She only hoped they would remember their conduct toward her for the rest of their days and come to feel sorry for it! Wiping away the tears that rolled silently down her cheeks, Theo finally gave vent to her overwhelming grief in smothered sobs.

*

The next morning at breakfast, Theo's eyes were dry, if a little red-rimmed. Noticing Mrs. Cherwell's grim expression as she banged the tea tray down on the table, she guessed their housekeeper was seething as much as she at the recent developments. Theo glanced toward her brother and sister to

20

see if they had noticed the venomous glares the housekeeper was directing toward the head of the table.

It was true that Felix looked a little flustered as he helped himself to toast from the rack. Certainly, he was studiously avoiding looking at the housekeeper, now employed in slamming small bowls of jam and butter onto the table. Disappointingly, Henrietta's attention was fixed on a letter she was reading, and she seemed oblivious to the tense atmosphere.

At this point, the door opened, and Harold Allsop entered the room in his usual apologetic manner with a murmured "Good morning" to all. Mrs. Cherwell's militant expression softened, and she pulled out a chair for the latecomer, bustling about to pour his tea and nudge the condiments toward him. Women usually rallied around Harold. He had a sort of sweet and helpless look.

Theo's lips flattened into a thin line, and she felt the strangest impulse to inform the housekeeper that Harold had also agreed with the household changes. After all, when you thought about it, he was no better than Felix, she thought bitterly. His inoffensive, mild manner clearly hid a propensity for treachery.

Feeling Harold's mournful gaze directed her way several times through breakfast, Theo stiffened her resolve and refused to look at the duplicitous wretch. Usually, she would be all smiles at this point, cheerfully asking him his plans for the day and telling him hers. This morning she pursued no such camaraderie.

Instead, she drank her tea in silence and ate half a slice of dry toast before realizing she had not buttered it. Smearing it liberally with damson jam, her least favorite but the closest one to her, she finished her breakfast and withdrew from the table without further comment.

Sadly, she could not flatter herself that either Felix or Henrietta had even noticed her manner was off. Felix had been frowning over something he was scrawling on his napkin with a small pencil. It had looked rather like sums, and Theo wondered if he was calculating what he would gain by denying wages to the three women in the room.

For her part, he would not be saving much, she reflected, as he paid her the merest pittance. She would not be remotely surprised to learn he paid far more to their housekeeper than he ever did her. She slowly climbed the wooden stairs and pictured herself delivering tea and toast to her brother and Harold in the future, as they ignored her presence and discussed theater business.

Henrietta would be living in some more fashionable residence by that point and would have left Juniper Row far behind her. As wife of the honorable Matthew, she would likely have a handful of servants to do her bidding and mercifully would not require her own sister to wait on her.

Theo maintained her coolness with her family by remaining in her room for the rest of the morning. Not that she flattered herself that either of her siblings would have noticed her avoiding them. They were entirely self-absorbed these days, she reflected indignantly.

She knew for a fact that if the roles were reversed, she would have been anxious to seek out the bone of contention. In the old days, Hetty at least would have perceived any change in her manner. The sisters had been close once upon a time. When had that changed? Theo pondered the matter as she cut out the pattern pieces for a new dress. Alas, she could find no easy answer.

She was not required to attend any rehearsal or read-throughs today as Felix had made it quite clear she would not be a part of the next production. As such, her day was hers to do as she wished with it, until she was required at the evening performance of *The Faithful Shepherdess*.

At elevenish, she opened her bedroom door and left it ajar to listen for the slamming of the front door signaling her siblings' departure. Sure enough, she heard the sounds of conversation in the hallway, followed by the sound of a closing door.

Theo hurried onto the landing and peered out of the window to see Felix and Hetty setting forth down the garden path in their outdoor things. She turned and ran up the next flight of stairs to the third floor where Felix's bedroom was situated along with a bathroom and her late uncle's room.

Once inside the large green-wallpapered room, she headed straight for his wardrobe, ignoring the piles of books stacked vertically at various points and the cluttered desk which was absolutely covered in papers and bottles of ink. Even Felix's sternest critic could not deny he had a strong work ethic.

She opened the right-hand door to his armoire and, ignoring the garments to the left, where his current favorites resided, she selected instead a brown Newmarket coat and a pair of trousers in a light beige that she had not seen Felix wear in an age. Possibly they were too snug on him nowadays, for the legs were very narrow-fitting and they had loops at the feet to keep them smooth and prevent them from riding up.

Casting these onto a chair, she rifled next through his shirts, waistcoats, and neckcloths. None of these were terribly inspiring, for Felix was a reserved dresser who believed the more understated a man's attire, the better. She would have loved a paisley or a tartan waistcoat, but sadly had to settle for one of somber dark green instead.

Luckily, she and her brother were much the same height, for she was tall for a woman at five foot ten, whereas her brother was only middling for a man. However, shoes *would* be a problem. Felix's feet were at least three sizes bigger than her own. She pondered this a moment, staring down at his black

23

and brown boots. She would slip and slide around in them as though they were clown shoes, she thought sadly, biting her lip.

The shoes she currently wore on stage were no good, for they were flimsy opera slippers and would look ridiculous with daywear. She would just have to stuff the toes with newspaper, she decided, and helped herself to the brown boots, tucking them under her arm. Hopefully, Felix would not notice, for currently he was mostly seen sallying forth in shades of black and gray. She had not seen him in his brown boots for a good while.

She was just closing his bedroom door behind her when Mrs. Cherwell loomed up out of the shadows, clearing her throat. "What you a-doing of with them there clothes, Miss Theodora?" she asked disapprovingly.

Theo almost jumped out of her skin. "Oh, Mrs. Cherwell, how you startled me. Clothes? These clothes, you mean?" she asked airily, glancing down at her arm. "I just—er—thought I would check them over for any possible repairs that might be needed."

Mrs. Cherwell looked unimpressed by this claim. "You and I both know Master Felix ain't worn them in a twelvemonth," she said severely.

Theo considered what reply to make. Moths perhaps? Then again, it might be simpler just to lay her cards on the table. "In truth, I mean to repurpose these garments for my own nefarious ends, Mrs. Cherwell," she admitted abruptly.

"To what purpose?" asked the older woman, narrowing her eyes.

"Revenge," Theo pronounced with relish.

"Revenge?" Mrs. Cherwell's head jerked back, her mobcap slipping to one side.

Theo nodded. "Yes, for despite the fact my uncle left me an equal share in The Parthenon, my brother has cruelly decided to force me off the stage. He has dashed all my long-cherished dreams and ground them in the dust." She did not trouble to keep the bitterness from her voice, and Mrs. Cherwell eyed her silently as she turned over these words.

Theo knew she was not the housekeeper's favorite, for Mrs. Cherwell favored the menfolk over her fellow women. Still, there was a chance she could win her over, given her brother had recently blotted his copybook. "In fact, Felix has been making a few unilateral decisions of late that I do not agree with," she continued coolly.

Two spots of high color instantly appeared on Mrs. Cherwell's cheeks. "You and me both!" she huffed. "Just between us, I fear Master Felix is getting a bit above 'imself!"

Theo nodded. "I'm afraid he is rather," she agreed. "Uncle Barnabus would never have countenanced such changes."

"I'll say he wouldn't!" Mrs. Cherwell responded, warming to the theme. "The old master would of never put me out on the street!" She touched the corner of her apron to her eyes before they fell once more on the clothing looped over Theo's arm. "What you going to do wiv 'em?" she asked with sudden curiosity.

"I would rather not make you complicit, Mrs. Cherwell," Theo said grandly. "That way, if my brother should ask, you can tell him quite truthfully you have no notion what has become of them."

"Huh!" replied the housekeeper. "As if I'd lose a wink of sleep over lying to the likes of 'im!"

Theo's lips twitched before she grew grave again. "Will you really be destitute, Mrs. Cherwell? If you lose your post here, I mean?"

The other woman's shoulders slumped. "As good as," she admitted flatly. "My 'Erbert ain't been able to work in nine months, not since getting injured at the warehouse."

25

"I *am* sorry," Theo said sincerely, then hesitated. "I do have a plan of sorts," she confided, "and if I should be lucky and manage to succeed, then perhaps…"

Mrs. Cherwell shook her head sadly. "If it's Master Allsop you're pinning your hopes on, then I fear you'll be sadly disappointed."

Theo felt herself color hotly. "Master Allsop?" she repeated. *Damn it, did everyone think she was sweet on Harold?*

"I got eyes in me 'ead, don't I? And even if you did manage to get him up the aisle, he'd never have the nerve to stand up against that brother of yours," Mrs. Cherwell pronounced glumly. "Not even though you'd own the lion's share of the theater between you."

The lion's share? Theo blinked, realizing Mrs. Cherwell spoke nothing but the truth, for Harold owned twenty-five percent and so did she. Between the two of them… She stared at the other woman with dawning appreciation. "Such a thing never once occurred to me," she admitted, feeling impressed the no-nonsense housekeeper was capable of such Machiavellian plotting. She gave herself a shake to gather herself. "But in any case, Harold does not figure in my stratagem at all."

Mrs. Cherwell looked skeptical, crossing her arms over her ample bosom. "What is it, then?" she asked, suddenly curious. "Your plan, I mean?"

"It's…well, it's rather complicated and hard to explain," Theo admitted, her gaze dropping.

"'Spose you think I'd be better off not knowing about this neither!" Mrs. Cherwell sniffed.

"Well, not until after the fact," Theo agreed.

Mrs. Cherwell huffed. "After all, what have I got to lose?" She shrugged after a moment's consideration. "You'll keep me updated, I daresay."

"I most certainly will."

The older woman gave her a hard look, then nodded and moved away. Theo slumped back against Felix's door, then rallied herself and hurried off to her room with her illicit stash of men's clothing. She could not wait to try them on!

3

Theo passed a very satisfactory day practicing her male mannerisms before the looking glass and trying on her brother's old clothes. They were not an exact fit but were close enough to perfect the illusion.

She remained in her room all afternoon, even when Felix and Hetty returned at about four o'clock. Dinner was served at half past five, and once again, conversation was desultory at the table. Theo took the dress pattern she was currently working on down with her to study for she could not make head nor tail of it at present.

She kept her eyes on this instead of engaging with anyone over their evening meal, and though she heard snatches of some murmured conversation between the other three, she kept to herself, pondering her thoughts. A reckless sort of plan was forming in the back of her mind. Whenever it swam to the front of her thoughts, she almost gasped at its audacity. Did she really have the nerve to do such a thing?

What had been the name of the music hall establishment Lil had said Clem Dabney ran? The Sun and Eagle? Or was it The Eagle and Sun? Whichever it had been, it was in Shoreditch, she remembered that much. Did she really have the nerve to approach the likes of Mr. Dabney with her scheme? He coveted The Parthenon. If he were to marry her, then he would get his hands on a quarter share.

Would that be incentive enough, she wondered, for him to accept her act and give her a spot at his music hall? Of course, if he married her, he would also get his hands on her. She almost dropped her fork as she considered this, fanning herself with her napkin. He would not be remotely interested in her person, she told herself firmly.

Quite the lady-killer. Was that not how he had been described? She felt a shiver of apprehension down her spine. A little voice whispered in her ear that perhaps Mrs. Cherwell's suggestion had more merit than her own. After all, she admired Harold and had even nurtured a small *tendresse* for him these past few years. Would it not be more sensible to approach Harold with an offer of marriage, rather than Clem Dabney, who was no more than a disreputable stranger?

Theo bit her lip. But no, her admiration of Harold was all in the past, she recalled, pressing her lips together. The sad truth was that she had never inspired a stronger feeling in Harold's bosom than mere friendship. Even that had proved no more than tepid, for he had conspired with Felix against her. She cast a brief look at Harold, so burning that he dropped his spoon into his bowl and splashed Windsor soup all up his front.

"Steady on, old son," Felix cautioned him as Harold murmured apologies and dabbed himself with a napkin.

Theo returned to her thoughts. No, it would have to be Dabney, she decided, stiffening her resolve. Even if by some miracle she managed to convince Harold to tie his lot to hers, Mrs. Cherwell was quite right. He would not have it in him to insist she retained her stage career; her brother would walk all over him. Dabney it was.

At six o'clock she headed for the hallway and donned her hat and cloak in readiness for Vincent's arrival. The hulking doorman always escorted her and Hetty to the theater for their evening performances. He was prompt as always, and Theo dropped behind as she always did during this walk to and from the theater.

This was not because she was shunning Vinnie's company, but rather due to her habit. She always allowed the great hulking doorman to have his few prized moments together with the object of his affections.

It was true, he barely spoke, and only allowed himself the briefest and most respectful glances in Hetty's direction, but still, Theo could tell, indeed she had always known that Vincent was completely smitten with Henrietta. It was evident in so many ways: the look in his eye, the softened tone when he spoke to her, a slight almost bashfulness that entered his manner whenever he was around her.

Henrietta knew it too, of course, Theo was almost convinced, although her sister, who was the soul of discretion and decorum, never alluded to it. Hetty's manner toward Vincent was kind, though perfectly correct at all times. She addressed him as "Vincent," never Vinnie, as most of the other theater folk did. Hetty thanked him prettily every time they reached their destination. She affected not to notice that his manner was different toward her than it was to anyone else.

Of course, she would never look upon him as a possible suitor, Theo reflected sadly. Vinnie's size and craggy face made him seem older than his thirty years. It was not just his plain looks, but his low station in life that were held against him. Hetty was the biggest snob in their family. Even Felix prized artistic endeavor above virtue of birth, but her sister did not feel the same way, and it was her biggest failing in Theo's book, for Vinnie was worth ten of that pompous ass Matthew Hillingdon!

The evening performance went off without hitch, though the paying public was in sparse attendance. In truth, Theo's role in *The Faithful Shepherdess* was only small. She still gave it her all on stage. How could she fail to do otherwise when every fiber of her being strained toward those few brief moments? However, the part of a naïve shepherd youth was far from taxing, and she barely had any time at all on stage in the last act.

She spent the time in her shared dressing room with a blanket thrown over her frilly shirt, frowning furiously and scrawling notes for her new act. There were several of the songs Harold had penned for The Turtle Doves that she thought could be adapted with little effort and without the aid of a professional songwriter.

30

Theo sat with the existing lyrics and painstakingly wrote her own above them. Music hall songs relied on a catchy tune, a rousing chorus, and a good deal of double entendre. What if she were to alter Harold's rather bland sentiments about pure love to something more suggestive, concerning the physical act of love?

Theo bit her lip and crossed out "He's never lost his heart before, but kept his mother's tenets hallowed" with "He's never dipped his toe before, just shilly-shallied in the shallows." Theo gave an undignified snort of laughter and expounded on the theme throughout the rest of the verses.

It was true, her cheeks felt a little overwarm by the end of it. Alright, so the song was now a little racy, but music hall *was* racy, was it not? One worry continued to plague her, which was whether or not Harold would be offended by her dragging his ditties into the dirt. She paused to consider this seriously a moment, gnawing on her pencil end.

On reflection, she did not think she *needed* to take Harold's feelings into account for he had made it very clear that he thought the songs he had penned were mere trifles, and she doubted very much that he would ever sit through her new act. Why should he when he so clearly did not prize her friendship?

Her concerns, however, could not be so easily dismissed. He might think them mere dross, but at the end of the day, the songs *were* his intellectual property, strictly speaking. She would have to speak to Harold at some point, she concluded with a sigh, before shutting her notebook and hurrying off to perform her last bow.

Her mind was elsewhere as the curtain swept down and Theo made her way backstage. She was still a few doors away from her own dressing room when she heard the muffled sobs. Surely that was Lil's room? "Lil?" She knocked softly on the door. "Can I come in?"

There was no answer, and tentatively, Theo pushed the door open. Lil never stood on ceremony, so Theo decided to take a leaf out of her book. She found her friend still in her shepherdess costume, scrambling for a handkerchief before pressing it to her eyes.

"Don't mind me, love," her friend sniffed. "Just feeling a bit sorry for meself."

"Whatever's happened?" Theo asked, shutting the door resolutely behind her. "Tell me."

Lil dropped down into a rickety chair. "I been let go, that's what. Your brother had a word with me this afternoon."

"What?" Theo gasped.

Lil nodded. "After *The Faithful Shepherdess* runs its course, I'm out on my ear."

"He can't *do* that!" Theo fumed.

"Afraid he can, love," Lil said sadly. "He already has." Her face crumpled. "What am I going to tell my old girls?" she asked, referring to her dependents. Her retired and near-blind ex-dresser Peggy and her mother-in-law, both of whom she had supported for years. The three of them lived in two rooms above a grocer's shop. "We live near enough hand to mouth as it is. Without my wages, we'll be out on the street." She balled up her tissue in her fist, blinking fiercely to hold back more tears.

"I'll tell you what you're going to tell them," Theo announced. "You are going to tell them you've thrown your lot in with mine. I need a partner for my new act and you're it."

That caught Lil's attention. She lowered her handkerchief. "Partner?" she repeated blankly.

Theo nodded. "The Turtle Doves are disbanding," she said, though in truth she and her sister had not been billed under that name for several years now. "Coincidentally, after this show finishes. Hetty's going to get married and give up treading the boards."

32

Lil gave a sour smile. "She ain't got him up the aisle yet, love."

"Well, that's none of my affair," Theo answered briskly. "Hetty's hell-bent on giving up this life, and I need to look to my own future. I've been thinking for a while now about how I want my act to evolve—"

Lil snorted, and Theo halted, sending her a level look. "Not you too, Lil," she said gravely after a moment's heavy pause. "I can take scorn from Hetty and even Felix, but I thought *you* believed in me."

The older actress reddened. "You know I've always said you was a clever mimic, darlin', and you know I ain't your sister's biggest fan, but the plain fact of the matter is that The Turtle Doves without your sister is a dud."

"It is," Theo agreed. "But I will be playing to my own strengths in the future, not Hetty's. I will certainly be using my talent for mimicry, but I've been on the stage for a decade now, Lil, doing breeches roles, and I want to build on that foundation."

"Your singing voice is pretty," Lil began patiently, "but it's sopranos they want front of stage, not altos."

"*You* would be my soprano," Theo pointed out. "Your voice is every bit as good as my sister's. Better in fact."

Lil gave a short laugh. "My voice may be, but my face ain't, not no more. It's been a few years now since I could lay claim to being a stunner."

"Well, I never could," Theo said roundly. "I was never more than passable, but that's not what the act will revolve around in any case."

Lil frowned. "Well, I'm in the dark," she admitted. "What will your act revolve around?"

"I'm talking about my male impersonation," Theo said levelly.

33

Lil made a choking noise. "Theo darlin'," she appealed. "*Male impersonator?*" She said the words with heavy skepticism.

Theo did her best not to bristle. It was hard, but she managed it. "That is how I consider myself," she answered with quiet dignity. "I have played the boy on stage since I was thirteen years old."

"Yes, but…" Lil hesitated. "Theo love, you was playing a pretty boy. It was pantomime stuff, *Babes in the Wood*, that sort of thing. Lord, you never convinced anyone you was anything but a girl in breeches!"

"I am aware of that," Theo replied calmly. "But I was never given free rein. My uncle would not have thought it seemly during his lifetime. Felix will no doubt take the same view, but I find I no longer care what my brother thinks." She lifted her chin. "You see, Felix has consigned me to the scrapheap as well."

Lil looked up sharply. "What do you mean?"

"He's told me after *The Faithful Shepherdess* finishes its run, my new place is keeping house for him," Theo said bitterly.

Lil shook her head. "Oh, Theo," she murmured sadly.

"And I'm not having it, Lil. I'm just not having it."

Her friend still looked doubtful. "But what can you do, my dear?"

"Do?" Theo echoed grimly. "Plenty, I assure you! But for now, I suggest we concentrate on developing the act. This is the direction which I am determined to take, Lil," she affirmed. "Whether you join me or not."

Lil regarded her in silence for a moment before shrugging. "So go on, tell me about it, then," she said resignedly. "And where do I fit in?"

"Well, Pure Percy," she said, gesturing to herself, "has all grown up. He's now a young man about town." She sketched

Lil an elegant bow. "I give you, Piccadilly Percy." Lil blinked at her. "Imagine me in full evening dress," Theo urged, "top hat, tailcoat, cravat, the works."

The fact that she did not possess this outfit yet did not deter her one bit. It would be hers, she vowed. One day.

"Go on," Lil urged her. "What about me? What am I wearing?"

"You? You're wearing the fanciest most ostentatious plumage you can imagine. I'm thinking purple silk and lots of lace, roses in your hair, and a daringly low décolletage."

Lil's nodded. "So I'm not playing your sister's role, then? That's a relief as I don't think I can pull off the artless ingenue at fif—forty-five," she corrected herself hastily.

"Percy is now a foppish young cad about town," Theo confided. "He has no interest in innocent young maidens. Quite the contrary. He is looking for a—a more *mature* lady for companionship. He's—er—how can I put this? Ripe for the plucking."

Lil went off in a coughing fit. "That's where you come in," Theo said brightly. "You are the experienced woman about town. Percy pursues you, makes up to you. You protest, cavil, and then finally, you pounce!"

Lil's eyes widened. "I turn the tables on him?"

"Yes, and poor Percy doesn't know what to do with you. That's the joke."

"The would-be seducer becomes the seduced?"

"Exactly."

Lil pursed her lips and seemed to consider. "I don't say as it wouldn't work as a turn, mind, but you do realize you're talking pure music hall, Theo my love. This wouldn't be what you and your sister's been doing all these years, skirting the edges, but keeping all respectable-like."

"I am aware of that, Lil."

35

"Are you?" Lil looked skeptical. "Because there would be no room for half measures, you know. You'd have to be proper bawdy with it for it to work. It would have to be more than just a bit...well, *saucy*."

Theo nodded. "It will," she agreed simply. "I'm not a complete fool."

Lil's gaze narrowed. "You think you could do that?" she asked. "Only I never seen you be risqué, my dear, nor even tell a rude joke. Not in the ten years I've known you."

"I *know* I could," Theo insisted, boldly holding her gaze. "I may not be that way inclined in...in my private life, but as a performance on stage, I assure you, I can be as bawdy as you like."

Lil chewed the corner of her lip. "Your brother would never let you do it. Not on stage in his theater."

"It is no more Felix's theater than it is my own," Theo fired up. "Or Hetty's, or Mr. Allsop's for that matter. You know the four of us all own a quarter share."

"That may well be," Lil sniffed, "but that brother of yours wields your and your sister's shares as if they was his own."

Theo had no answer for that, for Lil spoke nothing but the truth. On paper Felix *was* the head of their family. As a mere female, she would always be subject to her nearest male relative's rule. Aloud, she said, "It is true Felix has no love for music hall, but he will have to realize we need to move with the times."

Lil gave a *harrumph*. "You know how he hankers for respectability, Theo! Lord, even your uncle didn't try and cater exclusively to the middle classes, like what Felix does!"

Theo continued to avoid her gaze. "And how has that served him?" she asked evenly. "You've seen all the empty seats, night after night. If things don't pick up, we risk losing this place. He will have to cave eventually, Lil."

"Still can't see him ever agreeing to music hall," Lil said glumly. "He won't even countenance pantomime since your uncle passed. Thinks it's too vulgar and encourages the wrong crowd."

"Any crowd would be a blessing at this point. Things need to change," Theo resolved, echoing her brother's words from the day before but with a wealth of different meaning behind them. The two of them sat looking at each other before Theo's natural optimism reasserted itself once more. "I've already set about repurposing a couple of Mr. Allsop's songs for our new act."

Lil looked stunned. "You have? Did you get his permission first?"

"Not yet," Theo admitted cagily, "but I will, never fear. I doubt he will care now in any case. He's knocked out dozens of musical numbers for me and Hetty over the years." She hesitated. "I think, privately, he's always thought them a bit beneath him. You know his true ambition is to write an operetta."

"Lah-di-dah!" mocked Lil. "Well, what do I know? Mr. Fancy-Pants mayn't cut up rough if you think he won't. I'm an actress, not an artiste." Lil slumped in her chair. "Least, I *was*," she said, looking suddenly tired. "All me life."

"You've plenty more performances still to give, Lil," Theo assured her friend.

"Beats me how you can be so buoyant, girl," her friend responded dully.

"Trust me. Put your faith in me, Lil," Theo urged. "I won't let you down."

Lil gave a short laugh. "That's the best bit of male impersonation you done yet." She grimaced. "Ain't I heard that one before!"

"Not from me," Theo pointed out.

"How you even goin' get this act of yours on stage?" Lil asked. "Felix's next production is *Antony and Cleopatra*. How does your bawdy skit fit in with high Roman tragedy? Answer me that!"

"It won't be staged at The Parthenon, not initially," Theo admitted. "That will come later."

Lil's jaw dropped. "You're leaving The Parthenon? *You?*"

"I've got no choice, Lil. I have to be realistic at this point."

Lil gazed at her in stupefaction. "*Well,*" she said weakly. "You could knock me down with a feather." When Theo's gaze remained steady, Lil half turned in her chair. "You know, I'm starting to think you've actually got a plan," she admitted. "Have you?"

"Yes. Are you in or out?" When Lil did not answer at once, Theo thought of Mrs. Cherwell and added, "Let me put it this way, my friend, what do you have to lose?"

Lil snorted. "Absolutely nothing." She came swiftly to her feet and stalked across the room to stand in front of Theo. "I won't be waiting around for this plan of yours to come off, you know, love. I'll be knocking on everyone's doors, but all the same, I don't expect I'll find much joy. It'll be slim pickings for me these days. You're really serious about trying to get this scheme of yours off the ground?" she asked softly. Theo gave a nod. "You know what?" Lil extended her hand. "If you do get a taker for the act, then count me in."

Theo clasped it tight, vowing that in the morning she would pay a visit to Shoreditch.

4

The Office at The Eagle and Sun Concert Rooms,
Shoreditch

"It was a pleasure doing business with you," Clem told the
cool beauty as she shook his hand. Henrietta Fields smiled
perfunctorily and swept from the room without more ado. Clem
watched through the glass pane as her hulking great escort
straightened up to meet her. Through the glass, his cold eyes
met Clem's, and he stared at him balefully a moment. There
was a warning in that glare: *Keep your filthy hands off her.*

Clem found his lips crooking into a smile, and he could see
the other man did not like it one bit. Still, his hands were tied.
When his mistress started down the stairs, all the big man could
do was cast one last warning look at Clem and then follow her
down them, his neck bent to avoid the low ceiling.

The fact a haughty piece like Henrietta Fields consorted
with a bruiser like that made Clem think a little better of her,
though he doubted she used the man for anything more than
hired muscle. Thought a lot of herself, did that one, if he was
not mistaken.

She certainly thought herself too good for the acting life.
He picked up the document they had both signed and regarded
it with an air of satisfaction. The document proved he now
owned a quarter interest in The Parthenon. He had not
particularly cared for Henrietta Fields's manner, but she had
signed away her share of the theater without a murmur, true to
her word, and sailed out of his office with a substantial banker's
draft in her purse.

Thoughtfully, Clem locked it into his top drawer and
pondered the moment he would saunter back into that
establishment and wipe the smug smile off that bastard Felix
Fields's face. Fields would not like sharing ownership of his

precious theater with a guttersnipe like him, and that reflection gave Clem nothing but gratification as he pocketed the key and sat back in his chair.

It was less than two hours later that Jim knocked on his door again and announced, "There's a Miss Fields downstairs to see you."

Clem was startled. "Miss Fields?" he echoed in surprise. "Did she forget something?" He cast a quick look about the office for an errant umbrella or something similar.

"It ain't the same one," Jim told him, scratching his ear.

"Not the same one?"

"Naw." Jim shook his head. "This one ain't a looker like the first."

Clem's brain scrambled, then he realized what must have happened. Miss Henrietta must have broken her promise. She had blabbed to her sister of their business transaction and now Miss Theodora had turned up to give him a piece of her mind. "Fetch her up, then," he said resignedly. Best get it over with at once.

Jim disappeared, and Clem steeled himself for a second encounter with Miss Theodora Fields. He wouldn't even be able to console himself with a look at her legs this time, he thought, for she would be respectably clad this morning. When he heard the clatter of footsteps on the stairs, he dragged himself reluctantly to his feet and steeled himself to be heaped with scolding recriminations for his nefarious machinations for buying his way into their family business.

It was at this point that he received the first of his surprises. For one thing, Miss Theodora was *not* dressed respectably. He did not know what she was dressed as precisely, but if someone had told him it was another stage costume, he would readily have believed them. He would have taken her billowing outer garment for a cloak, if it had not also possessed sleeves and been matched with a strange velvet cap with a tassel.

40

The second surprise was that, instead of looking fired up with righteous indignation, she looked like someone about to face a firing squad.

"Miss Fields," he greeted her with wary politeness. "Come in. Please take a seat."

She gulped and thanked him in strangled tones before walking once around the chair he gestured her toward. Finally, she lowered herself into it and sat gazing at him with a faintly anxious expression on her face.

"How can I help you this morning?" he prompted when no further speech seemed forthcoming. She practically leaped out of her chair at this and started pacing about his poky office, cannoning into a packing case before wheeling about in the opposite direction, only coming up short when she barked her shins on the coal scuttle.

Clem stifled a sigh and glanced at Jim, who tapped his brow indicating he believed Miss Fields to be lacking in wits. Clem gave a slight shake of his head and indicated he could leave. Jim frowned and backed out of the room, shutting the door behind him. It was only at this point that Clem realized Miss Fields had already launched into a fast-paced speech he had not been listening to.

"...I know I'm not much to look at," she concluded earnestly, "but I understand perfectly what kind of man you are, and you may be sure I would not interfere with your carrying on or allow that to prejudice our arrangement in any way." She took a deep breath and looked at him hopefully.

Clem blinked, realizing at last whatever she had been twittering on about had *not* been burning accusations about his business practice. *Our arrangement*, he pondered. What the hell had she been talking about? "My…carrying on?" he repeated blankly.

"Your womanizing," she explained. "I only ask that you show me the same courtesy."

41

This time he leaned forward, giving her his full attention. Was this strange woman asking him to debauch her? Almost against his will, he let his eyes drag over her again in reluctant perusal. She was tall, almost startlingly tall for a woman, and very straight up and down.

He had noticed her lack of curves on stage, for she had slim boyish hips and no bosom to speak of, fantastic legs though. He had supposed that was why she was the one dressed as a shepherd boy, while her sister paraded in frills and bows. "You ask that I refrain from interfering in your affairs?" he said slowly, trying to dredge up some semblance of her meaning.

"Precisely." She sat back in her seat, looking flushed and pleased with herself. "I am so glad you believe in forthright speech, Mr. Dabney. I cannot tell you what a relief it is not having to beat about the bush."

Clem gazed at her, wondering if she really thought anything about her extraordinary speech was forthright. "I have no idea what you are talking about, Miss Fields," he admitted. Her face fell. "Except that you do not disapprove of extramarital affairs. Are you perhaps telling me that you have a lover?"

Theodora's face turned suddenly crimson. "No…er…no!" she stammered, lifting a hand to tug at her neck scarf as though her throat was suddenly constricted. "Oh dear, I do not seem to have explained myself clearly after all, and I practiced the speech most assiduously."

Clem took pity on her flustered state. Theodora Fields was a poor specimen of womanhood, but he liked women, always had. He was unfailingly polite even to old ladies as a rule. "You have a proposition for me, is that it?" he drawled, withdrawing his cigar case from his waistcoat pocket. "Perhaps we should start with that."

She took a deep breath. "Yes, thank you." She smiled at him gratefully. "I will endeavor to make my meaning plainer this time." In her enthusiasm, she let her handbag fall with a clatter onto the floor, resting a gloved hand on his desk. She did not even glance down at her fallen reticule, which had spilled a jumbled assortment of personal items onto the floor.

He noticed that her gloves did not actually match. One was black and the other navy blue. She was either very nervous or very eccentric. He remembered her somewhat combative speech from the theater the other night. She had not seemed scatty then, far from it. Maybe it was just nerves. He gave her his blandest, most nonthreatening smile. "You were saying?"

"You see, I own a quarter share of the theater," she said, and his ears did perk up at that. Had she come to him with the same offer as her sister? To sell her twenty-five percent? His brain scrambled. Could he raise the money if he rearranged some of his investments? It would be tight. Perhaps he could take on a few prizefights to cover the shortfall? Or maybe she would expect less money for her shares than her canny sister had.

"If you were to marry me," she said, her words breaking over him like a bucket of ice-cold water, "well then, that would put you in a shareholder's position."

Clem's hand froze in the act of opening his cigar case. "Marry you?" he managed to force out.

She nodded. "Yes, for you see, unmarried, my shares get managed by my brother. I barely get any say-so in the business. If I had a husband, however…" When he did not take the bait, she rushed once more into speech. "You would be able to espouse my cause."

Clem's mind worked rapidly. Theodora's percentage added to her sister's would give him a controlling interest in The Parthenon. He let his eyelids drop to hide the avaricious gleam no doubt shining from his eyes as he considered the matter. "You have discussed this matter with the other shareholders?" he asked casually.

The color in her cheeks once more ebbed and flowed. "N-no," she admitted. "My brother would be far from sympathetic. He—er—well, he has made it plain that he expects to rule the roost at the theater from now on, and that he expects me to fade into the background now Hetty is to marry."

"And that does not appeal to you, Miss Fields?"

She shook her head resolutely and he stifled a wince. He had thought Felix Fields a pompous prig, but in this instance, Clem did not think he was far wrong. The pretty sister had been the draw of the act and this one the dross. How old was she? It was hard to tell in her ill-fitting coat and shabby bonnet. She had looked younger on stage, but that could be achieved with lights and makeup.

Maybe she was desperate to get off the shelf? Even so, he was a poor prospect for matrimony. "I confess to an interest in your twenty-five percent," he said slowly, "but marriage has never held much appeal for me."

She nodded as though in perfect understanding. "As I said, I will not interfere in your established lifestyle, Mr. Dabney."

Oh yes, she had said something of that sort. He frowned. "A husband can be just as inconvenient as a brother, I think you'll find," he said wryly.

"Oh, but not you," she said quickly. "You have no desire for a wife, just as I have none for a husband."

"If you have no desire for a husband, I wonder rather at the nature of your proposal. You could just sell me your shares," he pointed out.

"Never!" Two spots of color had appeared on her cheeks. "I would never, *never* sell my share in The Parthenon!" Seeing his raised brows, she strove to collect herself. "No one from my family would ever countenance such a thing!" she claimed staunchly.

Well, there was the answer to his unspoken question. Her sister had not confided in her. Theodora was wholly unaware that, by marrying him, she would be gifting him with the majority share of The Parthenon's ownership. He felt a little trill of excitement at the prospect of pulling off such a coup.

"Besides," she continued bitterly, "Felix would only consult a solicitor and say I had been imposed upon or something of that nature. He refuses to consider me my own creature." She pursed her lips and shook her head. "No, I have looked upon it from every angle, and I simply cannot continue with my chosen career unless I have a husband who, at least nominally, supports it."

Clem had a struggle not to roll his eyes. He was strongly convinced her *career* without her sister would not last more than a few months before collapsing altogether. Or did she expect him to supply her with an endless collection of roles once he was at the reins? "You expect your husband to act as your manager, then?" he asked dryly. The thought gave him little pleasure. Was there a spot somewhere mid-bill he could stick a gangly spinster without raising too much scorn?

She would not actually be a spinster, a cold voice whispered in his ear, reminding him. She would be his wife. He gave an involuntary shudder. Still…a fifty-percent share. That was not to be sniffed at. He subjected her to another scrutinizing glance and managed not to grimace. "How old are you?" he heard himself ask, striking a match and lighting his cigar.

She answered promptly and without rancor. "Twenty-six."

Old enough to know better, he thought, blowing out a puff of cigar smoke. "Ever been booed off stage?" he asked, gazing at the tip of his cigar. Mayhap a cold dose of reality would be enough to shock her out of her crazy notions of going solo. Such as choking spectacularly on stage. He almost dreaded to think how a prim, sheltered miss like Theodora Fields would cope if she was thrust center stage at one of his own rowdy productions.

The Parthenon had been mostly empty on his own visit, but he had recognized they cultivated a particular crowd there. Their patrons were neither the aristocracy nor the working classes, but a middle ground as it were. They catered to the rising middle classes who pursued culture but expected it to be imminently respectable as they were.

How would Theodora Fields react if she had performed her insipid play in front of a crowd of hecklers at The Eagle and Sun? By either bursting into tears or wetting her drawers, was his own guess. He pondered this as a possible outcome. What if he allowed this to happen? Oh, he could be callous alright, in business, that was. Usually, he was far more gallant toward the ladies though. Still…he eyed her askance; she had approached him with this in the light of a business proposal, had she not?

He let a slow smile spread over his face and watched a hint of wariness enter Miss Fields's demeanor. So…she was not entirely without instinct, he was pleased to see. She was the rabbit to his wily fox, hopping around in front of him and showing him her fluffy tail in such an absurd fashion. "Why don't you tell me about this career you envisage for yourself, now your sister has upped sticks," he suggested in a friendlier manner.

She threw him a grateful look, and he guessed most people in her life had told her flat that she had no place front of stage anymore. Those people had her best interests at heart, he thought wryly. Him, not so much.

She took a steadying breath before beginning. "The Turtle Doves may have disbanded, but I was also raised in the business. I have performed as a male impersonator since I numbered thirteen years."

A male impersonator? Clem nearly choked on his cigar. That was a stretch. *Jesus Christ*, he was embarrassed for her. He had been too generous. Theodora Fields was every bit as deluded as he had initially feared.

"Miss Fields," he interrupted apologetically as soon as he had stopped spluttering. "Standing around in a pair of silk breeches does not a male impersonator make."

Theodora drew herself up at that. "If you would do me the courtesy of hearing me out, Mr. Dabney?" she suggested freezingly.

Very well, if she was determined to make an absolute fool of herself, who was he to stop her? "Go ahead," he said with a shrug. "Be my guest."

"I am aware that I work better in a duo." Well, that was putting it mildly. "And I have a new partner picked out—Mrs. Lillian Longdon. We have known each other for years so we have a good rapport between us. I think we will work together very well indeed."

Lillian Longdon? Clem nearly spat out his cigar. She was replacing her sister's beauty with an over-the-hill actress who was fifty-five if she was a day? He shook his head slightly. She was more than deluded. She was ready for Bedlam. "You have…er…been practicing this new act?" he heard himself say aloud. After all, what else could he say?

She lifted her chin. "We start on the morrow. I have some music picked out already and we will be easily worthy of mid-billing on your list of entertainers."

"Mid-bill is out of the question," he heard himself reply swiftly.

Some of the wind seemed to go out of her sails. "I…well, I suppose that was a bit much," she conceded. "But Uncle always said to aim high, so I thought…" She bit her lip. "Very well, Mr. Dabney, I would settle for bottom of the bill, so long as you give us our start."

Clem took a deep breath. "Have you ever been to a music hall performance, Miss Fields?" he asked skeptically.

She drew herself up in her seat. "I am not so naïve as you assume, sir," she insisted.

"That's a no, then," he observed.

"As a matter of fact, I have once! My uncle took me," she said defensively. "Though we left before the last act as he did not deem that one appropriate." She gave a small cough. "But in any case, I *have* met several music hall performers over the years, for my uncle's theatrical background was quite checkered before he settled down to respectability. I have met Miss Abigail Thewston herself and she gave me many pointers and tips of her trade."

He gazed back at her levelly. It had taken guts to come here and beard him in his den, but did she not realize that every word she spoke revealed how unsuited she was to this life? "I'm being blunt with you to be kind," he said abruptly. "At least it's kinder in the long run." This seemed to give her pause, and she gazed at him, her eyes very bright. He wondered if tears were threatening, and he softened his voice for her.

"I started out as a prizefighter, Miss Fields, as I told you before." Likely, she knew even less about organized fighting than she did music halls, but he had a point to make. "When I started out, I thought I had the makings of a champion, a true great," he confessed. "I truly thought I had it in me, but I got to a certain point in my career and looked about and realized that it just was not going to happen for me. That was when I started planning for a different future and sought out other opportunities in life. That is what you need to do now." And that was putting it generously.

"At least you had your shot," she said with suppressed emotion. "At least you came by that decision yourself, not by someone looking you over and telling you that you were not good enough to even climb in the ring. I tell you, I love the theater. It is in my blood!"

Clem shrugged. "And my mathematics teacher loved boxing ten times more than I ever will, yet he never climbed into the ring, not even once."

She gazed back at him. "Did he train for the ring or was he a mere follower of the sport?"

Clem removed his cigar from his mouth. She had him there. "He was a dedicated follower," he admitted. "But you seem to forget, I have seen your act, Miss Fields."

"No, you have not, Mr. Dabney! You saw *The Faithful Shepherdess*. I readily admit that I was nothing more than a prop in that role. I was not—" She grew choked. "I have not been given my chance in life to shine."

Jesus, she was stubborn. He lit a match. "You want to learn the hard way, is that it? Ever appeared before a hostile crowd?"

"You saw my sister, what do you think?" she shot back at him.

"Honestly?" The gloves were off now. "I think you had an easy ride in life, Miss Fields, and that free ride is now over."

She swallowed and stood up, the light dying out of her eyes. "I appreciate your taking the time to speak to me, Mr. Dabney, and your…candor." She looked as though the words half choked her, but she managed to get them out and thrust her hand across the table with an almost defiant look.

Clem glanced at her navy blue glove. The middle of three buttons was missing. Suppressing a sigh, he reached across and was surprised to feel her firmly grip his fingers. "Good day to you, sir," she said with freezing politeness. "I hope you remember this moment and look back on it with the bitterest regret."

His startled eyes met hers. "Regret?"

"For letting me slip through your fingers," she said, so boldly it almost took his breath away. He liked them bold. If she wasn't so respectable, he might have been tempted to pull her into his lap and kiss her, for all her plainness. Instead, he laughed and saw the ire spark in her eyes before she bolted from the room.

5

He had laughed at her. Theo blinked back hot, angry tears. *Laughed.* And the worst kind of laughter too. *At* her and not *with* her. She hated him, *loathed* him. He was a smug, rotten bastard who thought he knew it all after running his tawdry dinner and show outfit for eighteen months! *How dare he?* she raged inwardly as she plunged down another cobbled passageway.

Her chest burned with indignation and something worse than that. *Humiliation.* She had offered herself to him on a platter, and he had turned his nose up. That really smarted. She knew she was no matrimonial prize, but he hadn't needed to be so rude about it! Now what was she going to do? Lil would be out on the street with her dependents and so would poor Mrs. Cherwell and her Herbert.

It was no good appealing to her brother, for his mind was made up. For all his bohemian ways, Felix expected the utmost respectability from his sisters. He seemed to be getting worse as he got older instead of better. He had been pleased Henrietta was leaving the stage—*pleased!*—despite their rich heritage and the theater in which he had always been so proud.

It's no life for a decent woman, that was what he had said, the only time she had spoken to him of her burning aspiration to be a real male impersonator, not just a token one. When they were children, Felix had loved her mimicry as much as their uncle, and had taken great delight in watching her whistle a tune and do her impersonation of the butcher boy's swagger.

Even her uncle had prevented her bringing any of that swagger to the stage though. The Turtle Doves was strictly noncontroversial. Just two young girls singing their quaint ballads at the intervals and appearing in cameos in other productions. Henrietta had a sweet soprano voice and Theodora was a decent alto.

Of course, the real attraction lay with Henrietta's beauty. Likely their uncle had put Theo in breeches originally, merely so she did not suffer by way of comparison. He could not have dreamed at the time that it would become her life's ambition.

How vividly she remembered all of her uncle's theatrical visitors over the years, but Abigail Thewston was the one she remembered best of all. That diminutive old lady with her merry laugh and the twinkle in her eye as their uncle had pronounced her, "The greatest male impersonator of the last two decades. You would scarce credit it, my dears, but I assure you 'tis true." Then out had come the faded pamphlets, the printed bills announcing her as Sweet William and Billy Ballad and illustration upon illustration of Miss Thewston in the elaborate stage garb of breeches roles.

Theo had been immediately entranced. Abigail Thewston had been a giantess of the stage and not by dint of any great beauty or by some distinguished patron's espousing her cause. "Observation," the retired actress had told her when Theo shyly asked her secret. "You've got to watch how menfolk handle themselves."

"And not just when they know they're being watched," she had added, "but more importantly when they think they're *unobserved*. Watch their mannerisms, watch how they hold themselves. How they walk, how they talk, and how this is different, when they're among intimate or casual friends or business acquaintances, or their sweetheart. For they don't act the same in those situations, not by a long shot."

Miss Thewston had taken a sip of her wine and then tipped her head to look at Theo. "You're a fine tall girl and no mistake. I wish I'd had your inches," she'd sighed. "I could have taken real principal parts then and not just the breeches roles."

"That's what I want," Theo had confided.

Miss Thewston had laughed merrily at that. "You got to do more than just observe, then. In that case, you got to *perfect*

51

emulating them. Every day, pick one out, a man I mean. In the coffee house, in the street, even if it's only under your window. Then, when you're alone, in front of a looking glass, practice each look, each gesture, each nuance."

Theo had been wide-eyed. "I will," she had promised.

"I believe you." Miss Thewston had nodded before beckoning her closer. When Theo came in close, she'd whispered, "What you got to remember is, a lot of their front is just an act itself." She'd winked at Theo, then returned to reminiscing with their uncle about the old days.

Theo had taken every single word Abigail Thewston had said to heart and had never forgotten it. From that day forward she had become an avid observer and practiced her mimicry every night without fail. Paper boys, butcher boys, and boot boys had been her initial quarry. Once she had gotten their ways down pat, she moved on to larger subjects.

Clerks and costermongers, shopkeepers and streetsweepers, Theo stalked them all. On shopping expeditions, or walks in the park, she would spot a particularly distinctive walk and then fasten them with her deepest attention, sometimes following them for over a mile before she was satisfied she had the full gamut of their mannerisms.

When she got older, she added soldiers, sailors, bankers, and solicitors to her repertoire. Even the most discreet and unassuming could be found to have some interesting quirk or habit. Maybe how they flourished their handkerchief, or covertly tucked their betting slips into their pockets.

Even distraught as she currently felt, her pulse racing and her face flaming hot, Theo observed out of the corner of her eye a bandy-legged gait which caught her fancy. She slowed down automatically so that she fell in step behind the fellow. It felt like second nature to her now. She hadn't even made the conscious choice to follow him.

52

By the time her quarry had reached a public park and let himself through the wrought iron gate, Theo felt she had fully memorized his curious walk and her ruffled feathers had smoothed back down. Instead of following him into the neat gardens, Theo heaved a great sigh and retraced her steps to where she had been dropped off that morning.

She had failed. There was no getting around it. Her plan had fallen at the first fence. The taste of bitter defeat lingered on her tongue. All she could do now was retreat, lick her wounds, and regroup. She needed to think of a new plan.

It was not just a case of following her own dream these days. She had other people depending on her. Lil and Mrs. Cherwell were not as fortunate as herself; they had no guaranteed roof over their heads. Their landlords would throw them out on the street as soon as they failed to make rent.

Deciding against using any more of her dwindling funds on a hackney cab, Theo pulled her tasseled hat firmly down over her brow, hitched her handbag up to her elbow, and started her long walk home. It was a cold, crisp day in mid-February and Theo focused at first on the sound of her boot heels hitting the pavement and watching her breath puff out before her in the frigid air.

As she found her stride, her mind started to wander, playing over her recent ordeal and dwelling with horrible accuracy over minor details she had not fully appreciated at the time, so busily had she been concentrating on the task at hand. That smile that had played about Clem Dabney's lips, for one. Others might think it charming, but not she!

Her mouth thinned grimly as she recalled his tolerant expression of forced patience as she had pleaded her cause. It made her cheeks burn to think of it. Distractedly, she pressed her gloved hands to her face. Oh, she hoped she had not made a fool of herself, but she had the terrible feeling she had done just that. Certainly, Mr. Dabney had thought her a hopeless cause.

She swallowed painfully. The way he had laughed when she had finally thrown a little defiance his way made her ball her gloved hands into fists. Oh, he was monstrously arrogant! How dare he? She had given him the benefit of the doubt after their first meeting, thinking she might have been too harsh in her appraisal, but no. If anything, she had been far too generous!

She should have trusted her instincts, she seethed. Both times she had met him she had eventually abandoned her good manners to throw some kind of barbed comment in his face. Which was strange, now she came to think of it. Theo was not accustomed to outbursts of temper. If anything, she was known for the evenness and equanimity of her moods. Somehow, *that man* had an unfortunate tendency to bring out the worst in her.

She rued the day she had crossed paths with him! Theo dashed impatient fingers across her moist eyes. Now was not the time to fall into maudlin self-pity, she told herself sternly. At worst, Clem Dabney thought she was a figure for ridicule. At best, she had given him a good laugh that morning, and he would promptly dismiss her from his thoughts.

Her stomach clenched. Would he tell his friends and acquaintances of how she had propositioned him? Her step slowed a moment, and she breathed noisily in and out to steady her nerves and fight down the sick feeling clawing up from her stomach. He was no gentleman, so he likely would not scruple to repeat the tale to his cronies.

So what if he did? she rallied bravely, forcing herself to quicken her pace. It made no odds to her, and she would likely never hear of it in any case. Even if he was not a braggart, it would be strange indeed if he never breathed a word of it to another soul. After all, he must have been taken aback. He could hardly have realized he would receive an offer of marriage that gray February morning.

In all truth, she probably *had* appeared ridiculous to him. How could she not? Theo was under no illusions about how outsiders might view her. Uncle Barnabus had always encouraged them to follow the beat of their own drum, without heeding what conventional types might make of them. She had followed his advice the closest out of the three siblings.

Henrietta, the oldest, had always cared the most about public opinion. As for Felix, the middle child, he only seemed to care when it suited him, Theo thought bitterly. Out of the three of them, she, the youngest, was the one most likely to be seen as an odd fish. Was it so strange that Mr. Dabney should view her as such? He would not be the first or the last to do so, she reflected fairly.

Why, then, had it rankled so? For the *second* time, she realized dazedly, she had been put out by Dabney's dismissal of her. It was strange. Usually, she only cared what people thought when she liked or admired them. Neither of which applied to Clem Dabney. She had spoken nothing but the truth—she would dearly love to see him get pummeled in the ring!

It was unfortunate that his poor opinion of her seemed to bother her at some level. Unfortunate and *stupid*. She must put this behind her now and consign him to a place of little importance in her life. He was a mere footnote. A missed opportunity. Something that was not meant to be.

Theo lifted her chin and trudged on. She would rise to this challenge, she must. She would give herself a couple of days to recover from this blow and then she must resurrect her scheme from its ashes and redouble her efforts. That had to be a way, there just *had* to be. She simply refused to accept she was defeated.

She reached home, battered and worn with cares. Casting her hat and outerwear onto the pegs under the stairs, she wandered through to the parlor, wondering if she was the only one home. The house seemed very quiet.

Casting herself into the most comfortable chair, she decided she was glad neither of her siblings was home. Hetty was no doubt being squired about by Sir Matthew, and as for Felix, he would be about some business or other. He seldom felt the need to keep his sisters informed of his habits, though he invariably turned up for meals.

It was only when she found the letter propped on the parlor mantel addressed *Felix and Theodora* in Hetty's round handwriting that she felt the first pang of misgiving. Tearing it open, she found she had not been the only one strategizing for her future. Her sister had eloped to France with Sir Matthew Hillingdon.

6

It was a full three weeks later that Clem found himself rapping on the door in Juniper Row. When there was no response, he was forced to apply himself to the door knocker for a second time, with more vigor. Perhaps the Fieldses' housekeeper was half deaf? he reflected, considering a third attack on the olive-green door with the brass knocker.

It was then he thought he caught some movement behind the stained-glass panels. Finally, the door swung back, and an odd figure stood outlined in the doorway. It was Theodora Fields, he recognized, though her manner of dress was even more peculiar than the last time he had seen her.

She looked like she had donned something agricultural workers wore when they worked in the fields. What was it called? A smock? She also had what looked like a wet tea towel wrapped around her wrist. She gazed at him uncomprehendingly a moment before recognition dawned in those gray eyes.

"Mr. Dabney!" she exclaimed in astonishment, starting forward as though to join him on the step outside before pulling herself up short. "Did you come to see me, or…?" She glanced back over her shoulder. "Well, actually, no one else is home."

"In that case, might I trouble you to come inside?" he asked smoothly. He was almost sure that Miss Fields was wholly oblivious to any disturbance in her respectable street, but Clem fancied he had already seen some curtains twitching in neighboring houses.

"Oh, er, yes, I suppose," she murmured before dropping back to let him in. "I would take you into the front parlor, but…" She glanced down at her peculiar outfit.

"You were in the middle of something?" he hazarded. "Gardening?"

57

A look of surprise flashed across her face. "Gardening? Whatever gave you that idea? No, no, I was just in the kitchen, making a…well, a sort of pie," she said vaguely. "I'm covered in flour."

"I will be glad to accompany you there," he assured her smoothly. "Lead the way."

"Really?" She perked up at the suggestion of this social solecism and, shutting the door, led him past a dark wood staircase and down a narrow passageway until they reached an untidy kitchen. "I apologize for the mess. I am in the midst of preparing dinner." She gazed down unhappily at the kitchen table which was covered in a mass of unevenly rolled dough.

"Felix says he refuses to eat stew for a third night in succession and asked for steak and kidney pudding." Her tone was despairing. "I looked up the recipe, but there is *so* much faffing about with suet and the *steaming* of puddings that I could not face it. So, I thought a steak and ale pie would do as well, but I think pastry is probably *every bit* as difficult. I cannot tell if I have overworked or underworked it, but it does not feel at all as they describe in the book, and it keeps sticking to the table no matter *how* much flour I fling down on it." She gazed at him unhappily. "Tea?"

Instead of answering, he pointed at her arm. "What happened here?"

"I burned it on the range," she confessed, turning away as her eyes became suspiciously watery.

"Can I see it?"

"It's not really anything…" she protested as he propelled her toward a chair, sat her down, and peered under the tea towel at the large red welt.

"How about I make the tea and you just sit here awhile?" he asked. "That cloth needs soaking again in cold water."

58

Instead of demanding the reason of his visit, Theodora nodded and sniffed. "Tea would be nice," she admitted. "I have not had time for a cup since breakfast."

Clem approached the unwieldy kitchen range and eyed it a moment before making himself busy with the kettle. Once that was set on the stove, he peered into a large pitcher. "Is this just cold water?" he asked Theodora, who was now slumped in her seat with her eyes closed. She opened one eyelid to look.

"Yes," she murmured.

He poured some in a bowl and approached her again to resoak her impromptu bandage. She sat very still and docile as he performed these offices, though she did hiss through her teeth when the cold cloth touched her burned skin once more. Clem set her arm down on the table and looked about for a teapot and leaves.

Neither of them spoke again until he poured the brewed tea into two cups. Despite the fact they did not match their saucers, they were of the finest bone china. He pushed one toward her.

"Thank you," she sighed and promptly drained the cup.

"Now you've likely burned your tongue as well," he remarked.

She shook her head. "I only like it when it's piping hot."

Clem waited for her to ask him what he was doing there, but her gaze was now traveling unhappily around the kitchen. "Mrs. Cherwell would be furious if she could see the mess I have made in here," she admitted sadly.

"You mentioned her before I think."

She nodded but did not expand on this as her dull eyes finally finished running over the untidy dresser to land on him once more. A faint pucker appeared between her brows. "What *are* you doing here, Mr. Dabney?" it finally occurred to her to ask.

Something, he realized, had changed in Miss Theodora Fields since he last saw her. Today, he would not be subjected

59

to any outrageous comments. She was too miserable for that, and for some reason, he did not like to see it. Disappointment did not suit her.

Promptly, he abandoned the dry business proposition he had been about to lay before her. "I didn't want to let you slip through my fingers, Miss Fields," he said instead. Her blank expression told him she had not made the connection to her parting shot. "As soon as you walked out that door, I felt it."

"Felt what?" she asked with a faint frown.

"Regret," he uttered concisely.

Her forlorn expression slowly transformed before him. She sat up in her seat, her cheeks flushed, and her dull eyes swam into focus. "You did?" she gasped.

He nodded. "Of the bitterest kind."

A gurgle of laughter escaped her lips. "You're teasing me," she said uncertainly.

He shook his head. "No. I think your scheme is inspired. We both get what we want out of it, right?"

"You—my scheme?" She stared as though transfixed, as though she could not quite bring herself to believe his words. "Inspired?" she murmured at last. "You do not mean that?"

"Yes, I do. It was, frankly, so audacious that I could not comprehend its genius at first. You are very bold and direct, Miss Fields. I like that. Especially in a partner."

She licked her lips. "To *marry*?" she faltered, sounding entirely scandalized, even though the scheme had been of her own making. "You do not want to see me audition for you first?" She gulped. "Or—?"

"No." *Christ, no.* He didn't want to lie to her face about her abysmal act. He would just let it die a natural death out on the stage. Then he would console and settle her into something else. Anything else. The haphazard clutter of the kitchen caught his eye. Not housekeeping, he thought with a wince. No, definitely not housekeeping.

"Mr. Dabney, I—I hardly know what to say!" When his eyes snapped back to hers, he saw they were clearly brimming with tears again. Grateful ones this time, he hoped. She started to stand up, then sank back down into her seat. "How soon do you think—?"

"First things first, we'll have to get the banns read," he said simultaneously.

Her eyes widened. She looked, he thought, rather petrified at the prospect, though she was making an effort to conceal it. "Yes, yes, of course." She hesitated. "My own family are not regular churchgoers. Are you a member of a local congregation?"

"No," he admitted truthfully, feeling a little taken aback by her own confession. Maybe her family was not as respectable as he had imagined. "There is a church near my lodgings; we should probably get them read there, as we need to…er…keep our cards close to our chests." She nodded when he looked at her. "Could you slip away and meet me every Sunday for the next however many weeks it takes?" How many was it? Six? Eight? He had only the vaguest idea how it all worked.

She gulped. "Yes, of course. I suppose it will be a morning service. I could always tell Felix I was going to church, which would be perfectly true. He would probably approve of that," she admitted, sounding resentful of the fact.

They both clammed up, eyeing one another with a certain measure of wariness. "We should probably get married there too," he suggested, the words sounding odd coming out of his own mouth, however casual he tried to make them sound. "It's in Clapham. St. Thomas's."

"Yes, good thinking," she agreed in a croak. "Do we both meet with the vicar initially or…?"

Clem inserted a finger under his collar, which suddenly felt rather tight. "No idea," he admitted, clearing his throat. "Not my area of expertise. I will make enquiries."

61

"Perhaps you could send me word to let me know at what time I should meet you?" she said faintly, then inspiration seemed to strike, for her expression brightened. "Maybe we should devise a cipher for our secret correspondence?" she suggested excitedly.

It was his turn to look blank. "A cipher?" he repeated, tipping his head.

"Or," she said eagerly, "you could write to me under an alias. Such as calling yourself Clementine Darby."

Clem practically blanched. "Clementine…?"

Catching sight of his expression, she said quickly, "Or any other name you deem fit. You see, if a man was to write to me, it would surely raise eyebrows, and my brother would likely take issue with it."

Clem gazed at her again. To his surprise, he found *he* was taking issue with the idea of such underhandedness. He frowned. "How did you slip away to visit me in Shoreditch the other week?" he asked, suddenly curious.

"Oh, it was quite easy. My brother was at rehearsals and my sister—well, it actually turned out my sister was eloping, though none of us realized it at the time."

"Eloping?" Clem was startled. Surely that was the same day Henrietta Fields had signed over her rights to the theater to him?

"Yes," she agreed absently, seemingly oblivious to his surprise. "We had a telegram when she reached Calais a week ago, but we have received nothing else since. Felix says we should not be alarmed as doubtless, she is far too busy pleasure-bent to write to us. She promised to write again when she reached Paris."

Casting a quick look at her, Clem guessed Henrietta had still not confessed she had sold her interest in The Parthenon to either of her siblings. "Who did she elope with?" he asked curiously, thinking of the broken-nosed man mountain who had escorted her to his office.

"Sir Matthew Hillingdon," Theodora answered without much enthusiasm.

Not the bruiser, Clem realized and returned abruptly to the previous matter. "You should never travel to Shoreditch like that after dark," he found himself cautioning her. "Not alone."

"I know that," she answered without rancor. "We always have an escort to the theater in the evenings. *Had* an escort," she corrected herself. "When I still acted."

"Who was that?"

"Vincent, the doorman at The Parthenon."

"Would he carry messages for you?"

She paused as if to consider, then shook her head. "Alas, I could not be assured of his loyalty," she admitted. "My brother pays his wages, and it was my sister he was slavishly devoted to, not me." Her eyes took on a faraway look. "Poor Vinnie," she murmured, her mouth twisting. "He is quite heartbroken by Hetty's running off like that."

Briefly, Clem wondered if the bruiser and the broken-hearted doorman were one and the same. Then he dismissed the matter from his mind. "Do you have someone you *do* trust?"

"Well…" She seemed to think a moment. "There is always Albert."

"Albert?"

"He is a paper boy I am friends with who sometimes runs errands for me. He sells his papers near the theater, but he has fetched a parcel or two for me in his time and knows where I live."

This sounded more like it. "Have him come to The Eagle and Sun on a Friday afternoon to collect letters for you."

"Every Friday?" He nodded. "And will you pay him a tip?" Before he could answer she flushed and started fiddling with the tea towel wrapping her arm. "I only ask because I have divided what savings I had between Lil and Mrs. Cherwell, and I do not have much left."

"Lil and Mrs. Cherwell?" he repeated, a pucker between his brows.

"Felix has dismissed them both you see, and they will end up on the street without my help."

What he saw was that she had a hobby collecting lame ducks. He wondered if there was also a three-legged dog in the offing. "I will give Albert a penny every Friday," he confirmed, reaching into his jacket and withdrawing his wallet.

"I did not mean to appeal to you for funds!" she said hurriedly. "It is just that I need to be careful with my expenses, now I no longer receive a wage, however paltry it might have been."

He flashed her a smile, cutting off her awkward words. "You will need to catch a cab to my neighborhood," he pointed out. "We are getting married, are we not?" he said, placing two notes on the kitchen table before replacing his wallet and straightening his coat.

When he slid his gaze back to her, he found to his surprise that she had still not taken the bank notes from the table and her cheeks were bright red. "Mr. Dabney, that is a good deal of money," she pointed out.

"I'm sure you have a hundred things to spend your pin money on," he told her steadily, "and it is now my place to provide it."

"We are not yet married!" she pointed out, then glanced about nervously in case anyone should have overheard her compromising words. She cleared her throat. "It is…very good of you," she finished off awkwardly, still gazing at the money with a troubled expression.

"Perhaps bride clothes?" he suggested, hoping like hell she would not turn up to the church in anything like whatever it was she was currently trailing about in.

64

She reached at last for the money, though she still looked torn. "You are too generous," she murmured, before concealing it somewhere about her person. He looked away to give her a moment's privacy.

He felt a sudden conviction that the money would be spent neither on hats nor gowns for her wedding, but on some obscure cause such as over-the-hill actresses and unemployed domestic servants.

They both rose from their seats, and Clem was just opening his mouth to say something glib when she took an impulsive step toward him. "You will never regret this, Mr. Dabney," she said, seizing his hand, and this time she did not go for the handshake but instead clutched it to her chest as she gazed up at him earnestly. Clem blinked. She did not have much there, but what she did have was clearly uncorseted. He cleared his throat.

"Oh, I…er, do beg your pardon," mumbled a voice from the doorway, and Clem turned to find a scarlet-cheeked young man staring at them both with undisguised dismay.

"Oh, Harold," Henrietta faltered. "I—er—did not realize you were at home. Did you want something?" Then she seemed to notice she still held Clem's hand cradled to her bosom and hastily dropped it. "My friend is just leaving, are you not?"

Clem paused a moment, unsure of his cue. When the other man neither demanded his name nor his business there, he retrieved his hat which he had flung on a chair and allowed Theodora to shepherd him toward the kitchen door. Was she aware she was ushering him out of the tradesman's entrance? He wondered who the gentleman was, not the brother for he had met that prick.

To do him justice, Felix Fields would not have just stood there looking bewildered as his sister rushed a clandestine caller out of their house. "Thank you *so* much for visiting," she said loudly and practically banged the door in his face. Clem stood

65

frowning at the door for a moment before starting slowly down the garden path.

He felt more put out by the nature of their parting than he would like to admit. Was the fact they had been discovered going to cause a problem for her? Glancing uneasily over his shoulder, he found Theodora's anxious face was now watching him out of the kitchen window. When he reached the gate, almost obscured by an overgrown hedge, he raised his hand and gave her a wave. Her tensed shoulders relaxed at once, and she returned his gesture enthusiastically before turning away.

That, he supposed, was that. He was engaged to be married. He could not quite believe it and had to pinch himself once or twice to check he had not dreamed the hasty avowal. The Parthenon would make it all worthwhile, he told himself uneasily, but the rest of the week did not entirely dissipate the strange mood that overtook him.

He was forced to call at the church twice before he could get some private speech with Canon Bridgewater. That elderly gentleman scrawled down a few particulars and said he would expect to meet with them both before communion on Sunday. Clem felt another qualm which took all of five minutes to dispel. The unworldly clergyman would never suspect such a businesslike transaction was behind the holy sacrament.

On Friday, when Jim showed a skinny, sharp-eyed youth of twelve or thirteen into his office, Clem could not think who he was for a moment. He gazed at the boy, waiting for enlightenment, but to his surprise found the youth was subjecting him to a keen-eyed scrutiny.

"Gotter note for you, guvnor," the boy announced at last, shoving back his oversized check cap on his head. "I b'lieve you're expectin' it."

Clem's eyebrows snapped together, and he nodded a dismissal to Jim. "You must be Albert," he commented and held his hand out for the missive. The boy handed it over promptly. It was not scented, and the paper was of plainest white. Nothing about it indicated it was from a woman, let alone his affianced.

Dear Mr. D., she had written in a firm hand. *I hope this note finds you in good health. So sorry to hurry you out like that on Tuesday. I do hope you weren't offended. I did not wish to put Mr. Allsop into a difficult position.*

"Mr. Allsop?" he muttered with a raised brow. She had addressed the man rather more familiarly, if he recalled, as "Harold." He did not know why that caused him a twinge of annoyance, but it did.

I trust our plan is progressing nicely and we are still due to meet on Sunday as discussed. Kind regards, T.F.

He had already written his own note, which he withdrew now from his pocket. Glancing at it, he wondered if it was not a little brief in contrast to her own.

T. Meet me at the corner of Harlow Rd. where it meets Porton Sq. at ten thirty sharp on Sunday morning. C.D.

"Wait, while I write another line," he directed the boy, who was gazing about his office with interest. Albert nodded and crossed the room to peer out of the window at the street scene below. Clem picked up his pen and wrote scratchily underneath. *Plan all in hand.*

He folded the paper. "Albert, isn't it?" Clem asked, sliding the note across the table.

"S'right, guv," Albert said, reaching for the note.

"Do you read?" Clem asked, for he did not have an envelope to hand.

"Nah," the boy responded with a shrug. "Ain't never seen the point." He crammed Clem's reply into his jacket pocket and sent a speculative look his way. "If you don't mind me asking, sir, what's your game?"

Remembering the lad was a friend of sorts of Theodora's, Clem bit back his instinctive response. "I run these concert

67

rooms," he said instead and flipped him a coin which Albert was quick to snatch out of the air.

The boy gave a whoop and clattered to the door in his hobnail boots before whipping round, his hand on the door handle, plainly poised for flight. "'Ere you ain't sweet on 'er, are you, guv?" he asked disbelievingly.

Clem narrowed his eyes. "Be off with you!" he growled, and Albert promptly turned tail and fled.

Sunday dawned heavy with fog, which Clem supposed would be useful for their clandestine first meeting. Though, not if she lost her way before she found St. Thomas's, he thought wryly as he dressed in his most conservative suit of sage-green plaid. True, there was a mustard stripe running through it, but if he avoided the bright yellow waistcoat he generally teamed it up with and went with one of gray, he hoped he would not cut too conspicuous a figure among the sober churchgoers.

Clem made his way down to breakfast and wished a determinedly cheerful "Morning" to his landlady, who had been casting him reproachful looks ever since he had given his notice to leave at the end of March. He had spent a comfortable twelve months beneath her roof, but he was not particularly sorry to leave.

The other boarders were professional types, dentists and doctors, and Clem had very little in common with any of them. He had infinitely preferred its solid respectability and comfort to some of the squalid lodgings he had been forced to use in his early twenties. They had been little better than dosshouses, and he was determined he would never again sink to such depths.

He supposed he would need to engage a hotel room for their wedding night. They could hardly turn up at her brother's house as newlyweds. Not when they were likely to get a hostile reception. In any case, he could not have brought his bride back to his current digs, for no women were permitted into Mrs. O'Malley's, bastion of respectability that it was.

It was probably best if he did not raise this particular subject with Theodora just yet, he decided, wolfing down his breakfast of sausage, ham, and eggs.

By the time he had crossed the street to Harlow Road and reached Porton Square, he was on a sharp lookout for any approaching hansom cabs. The fog, however, was so thick by this point that he had to content himself with listening out for the sound of horses' hooves.

When he reached the prearranged meeting point, Clem reached into his jacket for his cigar case. By his reckoning, he just had time to smoke a half cigar before the service started. He had only just struck a match when he heard approaching footsteps. Clem cleared his throat to alert the newcomer to his presence. Sure enough, the steps faltered.

"Theodora?" he said aloud and heard her sigh of relief.

No sooner had she said "Yes, it's me" than she appeared before him in that coat and tasseled hat. He met her nervous smile with one of assurance, designed to put her at her ease. After a moment's hesitation, she took his proffered arm, and they strolled in the direction of the church.

"So," he began once they had exchanged greetings, "what is new with you, Dora?" He felt her nervous start. "I did warn you," he said with a lopsided grin.

She struggled a moment with her response. "No one calls me that," she said at last in strangled tones.

"I do," he said firmly and tipped her a wink.

She screwed up her eyes. "Last time we met, you did not actually address me as Dora," she said, nervously plucking at her sleeve. He noticed her gloves at least matched today.

"I expect I did; you were just rather preoccupied with your pie. How did that turn out by the way?"

She grimaced. "Do not even ask! Even poor Harold could not force down more than a mouthful and he would do anything to be polite."

69

"I thought your brother's name was Felix," he said slyly.

"Oh, it is. Harold is our—well, a sort of lodger. As a matter of fact, he is a fellow shareholder in The Parthenon."

Clem's ears pricked up. "Is he indeed?"

"Yes, for he owns a quarter share. My uncle Barnabus sold it to him five years ago to raise funds for a production he was convinced had the makings of a huge success." She sighed. "Alas it did not work out that way."

"I see," he murmured. "Unfortunate."

"You must not think that my uncle regretted letting Harold buy into the business," she said quickly. "My uncle was sort of a mentor to him, so it seemed to make sense, for Harold had lately inherited some money he wanted to invest."

"And now an outsider owns twenty-five percent of the theater?"

"Yes," she agreed, "though Harold has been with us so long he scarce seems an outsider to the family in truth."

"A sort of second brother?" Clem suggested, shooting her a shrewd look.

Theo had the grace to blush. "Well," she said evasively, "perhaps more of a cousin of sorts."

Clem supposed he would have to make do with that. "What did you tell him?" he asked, suddenly curious. "After he caught us together in the kitchen?"

She gave a small, uneasy laugh. "You make it sound so much more incriminating than it was, Mr. Dabney. We were hardly *in flagrante delicto*."

He could see she was trying to act like a woman of the world, but her shallow breathing told him she was nothing of the sort. Also, she had a thousand tells showing her nervousness.

"I think you had better call me Clem," he answered. "And I've never studied any Latin, Dora. You'll have to use plain speech around me. I'm not a gentleman, you see."

70

She gave him a swift, stricken look. "It means 'while the crime is blazing,'" she said hurriedly.

Clem frowned, for though he had spoken the truth and he was no scholar, he *had* come across that term before. He could have sworn it was to do with getting caught with your trousers down. "If he is any sort of family member at all, he ought to have called me out," he said heavily.

Theodora avoided his gaze. "Harold is not the confrontational type," she explained, "and you are quite an intimidating specimen. I do not think anyone could really blame him. And besides, things are a little awkward between Harold and me right now." She sounded, he thought, a little wistful.

"Why?" he heard himself ask, though it was actually none of his damn business.

"Well, he has been in my bad books of late, and I have been giving him the cold shoulder. Ever since Felix told me Harold supported him in the decision to make me housekeeper."

It trembled on Clem's tongue to ask if she had corroborated that fact with Harold or merely taken her brother's word for it. Then again, it suited his current purpose for her to be at outs with her family right now, even family in the loosest of senses. "So, Allsop said nothing about discovering you cozied up with a stranger in the house?" he persisted.

"Nothing whatsoever," she confirmed.

Sort of brother, my ass, thought Clem. "Is he courting? Engaged?"

She shook her head. "Poor Harold suffered a disappointment in life."

Clem almost rolled his eyes. He looked the type. "Oh?" he said aloud, leaving a convenient silence for Theodora to fill.

"His cousin Myrna and he had a…*an understanding*," she said primly, and he could tell the phrasing was not her own, but that milksop Allsop's.

"His cousin?" he repeated and was not sure he had managed to keep the derision from his tone.

"Not a first cousin," she hurried to assure him. "A second cousin, once removed."

"Another *sort of cousin*," he commented dryly, and she looked up quickly at his tone. He smiled to reassure her but could see from her expression she was not entirely convinced.

"Myrna contracted consumption and died of it on her twenty-first birthday," she explained. "They hired the best doctors, but nothing could be done to save her. It was all very tragic."

"And when was this?"

"Three—no, four years ago last Whitsun."

Clem forbore to comment further on this, and in any case, they had now reached the church gate. They both paused as one before it and eyed each other.

"Well," he said, "here we are."

"No going back now," she added with a clear wobble in her voice.

He paused and glanced down at her. "Do you need a moment?"

"Not at all," she assured him hurriedly. Strange to say, her own show of nerves settled any vestiges of his own.

Their brief meeting in the vestry with the vicar was surprisingly painless. Theodora looked extremely sincere and attentive, and Clem was at his most respectful. After this, they passed into the nave and sought out a pew at the back of the church. When they emerged an hour later from the gray stone church, they found that the fog had started to lift, and it had now started to lightly rain.

Theodora squinted up at the sky and then turned to Clem. "So…we have a wedding date," she commented, for Canon Bridgewater had said they could be married after four Sundays' worth of banns.

72

Clem nodded. "We do indeed."

She held her breath and turned very pink. Clem could not tell if she was thrilled or terrified at the prospect, and he rather fancied neither could she. After a moment she thrust her hand out again in that forthright gesture of hers. "Until next Sunday, then," she said bravely.

"I'll see you into a cab," he said. "My manners aren't quite so shabby that I would allow you to wander off into the fog alone." He took her arm and steered her in the right direction. "How is your arm, by the way?" he asked.

"My arm?"

He frowned slightly. "Where you burned it."

"Oh, that." She gave a slight laugh. "I completely forgot about it in all the excitement. It is quite healed." She cast him a quick smile. "Thank you for asking." The sound of an approaching cab had her wheeling about. "Stop! Cab!" she cried before Clem had the chance.

When it halted, Clem stepped forward and opened the door for her. He helped her up and leaned against the top of the door for a moment before it pulled away. "Same time, same place next week?"

She nodded so hard the tassel on her hat swung about and hit her in the face. "Yes please," she said, though she looked scared out of her wits at the prospect.

It was not until the cab pulled away that Clem realized he should have told her not to bother writing to him via Albert the following Friday, for they had already fixed their next meeting. For some reason, he was not unduly bothered about the needless exchange of letters.

In fact, he thought, suddenly brightening, he should ask her to Sunday lunch next week. He could take her somewhere respectable and convince her that he was nothing but a big softy at heart, then maybe she would stop trembling every time he touched her. The fact it was a complete lie did not bother him overmuch.

7

Theo spent the next week in a state of nervous anticipation. For some reason, instead of settling her nerves, her Sunday morning with Clem had set them all a-flutter. She could not remotely understand *why*, for he had been his most affable yet. Really, he had been almost agreeable company, if she had not been so terrified by what they were up to.

Maybe it was because the memories of their first two meetings still lingered, she pondered on Tuesday as she chopped haphazardly at two large parsnips. After all, they had met only four times, and for at least half those times, Mr. Dabney had been frankly unappreciative of her talent and person.

You have had a free ride in life and that is now over, she seemed to recall with unfortunate vividness. Oh yes, and *standing around in a pair of silk breeches does not a male impersonator make.* That one had held a particular sting. Still, they were on the same page now, and he did not seem to hold her in such contempt anymore. At least, not openly.

Theo wiped her brow with her forearm and surveyed the chunks of parsnip with disfavor. What was it she had been planning to do with them anyway? She debated a moment before scooping them up and throwing them into a pan of water. One boiled parsnips, did one not? Overall, Theo found boiling vegetables to be less hazardous than roasting them. They were less likely to shrivel up into blackened hard lumps that way.

Her gaze traveled doubtfully over the other ingredients lying nearby, but they looked similarly uninspiring. Had she had some particular plan in mind for this evening's meal? She stared blankly down at a leek, a stalk of Brussels sprouts, and a pair of mutton chops, before shrugging and reaching for the sprouts. She may as well peel and prepare them for boiling too. It was unlikely she would be struck with inspiration any time soon. One good thing about her preoccupation with her scandalous plans was that it had left her mercifully indifferent to Felix's scathing appraisal of her housekeeping skills, or lack thereof.

He had been most vocal about the dinners she saw fit to dish up to him and Harold of an evening. Breakfast was not too bad, for Theo could fob them off with toast, bacon, and eggs most mornings. Her one attempt at porridge, which had been very lumpy, had left her brother begging her never to try it again. The two men were expected to make their own arrangements for lunch, as it fell in the middle of their workday, so she was spared that necessity.

No, it was the evening meals that caused Theo's poor head to ache. Planning them, buying the ingredients for them, and—worst of all—cooking them. She was under no illusions that anything she had served at table so far had been remotely appetizing. The vegetables were usually limp and overcooked, the gravy watery, and the meat invariably tough.

She knew for a fact Felix had been fortifying himself with midday visits to the pie vendor near the theater. She had found pastry crumbs and telling grease stains on his cuffs and lapels when she had been struggling with the dreaded laundry.

She must be an undutiful sister indeed, for the information did not mortify her as she knew it would other women. As for Harold, her feelings still smarted enough for her to ignore the fact he managed to clear only half of his supper plate these days, and if this continued for any time, his clothes would soon be hanging off him.

Suddenly, she remembered she should have gone to the baker this morning, for they had finished off the last of the bread at breakfast. That was another thing Theo was finding difficult, staying on top of supplies. For the past two weeks, she had found herself running out of random things on an almost daily basis.

Monday had been eggs, Tuesday, milk, and Wednesday, butter. It was simply impossible to keep track of things. Yesterday she had noticed the flour tin was almost empty and she had been forced to scrape the sugar bowl this morning for her cup of tea. How on earth had Mrs. Cherwell managed to juggle it all?

Theo abandoned the sprouts and cast about with a harassed air for the piece of paper she had started scrawling her shopping list on, but when she discovered it, she did not think it was the right one. This one simply stated "Coal." Were they about to run out of coal? She glanced about at the coal scuttle. It did look a little low now she thought about it. *Bother*.

What day was the coal merchant was supposed to call? Mrs. Cherwell had been prepared with payment for every tradesman's visit, but Theo missed half of them and found herself short of the necessary coins for the others. It was all most vexing and dissatisfactory all around.

A sudden horrid thought occurred to her. Perhaps the coal supplier had cut them off for nonpayment? Felix would never forgive her if the household water was not heated. *Ugh*. She scrubbed at her tired eyes. She really must try to catch the coal wagon this week and find out if they were bad debtors.

Picking up a pencil, she found she had now forgotten whatever it was she had wanted to add. She studied it a moment, racking her brains. *Ah yes, bread*. Theo turned her head to look at the kitchen clock. Did she have time to rush to the baker? The nearest one was a half-hour walk away at least.

Biting her lip, Theo reached for the Staffordshire cow creamer off the top shelf on the dresser. She tipped it upside down, emptying it of money, and gazed sadly at what was left of her weekly household budget. Precious little, she reflected, and from this small pile of coins, she was still expected to purchase Friday's supper from the fishmonger.

Theo sighed and pressed her raw knuckles into her eye sockets. All morning had been taken up with boiling the laundry and her arms still felt itchy from repeatedly rinsing out the harsh soap she had soaked it in the night before.

This afternoon she had to wring it all out and put it through the mangle, a horrible contraption that lurked in the scullery. Then, there remained the starching and ironing to be done, and Theo had only the vaguest notions of how one starched shirt collars. Her previous attempt the week before had been lamentable.

Now that she considered it, laundry was even *worse* than cooking. Her existence would be bleak indeed if she did not have an escape plan in place. Her heart swelled with gratitude toward Mr. Dabney. Their marriage at least would deliver her from this never-ending procession of household tasks she showed no aptitude for.

She felt worn out with it all, and she had barely been keeping house for a month. Briefly, she thought of Henrietta and wondered what her sister was up to at this moment in time. Perhaps partaking of an elegant luncheon or strolling Parisian streets in search of diversion.

Or maybe she was simply sat at leisure in her hotel, enjoying her view and reading a book, Theo thought enviously. It felt like she had not had the liberty to indulge in a little recreational reading in forever.

The distressing reality was that she simply had no *time* to pursue her own interests anymore. She had not even opened a book in the last two weeks, and the gown she had started to make herself a month ago was still in pieces and folded atop her sewing box.

On Wednesday, Lil called around directly after Felix had departed and they commandeered the front parlor for their first rehearsal. Lil was tired, for she had been trudging around the theaters looking for work. Nothing had turned up, and she had been forced to pick up bar work in a "gentleman's grill" temporarily to make ends meet.

"My feet are killing me, darlin'," Lil had admitted, sinking down onto the sofa. Theo had made some sympathetic noises and drawn Lil's attention to the fortifying "cup that cheers" which she had placed on the occasional table in front of her friend.

Then, resolutely, she had whisked around the piano stool and taken her seat. "These are the numbers I've adapted for us from Harold's originals," she announced. Then, before she even had the chance to grow self-conscious, she had plunged straight into the first one. She did not even have time to feel embarrassment these days. Lil could only spare two hours a week for the development of their act.

"Oh, he's never dipped his toe before, just shilly-shallied in the shallows," Theo sang forth brightly as she plunked down on the keys. Her skill on the pianoforte was strictly minimal, but she could follow a tune right enough. Fortunately, she had rewritten the lyrics before she had taken up her new duties, which had turned out to be so time-consuming.

Lil's mouth had fallen open after the first chorus, and she had sat frozen throughout the rest of it, her eyes growing wider and wider. "You never wrote them words!" she gasped after the last rousing verse.

"I most certainly did!" Theo assured her, crashing down on the keys dramatically at the finish and then launching straight into the next number. "Oh, he may think he's cock o' the walk," she sang heartily, "but my fine fellow is nothing but talk."

Lil had almost choked on her mouthful of hot tea and then gone off in a coughing fit. Theo had finished the rollicking number before Lil had managed to catch her breath. "What does Allsop make of them?" the older woman wheezed at last, her mouth still quivering with mirth.

79

"I have not shared them with him," Theo admitted, "but when I intimated that I was working on a new act, he said I could repurpose them as I saw fit. He does not consider them of any import in his body of work, for they were mere trifles he wrote for us as a favor to my uncle."

Lil pursed her lips. "When he said that, no doubt he thought your 'new act' would never get off the ground."

"More than likely," Theo agreed. She hesitated. "What did you think of them?" she asked with a casualness she did not feel.

"I think they're bloody genius!" Lil said frankly. "I never knew you had it in you, girl. I don't even recognize those tunes, but with your lyrics, they're catchy as hell."

Theo breathed out a shaky breath and smiled her first genuine smile in weeks. "I'm so glad."

"You must know they're bloody brilliant," Lil said with a raised brow.

"They were a lot of fun to write," Theo admitted wistfully. Looking back on the time she had spent scribbling in her notepad of an evening, instead of passed out with exhaustion, she felt a yearning that was almost physical. She had felt bold and audacious and slightly wicked writing those songs. Would she feel the same thrill performing them to an audience? She hoped so.

"Plenty more where they came from, eh?" Lil said, looking increasingly cheerful. She was practically rubbing her hands together now in anticipation.

"Oh yes, dozens, it's just…" Theo looked down at her folded hands in her lap.

"What?" asked Lil.

"I have not had the time recently to work on such things. I'm a terrible housekeeper, Lil. Worse even than I suspected I'd be."

"Good!" snorted her friend. "Maybe it'll make them hire someone instead of turning you into their lackey."

"I don't know about that," Theo murmured. "Felix just complains bitterly and expects me to improve."

"I just bet he does!" Lil seethed. "Well, it'll be one in his eye when you end up the darling of the music hall, my dear!"

Theo flushed. "You really think we stand a chance?" she breathed, feeling unutterably grateful to have shared the songs to a receptive audience.

Lil nodded. "Oh yes, we stand a chance alright. I should say a good chance." She looked suddenly wistful. "If only someone would give us a shot at performing them."

Theo had cleared her throat. "As to that, I have it in hand. We shall have our opportunity."

Lil's face had frozen. "You've found us a spot already!" she gasped, setting down her teacup with a thud. Theo nodded slowly. "Where?"

Theo gave a small cough. "The—er—Eagle and Sun, as it happens," she said with a slight quaver to her voice, "in Shoreditch." She took a hurried sip of her own tea so she did not have to dwell on Lil's stunned expression.

"*Dabney's* outfit?" Lil uttered in hushed tones once she had recovered from her shock. "But however did you manage to persuade him, my dear?" Lil was utterly confounded. "I don't see as how that man's got a charitable bone in his body."

Theo fiddled with the collar of her blouse. She did not feel up to confiding in anyone yet about the bargain she had struck, even Lil. "As a matter of fact, he thought it was inspired," she said, scrupulously using Dabney's very words, though he had been referring at the time to their scheme and not the act at all.

Lil's eyebrows shot up at this, but before she could question her further, Theo had distracted her by telling her they had only a month to prepare. Then she had plied her with the music and handwritten lyrics and a dozen pages of notes about how she saw their turn unfolding on the stage.

Lil had been so overwhelmed with it all and their pressing time constraints that she had no time to further interrogate her friend about the whys and wherefores of it all. All too soon their two hours were up, and Lil was forced to hurry away with a sheaf of papers, promising faithfully that she would have committed the words and music to memory by the time of their next meeting.

Theodora had drifted back to the kitchen with a wildly beating heart and a hectic flush on her cheeks. She felt happy and scared and reinvigorated. Until Lil had climbed on board, she had not realized how exhausted she was of keeping hope alive all by herself.

Of course, she also had Mr. Dabney as a coconspirator. *Clem*, she thought, for he had told her to call him Clem. She had not quite worked up the nerve yet but perhaps this Sunday she would casually address him as such. At the thought of having two allies in her schemes for glory, she had to lean against the kitchen door and hug herself with glee.

It was happening. *Finally*, she would get her chance to be the actress she had always dreamed she could be. She would show the skills she had accumulated over years of study and practice. She let herself dwell on the incredulity and admiration Lil had showed over her reworking of Harold's songs. She had not even seen Percy yet, just a pale shadow of him. Theo could not *wait* to reveal him in his fully realized form.

Even the horrors of the kitchen could not fully dispel how much lighter her shoulders felt after the session with Lil, and in hopes of promoting this newfound serenity, she elected to eat her share of the evening meal by herself in the kitchen that night. This prevented Felix from destroying her new harmonious mood with his complaints.

So efficacious did this prove in maintaining her spirits that Theo continued this practice for the rest of the week, not only for dinner, but for breakfast also. She only ventured to the dining room to set down the dishes and then scurried back to the kitchen to eat her meals in solitude.

Instead of returning to clear the table while Felix and Harold were still seated, she waited instead for a good hour before venturing to collect the plates and condiments. This way she could avoid all conflict.

She was wholly successful in this endeavor until Saturday morning when she stood eating a piece of bread and butter for her lunch and gazing distractedly out of the kitchen window. Albert had brought her a note from Clem that morning, which had suggested they partook of Sunday lunch together after church. She had replied with a hasty scrawl in the affirmative, although the prospect filled her stomach with butterflies.

A cleared throat from the kitchen doorway made her jump halfway out of her skin. Turning with a muffled exclamation, Theo found Harold Allsop stood hovering in the doorway, an unhappy expression on his face.

"Oh, how you made me jump," she gasped with relief. "I thought you were Felix for an instant."

Harold scratched his ear. "May I come in?" he asked diffidently. "I—er—will understand if I am no longer welcome."

Theo blinked. "Did you want something for your lunch?" she guessed. It was Saturday so likely he had not gone into the city. She made for the kitchen dresser. "There is half a loaf still and some jam—oh, I just ate the last of the jam," she said with a wince and hurried instead for the cupboard. "There is marmalade, I think…"

Harold flushed. "Please, no, that is not why I came to find you, Theodora." He looked almost pained. "Will you not sit down?"

Slowly, Theo shut the cupboard door and turned to face him. She breathed in and out. "What do you want, Harold?" she asked, her voice cool. Almost, she was tempted to call him "Mr. Allsop," but something about his shamefaced expression prevented her.

"Can we not be friends again?" he blurted. "I know I do not deserve it, after…after all that has happened, but I hate this," he said, slashing a hand through the air and looking as flustered as she had seen him. "I hate that you have been turned into a servant in your own home!"

Theo gave a short, mirthless laugh. "If I truly was a domestic, I would have been dismissed weeks ago," she pointed out. "But Felix can hardly turn me out when I own a third of the house." Even she was shocked to hear the bitterness in her tone. Harold looked stricken by it.

"I—I'm so sorry, Theo," he said, sounding shaken. "I truly am. I had no idea…"

"No idea that I would take it so hard when you agreed to Felix's scheme?" she asked quietly.

He flushed bright red and hung his head. "You have every right to be angry," he said, drawing in a shaky breath. "I was…thoughtless. Wrapped up in my own cares. I did not consider your feelings at all. I was a bad friend."

"Yes, you were," Theo agreed, gesturing toward the table. "Will you join me? I was about to take a cup of tea. It should be brewed by now."

His expression brightened, and he hurried to pull back a seat and lower himself into it. Theo fetched another cup and saucer before she joined him and poured out two cups of the strong, hot tea. Harold accepted his with thanks, his anxious gaze watching her every move.

"There isn't any sugar," Theo told him unapologetically. "I could not find any East Indian at the store, and I did not wish to support the slave trade by buying the other kind. It seems I shall have to go further afield to purchase some."

"Oh—er quite right," Harold murmured hurriedly before lapsing into an awkward silence. Absently, he brushed some breadcrumbs into a little pile. "Will you—er—will you not take your meals with us again?" he asked hopefully. "Without you and Henrietta, we are a sorry pair at table. I miss the old days. How merry we were before Barnabus died."

Henrietta took a swig of tea, considering how to make a reply. "There is little cheer for me at all these days, Harold," she said truthfully. "And sitting with the two of you making faces over your every mouthful makes me even more miserable. I am wholly aware of how inadequate I am in my new duties."

"I—" A spasm passed over his features. "That is not your fault. Your uncle never intended for you to preside over the kitchen. You have not been taught any of the skills. It is too bad of Felix, and I—I should have stood up to him," he finished in a rush. "Our monetary woes should not have been made into a rod to beat you with."

They gazed at one another a moment in silence. "Thank you," Theo responded simply. She had already known The Parthenon was in trouble financially, but things must be even more dire than she had supposed.

"What can I do?" Harold said wretchedly. "I have tried to speak to Felix. This week when you started depriving us of your company, I realized I had to do something. But he is such a stubborn fellow, he simply will not listen to reason."

"We both know how Felix is," Theo agreed, topping up their cups from the teapot. "The only way of stopping him in his tracks would be a dose of arsenic in his supper." Harold's face paled. "That was a joke," Theo added dryly. His shoulders slumped with relief.

"I know that none of you has any faith in my stage ability," she said with as much dignity as she could muster and ignored

85

Harold's feeble sound of protest, "but I have not wholly given up on my chosen career in life."

She bit her lip and met Harold's gaze head on. "Can I trust you, Harold?" she asked.

He nodded vehemently. "I wish you would. You always used to."

"I have a scheme afoot. There is one who trusts in me," she said, swallowing. "Two actually," she said, remembering Lil. "And we are working on my…my debut. You once said that you did not mind what I did with all those tunes you wrote for Henrietta and myself…"

He waved a hand. "I make you a present of them. Truly, I do not care if you rip up the song sheets and rewrite them completely."

That was lucky, thought Theo. She gave him a cautious smile. "Thank you," she repeated. "I am truly grateful for that."

He smiled weakly back. "Is there really nothing else I can do?" he asked wretchedly. "To make things up to you, I mean? Those songs are really nothing. Far from my best work."

Theo shook her head. "I do not think so, unless you could start clearing your plates and pronouncing my cuisine fit for a king." Harold blanched, and she could not help but laugh at his reaction.

Harold gave a weak smile in rejoinder. "I have missed your laugh," he confessed in a rush, then seemed to clam up. "Is this person—the one who believes in you—is it the man who—?" He broke off with a quick shake of his head. "Forgive me, I ought not to have asked."

Theo propped her chin on her hand and surveyed him thoughtfully. "Did you tell anyone?" she asked. "About the day you came upon us together?"

"No, I was not quite such a heel as all that," he said, flushing.

86

Theo nodded slowly. "There is something else you can do, Harold," she decided suddenly. "Soon, something is going to happen," she admitted, making his face tighten with concern. "Felix will be furious and very shocked. But if you could stand staunch as my friend, and…and support me in my decisions, if you could only insist that I am in my right senses and that you have every faith in me, that would truly cement our friendship and wipe the slate clean."

Harold, who had looked increasingly alarmed with her every word, now looked torn. His expression wavered under her steady gaze. "Very well," he said at last, gulping and lifting his chin. "After all, it is the least I can do. Your uncle would want me to support you. I only hope that Henrietta…" His words drifted off, and Theo suddenly wondered if Harold had nursed rather more affection for her sister all these years than she had realized. For some reason, the thought did not pain her as it would have once.

She smiled at Harold when she realized he was not going to finish his sentence and thrust her hand across the table at him. He blinked, then shook it, his grip much laxer than her own. "Friends," she pronounced firmly.

"Always," he agreed, and Theo's heart felt considerably lighter to hear it.

8

Clem had not realized he was whistling as he sauntered down the Old Harlow Road. When he was hailed with a tentative "Mr. Dabney!" he turned to find Theodora hurrying after him.

"Hello, where did you spring from?" He cast about for her hackney but could not see one in sight.

"Oh, I asked him to drop me a couple of streets away, so I could—well—have a few moments to compose myself," she admitted, fidgeting with her bonnet strings.

He cast a critical eye over her pink cheeks and overbright eyes. She still looked like a terrified doe poised for flight. Why the hell did she think she was cut out for a life on stage when she was so timorous? "You are not wearing your hat with the tassel today," he observed with a lazy smile, hoping to put her at ease.

She raised a hand to touch her head as though unsure of what she wore there. "Oh, yes!" she agreed with a nervous smile. "I decided on my wool bonnet today. It seemed to me that last time my hat attracted some adverse attention in church."

He nodded gravely, thinking of her fright of a hat. "Perhaps they thought it rather fast," he teased, instead of pointing out it was hopelessly eccentric.

Theodora's eyes widened. "Do you think so?" she asked, sounding rather more gratified than horror-struck at this prospect. "No one has ever thought me fast before."

"I'm sure they must have," Clem protested. "You are an actress after all. A profession which has only been considered remotely respectable in recent years."

"I suppose that is true," she agreed, falling into step beside him, and taking his arm when offered, with only the tiniest of hesitations. "When it came to the theater, my sister and I were always under the aegis of our uncle, so we were protected from the seamier side of things." Clem digested this in silence. Well, he had suspected as much, had he not? "What was that tune you were whistling?" she asked suddenly.

"Hmm? Tune?"

"Just now," she elucidated, "when you thought yourself unobserved."

He cast a surprised glance at her. She looked genuinely interested in the answer. "I…ah, I'm not sure," he prevaricated, though he had a shrewd idea.

"It went like this." Dora pursed her lips and whistled the catchy refrain from a risqué number his star turn, Florrie Foss, currently performed.

Clem could not suppress his grin. "It's a music hall number called 'Oh Mr. Hipkins,'" he admitted. "You're a surprisingly good whistler."

"Oh yes, I practice daily. Who performs it?"

Realizing she would not be distracted, Clem relented. "A Miss Florrie Foss. She's top of the bill at The Eagle."

"Miss Florrie Foss," Dora repeated thoughtfully. "I should like to see her perform one day."

Clem winced. "I do not think her act would be to your tastes, Dora." She colored faintly, but whether from his casual use of the pet name or from the implication she and music hall were not compatible, Clem could not be sure.

"Is she very beautiful?" she asked suddenly, a strangely anxious look on her face.

"Beautiful? No," he answered, thinking of earthy Florrie with her roaring laugh and the too big gap between her front teeth. "But there is…something about her, I suppose. The paying public love her."

She relaxed. "Is her act very rude?" she asked shrewdly and shot him a sideways look that had Clem laughing again in spite of himself.

89

"Very," he admitted and was strangely gratified when she gave an answering laugh.

"I would still like to see it," she said, surprising the hell out of him, and then the church gate was in front of them. He was almost disappointed they did not have another street length to converse.

The service passed uneventfully, and their banns were read without anyone denouncing them. Dora quivered beside him when their names were read out, but he took her gloved hand in his and squeezed it tight. He gave her a reassuring smile and she seemed to breathe easier.

"Where would you like to go to Sunday lunch?" he asked her as they filed out of church after shaking Canon Bridgewater's soft, wrinkled hand.

"I hardly know," she said, brightening at the prospect. "It has been so long since I have been taken out for a meal. My uncle used to take us once a month as a high treat, but since he passed…"

"There is a new French restaurant opened near Piccadilly to favorable reviews," Clem suggested. "We could easily take a cab." Her expression wavered, and Clem could see she was not fully sold on the idea.

"That sounds very grand," she said, glancing down at her shabby paletot.

Perhaps she was not wholly oblivious to the strange figure she cut, Clem reflected. "Where did your uncle used to take you?"

"To a local chop house," she admitted, making him laugh.

"Well, there are plenty of chop houses round here. We can take our pick."

She looked relieved. "That would be wonderful," she admitted, and he realized Dora was not a champagne and filet mignon kind of girl.

"What do you usually have?"

90

"Roast pork with apple sauce," she replied promptly.

"I know just the place." He steered her to the left and, they headed for the establishment of Chas. Daneworth & Sons, a place he knew also served good steaks.

They were soon ensconced in a booth in a dark corner of a busy eatery, with conversation buzzing all around them from the tables interspersed with bursts of laughter.

"How's this?" he asked once she was comfortable, hat and coat removed and seated opposite him.

"Wonderful," she answered with a sigh. "Everything about it, the atmosphere, the noise, this cozy corner." She tipped her head to one side, considering him.

"What is it?" Clem asked, surprised to see her look at him so intently.

"How good you are at calming me down," she said slowly. "How did you cultivate such a soothing manner? Have you many maiden aunts?"

He laughed, an honest-to-goodness laugh, at this. "No, I have not. Two uncles only."

"How then are you so good at soothing nervous creatures? Do you keep cats?"

He grinned. "No. No pets allowed in my boarding house, I'm afraid. Mrs. O'Malley is a stickler for rules."

"I expect she serves all your meals on time though," she commented with a catch in her voice.

"Maybe so," he agreed, then added untruthfully, "but her gravy is often lumpy, and she serves artichokes with practically every meal."

Theodora brightened a little more at these outrageous lies. "You do not care for artichokes?" she asked, then pondered, "I would not even know how to cook them."

"You must never learn," Clem said, pulling a face and making her laugh. He wondered idly what other faults he could place on Mrs. O'Malley's blameless shoulders. He would not

91

scruple to malign his excellent landlady if it would bring a smile to Dora's face.

She cupped her chin now, looking thoughtful. Suddenly, she asked, "What line of work were you in before you were a stage manager?"

"Stage manager? Is that what I am?" he asked lightly. She looked up at him expectantly. "I already told you what I did before, Dora," he reminded her.

"Well, yes, you did, but I thought you might have had a profession or two in between prizefighting and owning a concert room," she clarified and then gave him a sideways smile. "I suppose it occurred to me that you might have flung the prizefighting thing in people's faces for shock value."

Clem's eyebrows rose. "Is it so very shocking?" he asked, though he knew damn well that it was. He was surprised that Dora seemed fully aware of the fact though. Up to this point, she had seemed so sanguine about marrying an uncultured lout.

"At least as disreputable as acting on a stage," she responded promptly, drawing a reluctant smile from him. "Do you know, I've never seen a prize fight," she added musingly.

"You don't say." His answer was possibly a little too dry.

"I suppose by that remark you mean that the audience is predominantly male," she said, apparently not taking offense.

"That would be one way of putting it."

At this point, they were interrupted by a waiter setting down their drinks before them. Clem had beer and Dora had ordered a large dry sherry which she immediately took a gulp of. For some reason, the fact she had ordered a "large" had amused Clem.

"Good?" he asked.

"Delicious," she affirmed, craning her neck to follow the waiter's retreat.

"Have you seen someone?" Clem asked, following her gaze, but failing to see what had caught her eye.

"Yes," she murmured, then blinked as though remembering present company and straightened up in her seat. "I mean, no. No one that I know. I just thought…"

"What?"

"That he had an interesting walk."

"An interesting walk?" Clem repeated with a frown, but Dora was now gazing all around them with a rapt expression. She leaned forward. "What a fascinating bunch of people," she breathed.

Were they? Clem glanced about. They looked like the usual mixed bunch to him. Some reasonably well-heeled, but the majority of them decidedly seedy. She nodded back at him, her eyes shining.

Well, hell, if he had known all he had to do was introduce her to the shadier side of life to please her, it would have made things a lot easier. French restaurants were clearly not required. He lifted his beer to his lips, still watching her, a faint pucker between his brows. "How is the cooking going?" he asked when he managed to catch her roving eye again. He still couldn't discern what it was she was finding so fascinating about their fellow diners.

"Oh." Her face fell at once. "Do *not* ask. It's the timing of it all that is my downfall, I think. By the time my mutton chops are cooked, my potatoes are stone cold, and my carrots have turned to a pulpy mush in the pan."

"Alas, poor Felix!" Clem teased lightly.

She gave a ripple of laughter. "It serves him right, the beast! In any case, I've decided it is the laundry that is my greatest bugbear. Men's shirts, specifically," she added darkly, taking a swig of her sherry. She plunked it down on the table, warming to her theme. "Let me tell you, starching collars is the very devil of a job! And there are so many exhausting and laborious stages you have to go through," she said despairingly. "You would not believe it. Tell me, have you ever heard of

93

bluing whites?" Before he could answer, she plunged on resentfully, "And really, why should Felix care what color his undergarments have turned when only he will see them, in any case? None of my own garments cause me such a headache to clean. I cannot for the life of me think why I was not Mrs. Cherwell's favorite all along!"

Clem considered this. Cherwell...she had mentioned that name before. One of her lame ducks he seemed to recall. "You were not her favorite?"

"Not at all! For Felix is the master of the house and she fairly doted on Harold." Clem, who believed Allsop to be another lame duck, decided not to comment. "Really, after struggling with their shirtfronts I cannot see why she held them in any affection at all," she muttered indignantly. "And Felix is not one bit grateful for my efforts."

"What about Allsop?" Clem could not stop himself from asking.

Her expression softened. "He has been rather a lamb about it, in all honesty. He never complains, even when I make a horrible job of it. In fact, I heard him tell Felix they should start looking for a laundress yesterday." She colored and hesitated before lowering her voice and adopting a confiding tone. "You will be glad to hear Harold and I have quite laid our quarrel to rest."

"Oh?" *Glad* was not the word he would have used. Even he could hear the edge to his tone, but Dora carried on, seemingly oblivious to it.

"He came to me in the kitchen on Wednesday night and apologized for siding with Felix. He takes it all back and means to support me in the future." Her expression was so open and relieved that he wondered at his own reaction, which was one of outright annoyance.

Mercifully, he was spared from having to comment on their reconcilement as a waiter appeared bearing a tray of their food.

94

After the two plates, a jug of gravy, and a pot of mustard had been set down in front of them, they were alone once more.

"Oh, this looks wonderful!" Dora exclaimed and sent him a beaming smile.

Clem felt his shoulders relax. Getting irritated over a poor specimen like Harold Allsop was patently absurd. "Do you think they will end up sending their laundry out?" he asked, pouring gravy liberally over his steak.

She pulled a face. "Chance would be a fine thing. Felix would not hear of it. The *expense*," she intoned in mock horror. "Really, I wish they would simply take to wearing more sensible attire as I do." She pointed her fork toward her own dress, which was another of her peculiar loose-fitting numbers which draped from her shoulders in a muted green crepe. It had a crinkled look to the fabric, and Clem wondered if that spared her the necessity of ironing it. "It is so much more practical."

Briefly, Clem contemplated what manner of dress she would have her brother and Allsop adopt instead of conventional suits. Handwoven smocks, perhaps? He gave a faint shudder and resolved never to ask. The rest of the meal passed pleasantly enough. Dora turned down a postdinner sherry with a regretful "Better not," and they exited the establishment with her companionably hanging off his arm.

"What will you do for the rest of the day?" he asked, feeling curious. "Not tied to a hot stove or turning a mangle, I hope. Not on the day of rest."

"No, for both Felix and Harold are out to dinner this afternoon, meeting with some backers for some production they are hoping to stage."

Clem's ears pricked up. "Indeed?" In the future, any such plans would need to be run by him, though neither Fields nor Allsop were yet aware of that fact. In any case, it was too early to declare himself just yet. He would be in a much stronger position once he had a ring firmly on Dora's finger.

95

"Yes, and that means it was agreed a cold supper would suffice, so I can work in peace on my own secret project this afternoon."

"Secret project?" Clem forced himself to ask, though in truth he was more intrigued by the other topic.

"I am attempting to alter an old suit of my brother's," she confessed as Clem flagged down a passing hansom cab. "It has been a lot trickier than I envisaged, but I am sure if I persevere then I will get the fit right. Eventually."

"To what purpose?" Clem asked without thinking. Her expression looked at once so wounded that it brought him up short. *Of course, the bloody stupid male impersonation nonsense.* "I mean," he said recovering quickly, "your build is surely quite different to your brother's?"

"Well, not greatly," she said with a brave smile, but he could see his careless words had shaken her. He had forgotten all about her bloody obsession with her "new act." "Felix is of slight build and middling height for a man, whereas I am tall for a woman. It means our heights are not terribly disparate."

"Your height, maybe not, but there are other considerations," he pointed out. He could see from the way she bit her lip and avoided his eye that he had screwed up quite badly. "Why don't you let me book you in with my tailor for next time?" he offered extravagantly.

She gasped, her face turning toward his again. "Y-your tailor?" she faltered. "You would do that? Take me to your tailor?"

"Why not?" He braced himself for his stab of regret, but it did not come. How could it, when she was gazing up at him like that, as though he had just offered to buy her a diamond bloody necklace?

Hectic color flushed her cheeks, and she parted her lips to draw in a ragged breath. "Oh, Mr. Dabney!" she exclaimed. "I hardly know what to say!"

"You want this cab or not, guv?" the cab driver growled from up on his perch. "I can't wait around all day."

Clem squeezed her fingers and led her toward the carriage, his hand at her waist to guide her up the steps. She kept trying to twist about to look at him, as though trying to assess if he really meant it.

"I'll make the appointment for next Sunday after church," he promised extravagantly. He'd have to pay double or triple rates to get Finch to open his shop for a customer on a Sunday. Then again, Finch would hardly want a woman waltzing into a gentleman's outfitters on a weekday, so it would work out better for him too in the long run.

He shut the door behind her and gave the address to the driver as Dora hung out of the window, still gazing at him with a painful look of intensity on her face. "Thank you," she said in a choked voice as they pulled away. "I had a wonderful time!"

Clem raised his hand to wave her off. Strange how he did not regret his extravagant gesture one bit. Stranger still, how often his thoughts kept straying to Dora Fields for the rest of the day.

9

Sunday dawned chilly but dry and Theo set out for church as soon as the grandfather clock on the hall struck ten. She hurried quickly down the garden path, pulling her paletot closer about her. She was glad of its thick wool and the big bell sleeves against the cold, even if Felix did think it was ugly.

Once again, she had left off the matching tasseled hat today in favor of her wool bonnet, so she would not get stared at in church. She managed to hail a cab in the next street, and after directing him to St. Thomas's, she sank back into the seat, catching her breath. The frigid air was almost painful to breathe into one's lungs, and she had run for the cab, so she was short of breath.

By the time they reached Clapham, her breathing had steadied, but her heart was racing with nervous anticipation. What was wrong with her? She had never suffered from stage fright. Had this past month really reduced her to such a nervous wreck?

Catching sight of a familiar stretch of road, she rapped on the side of the cab. "Just here, driver!" she called out, and they slowed to a still, and Theo clambered down. She was just congratulating herself that she had a good five-minute walk in which to calm her fizzling nerves when she recognized the tall, well-built male making his way unhurriedly toward her.

To her dismay, his slow smile of welcome deprived her once more of breath. Good grief, was she always to appear such a breathless featherbrain in front of him? Feeling exasperated with herself, she forced an answering smile to her lips and turned to him, wishing him a "Good morning," which almost sounded shy. Ugh! She was not remotely shy! *Theodora*, she told herself sternly, *pull yourself together!*

Clem reached up and paid the cabbie before she had the chance. "Oh, but I have the money you gave to me—" she started to protest, but he ignored this, presenting his arm. "Let's get church out of the way and then we can get you to your first fitting."

Theo could scarcely draw breath for a minute. "Y-you managed to book an appointment?" she gasped, clutching at his arm. She had hardly dared let herself believe he was serious about his flippant promise the week before.

He lifted an eyebrow. "Of course."

"On a Sunday?" she squeaked. "It only occurred to me as we pulled away that your tailor would scarcely keep such working hours."

Clem waved this aside. "I could hardly take you to a gentleman's outfitters on a weekday." He shrugged. "It would always have been by special appointment."

"Oh, yes, I had not considered…" She bit her lip and let her words die away as she fought down the excitement churning in her stomach.

"I'm guessing you know to the smallest detail what you require," he commented with lurking amusement.

Theodora's color flared. "I—well, would it be alright if I had a full evening suit?" she asked tremulously. She knew this was a huge ask as such an outfit would include an elegant frock coat and trousers as well as a silk waistcoat.

Clem shrugged. "Whatever you want," he answered.

Theo breathed noisily in and out and could scarcely pay attention during church. She would not even have noticed their banns being read if Clem had not nudged her gently in the side. She was floating on a cloud throughout the whole thing. He also had to steer her toward Canon Bridgewater for her to shake the clergyman's hand at the close of the ceremony.

"I've never known anyone so excited at the prospect of a new suit," he laughed softly as he escorted her toward J. Finch & Sons. It was a ten-minute walk, but Theo knew her conversation was lamentable. She was so excited; she could

99

scarcely string a sentence together. In the end, Clem took pity on her, and they walked the last stretch in silence.

Once they entered the tailor's establishment, Theo fell to earth with a bump for the place looked *nothing* like the gentleman's outfitters her brother frequented. There were no fancy glass-fronted cabinets to display the wares or upholstered chairs for the patrons to loll in. It looked instead shabby, bare, and functional.

Several large work-scarred tables were lined up to run along the center of the store with low-hanging gas lamps suspended above them. The rest of the interior was cluttered up with packing cases and tatty-looking drawers and smaller tables. Theo found herself having to work hard to swallow down her disappointment.

Clem let out a piercing whistle, and Theo heard someone moving around in the back room, then a curtain was swiped aside and a lean-looking man of about thirty-five years stepped out. He sported sandy-colored sideburns and wore a somewhat world-weary expression on his face. He eyed Theo impassively for a moment. "This 'er?" he asked, tipping his head in her direction.

"Dora, this is Charlie Finch who works wonders with a needle and thread. Charlie, this is my wife, Mrs. Dora Dabney."

Theo was so shocked by Clem's prematurely pronouncing her his wife that she was speechless for a moment. Mr. Finch's eyebrows rose, but he nodded in her direction, and before she could return the greeting, he crossed to the front door, pulling the shutter down and locking it.

"Know what you want?" he asked, turning abruptly and tucking his thumbs in his waistcoat.

"She does," Clem interjected smoothly. "She wants a full set of evening dress and also a day suit."

Theo caught her breath. *A day suit as well?* Had Clem guessed just how badly her alterations were going? Clem showed no sign that he had uttered anything remotely stupendous.

Mr. Finch sniffed and appeared to consider. "What sort of day suit?" he asked in his flat cockney accent.

Theo's head spun. She had not even dreamed of ever having a day suit made. Her eyes widened and flew to Clem in agonized appeal.

"It's for the stage," he said, "so it needs to be eye-catching."

Mr. Finch rocked on his heels, then he crossed to a set of drawers and deliberated a moment before withdrawing a bolt of yellow and brown check and another of blue and yellow. Both were very loud. Theo felt a little alarmed. She had imagined Piccadilly Percy as elegantly rather than brashly dressed.

Mr. Finch rejoined them with the cloth and wordlessly stuck them under Theo's nose.

"Er…" she hesitated.

"Either would be fine for the trousers," Clem put in, leaning against one of the tables. "But she would need a plain coat and waistcoat to team up with it."

Theo relaxed. Yes, that would tone down the florid check of the trousers, she thought with relief.

"Which?" Charlie asked.

"The—um—the brown and yellow, I think?" Theo mumbled, feeling rather daunted.

Mr. Finch spun on his heel and returned the violent blue and yellow to the drawer. "Color of waistcoat?" he asked.

"Yellow," Clem chimed in, picking up a pamphlet he had found on the table and flicking through its pages.

The tailor opened another drawer and withdrew another bolt of cloth without consulting Theo this time. Maybe they only had one shade of yellow. "Cut of coat?" he asked, sounding bored.

"Prince Albert," Clem again replied without looking up from his booklet.

Theo felt rather crushed by the exchange. Somehow it had not been what she had expected.

"What about the evening suit?" Mr. Finch asked, setting those bolts of cloth to one side.

"I want that to be very understated and elegant," Theo said, finally asserting herself. "Black frock coat, cut away to show the waistcoat, and narrow-legged trousers also in black."

"Single-breasted, then," Charlie said, withdrawing a pencil from behind his ear. He leaned over a table and made a few squiggles on a piece of paper. "Waistcoat?"

"I was thinking…a cream figured silk," Theo said boldly. She saw Clem look up with a frown, and she guessed his own tastes ran to something a lot flashier. "That is how I always pictured it," she said quickly.

Clem shrugged. "Whatever you want," he said and returned to his brochure.

"Alright," Mr. Finch said, throwing down his pencil. "You want to go out back and get ready for your measuring?" Theo nodded and hurried toward the curtain. "Give me a shout when you're ready."

After securing the curtain she found herself in a somewhat dusty back room with a stove and various paraphernalia littered about. Dragging her eyes away from the clutter, Theo concentrated on the matter at hand and stripped down in a businesslike manner to her loose chemise, linen knee-length drawers, and knitted stockings.

There was nothing fancy or embellished about her undergarments. Hetty liked a muslin frill on her chemises and wore the full regalia of corset and stiffened petticoats under her hooped skirts. Theo by contrast had always adhered to the principles of artistic dress. She congratulated herself now on how much quicker dressing and undressing was for her.

102

"Ready!" she sang out, and heard a hesitant step, then the curtain drew back, and Mr. Finch appeared, looking professional and stony-faced. He had his pencil and paper in hand once more and was brandishing a tape measure.

A cleared throat on the other side of the curtain made Theo jump. It must be Clem, though why he had moved from his spot by the table to stand directly by the curtain she could not imagine. Mr. Finch shot her an inscrutable look and then started the business of measuring her back and shoulders.

Theo had already taken the step of binding her bosom, though in truth, she did not have much up there to shatter the illusion. Still, it made her feel professional to have taken the extra step, and Mr. Finch probably appreciated it when it came to measuring her chest, which might otherwise have been rather indelicate.

He hesitated before taking her inside leg measurement. "You gonna put a sock down there, or something?" he asked.

"Pardon?"

He looked up at her. "Down your drawers."

Enlightenment dawned. "Oh! Oh, yes, that is a good idea," she enthused. "And really, it never occurred to me."

Mr. Finch adjusted his tape measure and muttered something under his breath which Theo did not catch. She had the distinct impression he did not think much of her in truth.

It was certainly interesting to see just how many measurements he took. She was not half so conscientious when it came to making her own garments. Then again, she tended to go for flowing gowns which were not at all formfitting.

The whole process took a good deal longer than she had anticipated, and Theo was glad for the heat the small stove threw out, for she was turning to goose pimples by the time it was over.

"That's the lot," said Mr. Finch, straightening up.

103

"Thank y—" Theo started to say, but he had already ducked back out of the curtain. Hastily donning her linen petticoat and billowing gown of moss green, she had no sooner fastened her belt about her waist than Clem coughed on the other side of the curtain.

"All decent?" he asked.

Theo drew back the curtain to show she was fully dressed except for her outerwear. "All done," she said, picking up her hat, coat, and muffler from atop a nearby packing case.

"You forgot your gloves," Clem pointed out.

"Oh! Silly of me." Theo snatched them up. "I'm always losing them."

He was looking at her keenly. "How was it?" he asked in an undertone. He looked, she thought, faintly concerned. Did he think she was flustered because Mr. Finch had seen her in her undergarments? She hoped he did not think her such a shrinking violet, but after all, she was always reduced to such a quivering wreck around him that it was no wonder he thought she might expire on the spot from maidenly modesty!

"Absolutely," she assured him, plastering a smile onto her face. "Mr. Finch was very businesslike."

He studied her face a moment longer and then nodded, as if satisfied. Then he motioned for her to hand over her paletot which he helped her into in a most solicitous fashion. Theo was quite touched. "Thank you," she said, pulling on her bonnet and fastening it beneath her chin.

They walked back into the shop, and Clem took Mr. Finch aside and withdrew his wallet from his jacket as Theo wrapped her muffler about her throat and pulled on her gloves.

"We are to return at the same time next week for your first fitting," Clem informed her, shepherding her out of the door.

"Goodbye!" she called over her shoulder to Mr. Finch. She did not hear him respond, but then again, the shop door did shut rather abruptly after them.

104

She bit her lip as they walked away from the tailor's. "Do you suppose Mr. Finch was a bit put out at having to measure up a female?" she asked.

"He's always like that," Clem observed. "Don't let it bother you."

"Does he make your suits?"

Clem cocked an eye at her. "You think I fobbed you off with a cheap tailor?"

Theo's face flamed. "No! Not at all, please don't think—"

He laughed. "I'm just teasing you, Dora, don't get agitated. And yes, he makes the majority of my suits."

As the suits she had seen Clem in looked well-fitted, if rather less conservative than those her brother wore, she felt heartened by this news. "I suppose I ought to hail a cab," she said, feeling a little flat for all she was so grateful. Despite the unkempt state of the outfitters, she fancied her fiancé would still have had to pay a pretty penny.

Clem glanced at his pocket watch. "It's still fairly early," he commented. "Is your brother expecting you home so soon?"

"No," she admitted. "He is going to a bar and grill this afternoon with some friends. And Harold is meeting his aunt for high tea."

"So then, you do not need to scurry back so soon," he pointed out.

Theo felt her chest flutter. Argh, she was doing it again! "N-no," she stammered and felt herself blush up like some little fool.

"While the cat's away…" Clem murmured suggestively. "We could have some fun. Why not let me show you a good time?"

"A good time?" Theo repeated, feeling a little light-headed. Clem smiled at her, and his smile was a little alarming somehow. Was that what people meant by a wicked smile? She had always wondered about that. She did not think she had ever

105

been the recipient of one before. "Yes, please," she said, and he laughed again, sounding delighted by her answer.

"Good girl, Dora," he said warmly, and somehow it made her feel all tingly inside. He cocked his head. "Or should I say, bad girl?"

Theo nearly tripped over her own feet. It was a good job she was clinging to his arm, or she would have been in a heap on the floor. "I—I suppose it is all a matter of perspective," she managed to choke out.

"Indeed," he agreed.

"Where pray are we headed for our good time?" she enquired, rallying her spirits as they crossed a street.

"I think," he said, subjecting her to a thoughtful perusal, "that I am going to take you to a hotel."

Theo's eyes nearly fell out of their sockets. "A hotel?" she squawked in dismay, dragging his arm until they came to a standstill on the opposite pavement.

"Yes," he answered calmly. "The one I am thinking of has a rather good cocktail bar." A smile played about his lips. "Now, what did you think I was suggesting, Dorabelle?"

Dorabelle? Theo felt herself blush a deep red. "I hardly know," she faltered. *Oh, good grief.* He certainly was not trying to allay her fears now, she thought, pressing a hand to her chest. Was he *dallying* with her? And if so, why was he bothering? Their arrangement was a business deal, not anything else.

Clem patted her hand. "I'm only teasing, Dora, no need for that expression." He turned and hailed an approaching cab. "Mayfair," he directed once as he had handed a flustered Theo up into the carriage. "Wards Hotel."

She only just had time to wonder what expression her face had worn when she gasped, realizing their direction. Theo had heard of Wards, for Sir Matthew had taken Henrietta there for lunch when it had its grand opening. Her sister had told her it was very opulent and luxurious indeed.

106

"Are we really going to Wards Hotel?" she asked, turning toward him in excitement. "I've never been."

He sat in the seat beside her. "Well, it will be my pleasure to introduce you to its delights."

Theo was fizzing with excitement the whole way there, and once they arrived, she gawped like a tourist at the splendid gray stone frontage with its cast-iron decorations and tall handsome windows.

Once Clem had escorted her up the front steps, a uniformed doorman bowed them inside, and she was struck once more with the grandness of her surroundings. Her heels echoed against marble floors as they navigated soaring columns, potted ferns, and velvet couches as Clem led her to a large rotunda bar saloon where they were seated beneath a huge domed ceiling decorated with stained glass.

"It's fantastic!" she breathed, wide-eyed as she stared around at the smart waiters, the bandstand, and the elaborate mahogany bar. "I've never been anywhere so fancy!"

Clem smiled at her, but as a waiter halted beside them at this point, he made no further comment, instead ordering two champagne cobblers and a selection of hors d'oeuvre. Theo sighed in perfect happiness and unwound the muffler from around her neck. Clem stood and helped her remove her coat, and another passing waiter took it and hung it on a coat stand.

"What is a champagne cobbler?" Theo asked with interest as soon as she was seated again.

"You're about to find out," he said, gesturing to an approaching waiter, who held a silver tray at shoulder level.

To Theodora's delight, their drinks were served in tall glasses and loaded with cold fruits, berries, pineapple, and orange slices. She was tempted to clap her hands as it was set down before her, so excited was she by the elaborate presentation. Another platter followed, elegantly laid out with tiny squares of toast and pâté, decorated with sprinkled herbs, devilled eggs, and small intriguing-looking bundles, speared through with wooden skewers.

"Why, it's devils on horseback!" she exclaimed after they had toasted one another, and she had sampled the first of the canapes which proved to be a stuffed prune.

Clem laughed. "I am sure they have a far fancier name for it here."

"It's very good. I think they have steeped it in brandy rather than tea."

"What do you think of your cobbler?"

"It's delicious," she answered truthfully. "It's quite the nicest fruit punch I have ever had." She settled back into her seat and let her eyes wander over the clientele. "Everyone looks very sleek and rich in here," she commented critically. For her part, Theo liked a mixed company best of all, as they had found in the chop house.

Clem glanced about as though only just noticing. Unlike her, it seemed he was not a devotee of studying his fellow man. "Half of them are probably faking affluence," he said airily. "Like me."

Theo's eye sparkled. "That does make them rather more interesting," she admitted. "Do you suppose any of them are confidence tricksters or card sharps?"

A smile lurked at the corners of Clem's lips. "Very likely," he admitted. "That fellow there looks like a bigamist hanging out for another rich wife."

Theo gurgled appreciatively. "Probably his fourth or fifth at least. It's those great handlebar moustaches that do it. They inspire trust in a woman."

"Oh really? Maybe I should grow mine," Clem debated, stroking his upper lip.

"Oh no!" Theo disagreed with a quick shake of her head. "You have such a lovely profile."

He laughed at that. "Now you're flattering me. My nose has been broken at least twice."

"Yes," she said, remembering she, too, had once thought this a bar to masculine beauty. "But somehow in your case, it serves to add character. You might almost be *too* good-looking without it. The bridge of your nose has not been smushed in like Vinnie's. Yours just has a bump—" She broke off her words, feeling suddenly self-conscious. "I'm so sorry, you should not let me rattle on so—" she started with embarrassment.

"No, don't apologize," he cut her off swiftly. "I like it. Hearing you think aloud, I mean."

"Really?" Theo asked doubtfully.

"Remind me who Vinnie is?" he asked as he gestured to the waiter. "Two more," he said pointing to their glasses.

Theo, noticing he had finished his, hurriedly took another swig of her own. "He is one of the doormen at The Parthenon," she explained.

"Ah yes, the one who escorts your sister about."

"Yes," Theo agreed automatically, though in truth she did not think Vincent squired Hetty about any more than he did her. "We still have not heard from her, you know," she added as the waiter plunked down another drink beside her. "Oh, thank you."

Clem leaned forward in his seat, lowering his voice, "Did her fiancé have flourishing moustaches?" he asked gravely.

"Sir Matthew?" she asked, blinking before realization dawned. "Oh, no, he is neither a bigamist nor a swindler, I am sure. His father is a banker."

"That's good. Try one of these." He nudged the platter toward her. "Angels on horseback."

"Really?" Theo helped herself to one. "Thank you. These used to be my uncle's favorite, but I never thought they would serve oysters wrapped in bacon at such a fancy establishment."

Clem gave a murmur of agreement. "Oysters must be coming into fashion, more's the pity. They'll be stealing all our working-class treats."

"Cockles and mussels?" Theo suggested.

"Eel pie and mash." He waggled his eyebrows at her, and Theo laughed.

"Felix dearly loves eel pie," she sighed.

"And have you tackled that particular recipe?" he asked lightly.

"I have not." Theo shuddered. "Pastry is not for me. I think my blood runs too hot, for I was reading an article upon the subject, and it said the best pastry chefs are naturally cold-blooded and that only cool hands should work the dough."

"Is that so?" He reached across the table and took one of her hands in his. "Hmmm, you do have hot little hands," he agreed thoughtfully. "For my part, I always prefer warm fingers to cold ones."

Theo really could not say why she felt her cheeks growing red. "You do?" she asked faintly, almost wishing she had not removed her gloves. Her hand felt naked in his. She almost yelped when he gave her fingers a lazy squeeze.

"Oh yes," he agreed huskily. "Don't you, Dora?"

Was he deliberately trying to fluster her? Maybe he was so incorrigible a flirt that it was just his habit around women? "Gloves help," she managed to splutter out before getting to grips with herself. What had she meant to quiz him about today? She tried to remember, giving herself a little shake.

She had realized only the night before that she knew precious little of his upbringing. Clem Dabney had made his money prizefighting. He had then invested in a supper and song outfit and had expanded this by investing in a set of concert rooms. This had done so well, he now wanted a theater. That was it. The sum of all she had learned.

110

The realization had been a little disquieting. He had told her nothing of his family or origins. Was he even a native of London? His accent was not East End, though there was a slight inflection. There was certainly a touch of something rustic mixed in there, perhaps Lancashire or Yorkshire. Other times, she fancied there was a hint of something even further afield, such as a touch of Irish brogue.

"Do you have any brothers or sisters, Mr. Dabney?" she asked brightly. "Clem, I mean," she corrected herself hastily and, to her annoyance, blushed again.

He released her hand with a show of reluctance. "A couple of half brothers," he admitted, "but we're not in touch."

Theo studied him in silence as she drained the last of her champagne cobbler. For all he was so pleasant and affable, he rarely let much information slip about himself. In fact, what *had* she learned about him in the past month?

He had two uncles, she suddenly remembered. He had told her that much. Were they paternal or maternal though? Why had she not pursued that topic? she wondered. It was not like her to monopolize a conversation by talking of herself. She rather thought it must be because Clem had skillfully steered her in other directions. "What about cousins?"

Clem sighed. "My family is…scattered. We are not good at keeping in touch."

"You mentioned two uncles before I think," she persisted doggedly.

"Did I?"

Theo frowned, ignoring the second glass she had not yet touched. "You are reticent when it comes to family matters, I find."

He shifted in his seat. "Not especially," he disagreed, then seemed to realize he was not proving his point. "The uncles I must have mentioned were my mother's brothers. They worked at the docks their whole lives. One, Miles, died five years ago.

111

The other, Dan, is a widower. I lived with him and my aunt Nancy for a while when I first came to London. They were a grand couple but never had any children. Miles had a couple of daughters. One married a barber, I think, and they moved away years ago. Up north somewhere. The other, my cousin Grace, looks after Uncle Dan now and takes in laundry to make ends meet."

Theo nodded slowly. "You said when you came to London. Where did you come to London from?"

Clem drained his glass and held it up, catching another waiter's eye. "I boarded at a school on the south coast from the age of six to fifteen years."

"The south coast?"

"Hampshire."

"Oh, I thought I could detect some sort of accent there… Nine years? That is a long time. All that time at one school?" He nodded. "And then you came to London?" He nodded again, and she was just starting to think she'd had her lot when he spoke again.

"My mother died when I was six," he said, catching her off guard. "That was when my father remarried and sent me away to school."

"Was it a good school?" she asked hopefully.

"No, not especially, though I was no scholar, so maybe they did their best. I learned my letters and my numbers and how to stand up for myself and then they turned me loose to make my way in life." There was an odd inflection to his words that Theo could not quite make out.

She shivered, as though a cold shadow had stolen over them, which had no place in their delightful surroundings. Suddenly, she wished she had not raised the specter of his past between them. "I'm sorry," she blurted impulsively. "I should not have pushed a subject you find painful."

112

"Painful?" He sounded surprised. "Nothing of the sort. I just find it…uninteresting."

"So then, let us talk of something else," she suggested heartily. "Something you do find interesting."

He shot her a genuine smile at this which touched his hazel eyes, warming them, and the next hour and a half flew by, though afterward Theo could not recall all too clearly what they had discussed. Whatever it had been, it had been diverting and amusing and had completely distracted her from her cares and woes at home.

She had certainly felt quite tipsy by the time Clem had handed her up into a hansom cab, kissed her hand, and sent her back to Juniper Row. She spent the afternoon sleeping it off in the most comfortable armchair before the biggest fire she dared to light considering their dwindling coal supplies.

When she woke three hours later, she found someone, probably Harold, had draped a woolen blanket over her legs and added the last of the coal scuttle to the fire. For the first time in a while, life felt, on the whole, pretty good.

10

Clem paused before a shop window to examine his reflection critically. If his jade green waistcoat was pushing the boundaries of taste, then his lucky horseshoe diamond pin was beyond the pale, but in truth, he was heartily sick of dressing conservatively. Besides, it was his wedding day. The more he got to know Dora, the less he thought she would be shocked by the fact her soon-to-be husband was a brash son of a bitch.

In any case, he had better ease her into at least a passing acquaintanceship with the real Clem Dabney or she was in for a hell of a rude awakening. One of these days, she was going to find out he was nothing but a calculating swine who now held a controlling interest in her family business. When that day came, there would be no more charming her with cocktails and luncheons out. For some reason, this put an irritable frown on his face as he crossed the road on his way to church.

It was likely poor sleep that had him feeling out of sorts, he reasoned. He had spent an uncomfortable night on a couch in his office at The Eagle and Sun after moving his belongings out of Mrs. O'Malley's. Up until this point, he had thought the sofa a perfectly functioning piece of furniture, but a night spent trying not to roll off it while a half dozen coil springs dug into his side had taught him otherwise.

Fortunately, he had the prospect of a comfortable bed ahead of him, for he had engaged a suite at Wards Hotel for their wedding night. It was an extravagance, but what the hell, it was the least he could do, he reasoned to himself. After all, his poor deceived bride deserved a little pleasure from her wedding day. A stay in a grand hotel would thrill her little heart to no end, even if sharing a suite with him would put her in a terrible fluster.

Her twenty-six years had afforded her precious little by way of treats as far as he could tell. He might almost say she had been deprived of them, despite the fact there was money or at least property in her background. That thought at least brought a faint smile to his lips. After today, he would have control of his own theater at last and an ambition of several years would be realized.

There was, however, another emotion lurking somewhere in the shadowy corners of his soul. He examined it now with some trepidation. Strange to say, it was not cold feet or regret or any of the conventional feelings a bachelor was supposed to feel on his wedding morning. In truth, he was not sure *what* it was, but if pushed he would have to admit he felt a little sad that his courtship of Theodora Fields was at an end.

This realization almost made him lose his footing as he stepped from a raised curb. It was *ridiculous* to be feeling sad when he was about to secure his claim on The Parthenon. It was just that, somehow, he had sort of enjoyed the role of indulgent fiancé during the past few weeks. He had been damned good at it too, and against all expectation, he had derived some gratification from the fact Dora so patently *did* think of him in that light.

Clem did not think anyone else in his life had considered him a kindly benefactor. He gave money every month to his cousin Grace to help provide for their uncle in his old age, but Grace clearly thought that was the least he could do, and he supposed she was right all things considered.

Uncle Dan had been good to him in the year after he had left school, providing him with a roof over his head, and Clem did not begrudge the money. He did, however, begrudge the time he spent in their cramped parlor every second Saturday, trying to hold on to the loose thread of the old man's conversation as Grace stood in the doorway and lectured Clem on the godless direction of his life.

Would Dora soon agree he was an immoral pleasure-seeker, steeped in sin and infamy? Grace disapproved of music

115

halls even more than she had boxing. Luckily, Clem did not much care what his cousin thought, and her haranguing rolled off his broad shoulders like water off a duck's back.

Of course, once Dora was his wife, she would not continue in such blissful ignorance of his character, but maybe after all, he should encourage her good opinion for as long as he could? His steps slowed as he considered this approach. It would certainly make things much easier for him to maneuver her along the path he saw lying ahead of them.

Not that he had been planning to start treating her with indifference as soon as the ceremony was done, but she would have to learn about his duplicity at some point. Need that be right away though? After all, there was no point in throwing barriers in their way before it was strictly necessary...

The poor thing would be in for a rough enough time of it when her dreams about a stage career came crashing down about her ears. No, it would be better if he was still the solicitous ally when that crisis came. That way he could console her and find her some other cause to throw her considerable energy into. Maybe motherhood, he thought casually and, once again, paused with shock at the direction of his own thoughts.

Motherhood? He stood stock-still on the pavement for a moment, breathing in and out of his nostrils as his thoughts raced. But that would mean...consummating their marriage, he thought slowly. He had not actually intended to do that, had he? *Or had he?*

After all, he pondered, why else had he booked the night in a premier hotel at an exorbitant cost? He certainly had not intended to sleep on a couch for the second night. Had he thought they would sleep side by side on their wedding night with nothing more than a polite peck on the cheek exchanged between them?

Maybe, just maybe, he had not wanted to look at his motivation too closely at the time of booking the suite. And maybe Dora expected a good ravishing, that was his reputation after all. The notion, though it pleased him, was not exactly convincing. Even his mildest flirtation threw her into a spin. As for Dora, she had been so focused on their goal of getting married that he doubted very much that she had given much thought to what logically followed their vows.

In truth, he had shied away from discussing postceremony plans with her in any detail. He suspected she would balk at his intention to brazenly move in with her family the following day, but she had informed him herself that the property was not her brother's and, in fact, belonged jointly, to all three of the Fields siblings. As such, the newlywed couple had every right to turn up there in a day's time and take up residence.

There would be some initial awkwardness, no doubt, for Dora. As for himself, Clem knew himself to be entirely shameless. He would not cavil at the idea of putting Felix Fields's nose out of joint, or that milksop Allsop. In fact, he would probably relish it.

That put a spring in his step if nothing else, along with the realization that he need be in no hurry to unmask before Dora. As for the seduction…he would play it by ear, he decided. Strangely cheered, he sped up, eager to arrive at the church on time.

By this point, he had reached St. Thomas's and recognized Dora hovering by the gate, looking both cold and pinched as she clutched at the railing and peered anxiously into the fog for him. To his surprise, he felt an almost overwhelming relief at finding she had not suddenly come to her senses and evaded him. Dora's fate was sealed. She was his. He could not stop the satisfied smile that curved his lips as he collected her and led her up the path to the church.

*

Clem felt surprisingly relaxed as they exited the church, Dora clinging tightly to his arm. Her breathing was fast and

117

shallow, and he could tell she was both exhilarated and terrified at what they had done.

"What now?" she asked in hushed tones. "I confess I had not actually dared to think of anything past the ceremony itself. I suppose we need to confront our families…" She blanched slightly at her own words.

Clem grinned down at her. "I thought it would be best if we spent tonight at a hotel. Then you can take me home with you tomorrow."

"To a hotel?" she squeaked, letting go of his arm and coming to a halt. "But what will everyone think when I do not return home?" she asked.

"Do you care?" he asked smoothly. "After the way they have treated you?"

That made her pause for thought. She worried her bottom lip with her teeth. "Well, but I—I should not wish them to start dragging the rivers for me," she joked feebly.

He reached out and tucked a lock of her hair behind her ear. "Have you really been as unhappy as all that, Dora?" he asked softly.

She stared up at him a moment, frozen into place, then color flooded her cheeks. "No, of c-course not," she stammered and gave an awkward laugh, finally able to look away. "Not when I knew we had our plan in place," she said bracingly, "though until that point, I do confess I felt rather wretched. As you know, I am not at all suited to the role of housekeeper."

Clem drew her hand back through his arm and felt the slight tremble in her fingers. She was full of nerves, and he should be soothing, not scaring the living daylights out of her. "We need to spend the night together to ensure our marriage is legal and not contested," he said carefully instead.

Her eyes widened, and he saw words trembling on her lips that she could not quite form. This was the point where he should reassure her that he did not expect her to fulfill all her wifely obligations. Except, the words did not come, as he had now realized this was no longer true and he had every intention of bedding her.

He was still not entirely sure when exactly he had decided that. They walked arm in arm along the Old Harlow Road, both deep in their own thoughts. Maybe it was since that day they had taken cocktails together. Nay, maybe before that even.

Since the chop house most likely, when she had taken such delight in her Sunday lunch. He *liked* putting that dazed and gratified expression on her face. More than liked it, he found he craved it. He wanted to see her look at him with that self-same expression when he showed her pleasures of a more...*carnal* nature.

The thought made his heart race, and he faced a few astonishing facts in quick succession. One, that the thought of seducing Dora excited him. Two, the fact that it would likely mess up his brilliant coup of The Parthenon did not put him off one bit. Somewhere down the line, he suspected he would pay dearly, but even as he considered the possibility of future regret, he could not dissuade himself from indulging in Dora's sweet body this night.

The thought almost jolted him out of his reverie. *Her sweet body?* When the hell had he started thinking of gangly and awkward Theodora Fields that way? He cast a quick glance at her face and found her regarding him nervously. He gave her his slow smile. "You're as jumpy as a little rabbit," he teased. "Do I need to keep a tight grip on you in case you try and give me the slip?"

"I daresay, though no one has ever thought me little," she said with another short laugh. "I'm exceedingly tall for a woman."

"Not compared to me," he said dismissively.

She glanced at their reflection in a passing window. "Yes, I suppose that is true. We do look in proportion, do we not, Mr. Dabney?"

He smirked. "We do indeed, Mrs. Dabney."

She gave another gasp of weak laughter, and he resolved not to tease her for the next hour at least. It was not really fair to make sport of her. She just wasn't equipped to deal with the likes of him.

"Is the hotel you booked near here?" she asked. Then her face fell, and she covered her mouth.

"What is it?"

"I did not bring an overnight case!" she said, clearly dismayed. "I did not realize—"

"It little matters. We can buy you a few necessities now." Clem shrugged. "What do you need? Toothbrush? Nightgown?"

Dora swallowed and nodded weakly. "Yes," she admitted, looking utterly dejected.

"I booked Wards for tonight," he said in the hopes of cheering her up.

"*Wards?*" she gasped in shock, coming once again to a complete standstill. "For us to *stay*?" He nodded, a slow grin spreading over his face. "Oh Clem!" she uttered, sounding quite choked and turning very pink.

Any qualms that might have lingered over the expense disappeared in an instant. "Of course," he said, lifting her gloved hand to kiss it. "I thought you might enjoy the experience."

He shepherded her successfully into a likely looking store to purchase what she needed, hanging discreetly back so she could make her selection. Up until the point of purchase that is, and then he took over, despite Dora's protest. She could not have much left of the money he had given her all those weeks before.

The nightgown looked to be a depressingly sensible affair of white cotton, but he paid up all the same. Now that he thought about it, Clem had not brought an overnight bag either, not seeing the need as he slept in the nude.

Seeing Dora's discomfiture, he reconsidered. Maybe he would keep his long underwear on, at least at the outset. He requested two toothbrushes and toothpowder, two washcloths, some lotion, and some face cream, the plainest he could find so they could both use it. He also picked up a smart leather bag to put everything in. Perhaps turning up at Wards without any luggage might have looked a little singular. "What else do you need?" he asked.

"That should suffice if we are returning to Juniper Row tomorrow," she responded quickly.

Clem frowned. "Really?" It did not seem a lot for a lady's toilette in his opinion, but then again, Dora's appearance was not exactly one of polished femininity. "What about a hairbrush?"

Her eyes gleamed at this, but she shook her head and he wondered at her sudden merriment. "I don't need one," she said, appearing to enjoy some private joke. "Unless you do?"

He ordered a comb instead and left it at that. After this, it was plain sailing. They checked in to Wards; Dora exclaimed over the hotel suite, though she kept her eyes firmly averted from the large bed. He did his best to put her at her ease, and Dora's nervousness seemed to be abating by the minute.

Clem suffered a slight setback when she removed her coat to reveal a very strange striped garment underneath with tassels and embroidered medallions. It was not so much the fabric and decoration that was jarring, as the shape and cut of it.

There was not enough volume by way of skirts, he thought, which he was used to being a stiff domed shape. Dora's skirts were long but fell to the floor in a softer incline, almost as if she only wore one petticoat instead of half a dozen stiffened ones.

121

The top half was not right either. Instead of a tight-fitting bodice trimmed with lace, hers was a modest high-necked affair with a fussy bow and oversized collar. Her waist was tidy but far from nipped in. If he did not know better, he would almost think she was not corseted at all.

This was nothing, however, to his reaction when she removed her bonnet, only for her ringlets to come away with it. Clem set down his hair comb with a clatter on the bedside table. "Your—er—*hair*, Dora," he murmured.

"Oh!" She made a grab for the two long ringlets dangling down from her bonnet and reattached them to the back of her head. "Silly me!"

Was that a thing that normally happened? Clem wondered in stupefaction. He had been with women who had removed padding from their hair before bed, but he had never been with a woman with actually *short* hair before. To his surprise, he found himself faintly shocked by the notion.

As though picking up on his reaction, she turned about to face him fully. "I had it shorn off three weeks ago," she confided. "After we formulated our plan. Albert took me to a barber he knows that doesn't ask questions. Lil recommended a wigmaker in Cheapside, and I sent him my hair and he made it into a switch so I could still wear it for respectability's sake. I only got it back two days ago, so I have had to wear caps at home for weeks. I told Felix I had an earache." She ran a hand over her long dark ringlets before tossing them back over her shoulder. "Rather good, isn't it? I thought it turned out well."

Clem stared at her head, trying to make it out. The front of her hair looked to be about jaw-length and was secured to her head at the sides with hair combs. The back, now that he really looked, was not twisted up as he had assumed into an up-do. Instead, it was cut into the back of her head and did not extend down her neck at all. The ringlets obscured this fact for the most part.

"That is your own hair?" he asked dazedly. "That you had cut off?"

She nodded. "I had the length cut off in a pigtail and then he curled one half into a ringlet and the other half he braided for me to wear in up-styles. He added loops and everything to them for attaching to my head."

Clem shook his head. "There really are experts in every field," he pronounced, not knowing what else to say.

Dora nodded. "He is a specialist wig maker and told me he vastly prefers working with human hair to horse's or sheep's hair."

"*Sheep's* hair?"

"Oh yes, and you know he makes pieces not only for theatrical folk but for fashionable society ladies too. Quite often their hairstyle needs some augmentation."

Clem regarded her with reluctant fascination. "Good grief."

Seemingly unoffended, she beamed back at him. "I knew you would not mind. For some reason, Albert seemed to think you would not like it." She sounded faintly baffled by the notion.

"I had thought impersonators usually wear wigs," he admitted.

"Oh, but I thought this seemed a good deal more practical, don't you think?"

"Why not?" he replied affably. "You do not...er...regret the decision to cut it off?"

"Not at all," she assured him. "It is so much easier to take care of now. I don't have to spend hours washing and waiting for it to dry. Really it only takes a fraction of the time it used to, and my head feels so much lighter and freer without the length."

Clem, who had always thought hair a woman's crowning beauty, was a little perturbed but gallantly strove to hide the fact. "I see."

123

"Would you like a closer look at it?" she asked, reaching up for her ringlets.

"No," Clem said quickly. "Let us preserve the illusion. Shall we go down to the restaurant? I'm ravenous."

Dora was quiet on their way downstairs, and it occurred to Clem that he might not have been as smooth with his deflection as he had intended. Once they had been seated at a table in the chandeliered dining saloon, he set about making reparations and soon had her smiling again.

"I doubt your poor brother and Mr. Allsop will be partaking of such a fine luncheon," he remarked, clicking his tongue when their elegant repast was laid out before them.

Dora went off in a coughing fit, which she smothered with a napkin, before turning toward him with watery eyes. "I have left them a very fine lunch, as it happens," she protested. "A cold collation which I have left under covers. Bread and butter," she listed, "stewed pears, a goodish wedge of Shropshire blue cheese, some biscuits which are only a little stale, and a big cold pudding. The pudding," she added with satisfaction, "was so large that it should last them for *days*."

"Ah," said Clem, glancing down with disfavor at the delicate tea sandwiches which he could eat in one bite. "You did not explain there was *cold pudding*. That, of course, makes all the difference." The fillings of the sandwiches looked to be insubstantial too, he observed: salmon, cucumber, fluffy egg salad, and cream cheese. Next to these was an elegant plate of iced petit fours, a bowl of mixed roasted nuts, and glazed fruits served on fancy china. God, he would waste away on this fare!

Dora's eyes narrowed at him. "I can tell you are being facetious, Mr. Dabney," she said archly, "but as a matter of fact, I have had a breakthrough in the kitchen. It turns out that baked puddings are my strong suit. Sago, tapioca, semolina, all of them are so much easier than the dreaded pastry." Her hand hovered over the sandwich platter indecisively before she

124

picked a cucumber. "My greatest success has been with bread-and-butter pudding," she said proudly. "Even Felix agreed it was very good. You make it with any stale leftover bread, just adding currants, sugar, milk, and butter."

Clem managed to keep his face straight by the greatest of effort. "Nursery puddings, you mean?"

"Nothing of the sort!" Dora protested. "Did you never like to eat pudding when you were at school?"

That sobered Clem up straightaway. "Indeed," he agreed gravely. "But we only had it on Sundays." Keen to dispel Drummond Hall from his mind altogether, he asked lazily, "Do you really have so much leftover bread? When I met you the other week you had none left in the house for you had forgotten to visit the bakers."

She grimaced. "Do not remind me; Felix will never let me live that down. I had rather a good idea, as it happens. I bought three loaves of bread to spare myself needless journeys throughout the week. Then the third loaf started to turn green and moldy, so I was forced to cut off the crusts and several mold spots, and Felix was most suspicious about why the bread was such an irregular shape."

"What a mistrustful nature your brother has." He smirked.

"He does, doesn't he?" she agreed roundly.

"How about Allsop?" Clem asked casually. "What does he think of pudding for supper?"

She smiled, causing Clem's gut to clench in a peculiar way. "I think Harold rather approves," she said, blithely unaware of his displeasure. "He always has a second helping, and frankly, it's a lot more palatable than anything else I've attempted. I know for a fact that Felix is scoffing down meat pies at lunchtime, so I fail to see why a nice stodgy pudding should not suffice for his evening meal." She turned on him impulsively. "How about you?" she asked. "Do you insist on meat at every meal?"

"Ah," Clem stalled, hesitant to admit he did not consider any meal complete without it. "I, too, am fond of pudding," he lied. The only pudding he cared for was steak and kidney. "But once we are installed at Juniper Row, we can reinstate your Mrs. Cheviot to the kitchen, so you will not need to make it again."

"Cherwell," she corrected him with a smile. "I cannot *wait* to write to her with the good news." A note of anxiety crept into her voice. "Are you quite sure you can bear the expense?"

"I'm quite sure," he assured her. He was damned if he was going to be eating cold tapioca pudding for his supper every night when he moved into her family home!

"Maybe I will have time this evening to drop her a line," Dora mused, swallowing the last bite of her sandwich and reaching for a dainty Genoese fancy from the petit four plate.

"On our wedding night?" Clem asked with a raised brow.

Dora almost dropped her tiny cake. "Oh, er, of course not," she murmured sheepishly, not quite able to meet his eye.

Her nervousness should be tiresome, but somehow…it wasn't. And why was that? Clem pondered as they moved into the grand salon once their meal was done. *Face facts, Dabney*, he told himself sternly, *you have a decidedly soft spot for her*. It seemed that somehow in the past five weeks she had managed to endear herself to him.

She was rather like a spaniel, he thought. Perpetually hopeful, good-natured, and lively, she would likely be loyal too, until she found out what a lying cad he was. He *liked* her. Which could be a problem, considering he was essentially gulling her right now.

How would she react when it all came out? He found himself wondering about this for the first time. This part of proceedings had not really seemed to strike him as important at the outset. Now though… For some reason, he felt a little

126

uneasy about it. He summoned a waiter and asked Dora to choose their next cocktail.

Of course, she knew that he had married her for a quarter interest, she was just unaware that she was gifting him the majority share. Was it really such an issue or was he making too much of it? It wasn't like him to get caught up on small details when there was a bigger scheme at hand. He watched as Dora ran her eyes up and down the cocktail menu, asking the waiter about the flavor of some cordial.

He could really do with a visit to the smoking room, he thought, glancing back over his shoulder, but he was reluctant to leave Dora unattended at this stage. What if she ran off and left him? Or bumped into some acquaintance who might drag her back to her brother? She was nervous enough to be spooked, he reckoned, though she had moments when she forgot what she had done that morning and relaxed. Then he would let something slip, usually some teasing remark, and she would immediately tense up again. He frowned.

"You do not like the sound of a Blushing Lady?" Dora asked, misinterpreting his expression. "Its ingredients sound quite nice. Pomegranate liqueur, grapefruit juice, and vodka," she read aloud from the menu.

"It sounds fine," Clem said swiftly. "And very appropriate for a blushing bride." There he went again; he could not seem to stop himself. Of course, he was naturally flirtatious, but he needed to rein it in.

"Clem," Dora started in a strangled tone as soon as the waiter retreated. "Could we please—um—" She glanced about them nervously. "Well, perhaps this is not the place."

"Place for what?" Clem asked.

"Renegotiating our terms," she said with a forthrightness that floored him for a moment.

"Renegotiate?" He stared at her. *What the hell?*

"You see, I thought that when you accepted my offer, it was on the terms I outlined. But now it seems you view things in a different light."

Clem leaned forward in his chair and cleared his throat. "Remind me again just what those terms were that you outlined," he said after a slight pause. He had some vague memories of her promising—what was it?—not to interfere with his *carrying on*?

Her expression cleared. "Oh, so you had forgotten. Well." She glanced quickly around. "I explained that I was aware of your—um…" He watched her turn very red and then clam up, a look of surprise passing over her features.

Strangely, Clem felt a pang of sympathy for her predicament. He fancied he knew exactly what was tying her tongue. When Dora had bearded him in his den that day and boldly called him a philander, they had not been, well, *friends*. They had been strangers, and she had not felt the smallest compunction in stating hard facts.

Things were rather different between them now. She shot him an agonized look, and Clem *almost* took pity on her. Almost. This talk of renegotiations had galled him somewhat. "Yes?" he enquired smoothly.

"The thing is you see," she blurted. "I don't want to get pregnant." Clem stared at her a moment, feeling quite dumbstruck. Well, that would serve him right for calling her bluff! He sent a quick look around the lounge, but, fortunately, no one seemed to be going off in a swoon or running to complain to a manager. "I am only just getting started on my true career," she continued apologetically, "and—"

"I understand," Clem put in swiftly. He would say anything to stem the tide of her confidences at this point!

"You do?" She breathed out a sigh of relief. "Oh, thank goodness. I know that there are"—she swallowed—"certain practices or *devices* that can be employed. I could ask Lil about them, for you know, she is a woman of the world and has no children. But perhaps it would be better if we kept things between the two of us." She bit her lip and looked at Clem for assurance.

"I agree that would be better," he answered quite truthfully.

"Oh good!" She flashed him a relieved smile. "So…will you secure the necessary items? Or perhaps point me in the right direction for an establishment that supplies such things? For some reason, the whole business seems enshrouded in the most unnecessary secrecy, especially from women, which is ridiculous. You would think, would you not, that we could simply walk into a store and purchase such things over a counter, should the need arise?" She sounded aggrieved. "But nothing so sensible!"

"Dora," Clem murmured warningly, "the waiter's approaching."

She lapsed into an obliging silence, and their drinks were set down before them. "Good health," Dora said brightly, picking up her own glass.

Clem hastened to lift his own drink. It should be called The Blushing Groom, he reflected wryly. The tops of his ears felt decidedly hot. Of course, she had a point. It *was* ridiculous that women had to jump through so many hoops to access preventatives.

As for Clem, he had never actually needed to obtain one before. Any previous company he had kept took care of that themselves. But Dora was not his mistress and up to every trick in the book; she was his wife. The realization that this was a different thing altogether was starting to dawn on him with startling clarity.

"You know," she started up again as soon as she had swallowed her first sip. He watched her in fascinated horror. What the hell was she going to come out with next? "When it comes to women's health, *everything* is invested with a—a most nonsensical level of *shame*. Somehow, we are not permitted to speak openly and frankly of matters pertaining to our own bodies because it is considered indelicate. You would not believe the lengths I have to go to simply to obtain patterns for my clothes."

Clem paused with his drink halfway to his mouth. "Is it so difficult?" he asked. He was sure he had seen dress patterns stocked on shelves. Then again, Dora's taste in clothing was decidedly unusual.

"Yes, for I subscribe to the notion of artistic dress," she said enthusiastically. "Years ago, I heard a friend of my uncle's speak on the subject one night at dinner. You would not have believed how uncomfortable my uncle and Felix grew by the conversation. And they are supposed to be artistic freethinkers themselves! When I told them I was newly converted to the cause, they said I should draw a discreet veil over such matters for the sake of womanly decency and not attempt to discuss such matters with them again."

When Clem continued to look at her blankly, she leaned forward. "I do not espouse the wearing of corsets," she explained. "Nor the adoption of uncomfortable and restrictive garments to achieve an unnatural silhouette."

Once again, Clem found himself dumbfounded. "You— er—don't?" he asked after a fortifying sip of fruity vodka. It was cloyingly sweet.

"No, for corsets, you know, constrict the organs to a dangerous degree and that is not even touching on the effect they have on one's ability to breathe. Would you believe that some people even recommend the wearing of a pregnancy corset?" she demanded without lowering her voice. "As for multiple petticoats, if you only *knew* the statistics for accidents and even *death* caused by them, you would be horrified, I assure you. I have heard such tales! Women bursting into flame if they stand too close to the mantlepiece or being cobbled up in wheels or machinery and unable to free themselves and quite *crushed*."

Hearing a gasp close by, Clem glanced around the salon and found two ladies staring in their direction with horrified expressions. One had a handkerchief pressed to her mouth. She would probably be quite attractive if she wasn't a hysterical eavesdropper, he thought irritably. He frowned at her, and she colored and looked away.

Hoping to distract Dora from the subject of grisly feminine deaths, he asked, "How *do* you get them? The patterns, for your—er—garments, I mean." He eyed today's gown again. Its odd appearance made more sense now she had explained her peculiar beliefs.

"Oh, I am subscribed to several magazines that run advertisements for their purchase via mail. It would be *so* much easier if I could simply walk into a shop and peruse them at will, but no. Apparently, they are too shocking to display in shop windows." She rolled her eyes, and Clem found himself smiling in spite of himself. "I am so glad you're open-minded," she sighed happily.

She had spoken that sentiment once before, he was not sure when. Perhaps at one of their early encounters, but whenever it was, Clem found himself wondering for the first time if she was quite correct in her assessment. It was true he had always considered himself broad-minded, but now he felt a little… He was unsure of the correct word for it.

He was not shocked, he told himself firmly. It would be absurd for the likes of him to be shocked by sheltered Dora. Taken aback maybe? His short-haired wife scorned conventional dress and desired a career over a family. It was a lot to take in all at once. A hell of a lot. He needed to smoke and get a real drink, he thought, discarding the cocktail with a grimace.

131

As though picking up on his thoughts, Dora leaned forward in her chair. "I am sorry I did not raise that other matter between us before now, Clem," she said earnestly. "You see, I did not initially think that—well—" She plucked at her skirts. "It would be something we would be navigating in our marriage."

Clem considered her a moment. He was damned if he was going to admit he had thought the same thing. "Don't give it another thought," he said instead. "Have you finished that?"

Dora glanced down at the glass in her hand. She nodded, setting it down.

"Let's go up to our room, then," he said abruptly. "I need to smoke."

11

Clem had ordered drinks sent up to their room, so no sooner had Dora settled herself in a chair by the window than there was a rap at the door. Clem, who had been removing his jacket, crossed the room to answer it. The waiter set down a sherry for Dora and a whiskey for Clem and, after being tipped, discreetly disappeared.

"Do you know, I think Dora Dabney makes a very good stage name," she said musingly. "It has a nice ring to it, don't you think? Better than Theodora Fields."

"You want to take that as your stage name?" For some reason, he was not entirely pleased by the notion.

"Unless you would rather I did not use your name," she said, noticing his frown.

That was when Clem realized that was not the part he objected to. Dora was what *he* called her. He liked that he was the only one to use it. *How strange.* To cover his confusion, he carried her sherry over and set it down on a small table for her. "Not at all. It is your name now, as well as mine."

She smiled and Clem picked up his own drink. "Sláinte," he said succinctly.

Dora hastened to pick up her glass. "Cheers," she agreed and took a sip. "What does that mean?"

"Good health, I believe. My uncles always said it."

"Are they Scots?"

"Irish."

"Ah. Do you know any more Gaelic?"

He shook his head. "They didn't raise me. I was fifteen when my uncle took me in."

Dora nodded. "We have that in common," she said thoughtfully. "Though I was only six when my uncle became our guardian."

"You liked him," he observed, watching her face as something snagged her attention out of the window.

She leaned forward, staring intently before answering him absently. "Oh yes, he was the best of men."

She had a good profile, Clem thought, though her nose was perhaps a little long. It would be pressed up against the glass in a minute. "Enjoying the view?" he asked lazily. She was too caught up to answer him. This time he knew better than to ask if she had spotted someone she knew. For some reason, Dora liked gazing at strangers. Who was he to judge how she found amusement in it?

He watched her in silence a moment before she turned her head to blink at him. "I'm sorry, did you say something?" she asked, coloring slightly.

"Let me see you without that hair piece," he said, surprising them both.

She reached up straightaway and unfastened the ringlets, setting them down and then fluffing her hair so it did not lie so smooth to her head. "What do you think?" she asked and bit her lip.

"Let me see the back."

Obligingly, she stood up from her chair and turned around.

Clem cleared his throat. "I think it is fortunate you have a shapely neck."

"Do you think so?" She sounded pleased with this, which was just as well, for Clem could think of no other genuine compliment. In truth, he was shocked as hell.

"Do you want me to grow it back?" she asked shrewdly.

Clem hesitated. He could not answer this truthfully without causing offense. Then again, once she had been through her disastrous debut, she would no longer have a reason to go about with a shorn head. "Of course not," he lied.

Clearly, this was the right thing to say, for she looked hugely relieved. He had thought once they repaired to their suite her stammering nervousness would return, but as always, she surprised him. It seemed now they had the pregnancy issue resolved she was at her ease.

"Shall we take our evening meal up here?" he suggested casually, testing her newfound calm. "That way you need not put them back in and I can undo this damnable collar."

"Of course, if you prefer," she said, glancing about their elegant surroundings. "It would seem a shame not to make full use of this lovely suite."

Clem was already tearing at his neckcloth, flinging it down in a chair with his jacket. He popped open the top two buttons and felt himself relax. To his surprise, Dora was watching his every move with interest.

"If my neck is well formed, then yours is certainly well developed," she commented.

Clem laughed. "Are you saying I have a thick neck?" he asked.

"It is very nice and manly," she said admiringly, making him blink. "I wish mine was more like it."

"I don't!" Clem answered with alacrity.

Now it was Dora's turn to laugh. She had a nice laugh, not too loud, not too quiet. "I only mean that after observing yours, I am not so sure my male impersonation will be too accurate." He watched her trace a finger down her throat, her eyes clearly fixed on his. God alone knew why, but it made his breath catch.

"You must have seen an Adam's apple before," he murmured, his voice far too husky.

"Oh yes." She blushed. "My brother's, though, is not as prominent as yours."

"Want to take a closer look?" he offered, fully expecting her to bridle.

"May I?" she asked eagerly, practically bounding out of her chair.

135

Clem was so surprised, he stood stock-still while she practically stuck her nose in the base of his throat. Her breath tickled his collar bone, and it affected him strongly.

"Can I…?"

"Yes," he answered too quickly. Whatever it was she wanted to do, he wanted it. Still, he had to steel himself not to jump when she placed three fingers to his throat and stroked them gently down. He could not hold back the stifled sound he made or stop his eyes from drifting closed when she repeated it.

"You like to be touched?" she asked curiously.

Fuck, he was getting way too worked up over such an innocent gesture. "Doesn't everyone?" he asked throatily. "Don't you?"

She tipped her head as though considering this. "I don't know," she admitted.

Every word coming out of her mouth seemed calculated to excite him even more. "*Jesus*, Dora," he groaned. "I thought I'd be seducing you, not the other way around."

Her gaze widened at this. "Is that what it seems like?" she whispered, a wistful look entering her eyes. "I wish I could, but I wouldn't even know how."

His cock disagreed; he made a dissenting noise in his throat. "You're doing just fine, love."

"Just stroking you?"

He wasn't sure his dick didn't leap in his pants at that. He gave a throaty rumble. "Stroking is good. Sometimes I stroke myself when there's no one else there to do it for me."

Her expression wavered. "By that…do you mean…?" She could not quite bring herself to say the words that hovered on her tongue.

Suddenly Clem wanted to hear them very much. "Say it, Dora," he encouraged her.

She took a shaky breath. "Between your legs, I mean," she whispered, her eyes darting down to that place. She had to notice the state he was in. Her eyes grew very round.

"See?" he rasped. "I told you you were seducing me. There's your evidence." When she did not drag her eyes away from his bulging crotch, Clem groaned.

"Would you—" she began hesitantly. "That is, could you—"

"Yes, to whatever you're asking."

"Show me?" Dora concluded shockingly.

Christ almighty. He licked his lips. "Show you my cock or show you...?"

"Yes. I mean both. I mean show me how you stroke yourself...down there."

He breathed shakily in and out again. Instead of answering her, he simply reached across into the holdall, withdrawing the bottle of lotion and inspecting it. A puzzled-looking Dora watched him unscrew the lid and sniff it. It did not smell particularly perfumed, so he took it with him and moved past Dora to the bed where he removed his waistcoat and cuff links, rolling up his sleeve. Then he slipped off his shoes and unfastened his trousers.

Dora seized a chair and dragged it across the carpet until she was directly opposite him, with only a few feet between them. Clem gritted his teeth. She was so fucking curious. He had not expected that, but if his brain was capable of functioning right now, he would probably find he should have. Dora was a never-ending source of surprise.

She sank into her chair. "I'm ready now," she announced, her rapt gaze on his crotch.

Clem wanted to laugh, but he did not want to hurt her feelings. He wanted to encourage this boldness in the bedroom, so instead, he unbuttoned his shirt, keeping a covert eye on his audience of one. Dora was frozen in her seat, her lips parted and her gaze steady on his fingers. He doubted her brother's chest looked anything like his either.

When he reached the last button, he opened his shirt, showing her his muscular belly before lifting his hips and peeling down his trousers, then his long underwear, until his cock was fully on display. It rose proudly to attention, and Clem looked at it, wondering for the first time how Dora would view it through her eyes.

Probably his size would be off-putting to a virgin, but when he glanced up, he found Dora leaning forward in her seat to get a better view. Her attention was fully trained upon his dick, and he had to blow out a puff of air to keep focus.

"I am not sure a sock would suffice after all," she murmured, color creeping into her cheeks.

"A sock?"

"Oh, um, nothing. Just something Mr. Finch suggested."

Clem tensed. "And why are you thinking of Charlie Finch at this moment?" he asked, narrowing his eyes.

Dora gave a wave of her hand. "It was nothing, ignore me," she said. "Pretend I'm not here." She smiled encouragingly.

The gesture was so ridiculous that it dispelled his brief annoyance. He gave a huff of laughter and poured a spot of lotion into his palm, rolling it around before wrapping his hand about the base of his cock. He could not resist another glance at Dora, despite her instruction.

Not that she noticed, for she was staring at his cock with a look of rapt fascination on her face. Clem caught his tongue between his teeth and started to stroke lazily.

"What are you thinking of?" she asked suddenly, breaking the silence between them.

"I'm not thinking of anything," Clem admitted. "Being here with you is stimulating enough."

She nodded. A thought occurred to Clem. "Do you want me to finish?" he asked. If so, he would need that washcloth.

138

"Not yet," she answered.

He bit off a laugh. "No, I mean, eventually."

"Yes," she answered, looking a little unsure.

"Then you need to pass me a washcloth out of the bag."

"Why?"

Clem shot her a searching look. "You just said you wanted me to finish," he said slowly. "I meant, spill my seed."

"Oh!" Dora turned scarlet, then turned to the holdall, fishing around in the bag until she found one. Quickly turning back, she hurried forward and flapped it in the direction of his free hand.

Clem took it from her, looking right up into her eyes. "Why don't you sit down beside me, Dora love?" He patted the spot next to him.

She frowned. "But I won't see everything then."

"You'll be right up close; you'll see more." Grudgingly, she dropped down onto the bed beside him. "Unless you don't want to." Dora was peering down at him again. *Fuck*. It was having an odd effect on him. He felt slightly dizzy.

"Did you just get bigger?" she asked critically.

"Possibly. My cock likes you being closer."

"Does it?" She sounded vaguely flattered.

"Can't you tell?"

She cast him a quizzical look. "It looks angry to me. Like it's throbbing. Does it hurt?"

He shook his head. *Ah fuck*. He wasn't going to last long. Not with her right next to him chattering away. He closed his eyes in an attempt to stave off the crisis point.

"Would it…would it like if I touched it?"

Clem gasped. His eyes flew open. "Yes," he wheezed. "Yes, it would, very much."

"Should I put lotion on my hand first?"

Clem whimpered; there was no other word for it. He nodded. "Quickly."

139

She fumbled with the cap a moment while Clem's labored breathing filled the room. He watched through half-closed lids as she poured the lotion, returned the cap, then rolled it in her palms. "Do I need to sit behind you and reach around?" she asked.

"What?"

"So I can get the movement just right."

Clem gave his head a quick shake. "Just wrap your hand about my cock, please, Dora sweetheart," he all but pleaded, reaching for her wrist and drawing her hand into his lap. "Fuck Dora, *yesssss*!" he hissed through his teeth as she took him firmly in hand.

"The angle is quite different so I am not at all sure this will feel the same—" she started.

"Ah!" Clem panted. "No, that's good, that's *very* fucking good."

"—and my hand is a good deal smaller than yours."

Clem had to stop himself from lifting his hips off the bed. "Use both hands," he gritted out. She was quick to comply. "Oh *fuck*, Dora." His head fell back, and he had to shut his eyes. Fuck, how was she so good at this? His hips were moving now; he couldn't help it, he needed more friction. But if he had more friction, he would never last. He felt perilously close already.

"Faster," he gasped, unable to stop himself. "*Harder*." She responded so thoroughly, he nearly jolted right off the bed. "*Unnngh, Dora!!*" The last words were a strangled shout, and Dora was still clasping him as he spurted all over his lower belly. "Oh *fuck*!" The note of astonished wonderment in his voice rang out in the room.

"Oh Clem," she said in a wobbly voice, gazing down at him. "Was that too hard?"

"No, it was fucking perfect," he groaned, collapsing back onto his elbows. "Christ almighty, woman. How the hell did you *do* that?"

A smile curved her lips. "I'm a good mimic and like to observe. I paid close attention to what you did, and I emulated it." She even sounded, he thought, a little smug.

His own lips turned up in an answering smile. "Well, you can watch all you like if I get to reap the rewards," he said throatily. "I can't remember the last time I came that hard. Especially to a hand job."

She looked back at him solemnly before her eyes strayed back to his crotch. "There is a lot of…seed," Dora murmured, her gaze wandering up to his belly.

Clem glanced down and winced. There sure was. Carefully, she released his now-flaccid dick and started to slip from the bed. "Where are you going?"

"To wet the washcloth," Dora said over her shoulder as she carried it into the adjoining bathroom. He listened to her pour water from a pitcher and then she was back. She hesitated. "Do you want to do it?"

"Only if you don't."

She started dabbing at him with the cloth at once. Clem watched her face the whole time. She looked so earnest as she gently cleaned him off, it made his chest grow tight. Suddenly, he realized he hadn't even kissed her. He did not count that brief salute he had dropped on her lips before the vicar. She slipped away again before he could remedy that, and he heard once more the slosh of water.

Clem scooted back onto the bed, pulling up his underwear and fastening his trousers. He left his shirt open though and laid his head on the soft pillows. *Too soft.* Clem flung one onto the floor. Hearing her tread, he patted the bed again. "Come and lie next to me, Dora."

She paused only to untie her ankle boots and then the mattress creaked, and she clambered onto the other side of the bed. "Does it tire you out?" she asked sympathetically.

"Only for a short time."

She punched a pillow and settled herself down beside him. "I couldn't sleep much last night; I was too excited," she confessed.

Again, her words had that same effect on his chest. A sort of *squeezing* sensation. "Will I fit in your bed?" he asked, using practicality to dispel the strange sensations. "Or do I need to buy us a new one?"

"Oh." She eyed him up and down. "Well, by rights, you *should*," she said doubtfully, "if you were a regular-sized man, but you're so large that I can't be entirely certain."

Clem grinned. "Think I'm large, do you?"

"You *must* know you are." Her gaze lingered over his exposed chest a moment before skittering away.

"A fine specimen?" he persisted.

"Now you are just fishing for compliments, Mr. Dabney."

He laughed. "Maybe I am."

She smiled back at him. "You're a fine figure of a man," she said warmly, but it wasn't enough. Not by a long chalk. He wanted her touch.

He rolled onto his side toward her, reaching for her hand and drawing it onto his chest. "Stroke my chest, Dora," he ordered.

"How do you like it?" This threw him, for he had never actually requested this kind of touch from a woman before.

"That's cheating. Why don't you experiment and find out?"

Dora gave a smothered laugh and then started lightly circling his chest. "How's this?"

"Nice," he admitted, rolling once more onto his back. "Keep doing it." He let his eyes drift shut.

"Maybe it's not so bad having hot hands," she observed aloud.

"Not so good for handling pastry," he agreed without opening his eyes, "but *very* good for handling dick."

142

Dora met his words with an astonished silence, then she burst out laughing. "I wonder if all husbands talk to their wives as you do," she mused aloud.

That struck him into silence. He cleared his throat. "You don't like it?" he asked.

"No, I do! What I meant was, do men start being much franker with women once they happen to be their wives?"

Clem shifted uncomfortably. "I wouldn't really know."

"But you're a married man now," she pointed out reasonably.

Well, that was true enough. Clem swallowed. "I suppose I am," he agreed dazedly.

Her hands stopped circling and were now rubbing gently back and forth. Clem had to suppress a groan.

"Clem?" she said softly.

"Hmm, what?"

"I lied earlier," she said quietly.

He turned his head sharply. "About what?"

"The touching thing. I know I like to be touched…I have touched myself, I mean." She was bright fucking red at this point, though her voice was steady. "Down there." The last two words were little more than a whisper.

He couldn't speak for a few heartbeats, not a single fucking word. "Between your legs?" Clem asked carefully, not using his usual word for it. She was a lady after all. She nodded. Clem clicked his tongue. "What a pretty little liar you are, Dora mine," he breathed admiringly. "Now as a penance, you have to tell me all about it."

"*Tell* you?" She sounded surprised. The tantalizing thought struck Clem that she might not have been averse to showing him. "Well," she started weakly, "you see, in our house we have *always* shared books. My uncle encouraged us to buy all the books we wanted and to discuss them freely over dinner. We've always done it."

143

"Never tell me you bought a dirty book, Dora," Clem teased.

She went even redder. "Not me. Felix."

"He surely never shared such a thing with his sisters," Clem objected.

"No, and that was just the thing that made me curious. You see, we found this obscure little bookstore one Saturday, piled from floor to ceiling with books, and it had the most intriguing set of rickety stairs, but would you believe it," she said with chagrin, "only gentlemen were allowed up them. Well, Felix ventured up, and Hetty and I had to make do with the selection downstairs. Presently, he returned with this little pile of books, all done up with brown paper and string, and that struck me as odd you see, for neither my own purchases nor Hetty's were parceled up, so that piqued my curiosity."

She lapsed into silence, and Clem reached across and took her hand, lacing his fingers through hers. "Then what happened?" he prompted. He was enjoying this story.

"Well, we had afternoon tea, and my sister and I regaled our uncle with what we had bought, but Felix was as quiet as mouse, most unlike him. Then after lunch, Hetty and I went into the parlor to read. Usually, Felix would join us, but that day he went up to his room. Then at dinner again, he spoke not a word about his books while Hetty and I spoke of ours at length. After a few days, we added ours to the communal bookshelves in the back sitting room, but none of Felix's ever appeared."

Clem, who had his suspicions about the content of Felix's books, smirked. "So how did you stumble on them?" he persisted.

Dora cleared her throat. "I waited until he was out at the theater one day and went into his room," she confessed. "I did not even have a notion what the books were, just that they were some forbidden knowledge, and that was enough to spur me on."

144

"What were they?" he pressed.

"They were illustrations of a risqué nature," she admitted. "Depictions of women alone and in a state of undress and they were…pleasuring themselves."

Clem breathed out. Well, he had expected women in a state of undress but not that! "How?" he asked, his tone already a little unsteady.

"With, um…their fingers but also…"

"Also, what?"

She reddened. "Other things." She lowered her voice. "Phallus-shaped things."

"Phallus?"

"Cock-shaped things."

Clem's gaze darted to her mouth. "Say that again?"

"Well, you see, they were using them…"

"No, the word you just used," he corrected her.

"Cock? Well, that's the word you have been using, so I—"

"Yes, that's the word." He steadied his breathing a moment. "You must have been very shocked," he continued lightly.

"I was," she agreed vehemently. "I set the book right down and walked out of the room, vowing I would never, ever, be curious again about gentlemen's secrets." Clem laughed. "But afterward, I thought about it a lot and…even on occasion snuck another look." She peeped up at him through her lashes. "Are you shocked?"

"Very," he said warmly. "Shocked and delighted."

"After seeing those pictures, I was curious," she admitted. "Curious about my own body."

"You touched yourself?" She nodded. "Will you show me, Dora?"

"I want to," she admitted, once more depriving him of air. "But it won't be as exciting for you. Not like it was for me to

145

watch you, I mean, because—well—you can't really see all that much."

"I can see your fingers working your—between your legs, I mean," he said hoarsely. "You don't need to worry about me finding it exciting, Dora. I'm already excited." Her gaze dropped down to where his cock was already stirring with interest behind his trouser seam and her mouth formed a soundless *oh*. Clem smirked.

"Well, that didn't take very long at all," she marveled.

"That's your fault."

She gave a huff of laughter. "Well, tell me when you're ready, then."

"Want me to go and sit in the chair?" he asked seriously.

She considered this a moment before shaking her head. "No." She drew her hand away from petting his chest and rolled onto her back. Clem breathed slowly in and out before rolling onto his side and propping himself up on his elbow to watch her.

To his surprise, Dora hitched up her skirts without more ado. Her progress was not hampered by any cumbersome undergarments, so she simply slid some very plain cotton drawers down to her knees. They were not the crisp white he would have expected, and he guessed this was due to Dora's lack of laundering prowess. They looked an indeterminate shade of blue gray and were entirely without embellishment.

"Are you ready?" she asked gravely.

He paused, enquiring, "Are you not going to remove more clothes?"

She shook her head. "No, I'm not corseted, so I'm perfectly comfortable like this."

He had not actually meant her top half. He would have liked to have seen her long, shapely legs again, especially just in stockings, but as he had not removed his own clothes, he did not feel he had the right to ask it. Instead, he just replied, lips twitching, "Ready when you are, Dora."

She slid a hand between her thighs. Had he rushed things like this? He wanted to tell her to slow down, but somehow, he could not bring himself to direct her, not when she was being so open with him. "What are you thinking of?" he asked softly. "The illustrations?"

She hesitated, then shook her head. "Not this time," she admitted. He could not decide where to direct his gaze, her flushed face or that juncture at her thighs where her fingers were busy. He was spoiled for choice.

"What then?" he asked. "What are you thinking about?" Her gaze locked with his, and he stopped breathing. She wasn't about to say what he hoped she would, was she?

"You, when you were…you know…" *Christ.* Clem's heart pounded in his chest. Her words were breathy and far more seductive than he had thought Theodora Fields would ever sound.

"Did you like watching me?" he asked, and his voice came out gravelly and gruff, not coaxing like he had intended it to be.

She nodded. "Yes." She didn't even hesitate.

She was so truthful, even in this, Clem realized with something approaching a pang. Then he heard it—her wetness. *Fuck.* His head was going to explode. He drew in a steadying breath before asking unevenly, "Are you stroking your pearl, Dora? Did the pictures teach you that?"

"Yes," she sighed. "They were quite lewd." She bit her lip. "I had not even examined myself down there before I saw them."

"You did not know you had a pearl?"

"No," she burst out, then gasped. "Clem, I c-can't talk and do this at the same time. I can't concentrate."

"Can't you, sweetheart? Do you need any help?"

147

Her eyes darted to meet his. "Help in what way?" she asked in a strained voice.

"My fingers…or my mouth," he offered.

Dora made a muffled sound, though it did not sound like a protest. Clem waited. "Um, yes, if you do not mind."

If he did not mind? Clem had to swallow as he shifted carefully closer, his body leaning over hers. He slid his hand over her own, between her soft thighs, though for the moment he did not do anything else. Then he leaned down and pressed his mouth to hers. She sighed against his lips, and Clem swept his tongue along the seam of her mouth. Dora froze, in surprise, he supposed. The lewd drawings had not dealt with tongue kisses, it seemed.

He sipped at her lips a while, before running his tongue along her lips again. Then he drew back. "Like it or not?" he asked.

"Your tongue?"

"Yes, my tongue."

"It's nice," she answered cautiously. "I was not expecting it, but it's surprisingly pleasant."

Clem bit back his laugh. "I'd like to put it in your mouth," he admitted. "If that's something you'd be willing to try."

"Your tongue?" Dora asked in astonishment.

"Yes, please," Clem all but begged, staring hard at her lips. By this point, he felt like he'd *die* if she didn't let him.

"And what do I do with it, when it's in there?" a flummoxed Dora asked.

Clem grinned; he could not help himself. "Whatever you want."

She shot him another mystified look, then shrugged. "Very well, if that's something you—"

Having gained her permission, Clem pressed forward and took her mouth thoroughly. Dora was passive for a moment or so, no doubt considering her options. Then he felt it, the tip of her tongue touch tentatively to his. Clem could not swallow his groan, which clearly startled her. He drew back. "That's it, love, give me more," he murmured before settling more comfortably over her and sealing his lips to hers once again.

Encouraged, Dora tangled her tongue with his with an increasing boldness that had Clem's pulse pounding. Not only that, but when her free hand suddenly skimmed his shoulder and clasped him firmly at the back of his neck, Clem had to concentrate not to lose it.

Instead, he pressed gently against her fingers which had gone slack between her legs. When Dora gave a little gasp, he knew he had found the right spot, and with a little gentle urging, she resumed her efforts there. Carefully Clem slid two of his fingers on either side of her own and rubbed her wet folds.

Dora whimpered into his mouth, and the sound had his nostrils flaring. Tearing his mouth from hers, he panted, "Give me your tongue now, Dora." Then he sought her lips again before she could make a reply. He was loud, too loud, when Dora's tongue ventured into his mouth, but holy hell, it was good.

He didn't hold back, kissing her the way he liked it, deep and wet, sucking her tongue and then plunging his own into her mouth in the expectation of her doing the same. She did not disappoint him. Hell, he was starting to wonder if she ever would. He shouldn't be this aroused, just from a good kiss and a little fingering, but he was hard as rock.

Between her legs, her wetness coated his fingers, making him groan again. Her hand squeezed the back of his neck, and fuck knew why, but he bloody loved it. Her tongue stroked over his, and he felt like he was on fucking fire for her.

Too soon, she was drawing back with a shaky "Oh, Clem!" She pressed her face to the side of his neck and made an explosive noise, half cry, half moan. She was there. And more to the point, so was he. In fact, if he wasn't careful, he was going to… Clem wrenched back with a panicked *"Dora!"* and reached for his crotch.

"Are you about to spill?" Dora asked with breathless interest.

Her words were the final straw. Clem groaned and grabbed the washcloth which was mercifully within reach. *"Fuck…"* he groaned again and thoroughly disgraced himself. That had been a close-run thing, and he had only one pair of trousers with him.

12

After a quick wash, a slightly shaken Clem made his way downstairs to order their dinner to be delivered to their room. He smoked a cigar en route and tried to pull himself together as he descended the staircase. That…had not gone the way he had expected. Not at all. In his mind's eye, he recalled a deliciously disheveled Dora propped up on her elbows watching him come his brains out into a washrag. *Jesus*, the expression on her face.

She was *so…* Clem didn't know the word for it. Before tonight he might have used words like *naïve* or *clueless*, but now, he was starting to think she was something else. *Forthright?* Was that the right word? *Fearless?* They seemed the wrong words to use for a twenty-six-year-old spinster, especially one as…not *dotty* precisely but definitely eccentric as Dora, but they were the closest he could come up with on the spot.

To be honest, he didn't think of her as remotely dotty anymore. She might sometimes wear odd gloves and her views on dress were outlandish, to say the least, but you couldn't think of anyone as a budding maiden aunt when they were so…well, *frank,* in the bedroom.

Something else had become apparent as well. Something he had suspected but could no longer ignore. She trusted him, implicitly. He had, of course, encouraged this trust over the past month and a half, but he had not realized at the time that there would be implications for him involved.

He felt *uneasy* being the recipient of such unquestioning trust. Something a ruthless bastard like himself had no right to feel. More than that, he felt sort of underhanded and furtive, a thing that had never bothered him in business before. In truth, he was faintly surprised it was bothering him now. He had known from the outset what he was doing was unscrupulous, but he had not cared. Now…he felt a nagging sense of discomfort.

He slowed almost to a stop, hand on the banister, gazing into the gilt-edged mirror hanging on the wall opposite him. Could it be the marriage part that made the difference? Why should it though? He had entered into sexual arrangements in a simple, no-strings fashion many times before. No, it must be Dora herself that was causing him this disquiet.

He took a deep breath and faced facts squarely. It wasn't like him to flinch from hard truths, but here he was. Deep down he knew what the problem was. Despite her delightful openness, Dora *was* naïve, and he had taken on this role of husband and protector in spite of the fact he was the one about to shatter her entire world.

Fuck. That was it. He met his eyes in the mirror. He was going to be a lousy husband and Dora had not the first notion of the fact. She thought he was her coconspirator, her confidant, her *friend*. In truth, he was none of those things. It gave him an oddly conflicted feeling as it both flattered and chilled him that she was now being so open with him. Telling him her secrets and trusting the wolf at her door.

There was no getting around it. He was going to have to keep a husbandly eye on her, he concluded with stirring unease. He, a shameless fucker most of the time, felt fucking *guilty* about misleading Dora. But not guilty enough to deny himself her sweet little pussy, he realized, starting back down the final flight of stairs. He was having Dora alright, just as soon as he could get his hands on some form of preventative. As for the rest of tonight, he was going to enjoy her every way he could think of that did not involve penetration.

He would just have to carry on being good to her until the truth came out and then he would have to hope Dora would take it on the chin. It wasn't even such a crazy notion when it came to Dora, he thought, a faint smile touching his lips. She took

152

everything else like a champ, he reflected, including his cock. Just the thought of how she had handled him made his breath quicken.

Automatically, he stood aside for two women slowly ascending the stairs in their wide crinoline skirts. They smiled coyly at Clem, and he gave them a cursory nod. Dora was right, he thought absently. If they slipped on a step they'd likely roll down to the bottom before they could turn themselves right side up.

When he reached the front desk, he requested clean water and towels and ordered a bottle of champagne to be delivered to their room. *That* was what they should have been drinking earlier, he thought, and could have kicked himself for being so damned thoughtless. Even though he knew Dora would never expect such attention, bless her.

He had a couple of stiff drinks in the bar to fortify himself for the patience he was going to have to exert over the next couple of hours when Dora inevitably turned shy. It only occurred to him when he reached their hotel room and quietly let himself in that he had waited too long.

Dora was stretched out on the bed in her virginal nightgown in peaceful slumber, a seraphic expression of contentment on her face. It was only after gazing down at her for a few seconds that Clem realized he did not have the heart to wake her. She'd had a long day and been such a sweetheart.

Instead, he drew the covers up to her neck and answered the door when the clean towels and water arrived. Later, he wondered if that might not have been the point at which he realized something was amiss, but at the time he just congratulated himself on doing a damn good impression of a considerate husband. Even if he did say so himself.

153

13

Theo woke with a fuzzy head and a vague sense of anxiety. *Something wasn't quite right*, was the thought penetrating the fog that was her sluggish mind. What was it? she wondered, then realized her pillow felt decidedly un-pillow-like in texture. She bounced her cheek against it. No, it definitely wasn't her pillow. It was... She raised her head. *Clem Dabney.*

The upper half of her body was sprawled across Clem's, and what's more, he was wearing only his long underwear. His massive chest was entirely naked, and she had been draped over it like a human blanket. Theo blinked and set out a cautious hand to grope around for the bedsheet in a somewhat futile attempt to dredge up a modicum of modesty.

"Morning," Clem murmured without opening his eyes.

"Morning," Theo croaked back. Why was her mouth so dry? She glanced at the bedside table and, instead of a carafe of water, found merely an empty glass. The cocktails had tasted heavenly last night, every single one, but the thought of them now made her feel slightly queasy.

Clem opened one eye. "Sleep well?" he asked lazily.

Theo felt her face fill with color. "Er, yes," she hastened to assure him, dragging the bedclothes up to cover her modest nightgown before being assailed by a vivid memory of some of last night's shenanigans. She almost dropped the bedsheet. Had she really let him put his hand between her legs? Had she really touched his penis? "Quite well, thank you," she quavered. "You?"

"A damn sight better than I did in my office the night before," he answered.

"Wh-why did you sleep in your office?" Theo asked, glad of any distraction from their predicament and the memories of being thoroughly debauched the previous evening. Had she really asked him all those dreadfully intimate things? Her cheeks burned and she almost groaned aloud. My God, had she really told him about sneaking those peeks at Felix's dirty book?

His eyes flickered open. "Because I am between abodes. More importantly, why are you stammering again, Dora?" he asked lightly and sat up. "You don't need to be nervous around me, sweetheart, remember?" He reached out and caught her hand in his, raising it to his lips before bestowing a smacking kiss there.

That brought a trembling smile to her lips. "My heart is pounding," she admitted. "And my pulse is racing, and I feel terribly thirsty and more than a little embarrassed," she confessed in a rush.

"That will just be the aftereffects of the alcohol," he said, slipping out of the bed and crossing the room to fetch a crystal jug filled with water. Theo tried to ignore the fact his underwear was riding low, and she could see the top of his muscular buttocks. Really, she didn't know where to direct her gaze, but she was pretty sure it shouldn't be glued to his backside the way it was.

She had managed to drag her eyes away before he returned to the bed, setting down the water. He cast a shrewd glance her way before pouring her a glassful and sitting down beside her. "Here, drink this."

"Thank you," she murmured, gulping it down.

"Better?" he asked, pouring her a second.

"Yes, I think so."

"Once we've had a good fried breakfast, you'll be right as rain."

Theo felt a light sweat break out on her forehead. "Fried?" she asked feebly.

Clem laughed at her expression. "Trust me, it'll sort you right out." His gaze traveled over her swathed body a moment before he cleared his throat and headed toward the bathroom.

"I'll get dressed," he said, sounding oddly reluctant. Only after the door had closed behind him did it occur to Theo that he had likely done it so she could dress without him around.

Feeling grateful for his consideration, she slipped from the bed and dragged on her chemise and drawers. She had washed her intimate areas last night before tumbling into bed. Congratulating herself once again on her sensible mode of dress and lack of tangled locks, she donned her striped ensemble and pulled on her stockings.

She was lacing her boots when Clem emerged, looking a little rumpled, for he had not yet done up his collar and cuffs and was sporting a little stubble. "Didn't bring my razor," he commented, stroking his jaw ruefully.

"Ah," Theo responded, still staring at him. He did not look as pristine as he had the day before in church, but somehow, it did not detract one whit from his attractiveness. Noticing he was watching her as he drew on his jacket, she jumped up from her seat.

"I'll just—" She disappeared into the bathroom and shut the door behind her, closing her eyes and leaning back against it a moment. She was feeling flustered again and she hated it! She needed to grow accustomed to the fact she was a married woman now. She was not some girl to be blushing and stammering like a little fool, no matter how astonishingly virile her husband was!

Squaring her shoulders, Theo made for the water pitcher and started sloshing it into the bowl. Her reflection in the mirror caught her eye, and she took a long, hard look at her flushed face. *Calm down*, she told herself sternly. *This is now your day-to-day reality, waking up in bed with your new husband.* She swallowed. She would need that comb after all.

They did not breakfast at Wards, but instead, Clem paid their bill, and they caught a hackney cab to Shoreditch. Hearing the direction he gave the cabbie, she turned to him excitedly. "Are we going to your concert rooms?" she asked.

He shot her a look, setting the holdall at their feet. "After, we will."

"After what?"

"After a hearty breakfast." He glanced down at her hands which were folded in her lap. For a moment, she thought he was looking at the gold band on her third finger, but then he said suddenly, "Put your gloves on; it's bitter out," dispelling that notion.

They partook of breakfast at a place called Finnegan's which was frequented by an interesting assortment of folk, most of whom seemed decidedly down at heel. Theo hoped she was discreet in all the avid observations she was making.

There was a disreputable man wearing a frightful hat by the window who absolutely fascinated her. He had a habit of sniffing and touching his nose while speaking to his companion that quite enchanted her. She had not realized how absorbed she was until Clem touched her hand. "Eat your breakfast, Dora," he said dryly. "Your sausages are getting cold."

She came to with a start and noticed Clem had nearly finished his plateful. "Sorry, just wool-gathering," she gave by way of hurried explanation. To her surprise, once the first forkful of eggs and fried bread reached her mouth, she found she was ravenous. "This is really good; you were right," she told Clem gratefully.

"How's the pounding head?"

"My head?" It hadn't been her head that was pounding, just her heart, but she did not point that out to Clem. He might misinterpret her words and think she had tumbled headlong in love with him like some foolish virgin and the last thing she wanted was to make him feel awkward. "It just feels a little tight around the top of my head now. Nothing to signify. How about yours?"

157

"Absolutely fine," he answered, still eyeing her a little oddly. Rather as though a pampered lapdog had wheeled about and bit his hand.

She lowered her fork. "Is…everything well with you this morning?" she asked, feeling a rush of color to her cheeks.

"Absolutely, Dora, why shouldn't it be?"

She hesitated, for how could she explain that she kept catching sight of him watching her out of the corner of his eye with a strange expression on his face? "I… Well, I hope I did not shock you last night, that is all," she said, and Clem promptly spat out his mouthful of tea and went off in a coughing fit.

"Oh!" She sprang up and rounded the table, smacking him squarely between the shoulder blades. Luckily, in this sort of establishment, someone could likely get knifed between the ribs and no one would blink an eye. She did love how this new husband of hers was broadening her horizons.

She slipped back into her seat once Clem had reined it in and regarded him with a concerned eye. "Better now?" she asked sympathetically.

"Fine," Clem wheezed, sitting back in his seat. "Dora…" he started in strangled tones.

"Yes?" she asked brightly.

He subjected her to that strange look again. "Eat your sausage," he concluded.

She beamed at him and set about clearing her plate.

After she had collapsed back in her seat with a satisfied sigh, Clem ordered a second pot of coffee. She was a little surprised as she had thought he would be in more of a hurry to get to The Eagle and Sun, but he seemed in no rush whatsoever.

Once the coffee arrived, he poured them both a cup, then faced her gravely. "Dora, I want to prepare you for what you'll find at my place of work." He hesitated. "It's a lot…rougher than what you're used to at The Parthenon." She nodded and

158

took a sip of the hot coffee. "My employees are not *genteel*," he stressed. "I make no apology for that. As my wife, you are going to be exposed to walks of life you have previously been sheltered from."

She nodded cheerfully; she was looking forward to it. Clem continued to look at her doubtfully, like she had no idea what was in store for her. Maybe he was right, but even so, she could not *wait*!

"You will need to make allowances for their…vocabulary and their manners," he continued, looking very serious. "Also…I have not told anyone of our association. So, when I introduce you"—he took a deep breath and looked her square in the eyes—"they will all be shocked as hell."

"Of course." Theo nodded. "I have not told anyone either." When he continued looking somber, she reminded him, "It was our secret after all."

He shrugged. "So long as you're not disappointed."

"Oh no," she assured him. "I'm sure I won't be." Then a thought occurred to her. "Felix and Harold will be unlikely to welcome you with open arms either," she admitted. "Felix might even be a little angry that I did not return home last night and that, well, I married without his approval. I hope *your* feelings will not be hurt by their reception."

Again, her words seemed to flummox him. "No, I won't be disappointed by that, Dora," he said dryly. "Though what business our marriage is of Harold Allsop's I fail entirely to see."

Dora lowered her cup. "Oh, Harold will not be angry in the slightest," she assured him quickly.

"I shouldn't care if he was!"

Clem's heated rejoinder threw her completely. She gaped at him, blinking rapidly. Was he annoyed? And, if so, why? She scanned back through her last few sentences with dismay. Had she inadvertently offended him?

159

Clem cleared his throat and straightened his jacket. "Let's not get sidetracked," he said, rubbing his brow.

Theo's puzzled frown cleared at once. He *did* have a headache! That explained everything. Hetty was always extremely snappy when she was suffering from "one of her heads." She leaned forward in her seat and impulsively reached to cover his hand with hers. "We will weather the storm together, Clem," she said warmly. "Never fear."

He gazed at their hands a moment with an arrested look on his face. Then he gave a brief smile that did not remotely touch his eyes. "Doubtless," he said and that was that.

Theo was buzzing with ill-concealed excitement the entire walk to the concert rooms. It was only two streets away from Finnegan's, so they reached it in no time. The entrance from the street was far from grand. It had no columns like The Parthenon, indeed it looked to have been converted from several terraced properties rather than purpose-built.

Still, to Theo's eye, it was the portal to the life she had always dreamed of, and she could find no fault with the modest black painted door and the small sign which hung over it depicting an eagle with its wings outstretched below the sun's rays.

Without more ado, Clem produced a key and unlocked the door which Theo guessed must be unmanned outside of opening hours. He hustled her into a small entryway and directed her to the narrow staircase, gesturing for her to go ahead while he secured the door behind them.

Theo mounted the stairs, looking about her with interest at the yellow paint which Hetty would likely think garish, but she found jolly and bright and indicative of the good time its patrons would find within its walls. She had a smile on her lips before she even reached the first floor, where she paused.

She knew already from her previous visit that Clem's office was on this level. Would he want to proceed there or show her the stage? She turned to find Clem already behind her. "Oh! You startled me." She gave him a considering glance. "You are exceedingly light on your feet, are you not?"

"My training," he commented, and at her blank look, he added, "Prizefighter, remember?"

"Oh yes, of course!" Theo felt unaccountably embarrassed how she kept forgetting that aspect of his life. "You must tell me more about it sometime."

He made a noncommittal noise in his throat and ushered her toward his office. "My things are in there." Sure, enough there were some bags and cases packed and piled up behind the door. Theo regarded them with interest as Clem added the leather bag to the pile.

"You must have told your employees you were moving?" she commented as Clem shrugged off his coat and tore the cravat from his throat before unbuttoning his collar.

Clem frowned. "I may have mentioned it to Jim," he answered with a shrug. "It's not really anyone else's business."

He flung open another case and picked out a different jacket. Theo leaned a hip against his desk and looked around the office curiously. That must be the sofa he had slept on the night before their wedding. It was a very bare office. A small fireplace, a big desk, some scuffed floorboards. She had seen it before, of course, but that time she had been overset with nerves. In truth, her memory of that occasion was patchy. She had a suspicion her self-respect depended on her forgetting the whole disastrous episode.

Vague memories floated to the surface of just how humiliated she had felt when she had stumbled down that same staircase, her eyes blinded with furious tears and Clem's laughter ringing in her ears. How funny that she climbed them now as his bride! Surreptitiously, she snuck another look at him now as he flung his neckcloth and dress coat into one of his cases and snapped it shut.

161

"Is Jim the heavyset fellow with sideburns who shows your visitors into your office?" she asked suddenly.

Clem looked up sharply at that, but when he spoke, his voice was mild. "Remember him, do you?" She nodded. "What else do you remember?"

"Barking my shins on your coal scuttle," she admitted with a wince. "I was a bundle of nerves that day." She hoped devoutly that Jim had not noticed she was crying when he had let her out into the street that day. She remembered he had reached out a hand to steady her arm before she tripped over the doorstep. "He was kind," she said suddenly. "I liked him."

"Kind?"

Theo turned her head at Clem's interrogative tone, but for some reason instead of explaining her words, she lifted her chin. "Yes, kind," she said staunchly, for she remembered with sudden vividness that Clem had *not* been.

The air turned tense between them as their gazes clashed. What was happening? Theo wondered. Was it the memory of last time making her antagonistic? Realizing she needed to let it go, she gave herself a little shake and dropped her eyes.

Clem gave a snort. "Jim's a broken-down fighter," he said, sounding irritated. "I gave him a job here for old times' sake. He's not known for being particularly kind, Dora. You can rid yourself of that impression."

He might as well have called her naïve, Theo thought, coloring slightly. Instead of responding, she moved away from Clem's desk to gaze out at the street below. Behind her, she could hear Clem moving about his office, opening a drawer before shutting it again. A rap on the door made her jump, and turning around, she saw the sideburns she had recalled.

"Didn't know you had company," Jim said, starting to withdraw.

"Jim! Come in a minute," Clem called after him.

Jim stepped inside with marked reluctance. At Theo, he threw only the most cursory of glances. "Somethin' you want doin', boss?" he asked gruffly.

"Just an introduction," Clem replied, then gestured to Theo to join him over by the mantel. She crossed the room to stand beside him. "Jim, this is my wife of"—he glanced at the clock—"precisely twenty-four hours, Mrs. Theodora Dabney."

A look of pure astonishment passed over Jim's features, but it was gone in an instant and his face returned to a slablike impassivity that Theo felt sure must be his habitual expression. "You've met before briefly," Clem added. "In fact, you seem to have made quite a favorable impression." This last was added dryly and drew a look of faint alarm from Jim.

The older man coughed. "Congratulations," he said finally, his eyes trained on neither of them but directed instead at the far wall.

"Thank you, Jim," Theo said cheerfully and extended her hand. Jim stared at it an instant as though unsure what it was. Then he took her hand carefully in his much bigger paw. This wouldn't do, Theo thought, unused to being treated like fine china. She seized his in a firm grip and pumped it up and down enthusiastically. "It's lovely to see you again."

Jim slowly blinked and then glanced at Clem again as though unsure of his cue.

"Perhaps you could spread the word, Jim," Clem suggested. Jim gazed blankly back at him a moment, said "Ah," and backed out of the room.

"I think you picked your emissary poorly," Theo commented as the door closed behind him.

"What?"

"Jim's clearly not a gossip."

Clem shrugged. "It's of no matter, I'll show you round and give whatever introductions are necessary." Theo nodded, and he moved toward the door, holding it open for her.

"Now?" She could not conceal her pleasure at this, and he gave her a mirthless smile.

"Why postpone the inevitable?"

She made no comment on his choice of words, though he seemed oddly reluctant to show her his empire, in her opinion. They passed out of his office and into the narrow corridor again. Striding past the other rooms on the first floor, he said dismissively, "These are all just storerooms," and led her to the staircase at the end.

Theo climbed the steps to the next floor practically trembling with anticipation.

"These are dressing rooms," Clem commented flatly, gesturing to left and right. Theo slowed her steps to read the handwritten notices pinned to the doors. The first one read "Roberto Russo." She turned her head to look quizzically at Clem.

"Magician," he said succinctly.

The next was labeled "Stimson & Holland." "Comedy act?" she hazarded.

"Quite right."

The next four doors were all labeled "D.G." "What do the initials stand for?" Theo asked in puzzled tones.

Clem cleared his throat. "Dancing girls," he explained.

"Ohhh." She nodded in comprehension. "Misc," she read aloud from the next three doors. "Miscellaneous what?"

"Acts. Temporary turns we're giving a trial run. We have quite a fast turnover. The paying public gets easily bored. You have to have real staying power to get your actual name on the door."

"Ah, I see. So, Lil and I will be in one of those rooms at first?" Clem did not answer. "Miss Florrie Foss," the next door boasted. "Your star turn," Theo remembered. Clem nodded. The final door read "L. Burgess." "Who is L. Burgess?" Theo asked.

164

"Larry, the announcer," Clem informed her. "He might be here, but none of the others will until tonight. I'll have to introduce you to the rest at some later time."

Theo was disappointed but not altogether surprised. Clem rapped at the door. "Come in, if you must!" called back an irritable voice.

Clem threw open the door to reveal a scruffy man sprawled in a shapeless chair and clad in a silk dressing gown which had known better days. His bare legs protruded from beneath it, showing a lot of hair and a pair of filthy-soled feet, propped up on a ratty-looking footstool. A smelly cigar hung from his mouth, and he was reading a newspaper with a sneer on his face.

The man's rather sour expression at once rearranged itself into one of affability. "Ah, Mr. Dabney!" he cried, casting down his broadsheet and scrambling to his feet. "Come in, come in." He subjected Theo to a quick look, before dismissing her altogether.

Clem caught Theo's elbow, and they took one step inside the room. "Burgess," he said coolly. "I came to introduce you to my wife."

Burgess's face froze. "Your wife…?" He glanced once more at Theo, clearly stupefied. Catching sight of Clem's face, he said quickly, "Delighted, delighted. I had no idea you were even married, dear chap."

Clem shrugged, and Theo noted he did not explain that this was a recent state of affairs.

"Mr. Burgess, I am pleased to make your acquaintance," she said politely.

"Dear lady," he said, approaching and taking her hand as though to kiss it. Theo hastily seized his in her customary handshake which seemed to confuse him. "Er quite, quite," he said, reclaiming his hand and wincing slightly.

165

Clem nodded and, tightening his grip on Theo's upper arm, firmly maneuvered her back out of the room.

"I imagine Mr. Burgess's charm must be more apparent when he is treading the boards," Theo commented as they reached the end of the corridor and Clem flung open another door to another flight of stairs.

He uttered a short laugh. "You could put it that way. He's a damn good compere, otherwise, I would not pay his wage."

"I do not understand why he is here at this hour when none of the other performers are. It is not as though he is practicing his craft," she pointed out when Clem did not answer at once.

"He has a wife and six children," Clem said briefly. "And he is not noticeably fond of any of them." He eyed her curiously. "Incidentally, where did you learn to shake hands like that?" he asked.

Theo tipped her head to one side. "I suppose I observed how you gentlemen do it. We women are never tutored in the art, you know. It always seemed to me that men do not let their hands merely lie limply within each other's fingers but instead take an assertive role."

Clem's lips twitched, and she thought for a moment he would laugh. "Quite right," he said at last and gestured for her to climb the stairs winding upward.

"Will we come along tonight?" she asked hopefully, looking back over her shoulder. "To watch I mean?"

Clem was quiet a moment. "Let's see how things turn out with your brother," he said at last.

"Oh yes." In all the excitement, she had almost forgotten about Felix. Her mood would have taken a decided downturn if not for the fact she had emerged into the auditorium. She gasped audibly and was still gazing about the large hall with its neat little stage and the row upon row of closely stacked wooden chairs when Clem emerged behind her. "Oh, it's *wonderful*, Clem!" she exclaimed, turning about. "You even have a gallery," she said, gazing up at the upper level.

He looked skeptical. "It's nothing to compare to The Parthenon," he said, scratching his neck. She supposed she knew what he meant, for there were no fancy flounces or pelmet on the plain black curtain, no wings even to conceal the next act. There were no elegant columns, no gold paint, and no chandeliers. Still, Theo could not disagree more strongly.

She shook her head. "It's living and breathing, I can *feel* it," she tried to explain. "I don't know how, but you can sort of tell when a place is thrumming with life. When it's *essential* to people. When it's needed. The Parthenon hasn't been like that in a long time. Not in my lifetime," she said sadly.

Clem was quiet, letting her take in every scuff on the skirting boards, every sign of wear on the well-worn floorboards, even the faint smell of cigar smoke that hung in the air after last night's performance. Every single feature spoke to her and told her that she was right about The Eagle and Sun. "You really pack this place out? Four days a week?" she asked finally.

"Twice on Saturdays and Sundays," he affirmed. "How can you tell it's alive?" This last question seemed almost dragged from his lips.

She focused again on him. He was watching her intently. "It's hard to explain," she said simply. "It's like a sort of atmosphere. Almost like being in church."

Clem snorted. "Church? You won't be saying that after you've seen Florrie Foss perform 'Mr. Mellar's Prize Marrow.'"

Her wonderment dispelled and she teetered a moment on the brink of surprised laughter. Instead, she pursed her lips and whistled the tune she had heard him whistling that day as he sauntered down the Old Harlow Road. "Is it that one?" she asked.

167

Clem stared at her a moment and then she found herself snatched up in his arms and thoroughly kissed. "Dora," he groaned.

"Yes?"

"Stop being so sweet, or I'll eat you up." She clung to his shoulders. She was being sweet? "Besides," he growled, "that's a different tune. That's 'Oh, Mr. Hipkins.'"

"Oh. Well, I think you should teach me that one too."

Clem had just opened his mouth to respond when a cough behind them made them both start. Her new husband tensed and set her back on her feet before he turned around to face the newcomer. "Sidney, is there something I can do for you?" he asked tersely.

Theo peered about Clem's bulk to see an impudent freckled face cocked in her direction. "This 'er?" Sidney asked, thrusting a thumb toward Theo. "Your new missus?" He was leaning on a broom with his shirtsleeves rolled up to his elbow and a bright red scarf tied about his neck. She liked the look of him immediately.

Before Clem could respond, Theo stepped around him and thrust out her hand. "Hello, Sidney, I am very pleased to make your acquaintance," she said. "I'm Dora Dabney." Clem breathed noisily in and out beside her, but she took no notice. She intended to start as she would carry on. Dora Dabney was her professional name, and she meant to be known by it in her place of work.

"Pleased to meet you too, Dora," Sidney exclaimed, tipping his cap back on his head and grasping her hand. He shot a speculative look at Clem. "I'm general dogsbody around here," he said cheerily. "You need anyfink doin', ask for me. Wivin reason like," he added as a qualifier. "I'm not a bleedin' miracle worker."

"I will certainly bear that in mind, Sidney," she responded gravely.

Sidney winked at her before eyeing his employer severely. "Good to hear you're on the straight and narrow now, boss, wiv the love of a good woman." He cast a knowing look at Clem before moving away, industriously sweeping his broom.

Theo shot a slightly apprehensive glance at her husband and found him speechlessly glaring after Sidney. "What a nice man," she said warmly.

14

Clem managed to gather up four of his sizeable suitcases without help and Jim grabbed the last two. Clem permitted her to carry nothing but the small leather holdall they had taken to Wards and her handbag. "Have you ordered a conveyance?" she asked, eyeing the amount of luggage as they trooped down the stairs.

"We can just take a hackney" was Clem's unconcerned response.

Theo had her doubts about this, but sure enough, after a moment's spirited arguing with the cabbie, and what she suspected was a sizeable bribe, Clem piled his cases into the small area available.

"What about me?" she was forced to ask when he clambered up before her.

He slapped his thigh. "You perch right here, Mrs. Dabney," he answered, reaching a hand down to haul her up. Jim took her elbow and helped her in, though he looked very embarrassed when she thanked him and took a hasty step.

It was a little undignified, and she only just fit. Indeed, she was forced to bend her neck, or her bonnet would be scraping the roof.

"Well, this is cozy," Clem commented, giving Jim a nod as they lurched off. Theo made a grab for his shoulders.

"Feeling nervous?" he asked sympathetically.

"Yes, I don't want to get whiplash."

He grinned. "I meant about confronting your family."

She pressed her lips together resolutely and shook her head. "No. I knew this moment would come. It is simply something we have to face together and get out of the way. When we inform your family, I shall stand just as firm, never fear."

"When we—?" He broke off his words, then gave a shrug. "My uncle Danny won't blink an eye. My cousin Grace is a tartar though. You won't win her over easily."

Theo felt herself relax. "Do you think it will take you long to win over my brother?" she asked, arching her eyebrows.

Clem laughed again. "He thinks I'm a boorish philistine and will no doubt be appalled that I've carried off his sister and mean to muscle in on his theater."

Theo smiled automatically. He spoke nothing but the truth. It was gallant of him to make mention of her before the theater in his list of acquisitions though. Gallant, but unnecessary. She did not want him to start thinking she was some deluded little fool with her head in the clouds.

"Clem—" she started awkwardly, but the hackney lurched at this instant, and she jolted violently and would have tumbled off his lap altogether if his arms had not closed about her like steel bands.

"Pothole," he murmured against her ear, for her bonnet had been knocked quite crooked. "Don't worry, I've got you."

Theo blinked down at him. "I'm not worried," she said simply.

"Aren't you?" He gazed back at her. "Not even a little bit?" She shook her head, and a faint frown marred his brow. "Well, maybe you should be."

"Why?"

He gave her a very level look. "You're taking a man home with you, Theodora. You ever done that before?"

"Of course I haven't."

"Well, your family is going to judge you on the manner of man you chose. They're going to be shocked as hell you spent a night with me and even more shocked that you gave me your hand in marriage." She opened her mouth, but he didn't let her get the words out.

171

"They're also going to be pissed that you've given me sway in the family business, and they're going to give vent to those feelings. Maybe not right away, with me stood by your side, but they're going to say things." He hesitated. "Ugly things. They're going to try and convince you that you've made a bad bargain taking me for a husband, Dora."

"Well, I've been 'pissed,' as you call it, for a whole month and a half with them by this point," Theo pointed out with spirit, "so I don't much care about their opinion on the matter!" Clem made a sound in his throat which sounded like half laugh, half snort. "And why do you keep saying 'my family' in any case? It is only Felix at home these days since my sister has eloped."

"Did you not say Allsop is like a sort of cousin?" he asked in a suddenly silky voice.

To her annoyance, Theo felt herself color up. "Yes, of course," she agreed, "but Harold really does not count, for he is on our side." Clem's face registered extreme skepticism. "It is true!" she insisted.

Clem's gaze slid from her face, and he shrugged. "If you say so."

"I do say it!"

"And I said that is fine," he replied smoothly, but somehow Theo did not quite believe him. Ah well, when he met Harold, he would soon see what a dear he was.

The rest of the journey seemed to take twice as long as usual, as it was so cramped and uncomfortable. When they finally pulled up at the familiar frontage of her family home, Theo breathed a sigh of relief. She started to clamber down from Clem's lap, but he tightened his grip on her, holding her in place. "I want you to remember what I said, Dora," he said in a low voice. "Remember how we entered into this, as equal partners. Don't let anyone tell you you're a fool."

172

She patted his shoulder. "You need not be concerned for me, Clem," she assured him. "Just let me do the talking and don't let Felix's bluster concern you. It is all just sound and air." A curious expression passed over Clem's face, but she forged on with what she wanted to say. "Just promise me you won't let any empty words offend you," she added, "for they certainly won't me. If Felix calls me a gullible idiot, or even a batty old maid, it really will not bother me."

"Maybe it won't you, but it will me," Clem responded with alacrity. "You cannot expect me to stand idly by while someone insults my wife, Dora."

Theo felt a momentary panic. "Clem, he's my brother, please do not punch him."

The tenseness left his shoulders at once. "Dora, my sweet, he's half my size, you really think I'd go toe-to-toe with him?"

She let out a relieved breath. "For a minute I confess it did enter my head—"

"'Ere, you lot gettin' out or wot?" called the indignant cabbie. "Only, I ain't got all bleedin' day to 'ang around!"

Clem released his hold on her waist, and Theo scrambled down from the cab, dislodging one of the cases in her awkward descent. She had only just retrieved it when Clem extricated himself from the hackney with athletic grace and dragged the other cases out. "Leave that there," he said. "Do you have a latch-key?"

Theo was just fishing around in her bag when the cab pulled away and the front door opened. Felix stood on the threshold, clearly in the grip of some deep emotion. He came striding out of the house without his coat or shoes and hurried down the front path in his stockinged feet.

"*Him?*" he shouted accusingly. "*This* is who you've been *consorting* with this past month? *Dabney?*"

"Consorting?" Theo echoed in surprise. She would have sworn Felix had been wholly oblivious to her every move.

173

"Allsop finally told me you had a—a *cicisbeo* in the early hours of this morning. After we sat up all night fruitlessly waiting for you to return, I might add!" he said bitterly. "I could scarcely believe you were capable of such folly! Even so, it never once entered my head that you could have taken up with this…this…" Words clearly failed him at this point.

Something brushed Theo's elbow, and she realized Clem was stood at her side. His stance was casual in the extreme, and he looked entirely at ease, but even so, the hairs on the back of Theo's neck stood up. She needed to keep things calm for Felix's sake.

"Let us not do this out in the street, brother," she said, glancing about them. If she was not mistaken, she could see shadowy figures had appeared behind several front windows. At her words, the wrath seemed to suddenly slide from Felix's frame, leaving him white and shaken.

"Tell me you have not married him, Theo," her brother appealed to her hollowly. "Only tell me that, and I swear I will forgive you all."

"I'm sorry, Felix, but you are going to have to face up to hard facts," Theo said gently. "I am indeed married. Clem is my husband," she said firmly as Felix began shaking his head, "and your brother-in-law. We are coming inside—"

"Over my dead body!" Felix bleated but was fooling no one at this point. Theo directed a speaking glance at Clem, then took her brother's arm, steering him into the house. When she glanced back over her shoulder, she saw Clem gathering up his cases to bring inside.

"You look shattered, Felix," she reproached, clicking her tongue. "You should not have sat up all night, especially after Harold explained I had likely eloped—"

"Hah!" burst out Felix as she led him down the hall and into the front parlor.

174

"I do not remember you sitting up all night after Henrietta eloped," she pointed out.

"Henrietta eloped with a respectable man," Felix pointed out sullenly as Theo steered him into the best chair before the unlit fire.

"Ugh!" she said, wrinkling her nose. "You and Harold must have been smoking disgusting tobacco in here all night! It reeks!" She hurried to the window and threw it open for some fresh air.

"Where is that blackguard anyway?" Felix asked crossly. "Do not tell me he has abandoned you already. Now he's got his filthy hands on a quarter share of my theater!"

"He is bringing in his luggage," Theo said calmly.

"Is he by God?" Felix rallied, puffing out his chest. "Of all the brass neck! Moving into another man's home, bold as you please!"

"The house is one-third mine," she pointed out mildly. "As well you know, Felix."

Felix eyed her with a jaundiced expression. "You do realize, I suppose, that is the *sole* reason he married you?"

"To move into a run-down residence on Juniper Row?" Theo asked lightly. "I had no idea the location was such a desirable one."

"Do not be facetious with me, Theodora!"

"I had something he wanted; he had something I wanted," she explained calmly, propping herself on one arm of the sofa. "Our marriage makes perfect sense, and we mean to deal very well with one another."

"My God, Theo!" Felix pronounced with disgust. He shook his head. "My uncle and I have done you a disservice in sheltering you so much. You're even more foolish than I gave you credit for!"

175

"Careful, Fields," growled Clem's voice from the doorway. "Have a care how you speak to my wife in future, or you'll answer to me." He turned to Theo. "Which bedroom is yours?"

"*Our* bedroom is on the second floor, dear. The furthest room to the right," she answered before turning back to her speechless brother. "Now, shall I make us all a nice pot of tea?"

*

Clem surprised Dora in the kitchen five minutes later as she was emptying the last of the tea leaves into a large pot. "I'm afraid it will be rather weak tea—" she started but did not finish, for Clem came right up behind her and closed his arms about her, holding her close to his chest.

"Clem?" she asked, sounding a little unsure.

"Hmmm?" He was inordinately pleased with his Dora right now. She had been a Trojan, striding into the house to claim him a place at the table. "Maybe I should have tried a little of this on the previous time we were in this kitchen together," he murmured in her ear before twirling her around in his arms. "And really given Allsop something to look at."

"Has Harold come downstairs, then?" she asked.

Clem treated this query with the contempt it deserved and ignored it. Instead, he swayed her in his arms as though they were dancing, even though there was no music to be had. "Where is his room anyway?" he grunted in far too confrontational a manner. Luckily Dora did not notice, likely because she always believed the best of him.

"Oh, Harold has the two attic rooms," she answered absently. "But I dare say he must have heard our arrival, for he keeps one of the windows open at all times. His great aunt greatly espoused fresh air for healthy lungs. He must have heard the commotion but not wanted to intrude." She tutted. "Poor Harold."

176

Poor Harold, my ass. "I should have kissed you, right here," he said, whirling her around and pressing her back against the kitchen dresser. "I wanted to."

Dora gave a gurgle of laughter. "No you did not, Clem Dabney!" she said stoutly. "You are misremembering on purpose. I had burned my arm, and you were forced to administer to my injury, wrapping a soggy tea towel around it. You were not remotely"—she hesitated before concluding— "amorous."

Clem caught his breath, and she must have seen the look in his eye for she said quickly, "And that was a very good thing, let me tell you!"

"Oh, and why is that?" he asked, seizing her about the waist and waltzing her across the kitchen floor. He was pleased to find she followed his lead with ease and clearly knew the steps. Her height made her a good partner for him. He would have to take her out dancing if only he could persuade her to wear something half decent for once.

Dora took a deep breath. "Because I had not quite made up my mind about you then," she admitted. "If you *had* taken any liberties, I would have been forced to bring a rolling pin down on your head," she joked, clearly striving for a lighter tone.

Clem made a sound of disagreement in his throat. "You promised to marry me on that occasion, Dora love," he reminded her. They were circling the kitchen now, their steps perfectly in sync. She had no problem dancing and conversing at once. Why had he thought she would blush and stare at her feet?

Dora pulled a face. "I was not sure of you though," she admitted ruefully. "Not at that point. I did not know you were wholly on my side. Not then. That came later." She smiled at him, and Clem felt his stomach clench.

What was he even doing? She had been right not to trust him. Why was he urging her now to ignore her instincts and

177

commit herself to his not-so-tender mercies? Then he remembered why he was doing it.

Dora was about to pitch herself off a cliff by performing at The Eagle and Sun and somewhere along the line he had decided, in his beneficence, that he was going to be the one to break her fall. In order to do that, she needed to accept him fully as her benevolent protector. Then her pride would not be entirely destroyed by the ordeal she was so intent on putting herself through.

To himself, Clem admitted that might not have been the original plan, but things changed. Now the plan included picking his broken wife off the floor and restoring some sense of purpose and comfort to her life in the aftermath of her shattered dreams.

True, he was not exactly sure yet *what* he was going to do with her or *where* he was going to clear a spot for her in his life, but he had the strangest feeling that wherever it was, he would not begrudge it overmuch.

Dora was not exacting in her demands; in truth, she required precious little to keep her happy, if you took the music hall career out of the equation that is. And very soon that would see to itself. That crazy ambition would die a natural death all too quickly. It would remain only an embarrassing memory that he would do his best to erase from her mind.

Maybe they would joke about it together when they were old and gray… Clem suffered a jolt, realizing he had just imagined a future with Theodora Fields where they grew old together. Fuck…maybe that was her place?

He could just stash her somewhere out of the way and keep her safe until he had made enough money. Then when he was done with the hustle and bustle of London and his drive and ambition were all spent, he could join her there. To live out his later years in comfort with Dora at his side.

He stared at her. Such an idea ought to scare the living daylights out of him. Why then, did it feel so peculiarly appealing?

"What is it?" Dora asked curiously, then her enquiring gaze shifted from his face to the doorway, and he turned to find Felix Fields regarding them both open-mouthed. When neither of them spoke a word or moved out of their clinch, his brother-in-law cleared his throat. "Thought I'd see how that pot of tea was coming along," he said lamely.

15

Clem's expectations were not high, but luncheon was a truly dismal affair. Allsop was coaxed down out of his attic and a pork pie was discovered in a cupboard that Fields had bought the day before and not yet demolished. This was cut up and set on the table along with some bread and butter, some jam, an almost empty jar of marmalade, and a thin wedge of cheese. To Clem's disgust, there were not even any pickles to be had.

The dining room itself had a shabby, neglected feel. Considering the huge oval table and proliferation of chairs that lined the walls, it ought to smell at the very least of beeswax furniture polish. The empty vases ought to be filled with flowers. There should be a crisp white tablecloth laid, but it was clear though that no one had thought of such things in a while.

Dora wielded the teapot and managed to keep up a little desultory conversation, but her brother sat alternating between outraged affront and melancholy despair, huffing and puffing one minute and then cradling his head in his hands and groaning the next.

As for Allsop, Clem could see no sign of his alleged support in the dejected-looking man who sat doing his best to avoid catching anyone's eye. He drank three cups of milky tea but the bread he so assiduously buttered and cut into triangles did not go anywhere near his mouth. If he had a mind to be generous, Clem would say he was nervy or high-strung. For some reason though, generous was the last thing he felt like being about the Fieldses' lodger.

Once the pie dish was emptied, the meal started to wind down. Felix looked up suddenly, clearing his throat. "I should like a private word with you after dinner, Theodora," he said pompously, "in Uncle's study."

"Certainly not," Clem interjected firmly. "You can have nothing to say to my wife that her lawfully wedded husband cannot hear."

Felix glared at him a moment before turning to his sister. "You must know why he will not allow us to speak alone together, Theo."

"Felix," Dora sighed. "You are being quite ridiculous! What's done is now done. We must all find a way to get along together."

"At any event, his only interest is getting his hands on my theater! Surely you see that, you silly girl?"

"It is not your theater," Clem corrected him swiftly. She also was not a girl, but he let that pass.

"Not anymore!" Felix agreed bitterly.

"It is *our* theater," Dora put in firmly. "And this way it still remains in the family."

"Is that what he told you, you poor deluded creature?" Felix demanded incredulously. He pointed a finger at Clem accusingly. "The things I could reveal about this man's reputation, but alas, not one word of it is fit for your ears!"

"Yes, yes, but that is all in the past now," Dora said hastily. "Mr. Dabney has turned over a new leaf." Clem frowned, remembering she had explicitly promised him he would not have to.

"Hah!" Felix cried bitterly. "A likely story! That type of man never reforms his ways."

"What type?" Clem asked in a dangerously low voice.

Felix clammed up and then shoved two forkfuls of pork pie into his mouth. Once he had furiously masticated them, he directed a baleful look across the table at his sister. "Well, at least you can resume your duties here," he huffed. "We ran out of eggs this morning and I don't have any clean collars."

181

Clem turned to her. "My love, am I to understand that you have been turning your hand to domestic duties instead of nurturing your own talent?" he demanded.

Dora met his gaze, before lowering her eyes demurely. "I do not deny it has been a struggle, husband."

Felix snorted wrathfully, but got no opportunity to expand on the theme, for Clem immediately assured her that never again would she turn her hand to such work. "You must hire someone at once," he said cavalierly which made Felix turn quite purple.

"I shall write to Mrs. Cherwell forthwith," Dora assured him, impulsively reaching across the table for his hand. Clem felt a little taken aback by the gesture, as she covered his with her own and squeezed it lightly before releasing him and returning to her plate.

Clem wasn't sure he did not faintly blush. Why had she done that? Because he had mentioned her possessing talent or called her "my love"? He was uncomfortably aware he had only done both things to infuriate her brother.

Then he recalled how she had called him "dear" earlier and realized she was likely playing up to her brother as well. For some reason, that did not please him as it should. Luckily, Felix's bleating soon distracted him from his conflicted feelings.

"And who is to bear the expense of such extravagance?" Felix demanded wrathfully.

"I will," Clem retorted coolly. "My business is doing extremely well, *unlike* yours." Fields looked like he would be fetched off by an apoplexy and Clem left it at that for now. There would be time enough later to demand a look at the accounts and start overhauling The Parthenon's future.

After dinner, Clem requested a tour of the house, and Dora obliged, leading him from room to room on all four levels. The ground floor mostly comprised of rooms he had already seen—

182

a small cloakroom, the sizeable kitchen and scullery, and the gloomy dining room. In addition to these was a large and ostentatious front parlor.

This last was stuffed full of heavy dark furniture, a large pianoforte, a loudly ticking grandfather clock, four massive bookcases, and a set of stuffed birds under glass cloches. To his eye, none of the faded red couches looked particularly comfortable, and the coal scuttle looked criminally empty next to the yawning fireplace. He could not see himself taking his leisure in there anytime soon.

The first floor was a little better. They viewed Dora's bedroom first, which Clem thought had likely not changed since she was a girl. It contained a brass bedstead, the obligatory bookcase (so far Clem thought every room he had seen contained at least one), a large ugly wardrobe, and a small desk covered in writing implements.

An elaborate wooden theater was displayed in pride of place before the window and sat upon a decoupage lacquered table. When she saw the direction of his gaze, she looked a little self-conscious. "I assure you I do not play with it anymore," she had hastened to explain. "It has strictly sentimental value these days."

Clem noticed a good deal of the cardboard players on sticks looked to be hand-drawn and painted, but he did not comment on this. He was just grateful she did not have a shelf full of creepy-looking dolls.

She opened the door to the next bedroom which was filled with a lot more lace and frills but otherwise was not much different in its layout. The desk had a mirror and a hat form instead of pens and ink and was covered in glass bottles and brushes and was clearly used as a vanity unit. "Hetty's room," she said briefly over her shoulder before shutting it again. If anyone would have had a doll collection, he guessed it would have been the sister.

The next room was an informal sitting room which seemed a lot more inviting than the parlor downstairs. The blue chairs looked to have lost some of their stuffing, but the cushions were broad and plump and not stiffly formal. The wallpaper looked to be more suited to a bedroom with its sprigged floral pattern, but it had a cheerful and lived-in look which Clem appreciated after the stuffy-looking parlor.

"Do you all use this room?" he asked, looking around.

Dora shook her head. "Just Hetty and I. When we were younger the three of us used this room when Uncle was entertaining friends downstairs. When we got older, Felix was permitted to smoke and drink with them, so us girls used it as our withdrawing room. We would lie on the sofas and read in our dressing gowns with our hair unbound and generally not trouble to make ourselves respectable."

Clem glanced at her hair but said nothing. Dora fell silent. After a moment she suggested tentatively, "I suppose now Hetty has flown the nest, we could repurpose it as our own private sitting room?"

Clem stirred. He liked that idea. Probably because Fields and Allsop were such abysmal company. "Good idea," he muttered, throwing another speculative glance about the room. Dora looked pleased and led him to the last room on that floor, which was a sewing room.

"This is where I make all my creations," she told him proudly.

The least said about that, Clem thought, the better, as he considered the bookcase stuffed full of outlandish patterns, the workboxes and dress forms, and the few bolts of drab-looking cloth stacked in one corner. "So, I see," he said when he noticed Dora's expression of expectancy. For an instant, he thought she looked disappointed, then she lowered her eyes and led him out of the room and up the next flight of stairs.

This floor held her late uncle's bedroom which probably had not altered much since his death, a large tiled bathroom with a large free-standing tub and an extremely dusty study which he doubted very much that Fields even used.

"So, this is where your brother was going to raise a scold over your head," Clem commented, looking at the large mahogany desk inlaid with green leather. It reminded him of another desk in another office, only this room did not contain a plaster of paris bust for him to smash or any portraits that he could see.

Dora laughed. "Felix likely thought it made him sound vastly dignified, but our uncle was never much of a disciplinarian." The final room was her brother's room which was crammed full of books. Sure enough, the desk next to the window was piled high with the things.

"I wonder how many of them are dirty," Clem mused aloud, making Dora turn quite pink. She threw a reproachful glance at him and primmed up her mouth in a manner that made him want to abandon the house tour altogether, but she was already darting up the next flight of stairs to the third floor.

To Clem's surprise, the third floor was not used, instead consisting of four dusty rooms filled with broken furniture, old theatrical costumes, and boxes and boxes of books and music. Seeing his reaction, Dora hastily explained, "We use this floor as storage really, as Harold lodges in the attic."

"It seems a waste of good space," Clem said with a frown, turning slowly around.

"I daresay, but it is simply another set of rooms to keep warm and clean with coal and domestics we cannot afford," she explained.

"Why is Allsop in the attics and not this floor?" Clem asked abruptly.

"Oh, he does not require four large rooms. He prefers the attic as it is a smaller space to heat, and he can practice his music up there undisturbed, especially as there is no one inhabiting the floor below."

Clem shrugged. "It still seems a strange setup to me."

Dora seemed a little reluctant to lead him up the rickety steps to the attic, but she did so all the same, and he gazed around at Harold Allsop's province. Sloped ceilings, a single narrow bed, a table covered in piles of sheet music, and a proliferation of musical instruments seemed to be the sum of Allsop's possessions.

It was scrupulously neat and tidy, and Clem could not say why several barbed comments rose to his tongue. He had to struggle not to voice any of them, but he managed to contain himself, with effort, and Dora led him back down the steps.

"I want to write that letter to Mrs. Cherwell," she said. "Shall I meet you downstairs in the parlor afterward?"

Clem frowned. "Where are you writing your letter?" he asked.

"At my desk."

His frown cleared. "I'll come with you. I need to hang up my suits," he added at her quizzical look.

"Oh, of course! I need to make you some room in my wardrobe."

So large was the wardrobe that this simply consisted of her sweeping her clothes along the rail to the one side and then turning to beam at him. "Enough room?" she asked. "If not, I can move some of my things into the sewing room. In truth, there are a couple of things that I wanted to alter and update in any case."

"Let me see how I get on," he answered. It should be ample room, but Clem knew he had a lot. He liked clothes and dressing to impress. Maybe he should have a clear-out at some point? He had never had to share a bedroom before.

"Meanwhile, I'll empty you out some drawers," Dora said, hurrying over to a large chest of drawers. She made short work of this, transferring a bunch of uninteresting white cotton garments from the bottom two of the drawers into the top, along with a bunch of lavender sachets. He noticed she struggled a bit closing them afterward. "Will two drawers suffice?" she asked anxiously.

Clem thought of his many shirts and neckcloths. "Yes," he lied. They would need more drawers and possibly even another wardrobe. Maybe her sister's room could become a dressing room at some point.

Of course, their cohabitation was not a permanent thing. He had always viewed it in the light of a temporary arrangement of about six months until their marriage was both established and accepted. Then other more suitable long-term arrangements could be made.

Clem had always seen himself in rooms somewhere a bit more central and not so solidly middle class. Juniper Row had an air of heavy respectability that Clem felt no affinity for. He liked nice things and didn't mind paying for them, but his taste did not run to stuffed birds and waxed fruit.

For now, though, he would get himself settled and see how best they could muddle along together. In truth, he thought, glancing back over his shoulder at Dora, he did not think it would prove so terrible an ordeal, though it was a bloody cold house to rattle around in.

"You can have the entire surface space on top of this chest of drawers for your brushes and colognes and things," she offered helpfully. "Shall I put away your handkerchiefs and socks?"

"No, you get on with your letter," Clem recommended. He guessed he would have to leave a good deal of his things in the cases, for now. He knew what he would need in the next week or so. "I'll be quicker about it if I do it myself."

Dora nodded, but before seating herself at her desk, she sat on the edge of her bed and removed her ankle boots. Clem watched her covertly as she pulled on at least three pairs of woolen socks one over the top of the other and then wedged her feet into a pair of shapeless, faded house slippers.

Next, she drew on a pair of fingerless mittens and a lumpy knitted shawl. Only once she had bundled herself against the frigid air, did she make for her desk and start unscrewing ink pots and rustling paper. Clem glanced at the tiny fireplace. It did not look like it had been lit in years.

"Where does your letter need delivering?" he asked idly as he opened a drawer and tossed a handful of socks in there. Unlike Dora's, his were of a fine knitted silk and in a variety of bright colors. Considering her outlandish taste in dress, he was surprised she surrounded herself with such muted colors.

All of her socks had been gray, black, or green. Her shawl was a grayish blue. The bolts of fabric in her sewing room had been of brown, a muddy maroon, and a mossy green. Not the sort of colors he would have thought would attract Dora at all. Not now that he knew her. He would have pictured her in bright, lively colors.

"The Cherwells live on Montague Street," she answered, interrupting his reflections. Her pen nib scratched busily over the surface of the paper. She tugged open a desk drawer and withdrew a book, consulting its pages. "Number 16b."

Clem nodded. "So, Whitechapel, then," he murmured. "What did you say her husband does?"

"Well, Mr. Cherwell was a meat packer in a warehouse, but he was injured last year in an accident and has been out of work ever since. Poor Mrs. Cherwell has been at her wit's end."

"She's likely at the end of your savings by now too," Clem pointed out.

"Yes, I'm sure," Dora concurred. "There was precious little to begin with."

"Maybe you should write to your other friend while you're at it."

"Lil?" Dora asked, turning her head. "You mean to tell her of our marriage?" She sounded nervous.

"Why not? It would probably be easier than in person. I can get them delivered at the same time."

Dora glanced over at the window, likely judging the hour. Clem glanced at his pocket watch. "It is now a little after three," he told her obligingly. "There's time enough."

She flashed him a grateful look. "You think of everything."

Clem cleared his throat. "The tip of your nose has turned pink," he commented. "You look like a little mouse." Dora laughed and hitched her shawl up over her head. "I'll pick up some coal while I'm at out," he added. "This house is cold as a morgue."

Dora bit her lip. "I never did sort out the coal delivery. I think we have been struck off by the local merchant. This house is run on the strictest principles of economy these days," she sighed. "Our candles are nasty and cheap too. They make your eyes water."

"Well, our rooms won't be," Clem vowed. He'd have to pick up candles too, he noted, as well as something decent to eat for dinner. "Tell me when you've finished your letters and I'll set off and deliver them."

He was as good as his word, though he did not return until past six o'clock and brought a wagon full of things back to the house along with two brawny individuals to carry it all in. He found Dora in the kitchen again, regarding half a loaf of bread and a dish of butter with a doubtful eye.

"Clem! Did you deliver my letters?" she asked eagerly.

"I did. Mrs. Cherwell vowed to be here tomorrow morning, bright. Your friend was not home so I left her letter with one of her elderly companions." He set down his box of provisions and waved the men through following in his wake. One carried a large sack of coal and the other another large packing box.

"What's all this?" Dora asked in surprise.

189

"Just some supplies," Clem answered vaguely. "Unpack this while I show them up," he said, pointing to the box he'd set down on the kitchen table. "There's things that will serve for our dinner."

Dora's expression brightened with interest, and she started pulling the straw out of the box at once to uncover the jars and bottles as Clem showed the men up the stairs to the first floor. The coal scuttles were soon filled to overflowing, with two new, bigger copper scuttles set down in their sitting room and bedroom.

The rest of the coal he had divided between the parlor and dining room. He should not begrudge it as there was ample, but frankly, neither Fields nor Allsop was his priority. Next, they returned to the cart to fetch up the large display cabinet and chest of drawers he had purchased. Clem had to help with these as they were large unwieldy pieces of burr walnut, carved and inlaid with marquetry.

He had got them at a knockdown price from a connection he knew in Clapham who bought lots at auctions when their original owners had gone bankrupt. Apparently, these two handsome pieces of furniture had once belonged to a wealthy silversmith whose son had squandered the family fortune and ended up in debtor's jail. His loss was Clem's gain.

He had the cabinet set down in the sitting room, where it put everything else quite frankly to shame, along with a large case filled with treats, wines, and liqueurs to go in it. Soon he would set about getting some new couches. Velvet, he fancied, in royal blue.

The chest of drawers fitted neatly into the bedroom on the other side of Dora's little desk. Returning downstairs, he tipped the men handsomely and saw them off the premises before returning to find Dora attempting to light the fire in the dining room. Wordlessly, he took the tinderbox from her and asked for old newspapers.

She trotted off to fetch some and Clem relaid the fire. When she returned, they sat kneeling before it on the hearthrug as Clem expertly rolled a jar full of spills and Dora scrunched pages to set on top of the pile of wood. "Will this be enough?" she asked.

He nodded. "Let's set it ablaze. Then you can shed some of those layers." He looked her over, and Dora beamed at him.

"Shall I fetch in the supper things?" she asked, leaping to her feet. "Which pie did you intend for this evening?" she called back over her shoulder.

"All of them," Clem answered promptly.

"*All?*" She blinked, then asked curiously, "What are they?"

"Game, ham and egg, and steak and ale."

"Well, you are certainly spoiling us!"

"It's a celebration, isn't it?" he answered. "We'll have a bottle of champagne too."

Once he had the fire flickering in the grate, he went into the kitchen, where he found her peering at labels. "Are these pickled eggs?" she asked, holding one aloft.

"There should be pickled eggs, pickled onion, and pickled beetroot," he informed her, rooting through the many bottles and jars to find the piccalilli.

"Which of the cheeses?" Dora asked, unwrapping a large piece of Wensleydale. She caught his eye. "*All* of them?" she said dazedly, catching his meaning.

"All of them," Clem confirmed. "I'm a man of large appetites." He waggled his eyebrows at her, but as Dora was now struggling with a box of crackers done up in string, his gesture went in vain. Once she had opened it, she fetched a large Staffordshire cheese keep off the dresser and an oval serving platter which she started piling the different cheeses and crackers onto.

Clem picked up a paper bag. "Here," he said. She looked at him enquiringly. "Grapes," he said briefly.

191

"Grapes? These must be from a hothouse," Dora breathed, taking them as reverently as if he had said "gemstones." "Why, it's a veritable feast!" She added the grapes to the platter and moved things around in an attempt to make things more picturesque. "I don't really have an eye," she admitted.

"It looks good," Clem said, picking it up and carrying it into the dining room without more ado. They had soon well laden the table up with the pies and the cheese board in pride of place, whereupon Dora started spooning the pickles into different decorative bowls.

It seemed setting jars on the table was not the done thing, so Clem helped her out, filling bowls with pickled walnuts and cheese straws and sliced apples and helpings of the other relishes and sauces he had purchased.

Clem knew his tastes were firmly lower class, but after hearing Dora's tales of culinary disaster he did not think Allsop or Fields would be turning their nose up at such basic fare. If they wanted the soups and consommé, the souffles and crepes of fine dining, they could take themselves off to a hotel for their meals.

As it was, the fire was roaring in the fireplace and Clem was polishing the wineglasses by the time Dora fetched the other two down. They seemed a little stunned as they took their seats and Clem popped the champagne cork. For a crazy moment, it crossed his mind to announce right here and now his fifty percent ownership of The Parthenon.

Glancing at Dora's happy, flushed face, he dismissed it just as quickly. Plenty of time for that. Might as well get over one hurdle at a time. No sense in trying to jump several all-in-one leap, that way led to disaster. At the moment, Dora was his willing accomplice, and the last thing he wanted to do was turn her against him before he was sure of his way.

"I propose a toast," he said, passing around the glasses as he filled them.

192

"To the founder of the feast?" Dora suggested helpfully.

"To us," Clem corrected her, picking up the last of the glasses. He turned to Fields and Allsop, who looked at one another and then clambered awkwardly to their feet. Fields looked sheepish and a little unsure of himself for once, whereas Allsop looked his usual awkward self.

His brother-in-law cleared his throat. "To the Dabneys," he proposed. "May you not live to regret what you have done," he said somberly. Allsop winced and turned crimson.

Clem's eyebrows rose and he looked to Dora, who at once pinned a smile to her face. "To health and happiness!" she said as though echoing a completely different toast.

"Health and happiness!" the other three repeated before resuming their seats once again. The champagne seemed to enliven things at least for Fields, who smacked his lips and glanced toward the bottle with a surprised look on his face.

"Dashed nice vintage, this," he muttered approvingly before drawing one of the bowls toward him with a gleam in his eye. "Ah! Pickled whelks!"

Not much more was said for the next twenty minutes as a fine supper was partaken by all. Even Allsop's appetite was tickled enough to take a decent plateful this time, and by Clem's reckoning, he ate more of the grapes than Dora.

The champagne was polished off and a second bottle opened. This time, Clem paused before the toast, and Dora jumped into the breach. "Sláinte!" she cried.

Fields looked a little surprised but gave a murmured agreement of, "Your very good health."

Inroads were made into all three pies and a quantity of cheese was consumed.

"Do you know," Dora commented chattily, "that someone once told me it was vastly unladylike to eat cheese?"

"Who the devil told you that?" her brother demanded.

"Mrs. Applewhite," she responded promptly.

Fields gave a disgusted grunt. "She would! Probably thinks it's too low class," he commented before glancing uncomfortably at Clem. "Your pardon, Dabney."

"Not at all, cheese is a working-class staple after all," Clem responded affably.

The rest of the meal passed without incident, and when Clem rose to help Dora clear the plates, the other two followed suit, and soon they had stowed the leftovers into the cupboards and piled the dirty plates next to the sink.

He followed Dora into the scullery, where she was working the pump for water. "Leave it," he said. "Mrs. Cherwell is coming first thing."

He could tell she was tempted. "I don't want her to walk in and for the first thing she sees to be a pile of dirty crockery," she said, biting her lip.

"If it was not for you, she would not be coming back at all," he reminded her, even as he reached past her to pick up the full bucket.

"It won't take long, for the plates are only covered in crumbs today, not gravy." When they returned to the kitchen, the others had disappeared and Clem put the water to heat on the stove. "You don't have to remain down here with me. Why do you not go on up?" she urged him. "Felix always secures all the windows and doors. He's likely doing that now."

Clem shook his head. "I'm content to wait," he told her, removing his jacket, and rolling up his shirtsleeves. He was elbow deep in soapy water when Fields reentered the kitchen a quarter of an hour later brandishing a large key.

He stood in the doorway, watching the two of them washing and drying the plates. "I've locked up," he said abruptly and hung the key on a hook. He hesitated a moment, then murmured, "Good night," before taking his leave of them.

Clem and Dora exchanged sidelong glances. "You see? He has accepted you already," she commented.

194

"Hmm, that was an interesting toast he gave."

Dora gave a gurgle of laughter. "He took it pretty well on the whole, you have to admit."

Clem would admit no such thing. They finished up, and he filled a bucket with hot water for their wash, carrying it up to the second floor while Dora changed into her long cotton nightgown. It would be a lot easier if they had a bathroom on their own floor, he reflected, as he first lit the fire in their bedroom and then took his own wash once she was done.

By the time he joined her under the covers, he fancied he could feel some heat from the fireplace.

"How about you take off one pair of socks, Dora," he teased.

She rolled toward him. "One pair?" she asked archly. "Well, as you asked so nicely…"

Ten minutes later, Clem rolled off her with a strangled expletive. *Fuck.* His chest was heaving like he had run ten miles. Just a bit of touching and kissing should not get him into this worked-up state.

"I am sorry, Clem," Dora said, misinterpreting his muttered curse.

"No, no," he said swiftly. "I am only annoyed with myself. I should have thought of getting you a—er—preventative before. I knew a career was your priority. You told me upfront. That was why you married me after all."

Dora bit her lip. "I should have thought of it too," she said disarmingly, "but I never considered that—well." She flushed and glanced away.

She had not thought their contractual marriage would include consummation, he reflected wryly. Of course, neither had he, at first. Then he had changed his mind. "We have both had a lot to contend with lately," he said, forcing a mirthless smile to his lips and fighting down the clamor of

195

disappointment from his cock. "I think we can be generous and let ourselves off the hook."

She brightened at this. "Yes, that is true," she agreed. "I do hope we will not have to wait six weeks though."

Clem lifted his head off the pillow to look at her. "Six weeks?"

"For mail order," she explained. "Sometimes my dress patterns can take as long as two whole months to arrive."

Clem exhaled noisily. "I can get hold of one if I put my mind to it. There are places in addition to newspaper advertisements."

"What places?" she asked, immediately curious.

"Places that no respectable woman would frequent," he admitted.

Her face clouded over. "It is so stupid how such matters are managed."

"Agreed," Clem huffed, blowing out a puff of air and leaning back on one elbow. "But I'm damnably glad I don't have to wait six weeks though," he admitted, glancing down at her relaxed body. His gaze lingered, and picking up on his mood along, no doubt, with his throbbing erection, Dora rolled onto her side toward him.

"Do you want me to—that is, shall I bring you to completion with my hand?" she asked. "I'm quite happy to."

"Yes, please," he answered thickly, and without even the slightest hesitation, she closed the distance between them and wrapped her hand around his cock. Clem could not hold back his relieved groan. Then she started working him, and it was so good his mind went mercifully blank.

He dropped his head back on the pillow and tried to shut his eyes to savor it, but for some goddamn reason, his eyes kept springing open to look at Dora's face. He wanted to check if she was really comfortable with performing this act upon him and was not repulsed by his inability to hold back his guttural grunts.

He had no idea what was acceptable or not acceptable to expect from your wife in the bedroom, never having had one before. He just knew it was fucking shameful how fast he was hurtling toward spending in her hand. He went from relieved to frantic in what felt like the blink of an eye.

All too soon he was a panting, heaving mess beneath her ministrations. Every time he thought he had reached his limit, she would pause and adjust her stroke saying, "Wait, no, I think I have it now," and the torture would start up again.

He watched her through half-closed lids, the expression of utter absorption and concentration on her face. Was she doing it deliberately? he wondered in bewilderment. How would a sheltered virgin like Dora know about the benefits of delaying pleasure?

"Is this the angle?" she asked, looking up at him suddenly.

Clem's hips jolted and he whimpered. "It all feels good," he gasped. "Everything you do to me." Dora's satisfied smile nearly sent him over the edge. "Fuck—I'm about to—"

Dora's eyes widened; she looked around in alarm. "Wait, I forgot to get a washcloth—" she blurted in panic.

Clem growled and rolled over her, caging her in with his body. "Dora," he groaned. "I want to come on your belly, can I?"

"My belly?" She sounded faintly astonished. "Well, yes, if that's something you—"

Clem levered himself up on his knees and barely got his hand to the base of his cock before he started releasing in a series of long, hard spurts. Dora gazed down between them to watch with a fascinated eye, but as for Clem, he planted his free hand next to her head and he kept his eyes glued to her face.

Only once he finished with a guttural half sigh, half groan did he lean back and look down at the glistening mess he had made of her smooth belly. He caught his breath and stared, letting his gaze travel up to her flushed face and back down again. He let out a shaky breath and swallowed. *Holy fuck.*

"Once my legs stop shaking, I'll fetch you a washcloth," he promised and collapsed back onto the bed beside her. For a few moments, there was nothing but his ragged breathing as his pulse calmed and his cock swooned against his thigh.

"Just how big is this sponge I'm supposed to insert between my legs?" Dora asked, breaking the merciful silence. His eyes sprang open, and he found her propped up on her elbows, regarding her stomach with interest. "Because—well—it seems like quite a *lot* to be absorbed."

Clem regarded her speechlessly for a moment, then he let his eyelids drop. He wasn't even feigning drowsiness. He was wholly unequal to such a conversation. A minute later, he rolled out of bed to fetch her that washcloth. "Just tell me one thing," he said, pausing at the door to scratch his belly. "What the fuck is a cicisbeo?"

Dora chuckled. "Felix was clearly flustered. From my understanding it is a *married* woman's lover, so he had that quite wrong."

"You are a married woman though," Clem pointed out. Then he ran up the stairs to the second-floor bathroom and fetched her that cloth.

16

Theo woke to someone moving around the room in the dark and, after a moment's confusion, realized it must be Clem and that the gray light breaking through the curtains was morning. By the time she had sat up, he had already left the room, and she hurried to drag on her dressing gown, some woolly socks, and her slippers and follow him downstairs.

He was busy with the stove by the time she caught up with him and greeted her with surprise. "Are you going to The Eagle?" she asked, reaching for the teapot off the dresser.

"Yes, but you don't need to see me off, Dora," he assured her. "It's still early, no more than seven."

"Can I not come in with you?" she asked, fetching the milk jug from the cupboard.

He paused a moment before answering. "What would you do there all day?"

"I could practice my act," she replied promptly, "and familiarize myself with the place."

Having lit the fire, Clem swung the stove door shut. "Have you organized a rehearsal time with your partner already?" he asked.

He knew full well she had not, and Theo hesitated before making a reply. "I asked for Lil to call on me at her earliest convenience," she explained.

"If she calls today, while you were out, you will miss her." Which was perfectly reasonable of Clem to point out, but for some reason, Theo had the distinct impression he did not want her to accompany him. He lifted a bucket of water and poured it into a pan to boil. "Do not forget you have Mrs. Cherwell coming today as well," he said, looking up. "You will want to tell her all of your news."

She managed a smile at that. Suddenly, it occurred to her that maybe Clem also wanted to catch up his particular

199

intimates at The Eagle with his new living arrangements. That would explain why he was so keen to shake her off. Jim and...whoever else he worked closely with. She did not exactly get to meet many of them on their fleeting visit the day before. The thought cheered her considerably.

"I'll take you along on Thursday night," he said, rolling up his sleeves and walking back into the scullery to take a wash.

Theo promptly set down the tea caddy and followed him into the scullery where he had already lit the copper to heat the water. "To watch the acts?" she asked breathlessly. He nodded, and though it must be an effect of the gray light, she thought his expression looked rather grim. "I will love that!" she told him gratefully as he soaped his neck and face over a basin of what could be no more than tepid water.

"We'll see," he muttered, and Theo remembered he had reservations about resilience when it came to bawdy humor.

"Lil thought the same as you at one point," she said impulsively, leaning her hip against the mangle.

"What's that?" Clem shook his head.

"That I couldn't tell a dirty joke to save my life." He lowered his towel and subjected her to a long, hard look. A sudden rattling in the lock made them both start and turn their heads. "It must be Mrs. Cherwell," Theo said, flying to the kitchen door.

"Mrs. Cherwell!" she cried, flinging the door open. "Welcome back! We have missed you!"

The older woman blinked at her a moment before bustling in. "Miss Theodora," she scolded. "Whatever are you a-doing down here in my kitchen at this hour of the morning?"

"My husband is just off to work," Theo told her, standing aside as the older woman removed her outerwear. She felt a little self-conscious referring to Clem as such. "So, I was attempting to be a dutiful wife and send him off with a cup of tea at the very least."

200

Mrs. Cherwell peered into the scullery with interest. "He spoke the truth, then," she said, lowering her voice to a harsh whisper. "That's 'im? The one wot you married?" Theo nodded, and Mrs. Cherwell looked her up and down as though reevaluating her. "Well, you been as good as your word, I'll give you that," she said with a nod. "My 'Erbert, 'e said as you acted proper 'andsome toward me."

"I'm afraid I've made a fearful mess of all your duties," Theo confessed. "The coal merchant no longer calls, or the butcher. I messed up paying them and they struck us off." To her surprise, Mrs. Cherwell seemed more gratified than not by this news.

She gave a dour smile. "I won't say as I'm surprised, Miss Theodora," she said, glancing around the kitchen with a jaundiced expression. "This whole kitchen needs scrubbing from top to bottom."

"I should not wonder," Theo agreed. "I've also made a wretched job of the laundry..." She did not get the chance to elucidate any further, for Clem emerged from the scullery at this point, towel still in hand.

"Clem, this is Mrs. Cherwell, our housekeeper. Mrs. Cherwell, this is my husband, Mr. Dabney."

"I introduced myself yesterday," Clem said mildly but extended his hand for her to shake in any case.

Mrs. Cherwell's gaze darted between him and Theo a few times before she answered, "Pleased to meet any husband of Miss Theodora's, I'm sure. Now, I see you've got the stove lit, so if you go up and dress, then I'll get a bit of breakfast on for you sharpish."

To Theo's surprise, Clem agreed to this without a murmur and disappeared up to their room to dress. "What do you make of him?" she asked Mrs. Cherwell curiously.

The other woman spluttered a moment before answering. "Well," she said judiciously, after a moment. "He ain't a gentleman born and bred, I can tell that much, standing down here in his bare feet, a-lightin of the stove, but he's a fine, broad specimen and no mistake. Where did you find 'im?"

"He owns a music hall called The Eagle and Sun in Shoreditch," Theo informed her, sinking down onto a wooden stool.

"'E never does!"

Theo nodded and resumed spooning the tea leaves into the pot. She could not remember how many scoops she had already done, but it probably did not signify if it was a little strong this morning. "Which room you put 'im in?" Mrs. Cherwell continued. "The old master's?"

"Uncle Barnabus's room?" Theo was startled. "No, of course not. I put him in my room. We're married," she reiterated.

Mrs. Cherwell's eyebrows shot up. "And what did Master Felix say to that?" she asked, taking eggs and ham from the cupboard. Theo was suddenly glad Clem had bought so many supplies or she would have had to confess to yet another area in which she had let the side down badly.

"After all, what could he say? We were indisputably wed by the time we returned here." Theo hesitated. "We spent our wedding night at Wards Hotel."

Disappointingly, Mrs. Cherwell did not seem familiar with the name of the grand hotel. Still, Theo gained the distinct impression she was squirreling information away to carry home to her Herbert. "What you a-done to your hair, Miss Theodora?" she asked finally, squinting at Theo as she scooped some lard into the frying pan. "Catch it in the mangle, did you?"

Theo could not help but laugh at this. She shook her head. "I wasn't *quite* that incompetent, though it was a close-run thing."

202

Theo felt decidedly flat after Clem departed directly after his breakfast. She drank two cups of tea with Mrs. Cherwell before drifting back upstairs to dress. She decided to settle herself in the sitting room today in case Lil should call. If she did not, then she could always pick up her dressmaking.

Theo lit a fire in the grate and then busied herself unpacking the large chest that had been left the night before. It was packed with fancy liqueurs and even fancier-looking boxes of sweets and bonbons all done up with pretty ribbons. Theo handled them with the greatest of care, placing them along the mirror-backed shelves. They must have been dreadfully expensive.

She was brought out of her thoughts by Mrs. Cherwell knocking briefly on the door before she came in bearing a tea tray complete with warm scones. "I brought you up some elevenses, Miss Theodora," she said briskly and set the tray down with a rattle. Theo was quite astonished, for Mrs. Cherwell had never done such a thing before. "I brought up an extra cup as you said you was maybe expecting your friend to visit. I'll be sure and show her up, should she deign to call."

Theo thanked her profusely and then gazed down at the fresh scones and jam. She had even been given the best china! She was just wondering if she ought to summon Felix and Harold down to join her when a rap on the door heralded Lil's arrival.

Theo flew out of her chair and embraced her friend. "Lil! I'm so glad you've come!"

Lil returned the embrace but drew back with a troubled expression. She waited for the door to shut after the housekeeper before she spoke. "Theo, my dear, what have you done?" Lil sounded half scandalized, half intrigued. "I hardly knew what to make of your letter! I could not decide if you were in the grip of a brain fever or were flat out intoxicated when you wrote it!"

"Neither, I assure you!" Theo took her friend's bonnet and mittens from her, setting them down on the nearest surface. "Now come and draw near the fire for you feel chilled through."

"Have you indeed married him? Dabney, I mean?" Lil demanded as Theo led her to the seat nearest the fire.

"I have." Theo nodded, seeing her friend seated. "If you had been in when he delivered your letter you would have seen him yesterday evening."

"My mother-in-law said it was a fine figure of a man, though no true gent," Lil said in a dazed voice. "What pray does Felix make of it all!"

Theo sat behind the tea tray and made haste to pour Lil a cup. "In truth, he took it quite well, all things considered," she answered. "There was a little posturing and a few cross words, but he soon caved when he saw there was nothing doing. We spent the wedding night at Wards Hotel," she added, casting a quick glance at Lil through her lashes.

"*Wards?*" Lil squawked, finally giving Theo the reaction she had anticipated from the name drop.

Theo nodded, her eyes aglow. "Oh, Lil," she said, setting down the teapot, "it was ever so fancy and quite the loveliest time I have ever had!"

Lil blinked, looking considerably taken aback by this confidence. "He treated you right, then?" she asked faintly.

"Oh yes! He could not have treated me more handsomely if he had tried. We had a beautiful suite, fine dining in the restaurant, and the most wonderful cocktails. I declare, I've drunk more champagne in the past three days than at any other time in my life! I cannot remember a time when I was so thoroughly spoiled."

Lil's gaze softened. "I can well believe that, my darlin'," she said wryly. "Well, I'm glad he managed to show you a good time, at least." She glanced around. "This room's a lot cheerier than the one we used last time," she commented.

"Yes, but there is no piano in here," Theo said regretfully. "Have you had much time to rehearse? How have things been with you?"

"I've learned all me words, never fear!" Lil told her. "I been practicing with Peggy," she said, naming her old dresser. "And she chuckles over every line, let me tell you! If she's any indication of the reception we'll get, then we're assured a hit."

Theo relaxed into smiles. "That's wonderful. Have you handed in your notice at the gentleman's grill? I shall have to ask Clem when we can start rehearsing at The Eagle and Sun. When he took me there yesterday, the place was as good as empty at midday."

They spent a half hour catching up. Lil did not feel she could give notice until they were assured a regular spot at The Eagle. Knowing Lil had two dependents living with her, Theo understood her friend's caution, and they spent the rest of Lil's visit running through the songs she had rewritten.

To her delight, Lil had the lyrics and tune down pat and even had a few gestures to go along with them which had Theo wiping tears of laughter from her eyes. The next two hours flew, and when Lil regretfully said she had to go, Theo accompanied her downstairs arm in arm and waved her off from the top step. They promised to meet again in two days, this time at Lil's lodgings where they could rehearse in front of Peggy as a test audience.

Theo was so excited; she ran upstairs to make a list of things she needed to run through to make ready. So caught up was she in her plans, that when Mrs. Cherwell knocked on the door bearing a cheese omelet for her luncheon, she was frankly astonished.

They had always been expected to shift for themselves when it came to the midday meal, for her brother and Harold were rarely at home for it. She thanked the housekeeper profusely and ate it while making scrupulous notes for her next rehearsal.

It was a little after four when Theo set her notebook down and considered how to fill the next hour or so until Clem's return. Dinner was always served at six o'clock, and she assumed he would be home sometime before that. By rights, she ought to resume her dressmaking. Her abandoned and half-finished gown lay in pieces in the sewing room, but she could muster no enthusiasm for the task.

She was growing sadly lazy, she told herself sternly, but it was no use. She simply did not want to sit puzzling over her latest pattern this afternoon. She was too excited at the prospect of performing in front of an audience, even if it was only Lil's old friend. In the end, she decided to simply go for a walk to clear her head and, with a bit of luck, spot someone interesting to observe in the nearby park.

17

Clem arrived back at Juniper Row by five o'clock with a pocket full of wallpaper samples, a case of delicate liqueur glasses, and a contraceptive device for Dora. He was consequently annoyed to find she was neither patiently awaiting him in their sitting room or, if he was honest, their bedroom.

He had half convinced himself by this point that taking Dora to bed was the right thing to do. It would go a long way to making her feel secure in their marriage, he told himself. Safe and secure before she came crashing to ignominious defeat on his stage that is.

Clem pulled a face. What a prince among husbands he was. Deep down, of course, he knew that was not the real reason at all. The simple fact was he wanted to introduce her to the delights of the bedroom, just as he had introduced her to many others.

He wanted to fuck her and see that look of appreciation and wonderment on her face for his cock. He loved that look on her, the way she embraced new experiences so wholeheartedly. The thought of taking Dora to his bed made him feel slightly light-headed and decidedly…needy. He was half inclined to go out and start looking for her.

Mrs. Cherwell told him grandly that "Miss Theodora" had gone to promenade in the park "as was her habit" and Clem was forced to make do with that. He went up to the sitting room, set down the case of glasses, and laid out the paper samples on the table side by side. He wanted Dora's opinion before proceeding, though his own preference was for an azure blue, punctuated by unfurling leaves of gold.

He paced impatiently throughout the room, noticing that she had unpacked the case, but had seemingly not helped herself to any of the treats on offer. For some reason, that irritated him too. Opening the cupboard door, he reached for the nearest box and untied the ribbons, setting it down on the table where it would be sure to catch her eye and tempt her.

Then he made for the bedroom, where he set the discreet cardboard box down on the dresser and wondered what Dora would make of the instructions printed in a cramped hand on a small card inside. He hoped she would not expect him to explain how things worked. After a moment's brooding on this, he realized by rights he ought to know.

Sliding the box open, Clem withdrew the card and read it frowningly three times until he thought he had the gist of it. Was it foolproof? He somehow doubted it. Should he withdraw as well? Maybe. He bore the burden of responsibility here, and it would be Dora who would face the consequences if the device failed. *Damn it.*

Withdrawing was the least he could do after she had made it plain that she did not want a child at this point. Clem groaned and lay back on the bed, wondering slightly at his impatience. If someone had told him two months ago that he would be lusting after a plain bit of goods like Theodora Fields, he would never have believed it. But there it was. He *was* lusting, and there was no use denying it, not to himself.

Maybe it was down to the uncustomary abstinence of late. He hadn't kept company with women in a while, as running his business had taken over his every thought and waking energy. He had resolved from the outset never to sleep with any of the women he employed; that was just bad practice and he liked to keep things straightforward.

In the past, he realized he had used sex as a way of blowing off steam, but the concert rooms did not give him the same rush as boxing, the same dizzying highs or crashing lows, so he found he had no pressing need to find an outlet for his excess energy anymore. How long had it been? Maybe eight or even nine months? Perhaps that explained it. He had deprived himself, and now he could not keep his hands off his own wife.

208

The simple truth was that he had been far too busy to think about pursuing women. Not that the women he usually took up with required much by way of pursuing. Clem had never been particularly interested in the chase. He liked to know the outcome was assured. He had never courted a woman in his life before Dora.

Maybe that was why he was champing at the bit? Then also…he did derive a strange kind of satisfaction from initiating her into new things. He wasn't sure *what* that was about, but there was no denying he enjoyed the hell out of it, whether it was a fancy lunch or something a bit more carnal.

A sudden noise had him sitting up. Was that the front door closing? After a moment, he heard footsteps running up the stairs and his name breathlessly called.

"In here!" he called back, and the door flung open, and Dora came sailing in, dragging off her hat and muffler.

"You got back before me!" she exclaimed, rounding the bed and casting her things down into a chair.

Clem stared at her, feeling a little winded. He wanted her to cast herself on him, he realized, and cover him with kisses. If she had, it would not have felt strange to him at all, for her face was shining with pleasure at the mere sight of him.

He felt an odd lurch in his chest. When had he wanted spontaneous acts of affection like that from women before? It wasn't like him at all. Of course, she would not do such a thing. The standard greeting between man and wife was likely a peck on the cheek. That was how one did it. But he did not get up off the bed. "Where have you been?" he asked, stalling for time, even though he knew full well already.

"Walking in the park. I like to take some daily exercise." She ruffled her hair and then started looking around, likely for her fake hairpiece.

"You left it in the sitting room," he told her.

"Oh yes, I took it off to show it to Lil. She thought it turned out rather well, though she said I should wet my comb to make the illusion complete." Clem made no comment. "Did you have a nice day?" she asked, pinning him with her gaze as though she had finally picked up on his strange mood.

Did he? Clem wasn't sure. He shrugged. "Tolerable." When she turned impulsively toward the door, he asked quickly, "Where are you going?"

"To get my hair."

"Don't bother. Leave it."

She stopped in her tracks to look at him in surprise. "Very well," she said agreeably, turning back. "But don't let me forget to put it in before dinner. Felix would be very shocked, I fear." She gave a gurgle of laughter as she climbed onto the bed to rest beside him. "Mrs. Cherwell thought I must have had an unfortunate accident—"

She did not get to complete her sentence, for Clem seized hold of her and kissed her as though he had been passionately longing to, which, of course, he had. Dora, after only the smallest of pauses, passed her arms about his neck and reciprocated with gratifying enthusiasm.

As he had rolled over her, Dora clearly thought her move was to respond in kind, so they ended up rolling to and fro and grappling with each other in a haphazard fashion which had Clem's misbehaving heart almost jumping out of his chest, along with other parts of his anatomy.

By the time he pulled back from their tussle to stare at her flushed face, the covers were hanging off the bed and both pillows had been knocked to the floor.

"I think you must have missed me today," Dora panted with a breathless laugh, which should have been like a splash of cold water, but fuck it, he *had* missed her, he realized, feeling dazed.

210

"Maybe," he answered cautiously. "What about you?" Her eyes flickered up, as though she was considering this. *What the fuck?* He should be incensed, but instead, he felt slightly anxious. Her reply was a sudden blinding smile and a nod, and Clem couldn't help it; he crushed her to him again with a groan. "Dora," he murmured, nibbling on her bottom lip and then pulling back. "I got the preventative today."

"You did?"

"It's over there on the dresser." When she made to get up and fetch it, Clem released her without an outward show of the reluctance he felt. He watched her peer into the box.

"It's more rubbery than spongelike in texture," she said in surprise before drawing out the tiny smudged card.

She gave a slow nod as she read it through. "Have you used something like this before?" she asked, just as he had known she would.

He had to force himself not to tense. "Yes, or something like it." It was ridiculous to feel so uptight when Dora was being so matter-of-fact about it. What the fuck was his problem? "There are a few different ones available," he added, scratching his neck. "If you don't get on with this one, we can get another."

Dora nodded again. "Well, it seems straightforward enough. Should I try it out for size?" When he nodded, she headed promptly for a lacquered screen she had against the far wall.

Clem rolled onto his back and slipped a hand under his head, gazing up at the ceiling. Likely he was making too much of this whole business and she would soon change her mind. This so-called career of hers was not going to last past a disastrous debut.

Maybe a baby or two would satisfy her just as well as a stage career. He wondered what kind of mother Dora would make. He could not really imagine it though. Any more than him as a father. No, it was probably better they were going to wait until they were both ready for such a thing.

"How often should I put this in?" her muffled voice asked from behind the screen. When he did not answer at once, she clarified, "Or do I just check with you of an evening?" Clem was still debating his response when her reappearance forestalled him. "All done," she said brightly, one hand still clutching the screen.

She was now clad only in her chemise and drawers which were the plainest undergarments Clem had seen on a woman. There was absolutely no reason why his chest should be pounding like a drum. "Is it…comfortable?" he asked, rolling onto his side to look at her.

She nodded. "I can't feel it at all now it's in. Though"—she bit her lip—"there is a ribbon hanging down. You might find it a little off-putting."

He smiled wolfishly. "I doubt that very much." He patted the bed. "Come here. Let me take a look."

She flushed, but joined him on the bed quickly enough, getting onto her knees and pushing down her drawers to show him. Something about the matter-of-fact way she revealed her bare thighs and pussy to him made him catch his breath. She had such trust in him; he felt a sort of tightness in his chest.

He ran a thumb down the thin white ribbon resting against her bare thigh. "Not remotely off-putting," he said huskily, his eyes riveted to where the ribbon disappeared into her dark curls. "Though I am very intrigued to find where this leads." He leaned forward and dropped a lingering kiss next to the ribbon and she caught her breath.

"Clem!" she whispered. "You know very well where it leads. What time is it now?"

He turned his head and reached for his pocket watch which he had discarded onto the side table. "Quarter to six."

212

"We only have fifteen minutes before dinner. I should not like us to be late after Mrs. Cherwell has been so obliging today."

"Has she been obliging?" Clem asked dryly as he dropped a last regretful kiss to her soft inner thigh before gently tugging up her drawers and refastening the drawstring. He needed longer than fifteen minutes when all was said and done.

"Oh yes, she made me fresh scones for Lil's visit and luncheon too. Nothing was too much trouble." She clambered off the bed, but instead of donning her striped dress again, she took a heavy velvet robe from her wardrobe with lots of tassels and drew it over her head. To Clem's eye, it made her look as though she was about to go on stage as a medieval witch, but he supposed it was warm at any rate.

"Don't forget your hair," he reminded her, though why Fields and Allsop should be spared the sight of her exposed neck he did not know. Of course, she *did* have an attractive nape, he reflected some minutes later as he followed her down the stairs. Graceful. Even her peculiar garb did not detract from it altogether. On second thought, maybe it was a good thing she bared it only around him.

Clem was distracted all through dinner, though he made short work of Mrs. Cherwell's capon in white sauce with attendant roasted vegetables. As there were plenty of leftovers from the previous night, he supposed she was making a point by serving a cooked meal from scratch.

Fields certainly seemed gratified, but as Mrs. Cherwell either ignored or talked loudly over whatever comment he attempted, it soon became apparent that she bore a grudge. Allsop was quiet, but that was nothing new, so Dora valiantly kept up a bright trickle of conversation. She managed this with a little help from him and a lot of help from the housekeeper, who found lots of reasons to remain in the dining room for the duration of dinner.

Clem found he sorely missed the tête-à-tête meals he and Dora had shared these past few weeks. He was glad to make his escape at the close of the meal, declining his brother-in-law's hesitant offer of a glass of claret following dinner.

"You should have gone with him!" Dora hissed as they climbed the stairs. "That is Felix's notion of an olive branch!"

"I would much rather spend my time with you than him," Clem answered with perfect truth. Was he supposed to be so open about his temporary infatuation? he wondered with vague unease. Everything he knew about interacting with women seemed to have gone out the window when it came to his wife. It was unnerving, to say the least.

Would Dora be hurt when he recovered from whatever it was currently afflicting him? He hoped not. With a bit of luck, he could shield her from his indifference when it inevitably kicked in. "What do you do while your brother and lodger smoke and drink claret in the parlor?" he asked, hoping to distract her from the fact he had snubbed her brother's overtures of friendship.

"I go up to my sitting room as a habit." She shrugged. "Why do you ask?"

"I would have thought, in such a forward-thinking household, you would not have to withdraw from the gentlemen's company at all."

Dora paused suddenly on her step, so he halted also behind her. "Do you know, I think that would be the sensible option. But sadly, I have often reflected that my uncle and Felix are only forward-thinking in matters that have no bearing on their own lives."

"Convenient for them," Clem remarked dryly.

Dora regarded him with interest. "Would you permit your wife to smoke and drink claret if we lived in our own house?"

Clem had to work hard not to let his expression show how startled he was at such a notion, for he had not meant that at all.

"Do you think you would enjoy such masculine pursuits?" he hedged, playing for time.

"Claret or cigars?" Dora asked, starting back up the stairs.

Clem's eyebrows shot up, and he was glad she was no longer facing him. "Either one."

"Claret is pleasant enough, but the one time I stole one of Uncle's cigars I was violently unwell afterward."

He should not be shocked by this, especially considering she fancied herself as a male impersonator. He should not be; however, he was. Rallying, Clem cleared his throat. "That is common for the first time. Persistence is key."

They had reached the top of the stairs now, and Dora pulled a face. "Even the *thought* of it makes my mouth sour. For the longest time, I could not abide even the smell. Are we going to the sitting room or the bedroom?" she enquired politely, looking from one door to the other.

Clem did not hesitate this time. "Bedroom," he answered with alacrity. Dora nodded and walked briskly through the door. Clem paused a moment, then walked into the sitting room where he unwrapped the pretty liqueur glasses and, grabbing two, extracted one of the fancy bottles from the cabinet. Only then did he join Dora in their bedroom.

She had already stripped down to her chemise and drawers and was under the covers awaiting him. He was glad to see she did not look remotely nervous but instead regarded him with interest. "What is that?" she asked.

"This," Clem said, brandishing the bottle, "is a very fine raspberry liqueur made with honey. It is delicious. And these are glasses I bought for the display cabinet in the sitting room."

"They're very pretty," Dora said approvingly.

"Hopefully," Clem said, breaking the seal, "you will like this better than claret. Though, if you do not," he added, considering, "I can always buy us a bottle of that too."

Dora sat up, plumping the pillows behind her, and accepted the glass with thanks, inspecting the hand-painted blue and yellow flower decoration. "They're even lovelier at close hand," she observed as Clem set his glass down and removed his cuff links and jacket.

"I'll need to take you back to Finch's this week," he commented without enthusiasm, unbuttoning his shirt. "You're due a fitting."

"Oh good!" Dora exclaimed. "That brings us another step closer to Lil and my debut. We had a good practice session today, by the way. I wanted to ask you when we can rehearse at The Eagle and Sun."

"We can negotiate that later," Clem answered absently, stripping off his shirt. "Your costume is not even ready yet."

"Yes, but it does not need to be a dress rehearsal," Dora pointed out. "This is very nice," she commented, lifting her glass to show him she had taken a small sip.

"Not too sweet?"

She shook her head. "Though a larger glass of it would likely be too much." She took another tiny sip and relaxed back onto her pillows with a contented sigh.

Clem stripped down to his long underwear, pulling off his socks before joining her under the covers.

"Are you not going to try your liqueur?" she asked with surprise when he immediately crowded into her.

Clem turned back and grabbed the tiny glass, tossing it down with one gulp. That way he did not have to taste the cloying stuff.

Dora laughed. "You may have to buy some claret, purely for you to take."

"Hmmm," he murmured in agreement, though taking a glass of anything was very far from his mind right now. "Should I have lit the fire?" he asked, glancing over at the grate, as the thought suddenly occurred to him.

Dora shook her head. "You can keep me warm," she answered so sweetly he had to catch his breath.

"I'd like that."

"So would I." They smiled at one another, and Clem felt like there was a bird trapped in his fucking chest.

"Finish your drink, Dora."

"Let me savor it," she protested. "I can't just knock it back like you did. That was a terrible waste."

Clem rolled his eyes and slid a hand down her stomach, before dipping down into her drawers. There was some advantage to her wearing them so loose, he decided as his questing fingers slid between her legs.

Dora made an interesting sound, part murmur, part exclamation, but as he simply cupped her there and propped his head on his hand to watch her face, she relaxed again and took another sip of her drink.

"You're spinning that out," he accused her lazily, but he did not really mind in truth. Not now his hand was where it was.

Dora gave a gurgle of laughter. "No such thing! This is delectable nectar and I mean to enjoy it."

Clem slowly traced the ribbon down her thigh and then slipped his fingers into her cleft. Her words held just as much relevance for himself. She was already delightfully slippery down there. Dora shifted against her pillows. "Tell me how you want me to touch you," he murmured.

She breathed out before replying. "Like last time," she confessed unevenly.

"Ah, but you were helping last time," he reminded her, sliding his fingers through her increasingly wet folds.

"You're doing fine," she assured him, even though he was deliberately avoiding her pearl. After a minute of these ministrations, Dora whimpered and started moving against his hand, trying to steer him right.

217

"Tell me what you want, Dora," he practically purred.

"Um—you—not there," she broke off frustratedly.

By rights, he should torment her more, but he was too keen. He tapped her clitoris. "Here?"

Dora gasped, shutting her eyes a moment. "Yes," she gasped. "Oh *yes*, please."

Well, fuck, he wasn't going to be able to deny her anything when she asked so nicely. Instead, he concentrated on teasing that pretty bud, any way he could think of. Dora sobbed and arched her back, sloshing the last of her raspberry liqueur over her breasts and staining her boring chemise with dark red spots.

"Oh no!" she squeaked in dismay. He plucked the empty glass out of her hand and set it down beside his own.

"Never fear," he said, leaning forward and sucking the first of the wet spots on her chemise. Dora's breathing hitched as he inched his voracious mouth closer and closer to her nipple.

"Clem," she repeated faintly, then gave a disappointed moan when he retreated and started licking toward her other breast. He repeated his tease until her hand closed about the back of his neck, making him draw in a sharp breath. This was what he had been waiting for, he realized, feeling stunned as he shuddered with pleasure.

"Guide me," he said thickly. "Tell me where you want my mouth."

Wordlessly, she tightened her grip, steering him toward her nipple.

He nudged it with his nose. "Here?"

"Please, Clem." He did not make her wait, and Dora made an explosive sound as he sucked her nipple through her chemise with almost an indecent amount of pleasure. Her fingers pinched on his neck, and he slid his middle finger right up inside her making her jolt. "*Clem!*"

"Never slipped a finger inside before?" he asked.

218

She hesitated, then cleared her throat. "Yes, but your fingers are much bigger than mine."

Clem had to take a deep breath. Damn, he liked how she told him everything. Liked it too much. "Anything else ever get in here?" he asked hoarsely.

Dora's eyes widened. "Like what?"

"Like...phallus-shaped things," he said, remembering what she had called it before. "I thought you might have taken inspiration from those ladies in the illustrations."

Her face turned even more scarlet. "No, never," she admitted in a choked voice.

"How does it feel?"

Her brow puckered. "It's fine," she said evasively.

Clem circled her clitoris with his thumb. "And now?" he asked.

She made a muffled sound. "That's better," she admitted.

"Tell me when it's not enough," he said, releasing her nipple to make his way toward the other one.

Her eyes fluttered open. "Not enough?" she repeated blankly.

"I'll give you two," he said and opened his mouth over her other nipple.

Dora's eyes drifted shut again. "*Ohhhh!*" After a few minutes, her fingers dug into the back of his neck and Clem looked up, quizzically. "I need to..." She whipped her chemise up and over her head.

Clem drew in a shuddering breath. "*Christ*, Dora," he groaned.

"What is it?" she asked, looking suddenly self-conscious. "My breasts?" She pulled a face. "They're not exactly impressive," she said with a nervous laugh.

"They're perfect," Clem disagreed.

"Perfect?"

"Your nipples..." he groaned. "Oh my God."

219

"They're rather large, aren't they?" Dora said unhappily. "Nothing like the tiny pink rosebuds you see in paintings."

"Nothing like them," Clem agreed huskily. "They're a hundred times better." She looked frankly astonished by his reaction. "I could tell they were dark through your chemise," he confessed, blowing out a ragged breath, "but I didn't realize what a beautiful color they would be."

"You—you really think so?" she said in a dazed voice, glancing down at them herself.

"I *really* fucking do," he said hoarsely. "May I?" He lifted his free hand and, when Dora nodded, touched her breasts gently, stroking and handling them with the reverence they deserved. Her large brown nipples were already stiff from his earlier attention, and he could hardly keep his eyes off them. Finally, he could stand it no longer and leaned down to kiss the sensitive peaks.

"Gorgeous," he sighed and felt one of her hands slide into his hair, petting him there. Clem opened his lips over the first of her luscious nipples and sucked it into his mouth, laving it with his tongue. After lavishing the same attention on the other, he began once more to slowly move his fingers between her legs.

"Ready for more?" he asked.

"Yes," Dora whispered, her gaze hazy with desire as he slid a second finger inside her. She bit her lip and closed her eyes.

"Are you close, Dorabelle?" he asked even though he could see she was from a million tells: the restless shift of her hips, the way her sweet cleft was clenching around his fingers.

"I—oh—*yes*," she gasped, and just like that, she tipped right over the edge with a broken cry. He swooped down to cover her lips with his own, but Dora was no screamer. She came with a hoarse whimper and a choked gasp. Clem was not sure why he liked it so much.

Carefully, he removed his hand from between her legs, but instead of rolling off her, he drew her further into his arms. Her

220

whole body was trembling and flushed, and holding her close in that moment felt like the most natural thing in the world to him. It was strange how protective of her he felt. "Breathe, Dora," he murmured against her brow.

She drew in a ragged breath. "Thank you," she murmured at last, her arms slipping around his neck. She pressed a kiss to his cheek. "That was lovely, Clem."

For some reason, that made him grin. "Yes, it was," he agreed throatily.

"You're not in any…discomfort?" she asked, trying to glance down between them, but his chest was in the way.

"I'm very hard, if that's what you mean. But not in any imminent danger of embarrassing myself."

"That's good," she sighed, dropping her head back onto his shoulder. "I'll get my breath back in a minute."

"There's no hurry. Do you want some water?"

"Yes, but I don't want you to move."

He hesitated. "Which is the more pressing need?" he asked. Dora's arms tightened about his neck, so he guessed his embrace was the priority. He was not sure how long they remained entwined. In fact, he was just debating if she had dropped off to sleep when she finally lifted her head.

"Water now?" he asked. She nodded, and he disentangled himself and made his way over to the chest of drawers where a pitcher of water was stood. He poured two glasses and returned to the bed. Dora sat up and took her glass, drinking it down in gulps. Clem drank his, then stripped off his long underwear and rejoined her in the bed.

Dora thumped down her glass and then wriggled out of her drawers, dropping them over the side of the bed. "We're both naked," she observed, turning toward him.

"Yes," Clem agreed.

"For the first time, with each other, I mean." Clem gave a rumble of agreement this time. "Do you think I could take a

221

good look at you?" Dora asked politely. "Only I've never seen one before."

"You've seen my dick before," Clem pointed out with a lazy grin.

Dora ducked her head, looking embarrassed. "I actually meant, well, an adult male," she explained. "Is that an odd request to make? I won't be offended if so. I did take a good look just now when you were pouring the water, but I—"

"I have no objection," Clem said, throwing back the covers and exposing himself to her. "You can look your fill, so long as you return the favor." Dora followed suit, neatly flipping back the counterpane. Clem sat up, drawing his knees up and resting his arms on them. As anticipated, Dora did likewise, so they were sat toe to toe.

"You have long legs," he observed appreciatively. "It was the first thing I noticed about you. That you had good legs."

Dora cocked her head to one side. "Likely because I was wearing silk breeches at the time. Yours are quite hairy." Her eyes traveled over him curiously. "Your chest and arms too."

"I'm hairy all over," he agreed solemnly.

"I like it."

"That's good. I like your hair too," Clem said, gazing fixedly between her legs. "It's nice and dark there."

Dora gave a surprised laugh. "I once heard—" She broke off awkwardly.

"Tell me." Her furtive look intrigued him. Had someone told her that some women shaved?

"About a famous cancan dancer in France," Dora said in a low voice. "She—well—when she performed, she did not wear any drawers. So, when she gave a high kick, her patrons got a tiny glimpse of—well—her hair, *down there*." Her eyes were wide and scandalized.

Clem could not help but grin. "For an extra thrill? Who told you that?"

"Well…" Her gaze slid away. "They did not actually tell me, but I overheard some actresses gossiping one time about it."

"And you filed that information away to think about later?" Dora gave an adorably guilty start. "I'm starting to get your measure, Dora Dabney," he teased.

She broke out in smiles but did not rise to the bait. "Have you ever…seen anything like that?" she asked tentatively.

Clem shook his head. "I've never been to France. Never had any cause to cross the channel."

"I'd love to go," Dora said, resting her chin on her knees.

"Why?" Clem asked. "You can just lift up your own petticoats if you want a glimpse."

Dora gasped. "Clem!"

He laughed. "None of theirs will be as nice as yours; I can guarantee it."

"That's not what I—" She broke off, narrowing her eyes. "You're teasing me!"

"Just a little," he admitted, "but I'm in earnest about how nice yours is."

"Is there another word for it?" she asked curiously. "I mean, like you have another word for your penis."

Clem paused. Well, she had him there. "If I tell you," he said slowly, "you must promise never to use it in any other company than mine, Dora."

"Of course I would not!" She looked so indignant at this that Clem could not bite back his grin.

"I don't know about that, Dora. You are *quite* forthright at times."

"When have I ever—?"

"You nearly gave a woman an apoplexy at Wards. Talking about corsets."

"Oh, well…" She trailed off awkwardly. "I did not realize anyone was listening to us."

"Hmmm."

"Did I embarrass you?"

He shook his head and lunged forward, capturing her hands with his and bearing her down on the mattress, stretching her arms above her head. Dora gazed up at him quite at ease. "Seeing as you asked so nicely, I will complete your education," he said. "These, Dora," he said, blowing on her nipples, "are your pretty tits. You have the most adorable and delicious nipples I have ever had the pleasure of tasting. They are the perfect shape and size."

Dora squinted down at them doubtfully. "Are you sure about that? I always thought they were rather large in comparison to how small my breasts—I mean, my tits are."

"They are large," Clem agreed huskily, "and I love it." He released her hands and shifted down her body. "Now this here," he said, breathing heavily, "is your hairy pussy which I like very much indeed."

"Hairy pussy?" Theo echoed, screwing up her face. "No, I don't think I like that one. It sounds...rather silly."

"You don't like that one?" He ran his nose through her nether hair, making her squawk. "Lucky for you I have another term you might prefer."

"What is that?" Theo asked, squirming slightly.

"Pretty little cunt," Clem breathed out.

"Hmmm." She considered this. "That might be acceptable."

"Never in public though," he stressed once again, glancing up at her and making her roll her eyes.

"Clem, I am not *completely* socially inept," she started but then gave a squeal when he lowered his head to slide his tongue slowly through her cleft.

"How about this? Have you heard of this, Dora?" he asked richly, smacking his lips.

"Yes," she admitted shakily.

"When?" Clem was unable to stop himself from asking. He really wanted to know.

"In the play *The Taming of the Shrew*, there is this one exchange between Katherina and Petruchio—"

Oh. He cut off her words with another slow, rolling slide of his tongue, and he heard the slap of her hands over her mouth as Dora gave a muffled groan. "That's a good girl, Dora," Clem approved. "I like how nice and quiet you are. It raises certain…possibilities."

"What kind of possibilities?" she asked after a heartbeat, just as he knew she would.

Clem grinned against her mons. "Distinctly interesting ones," he promised and set about reducing her to a melted pool of bliss. Toward the end, when she could stand it no longer, her hand drifted down to sink into his hair.

After a minute of this, she tightened her fingers, and it was Clem's turn to hover perilously close to the edge. He had to stop, even though he had planned to take her all the way to orgasm again. Breathing heavily against her pubic hair, he squeezed his eyes shut until he'd regained control over himself.

He was reeling. What had got into him? He'd always prided himself he was a good lover, but he'd never taken so much gratification in his partner's pleasure before. Pleasing Dora gave him the biggest thrill. His heart was beating fit to bust out of his chest, and as for his cock, it felt about ready to explode.

"Dora," he groaned, crawling up her body, "I can't stand it any longer, sweetheart, I need to be inside you."

"Yes," she murmured, looking heavy-lidded and flushed.

Clem caught his breath looking at her. "This part will probably hurt."

She looped her arms about his neck. "You won't hurt me," she said with such confidence it made his chest throb.

"Not intentionally," he said. "But this is your first time, and I hear it's not so good for women. I don't have any experience with virgins, so…"

She bent her knees and gripped his waist with her legs. "I don't think I could be more ready at this point," she said with her customary frankness.

Clem swallowed and reached down to align their parts. "Wrap those long legs around my back, Dora," he instructed, lowering his mouth to her ear. "That's where I imagined them, the first time I saw you." He brushed a kiss against the shell of her ear as she absorbed this with a small gasp.

"How outrageous of you," she replied, the smile obvious in her voice, and he had to take her mouth again as he felt her heels dig into his back.

"This is what I wanted to do on our wedding night," he admitted, tearing his lips from hers as he began to surge into her. "Before you fell asleep on me."

Dora's eyes widened but she did not reply, and he was forced to make do with listening to her breathing as he slowly sank into her blissfully tight depths. He paused a couple of times, feeling her fingernails bite into his shoulders.

"Tell me if you need me to go slower," he urged, but she only shook her head.

"Dora…"

"All is well, Clem," she burst out. "You do not need to hold back."

He drew his head back to meet her gaze. Was she in earnest? "I need your hand at my neck," he confessed in a low voice that shook. When he had her hand there, he would know.

Instead of questioning this strange request, she shifted one hand across his shoulder, gripping him firmly about the back of his neck. Clem almost groaned aloud. Fuck, why did he like it so much? "Slacken your grip on me if it hurts." She nodded.

226

He started to make torturous progress again, but Dora's hand only clenched harder. "Stop teasing me, Clem," she said huskily. "Don't make me wait."

Fuck. His self-control snapped, and he thrust right into the heart of her, once, twice, and on the third he was all in. Dora gave a lusty moan and arched her back. *Holy fuck.* Clem felt himself start to tremble violently. *No, no, no!*

He gritted his teeth but could not prevent the overwhelming bliss of release. "Dora!" he groaned, crowding in on her. Instead of the embarrassment he should feel at such a performance, he felt only shock, satiation, and an overwhelming sense of rightness as he spilled into her. *"Dora!"*

To his unspeakable relief, he felt an answering thrill run through her body and then they were both coming apart in each other's arms. Clem had never felt anything like it. He dropped his head to her shoulder and groaned aloud through his release. He was vaguely aware he was a lot louder than Dora, whose gasps and whimpers he completely drowned out.

The first thing he became aware of in the aftermath was her hand falling away from his neck. He could not help a disapproving rumble at this, but Dora ignored him, pushing at his shoulder. "Clem," she murmured. "You're crushing me."

He had to actively fight his own disinclination to move; instead, he rolled them so Dora was now atop of him. It was only at this point that he consciously acknowledged they were still intimately joined.

"Fuck," he swore. "I didn't pull out."

Dora blinked down at him. "I have the device in though. It says it acts as a veil against your—um…" she searched her vocabulary.

"I know," he said hastily. "But even so…"

"We had better separate?" she enquired.

Clem could barely meet her eyes. *Jesus*, she was so… He clasped her hips and started to lift her off him even though it

227

was the last thing he felt like doing. Dora, catching on fast, swung her leg over his belly and started inching across the mattress. "Where are you going?"

"To remove the device," she explained, picking up the candle from her bedside table.

"Get behind the screen. I'll go and fetch warm water and a washcloth," he said, climbing from the bed. He should have thought of that before. Once his feet hit the floor, he realized his legs felt surprisingly unsteady.

"You don't have to," Dora called out as she disappeared behind the screen, but he ignored her, pulling on his long underwear. His body was still buzzing and relaxed. It was strangely hard to coordinate himself.

Walking through the cold house was a shock, and he wondered if he should buy a damn dressing gown, something he'd previously never considered. Making his way down to the scullery, he mercifully found plenty of warm water in the copper. Soon he was back in their room, handing her the bowl and staying respectfully on the other side of the screen. "The cloth's in there," he muttered. "Let me know if you want more water."

"This will suffice," she said cheerfully. "Get back into bed. I'll join you shortly." Clem hesitated. "I'm perfectly fine, Clem," she insisted. "There's no blood or anything, I checked."

"What about the device?" he asked, taking a steadying breath. "Did…did you get it out alright?"

"Of course! It really is quite an ingenious invention."

He breathed out. "Do you need your nightgown?"

"Clem," she gurgled with laughter. "Stop fussing!"

"I'll leave you to it, then." She murmured some response, and Clem made his way back to bed. He could not settle for the next few minutes until she emerged, still naked, and crossed the room to climb into the bed next to him.

He scanned her face to check she had spoken the truth and, finally satisfied, passed his arms around her, urging her closer to his chest. Dora snuggled into his side, and they lay in perfect silence a moment. "I don't want you to think I'm making a huge commotion, but I would like some reassurance that all is well with you," he confessed heavily.

She lifted her head. "Perfectly well, I assure you," she said and lightly patted his chest. A thoughtful look spread over her face. "I understand how things work now. Even the slow buildup makes perfect sense. I mean, you were making me ready, of course, but also because the main act is over with so quickly. I thought you were needlessly teasing me," she confessed. "But now I comprehend."

Clem tensed. When he finally managed to speak, even he could hear the strain in his voice. "It's—er—not usually over with that quickly," he admitted. "I was too…excited. Next time I will last longer."

"Oh" was Dora's only reply. She sounded politely skeptical.

Clem cleared his throat and tried to think of a convenient change of subject. "Tell me about this dirty play of yours" was the only thing that sprang to mind.

"What dirty play?" Dora shifted against him, sounding startled. Likely she had been dropping off to sleep, but Clem wanted to hear her voice. He did not care to examine why.

"The one with the cunnilingus in it."

"Oh, that." She gave a chuckle. "It wasn't dirty. It was Shakespeare. The one character makes a sort of rude jest about it, scandalizing the other. It's part of their wooing."

"Sounds interesting." He might not know what intimate speech they could have at this point, but he knew one way to get her talking. "You ever put any Shakespeare on at The Parthenon?" he asked casually.

She took the bait at once. "I *wish*," she responded with more energy, propping a hand under her chin. "But Shakespeare is considered risqué these days. Do you know that in recent years people have started cutting huge swathes out of his text to sanitize his plays for public consumption? I consider it practically a crime. Felix agrees. He says if we can't put on Shakespeare in its entirety then it is better to avoid it altogether."

"Seems a shame."

"Yes," Dora agreed sadly, "but if the play gained notoriety, then it would not make any money anyway and likely respectable folk would boycott us altogether."

Clem considered her serious expression. "Sometimes," he said slowly, "notoriety can have the opposite effect, you ever think of that?"

"The opposite effect?"

"Audiences may not be actively boycotting The Parthenon," he pointed out, "but they're not exactly flocking to pack out its seats either, are they?"

"No, that is quite true," Dora agreed. She considered him with a fascinated expression that made his heart stutter to a stop. What was she thinking? "So…your idea is that we could draw a different crowd altogether?" she asked, and he felt his spirits plummet a little. Plainly, Dora had been thinking of his business acumen. He would rather some of his other skills had put that expression on her face.

He nodded, clearing his throat. "Your respectable dentists and barristers are not exactly keeping the place afloat, are they? If your middle-class patrons strike you off their calling card, there's still the upper and lower classes to appeal to."

Dora's eyes gleamed. "And Shakespeare would be so perfect for that, Clem, especially his comedies," she enthused. "In his day, he catered to the nobility and the peasantry alike. His plays are full of low humor as well as more classical highbrow themes. His characters run the full gamut of humanity."

Clem only loosely followed what she was saying. He'd had a schooling, but it had not been a particularly good one. Shakespeare was a mystery to him. Still, he liked how it lit her face up to talk about it. "Maybe we should suggest it to your brother and Allsop," he suggested lightly.

Her face clouded over. "We could," she agreed without conviction, "but Felix is so cautious sometimes, and it's hard to sway him once his mind is made up."

For a moment, Clem considered telling her the truth about just how much of the theater was now in his greedy grasp. Then he recalled that Allsop also held a twenty-five percent interest and was likely too weak to stand up to Fields. That would make a fifty-percent split of the board on any decisions. For this reason and this reason alone, he put off telling her.

It was absolutely nothing to do with the blissful postcoital glow he was enjoying right now or the fact he was basking in Dora's unquestioning faith these days. Dismissing any disquieting thoughts or rumblings from his unusually active conscience, Clem simply looped an arm about her shoulders and drew her in closer.

It wasn't cuddling, he told himself firmly. It was just…married things. There was a lot more to marriage than he had ever realized, was his last thought as his eyes drifted shut. Dora sighed against his shoulder, and Clem felt his body finally relax into sleep.

18

Theo awoke refreshed and invigorated the following morning. She felt wonderful, though she undoubtedly needed a bath. She had overslept, and her husband's side of the bed was already empty. He had snuck off to The Eagle and Sun without her, she thought wryly.

Of course, probably he imagined he was being a considerate husband, letting her sleep in, she thought, reaching for her cotton nightdress which was looped over the headboard. She was just struggling into it when a knock on the door startled her.

"Who is it?" she called out, hastening to pull down the fabric to decently cover herself.

"It's me, Miss Theodora," returned Mrs. Cherwell.

"Oh! Come in."

The door opened, and Mrs. Cherwell's head peered round. "Just to let you know the bath's full now." Theo blinked at her. "Your 'usband said as how you wanted one this morning," she continued, seeing Theo's blank expression.

"Oh! Of course," Theo replied with haste, throwing her legs over the side of the bed. "My wits have gone a-begging this morning! Thank you so much."

She had a lovely long soak in the tub and a speedy wash of her short locks. She had a sneaking suspicion that Clem did not care for her short hair, but really, she could not bring herself to regret the somewhat drastic decision.

She loved it personally, and besides, there were other aspects of her person that Clem seemed very appreciative of, she consoled herself, glancing down at her body as she toweled herself off. She spent a few moments lost in contemplation of his extraordinary appreciation for her mediocre charms.

It was too chilly in the bathroom to continue mooning over her husband, so instead, she hurried downstairs to dress and then down to take her breakfast. This consisted of ham and eggs, tea, and toast. A small pile of letters and cards was sat on the table, and Theo quickly sifted through them, hoping to see a telegram or letter from Hetty.

To her disappointment, there was nothing from France. She did, however, get an appointment card from J. Finch & Sons Quality Tailor, citing a time that very afternoon. Theo's eyes widened. It was not much notice, and she would need an escort. She pondered this as she chewed her toast.

In the end, rather than disturbing Clem at his work, she decided to see if she could engage Vincent's services instead. He worked the door at the theater for the matinee and evening performances, but he should be free for her four-o'clock appointment with Charlie Finch.

It seemed an ideal solution to her dilemma, and she could see how he was coping after Henrietta's desertion. Carrying her half-full teacup upstairs, she spent an hour sorting through her wardrobe, which was overfull now it was shared, and haphazardly pulled out a few garments that she had never been pleased with or which were falling apart. Theo's dressmaking skills were far from top-notch, and nothing she made ever lasted past the six-month mark. This had never bothered her overmuch as she liked selecting new patterns and fabrics to experiment with.

Once she had collected an armful of clothes, she moved them into the sewing room and deposited them on a chair for future projects. Then she made her way back and carefully washed the two exquisite liqueur glasses Clem had bought and took them into the sitting room.

To her surprise, she found the case with four more of them and promptly unpacked them and placed all six in the glass-front cabinet. That was when the wallpaper samples caught her eye on the table. She moved over to examine them and felt herself grow a little light-headed. They were so pretty and so decadent!

She glanced about the room, trying to picture the rich blues and golds on the walls, but the respectable chintz of the existing wallpaper hampered her vision. No doubt some might think them a little on the garish side, but Theodora had never shrunk from boldness. Would Clem really have the sitting room papered in such fabulous material? She felt a pleasurable anticipation at the thought.

That was when the open sweet box caught her eye. Now, who had opened that? It must have been Clem, she decided, drawing it closer and sniffing the heady aroma of chocolate and cherries. She closed her eyes. They smelled divine. Would he mind if she sampled one? She did not think so. He was always so incredibly open-handed with her.

Reaching into the lavender tissue paper, she extracted a perfectly round bonbon of dark, glossy chocolate topped with attractive reddish flecks of crystallized fruit. Raising it to her lips, she took a bite and had to sink into a saggy sofa to enjoy the burst of decadent flavors. The filling was a whole cherry, steeped in brandy, and combined with the rich chocolate it was a heady experience. Goodness, it was good.

Theo slumped back in the seat with a happy sigh. Before she knew what she had done, she had eaten four of them! Staring guiltily at the hexagonal box decorated with birds, she stuffed down the tissue and slid the lid back on before tying the luxuriant ribbon. They must have cost a fortune and were no doubt for important visitors!

Hearing the grandfather clock strike from downstairs, she glanced up at the old clock on the mantel which always ran twenty minutes slow. After making an adjustment for time accuracy she fancied it was now about a quarter to one. She would need to set out for The Parthenon. Running downstairs, she told Mrs. Cherwell she was going out.

234

"You've not touched your lunch!" the other replied, elbow deep in floury dough.

"Lunch?"

Mrs. Cherwell sniffed. "I put it under a cover for you in the dining room."

"I am so sorry," a stricken Theo replied at once. "My timekeeping has been awful so far today and I had an appointment come up unexpectedly. Perhaps Mr. Allsop could...?"

"Huh!" the housekeeper responded. "I'm not making lunch for the likes of 'im!"

"To be honest, Mrs. Cherwell, I had not the smallest expectation that you would make it for me on a daily basis," Theo admitted. "You never used to."

"Things is different now," Mrs. Cherwell responded staunchly, kneading her dough with ferocity.

"Well, I am very sorry to have put you to the trouble for nothing."

"It weren't no trouble for you, as it 'appens," Mrs. Cherwell conceded, climbing down off her high horse.

Theodora was touched. "Well, that is very good of you. I shall be back before dinner, never fear."

"What am I to say to that 'usband of yours when 'e barges in my kitchen demanding to know where you are?"

"Oh, um..." Theo considered how best to reply without scandalizing the housekeeper. "Tell him...tell him I had an appointment come up with Charlie Finch."

Mrs. Cherwell's eyebrows shot up into her mobcap. "Oh yes," she said with a marked tone. "*That'll* go down a treat, no doubt."

Theo hesitated; the other woman's comment surprised her, but in truth, sometimes Clem did seem a little put out about the most unexpected things. "If he looks concerned, tell him that I have taken Vincent for an escort." She whirled around at that and hurried into the hall, grabbing her paletot and bonnet off the hat stand. Forty minutes later, she was passing through The Parthenon's grand colonnaded entrance.

No one was on the door, but as only a few desultory couples drifted out of it, Theo guessed the matinee performance must now be over. She wasn't even sure what they currently were staging, so divorced from proceedings had she been these past couple of months. She was a little surprised that Clem had not already demanded a tour; he had been keen indeed to get his hands on a share of the place.

Then again, he had been busy lately, what with moving abode, running his own booming business, and seducing her. She flushed and cleared her throat as she walked through the familiar foyer. No doubt he would make his presence there felt soon enough. No doubt also, her brother would blow up again, but she could not bring herself to worry overmuch about that.

They would settle it among themselves eventually, and she was no longer concerned about it escalating into a physical altercation. Not after Clem's amused reassurance on that score. She was jolted out of her thoughts by Felix hurrying toward her with a frown on his face.

"Theo, how can I help you?" he asked, greeting her in a lackluster fashion with a wary look in his eye.

She resented the implication that she had no right to be in a theater she owned a twenty-five percent share in, but let it pass for now. "I am looking for Vincent," she explained.

"Vincent?"

"Our doorman," she reminded him crisply.

"What the devil do you want with him?" her brother asked with a bewildered expression. That quickly turned into belligerence as an unpleasant thought occurred to him. "If you mean to try and poach him for Dabney's damned fleapit—" he began wrathfully.

"Nothing of the sort," Theo tutted. "What a nasty, suspicious mind you have, brother." Someone else had said that once. Probably Clem. She wholly supported the sentiment in this moment. "Besides"—she cast her eye over the practically empty foyer—"the matinee performance seems to be over, and he will be off the clock from now until this evening." Felix made a noise of unhappy agreement, still eyeing her as he would a coiled snake. "If you must know, I wish for him to escort me somewhere. You never had any objection before, so I fail to see why you should now."

Felix relaxed. "Ah," he said, his expression brightening. "Capital notion. Capital. Glad to see you are not letting proprieties slide now you—er—now you have someone else dictating your behavior. You'll find that Vincent fellow somewhere about, no doubt."

Theo eyed her brother coldly, then swept past him without another word. "Pompous prig," she muttered under her breath as she proceeded through to the back and into the rabbit warren that was the staff quarters. She knew Vincent's usual haunts well enough and found him without too much trouble in a small dimly lit room, polishing his shoes. "Hello, Vincent."

He started at the sound of her voice and wheeled around. Theo saw the hope rapidly drain from his face and realized he must have taken her for Hetty in that moment. She winced inwardly at inflicting such pain, even unintentionally. "How are you, old friend?" she asked, pretending not to notice his disappointment.

"Very well, Miss Theodora," he told her dully, clearly trying to pull himself together. "Been keeping busy."

"So have I," she chimed in briskly. "I have lately married, have you heard?"

He looked surprised. "No, I ain't—haven't heard anything," he corrected himself. "Who's the lucky fella?"

237

She beamed at him. "A Mr. Clement Dabney," she responded.

"You *what*?" Vincent looked thunderstruck. "Not the bleedin' prizefighter?" he choked out, bridling. "Why he ain't—he's not fit to wipe your boots, Miss Theodora, if you don't mind my saying so."

"Well, as a matter of fact, I do mind, Vincent. I mind very much."

Hot color bloomed across his gaunt cheeks. "I apologize if I gave offense," he said stiffly. "But I can't fink wot that bruvver of yours was about and that's the God's honest truth."

Theo noted with interest that when he became flustered, Vincent's cockney accent intensified. "Very well, I accept your apology," she assured him wholeheartedly. "Now I hope you will stand my friend, Vincent, even if you do disapprove of my choice of husband. I was hoping you would fall back on your old role of acting escort, for I find myself in need of one."

Vincent visibly pulled himself together. "Of course, Miss Theodora," he said swiftly. "Where we off to?"

"Shoreditch," she responded promptly. "To a tailor called J. Finch & Sons. I have a four-o'clock appointment."

Vincent seemed to struggle a moment with how to respond to this, but he made a valiant effort and kept his expression and voice blank in his answering, "Yes, miss."

"Should we set off now, for I would like to cover the distance on foot if possible?"

Vincent glanced at the wall and then reached for his coat which was hung up on a peg. "Soon as you like," he agreed.

They walked briskly and the air was so cold that, for a while, Theo was happy to keep silent beside the hulking doorman. When it became apparent that they would arrive in good time, she allowed her pace to slacken a little and ventured a glance up at Vincent's granite-like profile.

"Did Felix tell you we received a telegram from Hetty when she arrived in Calais?" she asked, knowing full well that her brother would not have passed on such information to Vincent in a million years.

Vincent swallowed. "He did not." His throat worked. "She was…well?" he asked hoarsely.

"It was only a few words," Theo admitted. "Just confirming she had landed safely and was bound for Paris. She promised to write again once she arrived there."

"And you ain't 'eard from 'er since that first telegram?" he asked, clearing his throat.

"Not yet," Theo admitted. His face twitched, but he said nothing. She averted her eyes to give him some privacy as he struggled to rein in his feelings.

"Fank you for tellin' me," he said quietly. "That's 'ansome of you. You always acted 'ansome toward me, Miss Theodora, and that's the truth. I know I ain't got no right to ask after Miss Henrietta."

"Nonsense, you have every right," Theo told him. "You are an old friend of Hetty and mine. Of course, I will let you know as soon as we hear she has reached Paris safely."

He swallowed convulsively and ducked his head. Theo judged it would be kinder to let the subject drop. Instead, she started to brightly explain the reason why she had an appointment at a gentleman's outfitters.

Vincent kept up his stoic silence, but she saw from the way he pressed his lips together he did not entirely approve. "You're plannin' on takin' to the stage at Dabney's establishment?" he asked finally in a blank tone.

"I am, Vincent. Have you ever visited The Eagle and Sun?"

He shook his head. "It ain't to my taste, miss."

If he was not such a rough-looking customer, Theo would have thought Vincent's expression almost prim. "You prefer something a little more highbrow?"

Vincent frowned at this. "How do you mean?"

"You prefer the entertainment at The Parthenon."

He shrugged. "To tell the truth, I can scarcely follow what's 'appenin' on stage most of the time."

"What *do* your tastes run to?" she asked curiously. "Sporting events?"

His gaze brightened. "Now you're talking, miss."

"Have you ever seen my husband box?" she asked.

He looked cagey. "Might have done."

Theo gave him a sidelong look. "That means yes, I gather."

"Couple of times maybe. I prefer the 'orses, miss," he admitted, "when I get the time."

"Ah, I *see*."

They had reached J. Finch & Sons by this time, so they entered the establishment and Charlie Finch hurried forward to lead her into the back room out of sight of any of the other customers. He had tacked together an approximation of her evening suit and day suit, and Theo spent the entire time patiently standing around in both while he adjusted pins and added chalk marks to each of the pieces.

Vincent remained on the other side of the curtain, though she could feel his heavy presence the entire time. From the monosyllabic answers the tailor gave to any comment she made, Theo realized he would rather work in silence, so she held her tongue for the most part and regarded herself thoughtfully in the mirror. Her outfits were taking shape, but it was hard to determine fully how they would look.

She would need to steal Felix's old shoes again and restuff the toes. Perhaps, too, she could borrow Uncle's pocket watch and a pair of Clem's cuff links for the finishing touches?

"All done," Charlie Finch told her, straightening up. "I'll send for you when it's time for the second fitting."

"Excellent, thank you so much, Mr. Finch."

He nodded and helped her ease out of the partially assembled clothes, then left her to dress again. When Theo emerged, Vincent was still standing sentry.

"I'm so sorry to have kept you waiting so long, Vincent," she said sincerely. "I genuinely did not realize what a lengthy process a suit fitting was."

"Don't mention it, miss. Anytime."

She glanced at the darkening sky as they exited the outfitters and exclaimed over the time. "We had better take a cab, I think, Vincent. Where is best to drop you? I forget where you said you lodged these days."

He shook his head. "I'll see you safely home, Miss Theodora."

He was as good as his word, but to Theo's distress would accept neither tip nor her insistence that she pay his cab fare home. "I want the walk to clear my head" was all he would say as he waved the driver off. "I've got a lot to mull over."

From his bleak expression, Theo could tell it was Henrietta he would be brooding over. Impulsively, she reached for his large hand and squeezed his fingers. "I will let you know as soon as we hear anything, Vincent, I promise."

He swallowed and made a gruff sound in his throat. The front door opened, and Theo turned her head to see Clem's silhouette in the doorway. She turned back to Vincent. "Thank you so much for today," she said, releasing his hand and suppressing the sudden surprising instinct to stand on her tiptoes and kiss his cheek.

She could have reached it, thanks to her height, but Vincent was a stickler for propriety and would likely be very shocked. Indeed, he looked a little red around the ears from her just taking his hand. "I will see you soon, Vincent," she promised.

"Good night, miss." Without acknowledging Clem, he took off into the encroaching darkness, and Theo watched after him a moment, listening to the sound of his retreating footsteps. She

241

hoped Vincent had friends or family he could talk frankly to about his broken heart. Being so closed off must make such feelings a terrible burden to bear.

Hearing footsteps behind her, she turned to find Clem advancing toward her down the path. "It's getting dark," he observed.

"Yes," Theo agreed. "I had no idea a fitting would take so long. My suits are coming along nicely." When he said nothing, Theo took a second look at his face. "Has something happened?" she asked.

"No," he answered coolly, "not that I'm aware."

She relaxed. Perhaps it was not surprising that her sister was uppermost on her mind, but her thoughts had immediately leaped to possible news of Henrietta.

It was only halfway through dinner that she noticed Clem's small talk was somewhat sparse. He was also sporting a rather foreboding frown. Wondering if something was amiss at the concert rooms, she decided to be an understanding spouse and not demand too much of him by way of conversation.

Instead, she turned to Harold and asked him how his latest composition was coming along. He seemed grateful for a listening ear and poured out the difficulties he was having with his current piece as Theo made sympathetic noises.

After dinner was done, Clem once again declined to join the others in the parlor and instead followed Theo up to their sitting room. "I think you need to introduce me to this Vincent of yours," he said as soon as the door was shut behind them.

Theo turned to look at him, for though his tone was entirely neutral, every instinct within her tingled a warning. It was the oddest thing, and she frowned as he crossed the room to the cabinet and began pouring them drinks. He *sounded* relaxed, but somehow, she was not deceived. She needed to proceed with caution here. "He is not really my Vincent," she said carefully. "He is an old friend of the family."

"Funny, your brother does not speak of him as a friend" was his rather clipped response as he set the bottle back on the shelf.

His back was to her, but Theo took in the line of his tense shoulders with alarm. "Perhaps not. I suppose his relationship to Felix is more businesslike. Whereas with my sister and I..." she started, then tried a different approach when Clem did not immediately turn to face her but stood still with his back to her.

"In truth," she said with perfect frankness, "he belongs to Hetty, in both body and soul. I am concerned about him," she continued. "I think he is torn up inside about her disappearance."

Clem breathed out and turned with their glasses, moving toward her. This time he was carrying finely etched brandy glasses. "Your sister made her choice," he pointed out, placing their glasses on the table and sitting down beside her. "There is precious little you can do about that."

"I know," she sighed, "but I vastly prefer Vincent to Sir Matthew Hillingdon."

Clem gave a short laugh. "Vincent was never in the running with your sister, and you know it. She's a proud, haughty piece. I doubt she ever saw him as anything but her lackey."

Theo regarded him with surprise. "You made a quick appraisal of my sister's character from one brief meeting," she said with a brief frown.

Clem leaned forward to pick up his drink and took a swig before answering her. "I usually weigh people up pretty quickly."

"You must do," she said slowly, still scanning his face. Was it merely her imagination or did he look a little evasive?

Clem turned to face her. For a minute he said nothing, just regarded her so seriously that she started to feel alarmed. Then he leaned toward her. "I need you to introduce me as your husband to your friend Vincent, Dora," he said silkily. "Is that going to be a problem?"

"Of course not!" she responded swiftly. "I told him about you. I'm sorry; I should have introduced you just now, but— well, he was not at his best and it did not feel right to—"

"Next time, then," Clem said, cutting through her excuses.

"Yes," she agreed. "Yes, next time I will." He gave a nod and then drained his glass. "Clem," she said, shifting closer to him on the sofa. "Please don't be angry with me."

"I'm not angry."

She did not entirely believe him. Or if it was not anger, then it was something else not entirely dissimilar in nature. Her chest ached with the strangest pang. Suddenly, it was imperative for her to put an end to this strange gulf dividing them.

Theo could not have said why, but letting her tingling instincts guide her, she reached up to place her hand at the back of his neck. He nearly jumped out of his skin. He was sensitive there. "Clem?" she whispered.

When he would not turn his head to look at her, she tugged him there, lightly at first and then with increasing urgency, leaning right into him until he followed her promptings and turned his head so she could press her lips to his.

It was the first time she had initiated anything physical between them, and feeling his resistance weaken, Theo swept her tongue across his bottom lip. After a moment, Clem parted his lips in silent invitation, and Theo claimed his mouth with a boldness that shocked even her.

Clem groaned, and suddenly his hand was in her hair, wrenching out the hair comb that held her false ringlet in place and flinging it over the back of the couch. Then his fingers were back, massaging her scalp and tugging lightly at her hair as he took control of the kiss.

244

Theo allowed him his turn and then went back on the attack, pushing at his chest. She wanted to do the rolling around thing. She had enjoyed the push and pull of that last time. "Not here," Clem whispered against her lips, but there was absolutely no conviction to his words. Theo knew full well she had not the strength to topple him, and he now lay flat against the sofa cushions which showed he was complicit.

"Why not?" she asked, leaning down and nipping at his bottom lip, and making him gasp.

"Because…" Theo paused a moment when his words led nowhere, waiting for his reason. He huffed out a breath. "Sit astride me," he said in a sudden change of heart, his hands settling on her hips to urge her up onto his body. Having no objection, she dragged at her skirts to facilitate the change in position and swung a leg over him, settling over his hips.

Clem gazed up at her, his eyes heavy-lidded. "Kiss me again, Dorabelle," he practically begged her.

Her heart beating wildly, Theo leaned down over him and did just that. Being in charge of their kiss gave her a heady thrill, and she did not hesitate to capitalize on Clem's weakness, sliding one hand to the back of his neck. He groaned into her mouth, and she would have smiled if her lips were not already occupied in kissing him.

Whenever he tried to reexert himself, she squeezed at his neck, and he would shudder and turn passive beneath her. Theo loved it. She tried all the varieties of kisses she could think of—fast, slow, shallow, deep; Clem's hitched breathing assured her he was enjoying her creative experimentation.

At some point, his hands slid down from her hips to grip her backside, and he started moving his hips against hers in a slow grind. Theo's eyes flew wide. It felt wonderful. She wanted to hitch her skirts up further, to feel him there, but Clem's tight grasp would not allow her room to maneuver. Finally, Theo jerked her head back. "Clem," she panted.

"Yes, love?" His gaze was fixed on her mouth, his eyes glazed with desire.

"Shall I get it out?" At his blank look, she whispered, "Your cock, I mean."

His breathing hitched, and then he let out a shaky moan. "*Jesus*, Dora..."

She bit her lip. "I need to touch myself," she confessed shakily. "I'll *burst* if I don't."

His gaze caught fire, and for a moment his reply seemed to hang in the balance. "We need to take it to the bedroom," he groaned at last. "If I can walk."

"I suppose," she agreed, huffing out a breath.

He released his death grip on her hips and lightly pinched her bottom lip. "Don't pout."

Theo laughed weakly and crawled off him, stumbling a little when she got her feet to the floor. Clem reached out a steadying hand as he maneuvered himself off the couch. "Walk in front of me," he ordered, straightening up and settling a hand on her shoulder. She could only suppose this was for decency's sake as his disarray was evident.

As there were only a few steps from the sitting room to their bedroom, she thought his modesty was a little excessive. As soon as they reached the bedroom, Clem pointed to the screens. "Preventative," he reminded her, and Theo gave a start. She had not thought of it even once! Thank goodness her husband had his wits about him, she thought gratefully as she made haste to grab the little box and duck behind the screen.

When she emerged minutes later, she found Clem had already stripped down and was stood, hands on hips, waiting for her. He was still very aroused, she thought, looking at the bulge in his long underwear. She suddenly realized *that* was why he had been so determined she had to walk in front of him. It had been nothing to do with his ruffled hair and crumpled neckcloth.

With men, poor things, clearly a state of arousal was far more difficult to hide than women. She did rethink this a little as she caught sight of herself in the oval mirror hanging on the wall above her dresser. Her overbright eyes, hectically flushed cheeks, and red puffy lips entirely gave the game away.

Goodness, she looked most unlike herself, almost pretty, she thought dazedly, stripping down to her undergarments. It struck her that maybe that was why women wore cosmetics. Lil lavishly rouged her cheeks and darkened her lips before she took to the stage. Maybe she should try it sometime?

When Clem caught hold of her from behind and jostled her forward against the dresser, it occurred to her that she had tarried too long, and she gave a breathless laugh as he leaned his chest against her back, shoving her forward onto the dresser top. He kissed and nuzzled at her nape, lightly grazing his teeth there.

"Clem?" she murmured when his warm hand slid under her chemise to caress her belly.

"Rest your arms on the dresser," he advised.

"But your things," she objected, eyeing his expensive cologne and various other items.

"Do it; I don't give a fuck."

Feeling his hand dip down into her drawers, Theo took a deep breath and rested her forearms against the top of the dresser, nudging his combs and brushes out of the way. She exhaled noisily when he lodged his fingers inside her. She was so wet she could hear it, and Theo caught her breath in her throat. "Clem," she whimpered.

"Fuck, Dora," Clem groaned. "You're so wet, sweetheart." His thumb nudged her pearl, and she yelped before she could stop herself. Clem made a rumbling noise in his chest, and Theo met his eyes in the mirror. It was a mistake, looking at his face, for immediately Theo felt her legs start to tremble.

"Now you'll have to promise me that once I work my way into your tight little pussy, you're not gonna come straightaway," he cautioned. Theodora caught a whine in her throat. She really couldn't promise that. His eyes met hers with a glimmer of deep amusement. "Promise me, Dora, or I'm not giving you all this dick. Tell me you want it."

Her mind reeled at his crude words. Usually, he was much more guarded around her, but for some reason, she felt out of breath with desire. "Please, Clem!" she burst out.

"Good girl," he praised her richly. "So needy and I know just what will make it all better." He shoved down his long underwear and took out his long, thick cock. It curved up from his thick thighs, hard and insistent looking. Theo swallowed.

"Clem," she breathed. "Shouldn't we—?"

"Widen your legs," he said, stepping between them and wrenching her drawers down over her bottom and down to her knees. Lifting her hips like she weighed nothing, he settled the blunt head of his cock at her weeping cleft. Theodora's eyes locked on his as he lowered her down on him, forging through her folds, breaching her, and opening her up as she sank down onto his hard length. He bit his lip and his eyes fluttered closed as she took his every last inch. "Aw fuck, Dora," he whispered. "You've swallowed me whole. You're so fucking tight and wet."

Speech was beyond her at this point, but she could already feel herself start to flutter and clench around him. "Oh! Clem!" she gasped, arching into him. "I can't—! I can't stop."

His eyes sprang open, and his hands slid down to grasp her buttocks and squeeze her tight. "Bad girl," he growled appreciatively. "Coming already. Now, didn't you promise me you would wait?"

"Uhhhh, Clem!"

248

"And coming so hard too," he grunted, seizing her hips and jolting her against him. "Such a naughty little pussy. Don't you know what happens to girls who break their promises?"

Theo's fingers scrabbled at the dresser, but there was nothing to hold on to. She was suddenly terrified he would withdraw before she reached fulfillment. "Please, Clem," she shuddered. "I can't help it." He laughed low and wicked in her ear, his big hands still roaming over her backside and hips, squeezing and fondling her there.

"That's okay, Dora," he said soothingly. "I'll let you take what you need, but afterward you have to suffer the consequences." Theo nearly wept with relief. She pushed back against him as he murmured encouragement. At last, he placed his hand between her shoulder blades and pushed her down on the wooden surface, giving her a hard buck of his hips. Theo screamed and came so hard black spots appeared before her eyes.

She resurfaced moments later with her cheek still resting on the dresser. He was still hard and impaled inside her. She lifted her flushed face to meet his eyes in the mirror.

"All better?" he rumbled. His eyes were on fire with lust. *Oh God*, thought Theo. *I feel wrung out like a dishrag!* As if aware of her thoughts, he grinned at her wolfishly. "Now it's my turn, Dora."

"Clem," she said weakly. "I don't know if I have the strength to hold myself up."

"That's not something you need to worry about, my darling," he assured her huskily and shoved her forward again onto the dresser, and Theo gasped as several items were dislodged and bounced on the carpet below. Now she was fully bent over, the balls of her feet only just touching the floor.

"Open your eyes. I want you to watch yourself in the mirror."

Theo whimpered as she opened her eyes. Instead of her own reflection, she immediately sought out Clem's. "I said watch yourself," he repeated. She had just managed to drag her eyes back to her own face when he asked, "Ready for me, Dora?" She nodded, unable to form words in the moment. "Say it."

"Yes," she breathed out, and he surged forward again, letting her have it. Theo gave a low moan, and pushed back, encouraging his entry. Clem bit off a curse and slowly retreated again before surging forward with such strength that the dresser jolted beneath her, the wood surface biting into the tops of her thighs.

She could not bring herself to care in the moment, but Clem caught her hips and dragged her back onto his cock until her lower belly rested more comfortably on the edge. Theo ventured a quick glance at his face. His eyes were closed and his expression rapturous.

She knew he wanted her to watch herself, but she could not bring herself to tear her eyes away. His eyes fluttered open, and seeing the expression in them, Theo felt something tighten in her breast. *My God, he is so beautiful.* "You like watching me, Dora?" he asked softly.

"Yes."

At her words, his lips quirked up. "Well, then that's a fair exchange, as I certainly like watching you." They gazed at one another wordlessly for a minute, then Clem asked throatily. "Can you reach up and pull down your chemise for me, Dorabelle? I want to see those pretty tits of yours."

Theo went up onto her elbows again and reached up to tug loose the simple ribbon at her neckline; she drew down her chemise, so her shoulders were bared.

"A little more," Clem encouraged huskily. It was a good thing she wore them loose, she thought as she took hold of the fabric and yanked it down to her waist, baring her breasts. She

250

heard Clem catch his breath. "Ah, Dora," he groaned, moving his hands from her hips to grasp the edge of the dresser. Luckily, the hard press of his hips behind her bottom kept her pinned in place. "Dora, Dora, what am I going to do with you?"

"I think it's pretty obvious what you're about to do with me," she answered with a flicker of spirit.

"Oh yes, tell me, then," Clem said, his gaze scorching in the mirror.

"You're about to—well, spill inside me."

"Christ, I hope not. At least not yet. Last time was…" He winced. "Let's just say I was taken off guard."

"Taken off guard?"

He made a sound of agreement in his throat. "Whereas this time, I'm prepared for the tight perfection of your wet little pussy."

Theo frowned and opened her mouth to remind him of her preferred word, but the sudden thrust of his hips cut her off. "*Oh!*"

"You like that?" Clem asked, then thrust again.

"Oh." Theo closed her eyes and concentrated on the strange feeling. "Um…"

"Tell me you like it, Dora."

Theo was too busy at that moment shifting her forearms in an attempt to stabilize herself. Accidentally she dislodged a clothes brush, made a grab for it, but the blessed thing slipped through her fingers and fell to the floor.

"Leave it," Clem grunted. "Tell me you like it, Dora," he insisted.

Her breathing caught, then she let out a whimper. "I like it," she whispered, but clearly that wasn't enough.

"How much?" he urged. "Tell me." This clearly threw her for a moment. She jostled against him as she lost their rhythm, and he had to catch hold of her hips to get her back on course.

251

"Don't stop moving," he grunted. "Don't overthink it, just say what comes to mind."

"A-as much as champagne cocktails," she uttered breathlessly. "It's…it's much nicer, even than the grand saloon in Wards. *Oh!*"

He was starting to move his hips in earnest now, and everything on the dresser was starting to jump and shake. All of Clem's fancy jewelry boxes containing his cuff links and flashy tie pins were raining down onto the floor. For some reason, it was making Theo feel quite frantic.

"Clem, oh, *Clem!*" Theo panted, trying to move against him, but by this point, the hard slam of his hips prevented her from doing anything other than take the pounding he was giving her. And really, she was fine with that, though when the dresser started slamming against the wall, she knew a moment's panic her sister might wonder what on earth was going on. Then she remembered Henrietta was in France and gave herself up to the sensation of being so ruthlessly taken.

She was going to reach it again, she realized in amazement. It was meant to be Clem's turn for pleasure, but she was going to reap a second reward.

"Dora?" Clem's voice was harsh. "Are you close?"

"Yes," she panted. "I'm close, so, so close."

He lifted her slightly and slid his hand between the dresser and her stomach, working his way down between her legs.

As soon as she felt his fingers slide over her clitoris, she was *there*. Her vision swam, her arms gave out, and she collapsed forward, inadvertently sending a bunch more things flying as she cried out.

"Unghhhh, *Dora!*" Clem roared, collapsing over her, his breath hot against the back of her neck as he gasped for breath, his chest heaving. Theo lay slumped as she drifted gently down from the clouds. "Holy hell," Clem murmured, then after a moment, "Did I crush you?"

"No," Theo murmured, her eyes still closed. He said something else, but Theo was too content to listen. The next thing she knew she was being scooped up and carried over to the bed. She murmured discontentedly at being disturbed, but Clem ignored her, dragging off her drawers and laying her gently down on the bed and running his hands over her hips and pelvis.

"There's red marks here," he said regretfully. "Dora," he said more insistently. "Does it hurt anywhere?"

"Yes," she said irritably. "My ears!"

She heard him snort, then murmur, "Little wretch."

Then he disappeared again, and she wasn't sure how much later she felt him wiping between her legs with a damp cloth. She complained but he took no notice, other than murmuring, "Let me take care of you." She relapsed into silence, then felt him shake her. "Dora, you should probably take that thing out."

"What thing?" she grumbled, not even opening her eyes.

"The preventative."

"You do it," she said, opening her legs, and was met with nothing but a sharply indrawn breath. She opened her bleary eyes, feeling incredulous. "Do not tell me you are squeamish, Clem Dabney?"

When he did not move, she started to struggle upright, but his hand on her shoulder prevented her. "If you're really sure this is acceptable," he said uncertainly. It was Theo's turn to snort, and she did so, shutting her eyes again. There was a tug down below and then the cloth was back between her legs.

Hearing him move around the room and water being poured into a bowl, she drifted back into a peaceful doze until he climbed onto the bed and curled around her. This was a good deal more acceptable, and Theo relaxed into him as he covered them in bedclothes. She did not wake again for hours and hours, and when she did so, she found Clem had left the preventative in a bowl to soak and replaced all the items on the dresser.

19

Clem could not settle to a damn thing at the office the next day. His mind kept wandering back to the extraordinary woman he had married. She really whipped the rug out from under his feet the previous night. Well, if he was truthful, it was not just last night and not just in the bedroom either but practically every area of their life together.

It was annoying that her unconventional ways had such an effect on shaking him. He was hardly a model of respectability, far from it, but it was a good thing he was not easily shocked, for he was dimly aware that Theo's stance on most things went against society's strictures.

He was starting not to care so much about her graceless style of dress. In fact, there were distinct advantages that her underwear was so unstructured. What lay under her strange gowns more than made up for her peculiar choice of outfit.

As for her hair… Clem pondered this. He was starting to feel quite strange about the nape of her neck. He had never found that part of the female anatomy particularly attractive, but Dora's was extremely distracting. He had even found himself staring at it as he had her bent over that dresser and was frankly spoiled for choice where it came to places to look.

Christ, that dresser…

"Clem?" Jim's voice had him practically jumping in his seat. "You didn't answer when I knocked on the door," his friend and employee said, still hovering in the doorway.

Clem pulled himself together and motioned for him to enter. Jim launched into a bunch of things he wanted Clem's say-so about, and Clem gave him half his attention, nodding and responding with a yea or a nay as the case necessitated, his pen scratching away all the while on the paper.

"Didn't know you was an artist, Clem," Jim said finally, clearing his throat.

"What?" Clem looked up in bewilderment.

"Your picture," said Jim, motioning toward Clem's ledger.

Clem glanced down and, to his utmost astonishment, saw he had been drawing Theodora's shapely neck. *What the fuck?* He felt the heat rise to his face and had to resist the temptation to slam his book shut. Instead, he managed to preserve some dignity and responded, "I—er—was always considered pretty fair at drawing at school."

Jim nodded, still eyeing the page, and Clem's fingers twitched to snatch it out of view. "You should get her to pose for you."

"Who?"

Jim gave him an odd look. "Your wife, of course. That's who it is, isn't it? Plain to see."

Clem's collar felt too tight. *Fucking Jim.* When had he ever been so chatty? "Yes, well…" he said dismissively.

"Which changing room's gonna be 'ers?" Jim asked.

Clem drummed his fingers against the table. "She hasn't even got a date yet for her debut," he pointed out cuttingly. "Don't you think you're trying to put the cart before the horse?"

"Well, she was asking me about some props she wanted—" Jim began, and Clem started up from his seat. Talk of Dora's stage debut always made him damnably uneasy these days.

"Just give her the keys to the storerooms and let her poke around in there to her heart's content next time she's in," he snapped. "She's sure to find something," he added. "She's easily pleased." For some reason, his throat closed on these last few words, and he had to turn his head aside.

"You alright, boss?" Jim asked, sounding alarmed.

Clem nodded. "Just need some fresh air," he said shortly, snatching up his jacket. "If anyone wants me, I'll be back in an hour."

255

He had walked ten minutes in the bracing March air before he even realized where he was headed. Once he had reached the outfitter's establishment, he let himself in and scanned the busy room for Charlie Finch. Spotting Clem, the tailor came forward with surprise. "Wasn't expecting you," he said.

"What the hell do you mean by sending for my wife at such short notice, Finch?" Clem started coldly. "And in regular hours too. Thought that was absolutely something you could never accommodate at J. Finch & Sons when I set up the initial appointment."

Charlie shot a quick assessing look at him and led him through to the back room. "I did apologize to your missus," he said placatingly, "but knowing how keen she was to get the suits back…when I had a vacant spot come up, I thought—"

"Well, you thought wrong, damn you!" Clem burst out. "As it happens, I do not care for my wife having to be squired about by all and sundry, and I certainly do not care to have her visiting a gentleman's tailor unless it's on my arm, am I understood?"

Charlie nodded, looking a little pale and nervous. "As it 'appens you don't need to worry," he said, licking his lips. "That other fella was nearly as bad as you, looming on the other side of the curtain."

That did not make Clem feel better, something Charlie seemed to pick up on almost at once. He swallowed and lapsed into an awkward silence.

"Was she pleased with them?" Clem asked after a moment, his voice surly.

"Couldn't have been happier, though I don't fink she really has much of a clue how a suit's put together, like."

Clem grunted. "Very likely."

"You thought to get her any shoes, guv?" the tailor asked.

"Shoes?"

256

Finch shrugged. "Only she mentioned stealing her brother's old pair and stuffing the toes wiv newspaper. Be a crime that would, to team up a new suit, let alone a morning suit, wiv an old pair wot don't fit even fit 'er."

Clem considered this. "No, I had not thought of that," he said slowly. "By the way, what do I owe you?"

Charlie took him out front, and Clem paid the running balance and left the shop in a slightly better mood. He could not buy dress shoes at once, for he had no clue of her shoe size, but he would see to that later. There was plenty of time before Dora's ill-fated debut. If he could help it anyway.

After the first week, Clem fancied he was starting to get the measure of things at the house on Juniper Row. It was a household full of eccentrics, he realized. The four-story townhouse was well appointed but largely neglected. There had been money at one point, from what he could gather, their late uncle had bought the place with the insurance payout from their parents' deaths. That was probably the plumpest in pocket the old man had ever been, especially since he started sinking everything into The Parthenon.

Presumably, that short period of affluence was when Uncle Barnabus had paid for the wallpapers, rugs, and curtains, which, though now showing signs of wear, were of undeniably good quality. Likely the fancier pieces of the furniture too, though they were about fifty years out of fashion. These were mostly found in the front parlor or in the dining room, whereas other parts of the house were threadbare and sparsely furnished.

Her idiot brother and Allsop barely seemed to notice the freezing cold house or how rude their housekeeper frequently was to them. So long as they did not have to order the coal or prepare the food, they seemed willing to put up with all manner of discomfort. Sure, they would grumble, but then turn a blind eye from what Clem could make out.

At mealtimes, the other occupants of number six barely seemed to concentrate on eating at all. Now the formalities were done with, and his presence accepted, books were brought to table and pen and paper for sudden inspiration. Allsop's fingers sometimes ran absently over the edge of the table as if his fingers were playing notes. Fields wore a velvet smoking jacket and read extracts loudly from whatever play he was reading at the time, underlining passages with significant looks or a "Hah!" or a "You'll like this one" and then he would launch into a recitation and everyone would listen attentively.

Dora clearly found nothing amiss with this behavior, and Clem suspected that, before his installation, she must have behaved in a similar manner, perhaps planning her next bizarre outfit or cutting out pattern pieces between courses.

If a bowl of apples was laid out on the table in the parlor, they would eat them one after the other, but for the most part, Clem fancied they only seemed to notice their hunger when there were means of assuaging it at hand. Once the initial awkwardness of his arrival was out of the way, everyone seemed to accept him readily enough as a fixture in the house.

Mrs. Cherwell was the only one who seemed to continue regarding him through suspicious eyes whenever she thought he was not attending, but as she frequently snubbed both Fields and Allsop altogether, Clem was not so sure he had cause for complaint.

She made so many sarcastic and pointed comments about "hoping folks would be satisfied with her poor efforts" while thumping down dishes that Clem started to wonder if that was why his brother-in-law and Harold Allsop hid behind their books at table. He was half tempted to bring his own, though he was no reader by habit.

To Dora, Mrs. Cherwell could not be more attentive. Ignoring her married status, she addressed her exclusively as "Miss Theodora" and sought her approval alone in household matters. She reinstated the delivery of coal every Tuesday and the baker, the butcher, and many others besides. She also kept a tolerably well-stocked pantry, so Clem found that other than supplying a purse of monies for this purpose, he was not obligated to do anything else.

He contented himself instead with buying treats to tempt Dora with and setting them strategically either in their bedroom or in their sitting room. He watched her carefully to see which way her tastes ran, and it seemed to him that she had a decidedly sweet tooth.

If she did not like something, a brief expression of displeasure would pass over her face, then her expression would turn carefully blank, and she would cautiously eat it anyway. If she liked something, she would sit up, examine the label, and then carefully ration herself to make it last. He started to wonder if their uncle indulged them when in funds but otherwise stinted them on luxuries.

Clem glanced over at the sofa a couple of evenings later, where Theo was lying wrapped in a ratty old velvet dressing gown and a pair of knitted socks that looked like rotting cabbage leaves. She had also, to his distraction, carried on taking out her false ringlets whenever it was just the two of them alone and his strange preoccupation with her shorn head and neck still persisted.

He could not tear his eyes away from the pale column of her throat, rising out of the strange bronze robe she wore, the way her dark hair waved away from her brow. He wanted to draw her all of a sudden. It was an old hobby and one he had not indulged in for years. Not since he had left school. His fingers itched to commit those features to paper.

To Clem's irritation, she barely seemed to notice his frequent gazes. She was too busy scribbling away in her damned notebook with a dreamy look in her eye. He had a nasty suspicion it was new lines for her turn, the date of which they had still not negotiated.

Partly to distract himself and partly to drag her away from her fruitless occupation, he stated, "Those are the most hideous socks I have had the misfortune to lay eyes on."

"They are extremely warm though," Dora said, glancing down at them, as if unsure which socks he was maligning.

Clem sent her a withering look. "Should I add more coal to the fire?" This was nonsense, as the fire was a roaring blaze, and after glancing at it and then back at him, Dora reached down and slipped off her socks.

"I shall take them off if they offend you so much," she offered with a small smile. She had beautiful feet with a lovely arch to them; her toes tapered off to show well-shaped nails of perfect proportion. Stuffing such feet into those ugly socks was practically a crime, he decided.

Theo gave a sudden exclamation, and he looked up from her feet to her face questioningly. She was gazing down at the box of cherries dipped in brandy and dark chocolate with a horror-stricken look on her face. "Clem, I've eaten a whole tier of your fancy sweets!" she blurted out guiltily. "I'm so sorry; I will be sure to replace them the first chance I get—"

He shrugged. "I bought them for you."

"For me?" She sat up, blinking, a rosy color filling her face. "Did you really?" Her voice was husky with surprise, and it made parts of him perk up that had no business doing so. He watched the stunned expression on her face as her eyes pored over the fancy box embellished with lavender ribbon.

You would almost think no one had ever thought to buy her a box of sweets before. The realization made his breath catch in his throat as he watched her carefully lift the box to her chest and press it there, as though embracing it.

"Can I keep the box?" she asked, still in a hushed manner.

"You can do whatever you like with it," he answered. "It's yours."

Carefully she replaced the lid and carried it over to the display case, placing it in a position of prominence before returning to the sofa, walking backward so she could keep her eyes trained on it as she sank back onto her seat.

Clem watched her with a faint frown on his face. "Aren't you going to eat the rest?" he asked.

"Oh no! I shall savor them. Just one or two per evening to make them last."

"Why?" He shrugged. "There's four more boxes in the cupboard, and I shall buy you some more soon enough."

Theo's head whipped around, and she stared at him. "You will buy me some more?" she repeated.

"Yes."

His reply seemed to astonish her, before she decided he was joking with her. She gave a chuckle and shook her head. For the rest of the night, her eyes kept returning to the box in dazed gratification. Should he have presented them to her as a gift? Clem wondered.

She might have liked to open the box herself. On further reflection though, he decided she would probably never have opened them in the first place. No, he had better carry on opening them himself and setting them where they would catch her eye.

"When are you going to take me to your theater for a tour?" he asked abruptly.

Dora almost dropped her notebook. "Whenever you like," she answered at once, sitting up in her seat. "I think Felix said they were currently staging *The Duchess of Malfi*. It's a Jacobean tragedy."

Clem shrugged. One more play was as good as another in his view, and they fixed on the following evening. When the time came, to his surprise, Clem did not feel one bit of the

261

triumph he had thought he would on viewing The Parthenon through the eyes of a fifty-percent shareholder.

He finally got his introduction to Vincent, it was true, and both of them looked the other up and down as though sizing an opponent. There was a definite gleam of hostility in the other man's eye, and it belatedly occurred to Clem that at least part of the reason for that might be Henrietta Fields's secret visit to his office shortly before her elopement.

This man had accompanied her on that day, though he had not been privy to their business discussion. He guessed from what Dora had told him that Vincent would never betray her sister by telling this to Dora, but all the same, it caused Clem a moment's unease as he returned Vincent's steady, cold gaze.

"Vincent can seem a little unfriendly on first acquaintance, but when you get to know him, you soon realize that is not the case."

Clem merely grunted and busied himself glancing about the empty front of house. The place was like a mausoleum, he thought scathingly as they proceeded through, arm in arm.

"I see what you mean now about The Eagle being alive," Clem murmured in Dora's ear. "This place is dead."

"Yes," Dora agreed sadly. "It is, isn't it?"

After showing him the offices, plush though faded like everything else about The Parthenon, Dora led him up the stairs to the circle and one of the fancy private boxes which still looked quite grand in the dimmed lighting. From what Clem could tell, only one other box was occupied of the eight that were available.

The curtain was drawn up and the players began to tell their tale, and a damned dismal tale it was too. Clem folded his arms and leaned back in his seat, preparing himself for a trying evening. He thought he managed to follow it for the most part, but Lord, what a lot of fuss about nothing!

262

He could understand avarice as well as any man, but why two brothers should cut up rough about their sister marrying, even if it was beneath her, was beyond him. "This play is even worse than that dull shepherd piece I saw you in," he hissed. Dora winced. "Explain to me why this tragedy is more acceptable than that Shakespeare you spoke of?"

Dora leaned into him. "Webster's humor is dark, but never lewd," she whispered back.

"So, two brothers plotting against their sister is perfectly acceptable, but a bit of crude humor is beyond the pale?"

"Precisely," she answered him, straight-faced.

Clem shook his head and rolled his eyes up to the decorated ceiling. He owned half that ceiling, he reflected, examining his feelings, but no, he did not feel even a glimmer of satisfaction about that fact.

When the curtain fell on the first act, he let out a sigh of relief. "I suppose a drink is out of the question," he said without much hope.

"We are not licensed to serve alcohol," Dora said apologetically. "None of the theaters are to my knowledge."

"No one would see us in this box," he pointed out, glancing around.

"But where would you get it?"

"Depends on how long the interval lasts."

"A quarter of an hour."

He stood up. "Do not stir a step."

"Clem, are you really—?" But he had already ducked out.

He had to run into only three establishments before he could procure what he wanted, and Vincent's eyes did not so much as flicker when Clem passed him with a nod, carrying a champagne bottle and two glasses.

He lightly ran up the stairs and was back in his seat in the box just as the curtain was raised. He brandished the bottle and Dora laughed. "You said you'd find some."

"By hook or by crook," he agreed, popping the cork. Dora looked around at that, wide-eyed with alarm, but Clem could not bring himself to care about the few turned heads. "Tell me this at least has a happy ending," he murmured, passing her a glass.

Dora screwed up her face. "I'm guessing you have not much experience with Jacobean tragedy."

"None."

"It does not end happily for anyone," she admitted. Clem groaned. Dora placed down her glass carefully. "Clem, shall we go and tour the back instead? I was thinking while you were gone, and you have already sat through one play here, so this isn't exactly treading new ground for you—"

"No, I have no interest in seeing a bunch of dressing rooms and storage rooms," Clem interjected smoothly. "You can alleviate my sufferings some other way."

"Alleviate your sufferings?"

"For my ordeal." Dora regarded him in bafflement as he drained his glass. "Drink your champagne," he recommended.

She took another sip. "It might help if you gave me a clue how I might do such a thing."

Clem considered. "Why don't you let down one of the curtains," he suggested, "and give us some privacy."

Dora glanced up at the fancy fringed curtains suspended above the box. They were tied up with gold tasseled ropes. Casting a quick glance at him, she tugged one loose and caught the curtain as it swooped down. "And now?"

"Now come and perch on my knee, Mrs. Dabney. I've an idea you might make this next hour more bearable for me."

"I would just like to point out," she said archly as she slid across into his lap, "that this is highly disrespectful of the actors below."

"Hmm, I daresay. Do you know any of them?"

"I know Lance Pevensey," she whispered back. "He plays the Cardinal. Oh, and Lionel Greenf—"

As he chose that moment to claim her lips, Dora promptly abandoned her recitation of cast members.

"And in any case," Clem said, just a trifle unsteadily as he drew back his head after a minute or so, "you should get used to it. In a music hall, your audience will be up to all sorts."

"All sorts," Dora echoed, her eyes on his lips.

Clem quickly scanned the auditorium, but they were out of view of even the other occupied box in the circle. He rested a hand on her velvet-clad bosom. "What's under this, Dora?" he asked lightly. "One of your cotton chemises?"

"That's the only kind I wear."

He clicked his tongue. "There's some distinct advantages to your principles regarding dress, I find."

"Oh really?"

He nodded slowly. "Care to show me?"

"My chemise?"

"For starters." Dora glanced around. "No one can see us, Dora. I checked."

She reached up and undid a row of decorative buttons that fastened the bodice and showed the top of her chemise. Then, without prompting, she caught hold of the white cotton bow and tugged it loose. "More?"

Clem swallowed. "Yes, please," he said, reaching across for the champagne bottle. He kept his eyes on her the entire time. To his delight, she dragged her chemise down over her breasts, exposing them to him entirely while boldly meeting his gaze.

With slow deliberation, Clem pressed the cold champagne bottle to her breasts, making Dora gasp. Then he rolled it from one peak to the other. "You have the prettiest nipples I've ever seen in my life, Dorabelle," he uttered with perfect truth.

Though she was not overendowed in the bosom department, her nipples were magnificent and extremely sensitive, standing out proudly for his fingers to tweak and fondle. He trickled a little of the champagne for good measure, making her softly moan, and then supped and licked the droplets from her breasts. "Delicious," he pronounced richly.

"Do try not to get any on my chemise," she whimpered. At his arched brow, she added with embarrassment, "Mrs. Cherwell."

"I refuse to allow thoughts of Mrs. Cherwell to intrude in this moment," he said, sloshing a little more of the champagne to trickle down her cleavage. "I want to put my hand under your skirts. Can I?" Dora's eyes sprang open. She looked faintly scandalized. "Why, Dora, I do believe I've finally shocked you," he drawled, pleased for once that it was not the other way around.

"Here?" she whispered.

He nodded. "I did speak of possibilities," he reminded her. "Due to how nice and quiet you are when you come."

"Here, though?" she repeated, faintly shrill.

"Unless you'd rather not."

Clem tried to look unconcerned as she considered. Finally, she gave him a small nod. "But if I tell you to stop…"

"I will at once," he promised, bunching her trailing skirts up to her knee and slipping a hand underneath. Thank God for loose-fitting drawers, he thought as his hand slid between her legs to cup her there. "Have I told you how much I love your hairy pussy, Dora?" he groaned. "I don't think I could go back to a shaved one now."

"Shaved?" she squeaked.

"Yes, shaved."

"Some ladies do that?"

"Yes, they do."

"They would not be popular at the cancan," she said so seriously that Clem could not stop his shoulders shaking with laughter.

"Dora," he whispered, passing his thumb through the curls covering her mons. Dora whimpered faintly, and he lowered his head and fastened his mouth lasciviously to one of her nipples.

Dora jumped in his arms. "Clem," she gasped as his fingers sought out her drenched folds.

"Oh fuck, Theodora, I could just play with your nipples all night and be a happy, happy man. I love how wet it gets you."

And that is precisely what he did for the next half hour. His fingers worked her expertly as Dora squirmed and held her breath, but every time he got her worked up to the point of orgasm, he would stop and concentrate on her breasts again until he thought the dangerous moment had passed. Then he would set his fingers to work again.

"Clem," she panted after another attempt to wriggle where she wanted his fingertips, only for him to still them, thwarting her attempts.

"Yes, Dora?"

"Are you doing it deliberately?"

"Doing what?"

"Withholding my pleasure?"

"Oh yes, Dora mine."

"Wh-why?"

"Sometimes it's nice that way."

"Nice for *you* or nice for *me*?" she forced out, her face turning very pink.

"For both of us," he whispered in her ear. "If it feels a little frustrating for you, let me tell you how much I want to pin you against that wall right now and take you there, behind the curtain, but alas, I know I'm not as quiet as you."

Dora glanced at the wall slightly desperately and then back at him. "You could try," she suggested, and Clem's grin broadened.

"You haven't got your preventative in," he reminded her.

"Oh yes," she said, looking so disappointed Clem could have kissed her. So he did. "Clem, I'm sorry," she blurted once he drew back, "but I don't think I can do this for much longer."

"Oh? Shall I let you come, then?" he asked lazily.

Dora's expression wavered. "Is this a trick question?"

"Just ask me nicely."

"Please, Clem, let me come."

He caught his breath. "Of course, my sweet Dora, anything for you." He had her there in an instant and this time let her soar. She jolted violently in his arms, gave a stifled cry, and then went so slack he thought for a moment she had gone off in a swoon. "Dora?" he asked, gathering her close.

"Clem," she whispered, her head lolling against his shoulder.

He withdrew his hand from her skirts and started refastening her buttons. A lot of shouting and rushing about was going on below, so he guessed it must also be the climax of the play. About time, he thought as Dora stirred and struggled to sit up.

Not that he could complain about his evening's entertainment, far from it. Wordlessly, he topped off her glass and passed it to her. She sipped the last of her champagne, watching him out of the corner of her eye.

"Shall I get off your lap?" she asked.

"No." She relaxed against him, and he passed an arm about her waist. "What the fuck is going on on stage?" he asked conversationally after a moment.

"Essentially, they have all killed one another."

Clem sighed. "Of course they have."

He didn't want to hang about once the play was done but led her straight out to summon a hackney and kept his arm about her in the cab ride home.

Once home, Clem fetched them up washing water, and they changed out of their evening finery for bed. Once he had hung up his evening suit, he turned to find Dora regarding her chemise guiltily.

"We certainly spilled champagne on this," she said regretfully. "What will Mrs. Cherwell think?"

"She'll think you're somewhat clumsy with a wineglass," he remarked.

"Yes, and not for the first time. She said she had a devil of a job getting those liqueur stains out of that one the other day."

Clem snorted. "It's a good thing you're her favorite, then, isn't it?" He took the chemise from her hands and cast it over a nearby chair, then took her back into his arms. "Shall I light the fire?" he asked, feeling her shiver slightly.

"You take such good care of me," she commented, laying a hand on his cheek. He turned his face to kiss her fingers.

"And I'm going to continue to take very good care of you," he promised lightly. "Both of us are going to be oh-so-careful, until one day, when the timing is right…"

"What happens then?" she asked breathlessly.

"Then I'm going to put my baby here," he said, spreading his hand across her flat belly. "And you won't even have to buy a new wardrobe," he promised her softly. "Because all those dresses of yours and your height will hide our little secret until you're too far along for anyone to voice any objections at all."

Theo gave a hitched laugh. "Who would object? You're my husband and also my employer," she pointed out. "You can hardly sue me for not fulfilling my obligations now, can you? Not after you're the one who…"

"Knocked you up?"

"Is that a colloquial saying for it?"

269

"It is. Now you try it." He could not say why he suddenly wanted to hear that rather vulgar term on her lips.

"You can hardly sue me after you've knocked me up, Clem Dabney," she pointed out.

He swallowed. Christ, why did that sound so…? "I think you'll find men can be massive fucking hypocrites," he said thickly. "But even if the paying public were pissed, I wouldn't even care. You know why, Dora?"

"Because you want a baby?" she asked, tipping her head to one side.

He felt the oddest sensation at these words. That wasn't right, was it? Did he want a baby? He gave his head a slight shake. Of course he did not want a baby. That was ridiculous. He wanted her to be content in her life, that was all. Dora smiled and leaned into him for a kiss. Immediately, Clem followed suit, chasing the strange thrill.

He could never anticipate a damn thing this woman would do, so her placing a gentle hand to his cheek should not make him breathless with want like this. He tore his mouth from hers, simply so he could get a look at her expression. Not scared, thank Christ for that. Not nervous around him now, when she probably ought to be.

Instead, she smiled dreamily up at him, and Clem felt all his innards lurch in the strangest way. "Let's lie on the bed, Dora," he said thickly, grabbing her hand and tugging her in that direction like some untutored, clumsy lad. Luckily Dora had no idea of polished seduction and simply followed his lead, sinking down onto the bed, gazing up at him with a steady trust that should have killed his ardor stone dead.

Almost, but not quite. She *was* his wife after all. He was obligated to take care of her, so it was not foolish for her to trust in this. That's right, she was a wife, and this actress malarkey was never going to work out. She needed a new purpose in life and a baby was the obvious choice to fulfill that purpose. That was all. He broke their kiss. "How *do* you feel about babies?" he demanded, suddenly spotting a flaw in this logic.

"I don't know any," Dora admitted cautiously. "But as a concept, it might be nice at some point in the future."

Clem relaxed. The future could be as near or far away as one desired. To the hypothetical cottage that he meant to stash Dora in, he now added a child. That would keep her busy alright, feeding it pudding and reading it pamphlets about rational dress. A sudden thought occurred to him.

"You had better put your device in, love."

He wasn't quite ready for her to disappear off to that cottage just yet.

20

The next morning, Theo woke early enough to wring a
promise out of Clem to take her with him to The Eagle.
Perhaps, too, he felt he could not fail to reciprocate after she
had taken him to The Parthenon the night before.

She chattered excitedly all through breakfast until Felix
begged her to give them all some peace and then caused a delay
in their departure, first flying upstairs to fetch her notebook to
take with her and then failing to find one of her shoes. Clem
bore all this patiently, though Dora fancied she heard her
brother make some crack about her being scatterbrained.

Clem was quiet on their journey there, reminding her more
than once that he would be busy, and she would be left to her
own devices. She assured him this was no more than she
expected and beamed at him, even though he looked unusually
serious. After that, Theo sneaked a few looks at him but
otherwise held her tongue. He was in a strange mood, she
thought.

Maybe it was something to do with confiding in her his
longing for a family the night before. That had been a bit of a
surprise, and she considered it now in the gray light of morning.
Could he have been in earnest about a baby?

He had seemed very excited by such talk, but then again,
maybe it was just a passing whim. He had not mentioned
children before when they had arranged their union, and he
certainly had raised no objection to her request to use
contraception.

When they reached the concert rooms, he took her straight
to his office and helped unbundle her from her paletot, muffler,
gloves, and bonnet. The latter she managed to remove without
taking out her hairpiece at the same time. He hung these up and
then regarded her moodily. "Now how are you going to occupy
yourself?"

"I am going to see if anyone is using the stage, and if not, I am going to take some measurements," she said, holding up her tape measure, pencil, and notebook.

"I see," he said skeptically, then waved a hand. "Well, by all means, be my guest."

If she wasn't mistaken, his eyes dwelled a moment on her moss green dress with disfavor before she took herself off. In fact, she really wasn't sure Clem appreciated her clothes at all, except for the fact he found them unusually easy to access.

Theo did not think he had truly liked even her outfit the night before which was a shame, for she thought it became her well. He had complimented her, it was true, but he had made no mention of her favorite gown with its high fitted bodice in a rust-colored velvet and trailing skirts in a sort of pale tea color.

She had teamed it up with long evening gloves, and in truth, that was as glamorous as her wardrobe got. Perhaps he would prefer it if she *did* have a nipped-in waist and big full skirts? The thought was a depressing one, and she was pleased to bump into Sidney, who hailed her cheerily and distracted her for a few minutes with his banter.

"Want me to go down there and clear 'em off the stage for you, Miss Dora?" he enquired genially, poking his thumb over his shoulder.

"No, no nothing of the sort," Theo hastened to assure him. "I am more than happy to wait my turn." Really, the last thing she wanted to do was put everyone's backs up. Already, she fancied she had been the recipient of a few wary looks.

Sidney happily introduced her to Reginald Stimson, one half of the comedy double act Stimson & Holland. When Theo had briefly spied him before, he had seemed the very picture of rotund amiability. Today, however, he seemed tetchy and irritable. "What?" he squinted bad-naturedly.

"This is the guvnor's wife, Mrs. Dabney," Sidney repeated loudly.

"Is she?" Stimson looked her over critically. "I'll take your word for it though thousands wouldn't."

"Don't mind 'im," Sidney sniffed as the comedian bowled away. "Comic," he said, leaning in closer. "They're always a bit peculiar. Nuffink like wot they appears on the stage."

Theo agreed that stage personas were often vastly different to those performers possessed in their private lives. After watching a dance troupe practicing their formation for three-quarters of an hour, she finally got her turn to measure up the stage and jot the figures down in her notebook.

"Right," she said brightly, sitting up on her knees and turning to Sidney, who had elected to lean on his broom and watch her. "That gives me exactly the information I need to set about obtaining my props."

"Props, did you say?" Sidney moved his cap back and scratched his head. "They got rooms full of the stuff out back. When someone's finished wiv somefink, they just chucks it in there. Needs a good going over and an inventory done really, but well, who 'as the time?"

"How do I procure the key to these prop rooms?" Theo asked eagerly, scrambling to her feet.

"Storerooms," Sidney corrected her. "Jim's got 'em. Though getting anyfink out of him's like drawing blood from a bleedin' stone!"

"Jim," Theo said, brightening. "Oh, I'm sure he'll oblige me. Tell me, where can I find him?"

"Well, usually he's doggin' yer 'usband's every step," Sidney said. "While 'e barks out orders so to speak."

"So, I'll likely find him if I head back in the direction of Clem's office," Theo decided and took off like a hare.

She duly found Jim, who escorted her with a bunch of keys to the storage rooms where she spent an interesting couple of hours sifting through the various preused stage props. By the end of it, she had picked out a flimsy table and a pair of decorative screens with the hinges hanging off. Both were light enough for her and Lil to carry on stage before their performance, and Theo felt well pleased with her discoveries.

She was just attempting to disentangle them from a dozen other items when Clem appeared in the doorway. "Dora?" He frowned. "What are you doing in there?"

She turned. "Clem! Only look what I have found." She gestured to her discoveries. "The perfect props for my act. The screen just needs a few new screws and this table a fresh lick of paint and we'll be all set."

Clem looked the items over without comment. "You're covered in dust," he said abruptly, stepping inside the room and holding his hand out to her. "Come here. Sidney can fetch those out for you."

"Oh, but—"

"Come here, Dora," he said shortly. "It's time you were fed."

Dora gave a start. "What time is it? It is surely not after twelve?"

"It is half past twelve," Clem corrected her, "and I need to feed you before you start painting and renovating."

She stepped over a pile of tangled rope and reached out for his hand. "I had not realized; I must have lost track of time."

He held her steady as she negotiated her path through the numerous boxes of odds and ends. Once out of the muddle, she brandished the bunch of keys. "I need to return these to Jim first."

"Jim can wait," he said, plucking them out of her hand.

"Well, then, if I might just have a quick word with Sidney…"

"Lunch, Dora," Clem insisted. "No one is going to rush up here and steal your pieces of junk. They've been moldering in here for months. Besides," he reminded her, "I have the key."

275

Theo bit her lip rather than argue that her new treasures were not junk but an essential part of her stagecraft. "Very well," she said agreeably but gave him a sidelong look as he locked the door behind them. He still seemed rather tense. Had he had a bad morning?

"Hold still," he said, dropping down to swipe at her skirt with the flat of his hand. "Your hem is covered in dust."

"I'm sorry you had to come looking for me," she said contritely. "I should have kept track of time."

He shook his head. "Don't apologize," he said, standing up. "I should have checked what you were up to." She was surprised when he took her hand in his and led her down the corridor.

"Why though? I was perfectly happy left to my own resources." Clem shook his head again, and Theo was just opening her mouth to continue when the magician and his assistant came down the corridor, eyeing them curiously. Clem gave them a brief nod but otherwise ignored them. Theo gave them a smile which was not returned. She sighed. She was not imagining it. The other acts were decidedly cool around her.

Clem took her lunch at a nearby grill room and plied her with roasted meats and ginger beer before they returned for the afternoon and Sidney found her some paint and a brush and promised he would fix the screens for her "wiv 'is own fair 'ands."

Theo had just applied the first coat of white paint to her table when she was interrupted in her task by her old friend Albert the paper boy, who had called by in the hopes he might find her. Sidney led him to the second storeroom where Theo had set up shop.

"Only you ain't given me any commissions in a couple of weeks, Miss Theo," Albert reminded her with an injured air.

"That's true, Albert," she agreed, urging him to take a seat. "Not there, that seat only has three legs. This one is wholly

276

intact, if a little threadbare." He plumped himself down. "You see, we do not need you to carry our notes to each other, now we are married," Theo explained apologetically.

"Coo, fancy 'im marryin' you," Albert exclaimed ingenuously.

"Yes, I know," Theo replied, not taking the slightest offense. "Now tell me all about how your nan is managing with her leg and what that vexing older brother of yours has been up to."

Nothing loth and having sold all his newspapers that morning, Albert settled into his seat and was still there three hours later when Clem ventured up to check on her. They were sat on the floor and cheerfully chatting away as Albert demonstrated his superior skill with a boxwood screwdriver.

"Yes, I see," Theo was murmuring. "I *had* thought you might try to reuse the preexisting hole."

"Too small," Albert responded cheerfully.

"Yes, but Sidney gave us a variety of screws in different sizes," Theo pointed out. She was not sure that the screen did not look rather worse for Albert's attempts at fixing it.

"Making progress?" Clem asked dryly.

"Oh yes!" Theo assured him blithely.

"Have you enough to keep you occupied for another couple of hours or should I ask Albert to accompany you home?" he asked.

"Home? Certainly not! I've dozens of things to keep me busy."

"Only I thought you might be rather tired of sitting around on a dusty floor."

"Not at all! As soon as the paint is dry, I want to start decorating that table, and I still need to write a letter to Lil. Albert said he would deliver it for me." She lifted her chin. "How soon do you suppose I can ask her to start rehearsing here with me?"

277

Clem did not speak for a moment. "Next week?" he offered.

"How about this Wednesday?" When he eyed her coolly, she explained, "We need to work around the hours she keeps bar, you see."

"Very well, this Wednesday," he agreed and moved away from the door.

Theo did not realize she was staring after him until Albert spoke. "Ain't very keen to give you your break, is he?"

She gave an awkward laugh. "It's not that, Albert; you mustn't think that. He's actually been wonderfully supportive."

"Could have fooled me," Albert sniffed, and for the first time that day, they sat in perfect silence. It was at this moment that Theo heard the brush of long skirts approaching along the corridor.

"That's wot you fink. 'E's been courting 'er on the sly," they heard someone pronounce with relish. "They been spotted going about togevver all sorts of places. Taking her out to eat in the chop 'ouse and even at Wards! He ain't been near any of his regular 'aunts in an age."

"You mean he ain't been to see Goldie of late?" asked another voice with interest.

"Lord, he ain't seen her for months," another said scornfully. "She's got a banker now, set her up in style he has, somewhere along the embankment."

"Good for 'er," said another. "She'd have caught cold waiting on the likes of Dabney."

"Well, but he married this one though," the other pointed out thoughtfully.

Theo cleared her throat and moved forward to shut the door which had been standing ajar to dissipate the smell of paint.

"Dancing girls," said Albert, who had leaned forward in his chair to peer out. He turned back to Theo curiously. "Did he really take you to Wards?"

278

21

Over the next two weeks, Dora accompanied Clem to the concert rooms every morning without fail. She bustled happily about the place keeping herself busy while Clem found himself increasingly on edge. He had finally taken her to an evening's performance there, and she had sat through every act with her eyes glued to the stage and an expression of rapt attention on her face.

She did not laugh out loud once at Florrie Foss's vulgar humor, but she squeezed Clem's arm when "Oh Mr. Hipkins" started up and whispered, "She's very good, isn't she? I can see why she's so popular."

"Can you?" Clem asked, eyeing her doubtfully.

She nodded furiously. "Oh yes, I can't take my eyes off her." At the close and third encore of "Mr. Mellar's Prize Marrow" she had clapped furiously along with the crowd and drummed her feet against the floor as loudly as any man present.

At dinner the following night she could not speak highly enough of the entertainment at The Eagle and Sun. "You must visit it when you can," she had urged her skeptical brother and Allsop without reservation. "It is so inspiring to see how the crowd embraces it."

As for his star act, she sang her praises. "Oh, Miss Foss is wonderful," she had enthused. "So exuberant and magnetic even. You feel as though you could watch her recite a laundry list and be entertained. Her manner is so exceedingly inviting and—and...*warm*. Even when she is being quite crude, you cannot take it amiss, for she is so likeable."

Allsop dabbed a napkin to his lips delicately and enquired if she had yet managed to obtain a pianist to accompany her act.

A frown marred Dora's brow. "Not yet," she admitted, and Clem meant to ask her about it after they went upstairs but forgot. As it happened, Dora raised it herself the next day, when she announced after breakfast that Allsop, of all people, had offered to play for her and Lil on The Eagle's piano, for the regular pianist had declined to learn their musical numbers.

"What do you mean, he 'declined to learn them'?" Clem asked sharply.

"Well, it seems the poor man is quite inundated at present. Apparently, there have been so many new acts come and go recently that he can scarcely keep up with the musical score."

"If he can't keep up, then I'll sack him," Clem said crisply. "There has always been a high turnover of acts at The Eagle."

"Harold volunteered," Dora murmured. "And he really is an excellent performer, Clem."

"He may find music hall rather different to his tame musical recitals," Clem pointed out tetchily.

Dora tactfully made no reply to this, but Clem caught sight of Allsop at The Eagle twice that week, looking a damn sight more out of place than she ever did. He managed to nod at Clem before lowering his eyes to his music and keeping in Dora's shadow.

For some reason, Clem felt himself bristle all over like an alley cat, seeing an interloper in his territory. "Keep an eye on that new pianist," he told a startled Jim. "If he puts one foot wrong, sling him out."

"He seems inoffensive enough," Jim protested, throwing a bewildered look over his shoulder. "Besides, I thought he was a friend of your wife's."

Clem gave him a pointed look. "Precisely," he muttered and flung off before Jim could respond. Collecting his jacket from his office, Clem went out to get some fresh air. He had to face facts. He was bloody *dreading* Dora's debut at The Eagle.

She was going to be disgraced, and he was going to have a problem with it, because for some reason she had brought out a protective streak in Clem that he hadn't even known he possessed. He needed to be careful how he handled this disaster, so everything did not blow up in his face.

Maybe if he made her think he had a need of her, that she was somehow useful to him, then she could carve out some other role in his organization. Maybe in some advisory capacity, though God knew she was not remotely qualified to even set foot in the place, let alone have any authority there!

Still, if anyone said anything, he could soon let them know they'd be out on their ear. How did one console a distraught woman anyway? Clem's past liaisons did not cover such eventualities, for they had been in no way serious. Jewelry? Would that do the trick? He stopped to gaze in a passing window. None of the trinkets displayed seem appropriate for Dora.

She admired his cuff links, he knew that, but once she realized her male impersonation was a failure, they would hardly be useful to her. Maybe they would even be an unpleasant reminder. Still, he found himself drifting toward the window displaying gentlemen's wares in any case. He had already taken Charlie Finch's advice and bought her a pair of smart leather men's shoes and hidden them in the bottom of the wardrobe along with his own.

Perhaps he could pick her up a tie pin or some such trifle. Anything to assuage the guilt that was starting to gnaw at his gut. Some of them were decorative enough for women to wear. He could imagine Dora pinning one to her breast. Perhaps the more ornate among them could double up as a bar brooch?

On impulse, he made his way inside and a smiling assistant swooped down on him. Clem asked for a closer look of a cerulean blue pin with six seed pearls set down the middle. "It is a pretty pin is it not, sir? There are cuff links to match."

Clem found himself exiting the store with the full set in his pocket. *Ah, what the hell*. She would need cheering up. He slid the gift box into his pocket and made his way back toward The Eagle, his expression still set and stern.

It was strange how much the business was playing on his mind, but he could not be easy about it or seem to relegate it to its proper place. It did not matter how much he tried to put it out of his mind, feelings of impending doom kept creeping into his head. Every day he seemed to wake up with a gnawing sense of unease about it. *Goddamn it*. He was far more concerned about Dora's upcoming humiliation than he had ever been about getting seven bells beaten out of him in the ring.

He shook his head. He needed to get a sense of proportion about the business. After Friday night, Dora's theatrical aspirations would lie in tatters around her. What could he do about it? Realistically, he knew there was *nothing* he could do to spare her. She needed to face up to harsh reality, and the minute he had agreed to uphold his side of the bargain, he had *known* she would face this.

Somehow, though, he had not realized it would eat away at him the way it was. He almost felt guilty, which was fucking ridiculous. He wasn't the one who had insisted on putting her on a music hall stage where she would be a fish out of water. It was Dora herself who was hell-bent on the scheme. Maybe it was better that she faced a short humiliation at The Eagle than suffer slow disillusionment over a number of years at The Parthenon?

He had watched her carefully this past week. If she had voiced the slightest misgiving about the scheme, had admitted to any second thoughts, he would have been there, coaxing her out of this disastrous course of action, but there was none. She had not even the smallest or momentary doubt regarding the wisdom of it.

When the subject was broached, her eyes gleamed, her voice grew warm, and whenever she pulled out her notebook to hastily scribble some new idea in it, she was practically vibrating with excitement. Reluctantly, Clem was forced to conclude that Dora possessed not one ounce of sense when it came to this subject.

It was her blind spot. He might almost call it an obsession. The only thing that would snap her out of it was the short, sharp shock of a bad reception. He had no doubt that the audience of The Eagle and Sun would give her that like a sock to the jaw. All he could do was be around to pick up the pieces. He slowed his step as he considered this.

Yes, he would focus his attention on that. She would need a bolt hole to retreat to, in order to lick her wounds. Very well, he could provide that for her. What would be best? A hotel suite? Or the familiarity of her own home? Perhaps her home on Juniper Row would be better, he decided on reflection. It was not as though anyone there would have borne witness to her humiliation.

Well, except for him, of course, but he could assure her on that score. It wasn't as though he was some arbiter of taste when it came to the stage. She needn't worry that he would judge her and find her wanting. He just knew what the rank and file wanted, that was all. He could assure her his opinion didn't count for much. Either that or just lie and say he'd loved her act.

He called in at a couple of places on the way back to the concert rooms. First out he finally hired a painter and decorator to come and paper those walls in their sitting room. Dora had deliberated over those samples many times. Each time she said regretfully that the blue and gold was too overpowering and that they should likely go for something plainer like the cream, but all the same, her eyes kept returning to the blue and her fingers reaching out to brush the textured surface.

He knew she preferred it. Dora's tastes were no more timid than his own. If it was brash, then what of it? It was their sitting room at the end of the day, and no one else had to sit in it. Hang the expense. Next stop was his acquaintance in Clapham. He had sent him word at the concert rooms the previous day, saying he'd had some fancy couches fall into his clutches, something like Clem had described.

On inspection, Clem liked them very much and paid for them on the spot. Dora's safe harbor was coming along nicely. Last of all he put in orders for flowers to be delivered both to Juniper Row and the concert rooms for Friday. Then he called it a day. All he could do now was make sure he caught her when she fell.

22

The Eagle and Sun

Clem paced uneasily up and down the length of noisy hall. The seats were already spilling over with customers, and the performers were not due on stage for another half hour. The tone was rowdy and loud. Most of their guests had spent at least an hour in the public house before transferring their patronage to The Eagle and Sun, where the beer continued to flow.

Clem's growing tension had risen all week until it was now at an all-time high. He had been unable to spend longer than five minutes in the dressing room where Dora had been in raptures over the shiny leather dress shoes he had wordlessly presented her with.

She had almost started crying when he had produced the jeweler's case. "Clem, you are too good to me," she had said, jumping up from her chair and attempting a clumsy embrace. Clem had moved away, so all she managed was a brief hug of his arm. He could not bear her affection in this moment, not when he was about to betray her trust by setting her before a baying crowd.

"It's nothing, Dora, just a…good luck gesture," he had said awkwardly. He hated this. Hated that she was in a dressing room marked "Misc" and that she was so fucking grateful for her secondhand props and the opportunity he was giving her to humiliate herself. "I'll be out front."

"I'll look for you," she promised, her eyes bright and shining.

Jesus Christ, he felt like he was going to be sick. He could not quell the twist in his gut whenever he thought of Dora coming out on that small stage and exposing herself to the scorn of the crowd. He supposed the place always had the same undercurrent of hard-edged, hectic gaiety on a Friday night, but strange to say he had never really noticed it before.

The place, as always, was teeming with working men, all determined to blow off steam in their precious downtime. A good time for most of them meant the opportunity to forget their squalid living conditions for a few hours and the hard labor they submitted their bodies to in order to eke out their existence in this harsh world. What they really wanted was to forget reality for one night a week.

They wanted a pretty girl on their knee, a strong drink at their lips, and a good laugh. Clem had never had a problem catering to this. Well, the drink and the entertainment that is. He put plenty of pretty dancing girls up on the stage, but he was no pimp. There were ladies of easy virtue milling about the crowd, but they paid their admission same as everyone else, and whatever else they provided on the side was no business of Clem's.

The fact remained that The Eagle and Sun was a powder keg waiting to blow at any time. The determination, even desperation of their punters to find a good time, could go awry at any point. Wherever alcohol flowed freely, things could flare up quickly. It was inevitable that fights broke out every Friday and Saturday night, and sometimes other nights too.

This never bothered Clem, for he kept plenty of doormen on hand to break things up and sling people out on their ear. Coming from his fighting background, he knew plenty of brawlers who might not have been good enough to make their fortune in the ring but could more than hold their own in a skirmish.

Blood could be mopped off the floorboards the next morning and broken chairs replaced. He kept "the décor" of the place minimal. The walls were refreshed with paint every few months and the lighting was kept low. Early on, he had tried hanging a few gilded mirrors and fancy lamps, but once the first couple had been smashed, he had abandoned all such attempts. The Eagle and Sun was just not that kind of place. Later, when he got his hands on The Parthenon, he could indulge in such fripperies, but for now it was bare basics.

Usually, he felt entirely impervious to the atmosphere of the place, but tonight he was on edge. He felt jumpy and ill at ease. There was a good chance that if someone tapped him on the shoulder, he would wheel about and slug them right in the jaw. He was, he realized with surprise, primed for violence. It would almost be a relief to give vent to it at this point.

As soon as the crowd started to turn ugly, he wanted Dora off that stage and whisked into the safety of one of the back rooms. Maybe his office would be best, where he could give her whatever she needed to get over the shock of her rejection. A stiff drink, a good kissing, he did not care, whatever it took. He would give it to her, whatever the hell she wanted. So long as she picked herself up, he would dust her down and soothe her ruffled feathers.

Then he would encourage her to form some *new* ambitions. He was not sure precisely what shape these would take yet. Maybe some godawful emporium where she could sell peculiar garments to clothing reformers, he thought with a hint of desperation. Anything she wanted, so long as she gave up chasing this damned fool dream of hers where she could only get hurt.

"'Ere, Clem."

He turned abruptly. When Jim took a hasty step back, he realized he was glowering. "What is it?" he forced himself to relax his jaw enough to ask.

"Nat Jones is here," Jim told him, gesturing over his shoulder with his thumb. "I told him I'd let you know. He's brought a few of the lads in wiv 'im."

Clem bit back his irritated response at the news some of his boxing brethren were present tonight of all nights. Usually, he comped them a few drinks and caught up with their news. He liked to keep his hand in, after all there was always a chance this entertainment lark could go belly-up. There were businesses going bust almost every day somewhere in this city. Coming from nothing meant Clem always appreciated an alternative source of money to be held in reserve.

"I'm busy right now," Clem said brusquely. At Jim's surprised look, he added, "Dora's on soon."

Jim's eyebrows rose. "You've never put 'er on first?" he asked uncomfortably. "Like a lamb to the bleedin' slaughter."

Clem tensed. *Jesus*, he wasn't that cruel. "No, she's on third. After Collins and Farmont." Jim pursed his lips disapprovingly. "It's best she gets it over with," Clem heard himself point out. "Then she's got the rest of the night to recover." Why was he even justifying his actions? She was his damned wife at the end of the day.

His old friend blew out his cheeks. "If you say so," he muttered belligerently. Clearly, Jim did not agree with his outlook.

"As soon as…things start to go south, I want her off that stage, do you hear me? Have Eddie and Sam down the front, ready to hustle her off," he said, naming his two most formidable bouncers.

"Where are you going to be?" Jim looked faintly indignant as though he thought Clem was shirking his duties, though whether as husband or manager, he was not sure.

Clem glared back at him. "Around," he said succinctly and turned on his heel, leaving Jim frowning in the aisle.

In truth, Clem did not know where best he should be situated when Dora spectacularly failed. Perhaps it would be easier all around if he did not witness it. She could likely forgive him better if he had not observed her fall from grace. Then, too, there was the fact that he felt slightly murderous about anyone heckling her. It would not do for him to forget himself and get involved in a punch-up with his own customers.

Still, he wanted to be close at hand. In the end, he compromised by lurking at the back of the hall, determined to plunge in and out at will with an ear cocked for the moment the crowd turned ugly. Then he would sprint back in there and whisk her away.

He managed pretty much to follow this plan through the first two acts, though his palms were clammy, and he was not sure, but it felt like sweat was breaking out on his top lip as Larry the announcer gave his spiel about a new act debuting that night. Clem swallowed hard and turned, emerging into the corridor outside where he closed his eyes briefly and stood, breathing deep, striving for a modicum of calm.

"You alright, Clem m'boy?"

Clem turned at the unwelcome greeting, recognizing the tones as those of Nat Jones. Sure enough, the fight promoter's flamboyant figure stood before him in a pale blue frock coat, seemingly oblivious to the fact that nearly all of London now exclusively wore evening wear of deepest black.

Nat surveyed him with eyebrows lifted as he held out his hand. "You look a little green around the gills." Clem took his hand in a firm grasp, and they shook. "Heavy night last night?" Nat eyed him shrewdly. "You have the look of a man who's suffering the aftereffects."

"Nothing like that," Clem replied, wishing his old acquaintance would go to the devil. Nat looked like he had something up his sleeve and, really, talking business right now was the last thing Clem wanted.

"I asked Jim to tell you I'd looked in, but maybe he did not get the chance," the other responded affably. "Glad I ran into you as I wanted to put something to you," Nat continued, and Clem nodded as his ears picked up on a smattering of laughter. He stiffened, listening hard, but of course, from out here, he could not discern the nature of the crowd's amusement. He pictured Dora nervous or stumbling awkward on the stage and felt his stomach lurch.

"…I told him what you were up to these days," Nat continued easily. "Said as how he'd always had a fancy to see you in the ring with Stevens and was disappointed that never came to pass before your unofficial retirement…"

Clem nodded again. "Oh aye," he murmured. *Another gale of laughter.* He turned his head sharply and concentrated. Were they laughing along *with* or *at* the object of fun? That was the question.

"…so I told him I would put it to you, though I could not guarantee you would be interested in such a bout. It's good money though, Clem. I thought, under the circumstances—"

Clem could not stand it any longer. "Excuse me," he said shortly and strode away leaving Nat open-mouthed and staring after him. No sooner had he entered the concert hall than another louder burst of laughter regaled him. Clem nearly jumped out of his skin, his startled gaze darting over the seated audience.

"Look at 'im!" hooted an older-looking woman in an aisle seat to his left. "'E don't know what to do wiv 'er, now 'e's got 'er where 'e wanted 'er!"

"Bitten off more'n 'e can chew!" her companion agreed, nudging her in the ribs. They both guffawed.

Clem's eyes sought out the only person who counted. Dora, or rather Piccadilly Percy, was sauntering with seeming insouciance toward a lacquered screen, behind which Lil was elaborately refreshing her toilette. Clem could have sworn Percy gave an almost audible gulp, though how he could hear such a thing at this distance from the stage was debatable.

The crowd tittered. Percy adjusted his too-tight collar and peered over the top as Lil adjusted how much of her ample

290

breasts showed above her low-cut neckline, squeezing her bosoms together. Percy's eyes practically stood out on stalks.

The crowd chortled again as Percy reeled back from the screen and, to Clem's astonishment, reached down to adjust his breeches in a casual move that spoke of an intimate knowledge of the male anatomy. In a man, such a move was self-explanatory, from a male impersonator, it was frankly shocking.

A spurt of startled laughter burst from the audience that developed into a rolling belly laugh as Percy glanced about self-consciously before assuming his previous swagger and approached the screens once more for a second look. It was tame enough stuff, Clem told himself uneasily, as he watched Lil lavishly applying the powder brush.

On noticing she was observed by her young swain once more, the older woman cocked a knowing eye at the audience before fluttering the brush teasingly across her décolletage. Once more the audience abrupted into gales of laughter at Percy's exaggeratedly stricken response. Clem had to admit, they were both putting it over well.

The audience, he noticed, was entirely captivated by the turn. This was no easy thing to achieve in such an unruly place as The Eagle and Sun. Usually, only the most popular and top-billed turns could command the entire audience's attention like this. The rest had to put up with the fact that, at any one time, there would be a fracas going on in one corner and a private joke in another.

But right now, all faces were turned toward the stage, utterly diverted. They were lapping it up. The piano keys jangled under Allsop's fingertips into a catchy tune with the refrain, "Oh, he may think he's cock o' the walk, but my fine fellow is nothing but talk." He had to admit, Dora had spoken perfect the truth about Lillian Longdon's voice. It was fine and strong and soared out with a purity he had not expected. In her day, Lil must have been quite a looker and that teamed with her voice should have got her to the top.

She also didn't hold back with the innuendo and was entirely unblushing as she collared hold of Dora's skittish dandy and dragged him mercilessly into her boudoir. Strange to say, Clem did not find himself remotely inclined to laugh along with the crowd. He supposed he was wound too tight to appreciate the humor of the situation.

He was also far too distracted by the crowd's appreciation, which was almost jaw-dropping. Was it possible he had lost his impartiality or was the act really going down as well as he seemed to think it was? He gave his head a quick shake before returning his bemused gaze to the stage.

Nervous Percy was a tottering mess by this point as Lil pushed herself up against him at every opportunity, squeezing herself past him one minute and seizing hold of his trembling hands to place them on her hips or the bodice the next. She serenaded him with a number called "Oh, he's never dipped his toe before, just shilly-shallied in the shallows." The crowd whooped and hooted with laughter as Percy squirmed and stammered out his responses.

Percy's hands shook so hard as he gulped down a glass of water that he spilled almost the entirety before collapsing into the chair, overcome with a heady combination of nerves and lust. Clem almost found himself wincing in sympathy at Dora's portrayal of a young man untutored in the ways of the world. The way she hit on the uneasy combination of bombast and vulnerability was almost uncomfortable for him to watch.

Moreover, how the fuck did she know how to work a crowd like that? He could accept that Lil was an old hand, but Dora, his own sweet and slightly clueless Dora, embodying a young man at risk of shooting his shot prematurely—and doing it for laughs—was mind-boggling to Clem. He knew how inexperienced she was with the opposite sex, so how the hell was her portrayal so accurate?

The crowd was warbling along with the chorus now as the piano struck up a last refrain. "Oh, he may think he's cock o' the walk…" Clem stood frowning deeply, his arms crossed as their turn came to an end. As the last line died away, Lil hitched her skirts and straddled the seated Percy as the curtain came down.

The hall burst into delighted laughter. Moments later, the curtain lifted to show Percy still sat looking dazed, with his collar burst open and lip stain all over his face. Lil was now kneeling at Dora's feet, wiping a finger around her lips suggestively. The crowd roared with hilarity. *Jesus Christ*, Clem thought. He supposed he should be glad her breeches weren't unfastened.

Dora swiftly rose from her seat, taking Lil's hand and kissing it theatrically. "Mrs. Lillian Longdon," she proclaimed, beaming as the crowd gave thunderous applause. She led Lil to the side, front and center of the stage, where Lil curtseyed again and again to rapturous appreciation before turning back to Dora.

"And Mrs. Dora Dabney as Piccadilly Percy!" Lil shouted, raising her own hands to clap in Theodora's direction.

Before Clem's bemused gaze, half the hall clambered to their feet, whistling and clapping and shouting for an encore. "Give us another one, Perce!" someone roared loudly from the back. "Another!" went up the cry which echoed about the hall. "Another one!"

Larry, his announcer, was hovering at the side of the stage. He turned an enquiring look in Clem's direction. Clem gave the nod, and the pianist broke into another rendition of "He's Never Dipped His Toe Before" as Clem turned on his heel and strode back out of the hall. He needed a stiff drink. Maybe two of them.

She'd looked more than comfortable up on that stage. She'd looked *good*. Damn good. He had thought he would be consoling a distraught Dora in his arms by this point. Now, as things stood, he was not sure he did not have a sensation on his hands. It would take him a moment or two to wrap his head around the fact.

Dora might make a tall and rather gangly female, but the joke of it was that she made an elegant, fashionable young man. He had found it hard to even *see* his wife in the dapper, debonair figure she cut, swaggering about the stage, before the abrupt turnabout when she switched to bashful puppyhood, showing Percy was all talk.

Clem had no sooner swallowed down his first whiskey than someone appeared at his elbow. "Dabney," said a deep, familiar voice.

Clem turned. "Ben!" he exclaimed, snapping abruptly out of his strange mood. "Finally, you come to see us up and running!" He gripped his friend's shoulder. "Took your sweet time about it!"

Benedict Toomes grinned. "Aye, well, I've had a few other things on my mind," he admitted.

Clem grinned, for his friend had lately won the English Heavyweight Championship in eight rounds. "Congratulations, by the way."

Ben looked surprised. "Someone told you, then?" He looked faintly disappointed.

Clem frowned. "I was there, you fool. On Epsom Downs. Didn't get the chance to shake your hand on the night but—"

"Not that," Ben laughingly interrupted him. "I'm to be a father this summer. Lizzie's expecting."

Clem's expression wavered as he took in Ben's air of quiet pride. "Then double congratulations, my friend," he said, slowly pumping his hand. "You must let me buy you a drink."

"I can't be long," said Ben, looking back over his shoulder. "I've left Lizzie with Nat."

"You've brought along your wife tonight?" Clem was faintly startled. He had met Mrs. Lizzie Toomes on a few occasions now and that lady was staunchly respectable. He almost winced imagining her reaction to tonight's acts.

"Aye, for she had a fancy to see the business you so nearly had me investing in."

Clem laughed again. "You were never more than lukewarm in your interest," he pointed out.

"I almost regret that seeing the roaring trade you're doing," Ben admitted. "You're doing well for yourself, Clem. Good for you."

"Not bad," Clem said cagily.

"Not bad!" Ben mocked as Clem gave his order at the bar to Jessie. "To grow all this from a miserable six-man supper and song outfit!"

Clem was almost tempted to confide that he now owned the majority stake in a West End theater, but this was neither the time nor the place. "You've not seen anything yet," he contented himself with murmuring instead.

"I'll get these," Ben interjected as the barmaid plunked two whiskeys down. "And a bottle of champagne to take back to our table. You'll come back with me?" he said, turning back to Clem. "I've got some of the old crowd along with me," he said, noticing Clem's frown. "My brothers are here along with Nat and Jeb, and Nye's come all the way up from Cornwall for a visit."

"These are on the house, Jessie," Clem said, waving Ben's money away. "Better make it two bottles of champagne. I've already seen Nat tonight," he prevaricated, wondering if another swell of applause meant Piccadilly Percy and Lillian Longdon had been allowed to retreat now from the stage.

He fancied he heard another tune start up and recognized "Oh, he may think he's cock o' the walk." *Another* encore, he marveled. The early acts were supposed to stick to a strict time schedule. Then again, maybe Larry was being more accommodating for the owner's wife.

"Nye's brought his wife along and all," Ben told him. "Now you know you have to come and make up to the ladies, Clem, if nothing else. You know what a charming bastard you are."

Clem appeared to consider. "Mrs. Nye, you say? As well as Mrs. Toomes? Never let it be said I'd ever willingly disappoint the ladies."

"There he is." Ben slapped him on the back. "The Clem I know. Nat said you were playing hard to get tonight. He reckons you're trying to drive up your appearance fee." Clem shrugged, snatching up the two bottles of champagne before they made their way back into the midst of the noisy hall. To Clem's relief, the curtain was lowering again, so he was not subjected to another glimpse of his wife covered in Lil's lip stain.

The table of prizefighters was about halfway down, and Ben waded into the audience with all the assurance of a man who could back himself up with the best right in all England. Clem was content to follow in his wake, and they soon found the prizefighters' table.

"Look who I've found," Ben announced loudly to be heard above the clamor of the crowd who were still clapping enthusiastically.

"Clem!" he was hailed simultaneously by at least three people. He shook hands with Jack and Frank Toomes, who were nearest to him, and Jeb Morris. Nat, Clem noticed, was eyeing him narrowly. He ignored this to bend over Mina Nye's hand as he welcomed her to the capital.

296

She thanked him gravely, but her eyes danced as she returned his greeting. "Nye always promised me that he would bring me to see the dancing girls one day," she commented, glancing enigmatically at her husband.

"You're looking well, Mina," he told her, sweeping an appreciative eye over her dove gray gown of silk taffeta. She now only appeared to be in half mourning. He thought Mrs. Nye a handsome woman but her drab mourning dress had never done her any favors. "It's good to see you out of your black."

"Why thank you, Clem. You look well too. Success suits you it seems." He grinned back at her.

"Stop making up to my wife, you smarmy bastard," Will Nye growled, only half in jest as he rested an arm along the back of his wife's chair.

"Ah, but you'd hardly know me if I did not," Clem pointed out with a grin as Nye reached up to shake his hand. "Been a while, Nye. How's The Merry Harlot?" he asked after Nye's coaching inn.

"It's not called that anymore, which you would know if you ever made time in your busy schedule to come down for a visit," Nye grouched. "You've not made an appearance at one of our fight nights in six months!"

"Has it really been that long?" They assured him it had been, and after asking after their prickly maid, Edna, and Mina's nephew, who was a huge boxing fan, he moved down the table.

Next was Ben's wife, who was pink-cheeked and vigorously fanning herself with a mother-of-pearl fan. Ben was standing at the back of her chair, with his hand on her shoulder, murmuring into her ear. She nodded and gave Clem a perfunctory smile when he kissed her hand.

"Mr. Dabney," Lizzie Toomes murmured politely. "Business is booming for you, I see."

"And you are blooming, Mrs. Toomes," Clem responded gallantly as he took in her filled-out figure. She wore a dress of soft mauve which became her well, and her blond chignon was dressed with fresh violets. Clem had never thought much of her looks, but he had to admit she was displayed to advantage tonight. "May I offer you my congratulations on your good news?"

Her smile warmed. "Thank you, you are very kind."

"You are not too hot?" He darted a quick glance at Benedict, who hovered proprietorially over her.

"Not at all. There is no need to fuss," Lizzie responded quickly.

"We'll be leaving long before the crush at the end," Ben assured him. "I have to get this one home to bed." Considering how bawdy his highest billed act, Miss Florrie Foss, could be, Clem could only be glad of that fact. He did not think Benedict's wife would approve of her at all.

Next, he spent a few moments with Frank's wife, Maggie, whose beauty made up for her lack of sparkling conversation, and with Jeb's partner, Effie, who Clem had always had a soft spot for. Effie laughed uproariously at any joke he made and nudged him in the ribs with her elbow. "Go on with you, you rogue!" she scolded. "We know better'n to listen to a charming rascal like you. Ain't that right, Mags?"

Clem could not fail to notice the wistful glance Effie shot toward Jeb, who alone out of the men did not seem to think he needed to keep a close eye on his woman. Maggie Toomes smiled her lovely smile before looking to her husband, Frank, who was filling up her glass. Frank shot her a wink, and she blushed as though they had not been married for years. Frank, Clem noticed with interest, was the only one drinking orange juice along with Lizzie. Had the oldest Toomes brother become a teetotaler?

He spent the next ten minutes or so catching up with old friends and wondering how to effectively make his escape. He had seen the magic act that followed Dora's a dozen times before at least. The Great Roberto Russo was very polished and professional, but tonight he suffered by way of comparison to the turn that preceded him.

Even the magician's pretty young assistant could not save him, for all she pirouetted about the stage, presenting top hats and silk scarves and disappearing bouquets. The crowd was restless and unappreciative. They had seen something new and fresh, and they wanted to carry on with their rollicking evening's entertainment. Dora and Lil needed bumping up the bill, Clem thought. There was no getting around it.

"Clem?" He turned in surprise to hear Dora's voice close at hand. He found her stood behind his chair, once more dressed in her dark green gown, though her face was flushed and her eyes shining.

"Dora!" He sprang to his feet at once and rounded the chair. Dora stretched her hand out to him, and he captured hold of it, drawing her close against him. She was quivering all over, with excitement he guessed rather than nerves. He cast a quick glance about but no one in the audience seemed aware this tall female in drab olive green was one and the same as Piccadilly Percy.

"Clem," she repeated breathlessly, her eyes fixed on him alone. "Oh Clem, what did you think?" She looked so open and vulnerable at that moment that he could tell her nothing but the truth.

He should have been waiting in her dressing room to congratulate her, damn it. What the hell had he been playing at? "Top billing," he admitted, and as soon as he said it out loud, he knew it was nothing but the truth.

She gave a hoarse cry and threw her arms about him. After only an instant of feeling her body's violent trembling and her hot face against his neck, he circled his own arms about her, holding her tight against him. He didn't give a damn about the fact he could feel the entire table of his boxing friends' eyes boring into his back. Not at this precise moment.

"Dora, sweetheart," he murmured in her ear nonsensically. "*Dora.*" He ran a hand up and down her back soothingly. He marveled that she had been so calm earlier only for the adrenaline to affect her now. Pfeiffer was like that, he thought suddenly, thinking of a fellow fighter. Bastard wanted to punch down a wall long after his foe had been dragged away, bleeding and broken. Then he dismissed the obnoxious Claude Pfeiffer from his thoughts altogether.

"You're shaking," he said after a few heartbeats. "Come and sit down." He maneuvered her to his own chair and saw her seated before acknowledging his friends' openly curious stares. "Dora," he said, crouching down beside her and threading his fingers through hers. "These are my friends from the boxing world. Everyone, this is Theodora. My—er—wife."

Clem heard a sharply indrawn breath, but he kept his eyes trained firmly on Dora, whose mouth had fallen open with dismay. "Oh, I—I'm so sorry, am I interrupting your gathering?" she stammered, trying to rise from the chair.

Clem kept a firm grip of her hand, anchoring her to the seat. "Not at all," he said smoothly. "You would have to have met them sooner or later. It may as well be sooner." He gave her his easy smile, but she still looked stricken.

"I just barged right on in here," she said apologetically, darting her gaze about the table. "I'm so sorry."

Her words were met with a blank silence. Clem tore his eyes from Dora to level a frown at his friends. What the fuck was wrong with them?

Nat Jones was already leaning forward. "Not at all, dear lady," the fight promoter said jovially. "Not at all. I must admit that ever since I heard the compere announce your name, my curiosity was piqued. I thought perhaps a sister, but—"

"I don't have any sisters," Clem responded. From the consternation of everyone else at table, he guessed Nat was the only one who had picked up on Dora's stage name.

"May I congratulate you, my dear Mrs. Dabney," Nat continued. "Your act went down a positive storm."

"Thank you," Dora answered, a fresh wave of hot color washing over her. Clem reached to pour her a glass of champagne. Had no one thought to take care of her once she came off stage? he seethed. Where the fuck was Lil? Or even that dishrag, Allsop?

He pressed a glass of champagne into her hand. "Drink this," he urged. "And take a few deep breaths."

Effie was whispering in Nat's ear. Clem thought he caught a bewildered "What act? Who is she?" Nat muttered something back under his breath.

Effie clapped a hand to her forehead. "She never is!" she burst out. "That was you? That dapper young sprig? I'd never believe it!"

Clem sent Effie a quelling glance, but she had turned and was babbling into Jeb's ear. Jeb turned a frankly disbelieving gaze on Dora and shook his head. "I don't believe it for a minute," he said, narrowing his eyes. "You're trying to pull a fast one, Dabney."

Clem rubbed his hand over the small of Dora's back in what he hoped was a soothing gesture. "Dora, eyes on me," he murmured. She swallowed and turned to face him. "Do I need to take you back to the dressing room?"

"No, no," she said quickly and took a gulp of champagne. "I will be fine directly. I'm still just a little…" Her words trailed off, and she flashed a quick smile about the table.

301

"It *was* you, weren't it?" Effie marveled. "Piccadilly Perce, I mean. Lord love you, you was a rare caution up there, I could scarce draw breath for laughing!"

Dora's panicked smile broadened to a more genuine one. "Yes, it was me," she said with a hiccup. "I'm so glad you enjoyed it."

Around the table, the urgent whispers were still doing the rounds. He heard an incredulous "*Wife* though, did he say *wife*?" from Jack Toomes.

Benedict cleared his throat. "You will have to excuse us, Mrs. Dabney. Clem kept the news of your marriage close to his chest." He reached down to extend his hand to her. "I'm Benedict Toomes, Ben to my friends. This here is my wife, Lizzie."

Dora shook his hand, though Clem would have been surprised if she would remember any names afterward. She still seemed to be riding a high, and if his observations were anything to go by, she would barely remember any of this interaction.

"I am happy to meet you both," she claimed unevenly, her gaze darting between Benedict and Lizzie as though she could not focus clearly on either of them.

Lizzie Toomes, to Clem's surprise, was warm in her greeting and clasped hands with Dora. "I think she needs water, not champagne," she said, turning to Clem directly.

He jumped to his feet. "I think you're right. Can I leave her with you a moment?"

"Of course."

When he returned minutes later, carrying a pitcher of water and a clean glass, Dora was flanked on either side by Mina and Lizzie, who were talking to her in low, calming tones. Dora's eyes were still unnaturally bright, but she seemed less agitated and was nodding in agreement to whatever Mina was saying.

Clem knelt beside her and poured the water. "Everything alright, Dora?" he asked in a low voice.

She nodded and took the proffered glass, drinking deeply. "Sorry to cause a scene."

"Nothing of the sort, Mrs. Dabney," Mina responded briskly. "It's so hot in here, it's no wonder you're a little overcome."

"Fetched you a chair," Nye put in, shoving a seat in Clem's direction. Considering how packed the hall was, Clem did not want to ask how Nye had got hold of one. He knew for a fact it would not have been by fair means, but foul.

Clem plunked himself down on the wooden chair and passed an arm about Dora's waist. She leaned lightly against him and smiled gratefully up at him. "Your friends are very nice," she murmured, and Clem could see she had picked up because her eyes were now roaming over them with interest.

"Mmmm," he rumbled by way of response, casting a jaundiced eye over the company at large. Hardly any of them, it seemed, were paying much heed to the action on stage. Not when there was a much more diverting spectacle to be had closer at hand.

Frank was whispering in Maggie's ear, while Jack was frankly staring like an idiot. Jeb smirked as if at some private joke, while Nat was casting a benevolent look in their direction and puffing on his cigar. Only Nye and Benedict seemed to take the development in their stride. Oh, and the womenfolk, of course.

He wondered if he could persuade Dora to let him take her home, but one glance at her exhilarated expression told him that was not an option. Well, he thought, she did deserve to celebrate her success, even if it was just some strange kind of fluke.

Theo woke late, and to her surprise, Clem was still in the bed beside her. Her bleary eyes alighted on the mantel clock which told her it was close to midday. Theo almost gasped. Why were they both still abed? Then memories of the previous night filtered through her confused brain. *Of course.* They had not got in until three in the morning after staying out all night carousing with his prizefighting friends.

The one with the kind wife, who Clem later told her was the current champion, had left early, but as they were expecting a baby that had not been surprising. Then the couple from Cornwall had left halfway through Florrie Foss's act. Theo did not think that the wife had been enjoying Clem's star act, for she had cleared her throat several times and her husband, who had been laughing, passed a brawny arm about her waist and started whispering in her ear to distract her from the on-stage antics.

In any case, Theo did not think he had seemed particularly disappointed to leave early for he had been more interested in his wife's blushes than Florrie's lewd jests. He had stood up first and then pulled his wife to her feet and they had taken their leave, making Clem promise he would bring Theo down to their inn for a visit in the summer for they were returning home the following morn.

The rest of them had stayed out on the town. They had been to three, no, she thought it was actually *four* different drinking establishments and met up with several other fascinating types, most of them fighters, who Effie had enthusiastically introduced her to, praising her act to the skies. And there had been dancing, so much dancing.

Theo could not remember hardly any of their names, but a good deal of them had promised to come and see her at The Eagle. Clem had danced with her the most, but she had also danced with a boxer with a French name, who when he talked had sounded no more French than her. He had complained that she was too tall for a showgirl, and she had pointed out that she was not a showgirl but a male impersonator.

He had scoffed at that, and Theo, using the man's own slightly contemptuous manner, had scoffed right back. He had been so surprised, he had laughed and told her to show him more of her impressions. She had not had the chance, for Clem had cut in at that point and borne her off. "Stay away from Pfeiffer," he had said warningly, and Theo had wanted to ask why, but she had been so distracted by the sublime music and being in Clem's arms that she had forgotten all about it.

There had been a few others besides, the most interesting of which was young Bartholomew Ewell. Theo had been particularly interested in him, as he was not of the same large powerful build as her husband and a good deal of the others.

Barty, as the others called him, was svelte, and his height was not so very far off her own, though he was undoubtedly broader in the shoulder. Still, this was something she could easily get around with a little judicious padding.

Seeing the casual assurance, even arrogance with which Bartholomew Ewell had carried himself, had utterly enchanted Theo. Trying to imitate Clem in anything other than small gestures would be impossible as his body type was far too disparate from her own, but Barty…*he* held distinct possibilities.

Even thinking of it now, she fervently wished she could get in a few good hours studying him. She felt sure, with a little practice, she could pull off that cocky, self-assured manner of his. She felt a little giddy at the idea of having such a character at her disposal. It could be so *useful* to her repertoire.

As she reached for a glass of water off the bedside cabinet, Clem stirred in the bed beside her, and she held still, swigging down her water. There had been lots of champagne and possibly

305

he might have a sore head. Suddenly, she remembered his cryptic comment in the early hours before he had fallen asleep.

"Dora." His voice had almost startled her, for she had thought he had drifted off to sleep.

"Yes?"

"Make sure Lil's not kneeling at your feet next time you get your curtain call."

"Not kneeling? Why?"

He was quiet for a moment. "I'll let you in on the joke sometime."

His voice had sounded funny, Theo thought, frowning. She wished she could have seen his expression clearly, but he had his forearm flung across his face. Before she could question him further, he had muttered, "Take my word for it. If you don't tone it down a bit, you'll have us hauled up before the Moral Decency Board."

She must remember to ask Lil what he had been referring to. She had still been too excited for sleep when they had stumbled in, so she had spent another hour scribbling in her notebook and sipping on water before she had blown out her candle. Doubtless, that was why she was not feeling seedy herself, though the balls of her feet did ache a little.

Setting down her glass, she let her mind flood with memories of the previous night's performance. Applause, congratulations, and Lil's high glee afterward in the dressing room. Her friend had practically danced along the corridor as they had made their way back to change out of their stage clothes.

"Three curtain calls, Theo!" Lil had caroled with delight, seizing her, and then enfolding a startled Harold into her perfumed embrace. "Three!"

Harold had seemed a little dazed by their rapturous reception, and she knew full well he had been shocked as anything by the lyrics she had put to his music. Still, he had not murmured a single disapproving word on that subject, bless him, merely polished his eyeglasses and cleared his throat a lot during rehearsals.

Theo smiled now as she thought of it. Lil had been ecstatic, and she had not yet told her what Clem had said about top billing. Her toes curled with delight. Of course, he might not actually *give* them top billing, she reminded herself firmly before she grew quite carried away. Florrie Foss, his current star turn, might be under contract after all. And in truth, she was not sure she was yet ready to topple the mighty Florrie from the top spot. She was sure she had room for improvement.

She hugged herself a moment, letting the sheer joy of her success wash over her. Everything had turned out better than she had ever dared dream it would. Every joke had landed, every nuance had been savored, every song had been a hit. Their audience could not have been more appreciative, even if they had been coached. She already knew what tweaks she wanted to put in place for the next performance.

"Mmm, Dora?" Clem's husky morning voice startled her.

She turned her head quickly. "Yes? I did not realize you were awake."

"I am now," he sighed, his eyes still closed as he reached down to scratch his muscular belly. His long underwear was riding low on his hips, and Theo tried not to ogle him. She was not sure she would ever get used to sharing these private moments with him.

He turned his head toward her, a pucker between his brows, though his eyes remained closed. "It's early," he complained. "Why are you awake?"

"It is not early," she gurgled with laughter. "We got in so late, Clem; it was after three, you know."

He frowned, still without opening his eyes. "What time is it?"

"Almost half past eleven." He grunted. "Water?" she asked. When he shook his head, Theo poured herself another glass and tossed it down. She could feel his eyes on her as she swallowed her drink, and after replacing the glass on the table, she turned back to him with a quizzical look.

Clem cleared his throat. "How about I take you out to breakfast? Well, I suppose it's near enough lunch now," he said, glancing at the window.

Theo's spirits lurched crazily. "I would love that, Clem," she admitted, drawing her knees up and hugging them tight.

To her surprise, he did not turn to kiss her cheek or indulge in any of his customary affection when they lay in bed together. Usually, he could not keep his hands to himself. This morning, however, he simply sat upright and swung his legs over the side of the bed. "What happened to Allsop last night?" he asked unhurriedly.

"I'm not sure. I think he fled after our second encore. He seemed a little overwhelmed in truth. He's quite shy and retiring after all."

"And what about Lil? Where did she disappear to?" he asked, still in his casual tone.

"Oh, she had to get back home," Theo explained as Clem sauntered across to the wardrobe to pick out a pair of trousers. Today he chose some of the blue and gray check plaid. "One of the elderly ladies she lives with has been under the doctor. Lil wanted to get back to make sure all was well. I expect they were agog to hear how our act went down as well," she confided. "They would have been waiting up for her, to hear the news."

Clem's eyebrows rose as he reached for a shirt. "She supports them both?" he asked.

Theo nodded. "Yes."

"Where is Mr. Longdon?" he asked, threading an arm through one sleeve. "Does he exist?"

308

"Oh yes, one of the old ladies is his mother. Lil had to take her on after her investments hit rock bottom. The other is Lil's old dresser who had to retire from the business. She's now blind as a bat, poor thing, and can't fend for herself anymore. Lil's husband left for the Americas years ago. He went off prospecting."

"And abandoned his old mother at the same time?" Clem asked, starting on his buttons.

Theo lowered her eyes which had been following his progress with a little too much interest. The close fit of Clem's trousers showed quite clearly the size of his muscular thighs. Aloud she continued, "There is a sister who works as a companion, but she finds it hard enough to make ends meet without contributing to her mother's upkeep. Funnily enough, old Mrs. Longdon did not care for Lil above half much before her Johnny left. It is only in the years since that they have grown so close."

Clem snorted. "What's 'funny' about it?" he asked dryly as he tucked in his shirt. "I imagine it's hard to remain disapproving of a daughter-in-law that's keeping a roof over your head and food in your belly."

Theo smiled wryly. "Yes," she agreed. "Lil has always had a heart of gold."

Clem grunted. "Maybe, but she and Allsop ought not to have left you to your own devices last night when you were done on stage."

Theo straightened up. "What do you mean?"

He cast her an unreadable look as he drew on his royal blue waistcoat. "It's a rough crowd we get at The Eagle and Sun," he said abruptly.

"You mean that I ought not to have sought you out in the audience after?" Theo asked, biting her lip. "As a matter of fact, Lil did try to dissuade me. She told me to wait in the dressing

309

room until you sent for me, but I—" She broke off, looking embarrassed.

"You what?" Clem asked gruffly.

"I just wanted to see you," she admitted lamely. "No one else would do in that moment."

Clem was silent for a couple of heartbeats, then he said, "Come here and fasten my cuff links."

Theo threw back the blankets and hurried to his side. Wordlessly, he extended his wrist to her, and she bent her gaze to the lapis lazuli links, threading them through and fastening first one cuff and then the other. Only then, did she raise her eyes to meet Clem's steady gaze.

"I'll get dressed," she said, averting her eyes, but he caught her chin, tilting it up so she met his eyes with hers.

"Only I would do?" he asked softly. Theo nodded. "So, say it, then."

"Only you would do in that moment," she repeated. He stood gazing at her intently before releasing her. "Are you cross with me, Clem?" she blurted.

He shook his head. "Cross with myself."

"Why?"

"Because I should have been waiting there for you."

"But your friends—" she began.

"They would have waited."

He took her to a newly opened establishment in Piccadilly. It was a little fancier than the eating houses they had frequented of late, and Theo found herself gazing about at the smart interior and the fashionable patrons with interest as they waited for their food.

Clem cleared his throat. "How is it that you—?" he started before apparently deciding against his choice of words. "I understand that you were acting, but some of those physical characteristics of yours looked very…authentic."

Theo beamed at him. "Did you really think so?"

"I did." He spoke carefully. "I've seen male impersonators before, of course," he continued. "I've even seen that same scenario played out, or something close enough, but I've never seen anything quite like that before." He looked faintly puzzled as he gazed at her.

Theo felt herself flush with pleasure. "I'm so glad," she said. "That's what my uncle always said you had to do, to have longevity in this game. Find something unique, I mean." When Clem did not speak, just continued to watch her with a faint pucker between his brows, she plunged on. "Of course, the tunes were very catchy, and we were very fortunate that Harold agreed I could change the song lyrics."

"It wasn't the quality of the songs," Clem said dismissively.

"And Lil has a lifetime of treading the boards behind her," she rattled on. "She has a marvelous voice and performs with such confidence and verve."

"She was very good," he agreed briefly. "But I wasn't talking about her."

Theo felt her cheeks grow hot. She traced a finger along the tablecloth. "Are you saying you think I have what it takes to make it in the business, Clem?" she asked, suddenly breathless. Instantly, she was desperate to hear him say just that. She waited with bated breath, but he did not even appear to have heard her.

"It was almost like you disappeared from the stage altogether," he mused. "I could scarcely recognize you, and I don't mean your features. They, of course, remained unchanged, but somehow even the way you stood was completely unrecognizable to me."

Theo thought he sounded a little unnerved. "All of my mannerisms are observed from life," she hastened to explain. "I have hundreds now at my disposal." When Clem gave her a hard look, she felt a little self-conscious. "Of course, I

311

exaggerate some of them for comedic effect," she said quickly, in case he should think she took herself too seriously. "It's the simple art of mimicry really."

He opened his mouth as though to speak, but then seemed to change his mind. She watched him tap a finger against the tablecloth and, almost without thinking, stored away the gesture to try at some later point. "I did not realize that your character was studied from life," he said at last. "So, Percy is a real person? Someone you know?" He did not sound pleased by the notion.

Theo gave a startled laugh. "No, no, nothing of the sort. He is simply a comical caricature I have developed."

"You based him off someone real though?"

"No...it's not like that," she assured him. "He's a composite of many, many young men I have observed over the years. You see, I make a point of studying a stranger every single day. I picked one habit from one and another from another, combined a whole bunch of them together, and came up with Percy."

"But you—" Once again he bit off his words. "I get that he's an exaggeration, Dora, and made up, but the way you walked and talked. Your bearing...everything. It was so..." He broke off as though unable to think of the right word. "Completely unlike you," he said finally, sounding dissatisfied with his own choice of words.

She nodded. "Right, for I was not being me on that stage. I was being Percy."

Clem was silent a moment. "And it is only men that you observe?" he said at last.

"Yes, usually, for my intention was always to take this to the stage. Male impersonation I mean. From a young age."

"I don't see you as a mimic somehow," he said shortly. "I've never seen you do an impression of any of your family or acquaintance in the entire time I've known you."

Instead of pointing out he had only known her for less than three months, Theo tried to explain. "No, I don't do impressions of people who are already formed. That does not interest me." She hesitated. "It's more like I *collect* different characteristics and then store them away for future use. So that at a later point, I can create characters incorporating the different features I have stored away."

He appeared to turn this over a moment. "You do not see yourself embodying Piccadilly Percy then, for the rest of your career?"

"Oh no! Percy will be just one character of many. I hope to have a whole arsenal of them to pick and choose from in the future. In fact—" She hesitated.

"What?" he said quickly.

Theo fiddled with the folded napkin on the table. "It is only that one day, I always hoped I might pick up some actual roles in real plays," she confided in a rush.

"Male roles, you mean?" Clem asked.

"Yes." She nodded. "Not breeches roles traditionally played by women, but actual *male* roles. I could carry them off, you know," she said with all the quiet confidence she felt deep down in her soul. Clem said nothing. "I often read plays and think how I would play the parts," she admitted. "As a braggart, or perhaps a secret drinker, or even a man with a tragic past which drives him." Clem was still eyeing her as though she had suddenly grown an extra head. "Does that sound strange?"

He leaned back in his chair. "If all this is true, then I don't understand why that shepherd character you played was so nondescript."

Theo felt herself color hotly at the criticism, even while she owned it was nothing but the truth. "That was not my fault! I would have dearly loved to have played Daphnis my way, instead of as a mere cardboard cutout. Felix and my uncle always made it quite plain that I was not allowed to fully realize

313

my characters on stage. They did not think it…appropriate somehow."

Clem was silent a moment, the expression on his face unreadable. "Tell me how you would have played him," he said suddenly.

Theo felt her pulse quicken as she leaned forward in her chair. He really wanted to know? She did not even have to think twice about it. "That's easy, I would have played him as an earnest young puppy nursing a terrific crush on his shepherdess. He would not have been remotely lecherous like Percy but would have elevated his beloved onto a pedestal. He would have avoided her eye whenever he spoke to her, and I would have had his voice crack occasionally over his dialogue. They do that sometimes, you know," she said eagerly. "Male youths, I mean."

Clem gave a brief smile at this. "I am aware," he said dryly. "It just seems a little disconcerting that *you* are. Some of your observations…" His words trailed off.

"Yes?" she prompted eagerly.

"They're a little *too* accurate, if you know what I mean."

She did not know what he meant. Not really, but she took a stab at it in any case. "You—you think it is improper too, don't you?" she blurted, feeling ridiculously crestfallen.

When he did not answer at once, Theo felt her spirits plummet to her feet.

"It's not that," he said at last. "God knows, I'm no prude, and music hall is all about being improper. I've seen far worse," he carried on, almost as though he was trying to convince himself.

Worse, thought Theo, her heart in her throat.

Catching sight of her expression, he waved his hand. "You know you went down like a storm, Dora. I meant no criticism of your turn."

"But you—you did not enjoy it? Personally, I mean," she heard herself ask in a small voice.

He straightened up in his seat. "No such thing. I thought it was masterful," he said heartily and reached for the strange drink the proprietor had brought them of tomato juice and something else she could not identify. Clem had told her it was supposedly good for the morning after a night of indulgence. He drained his glass. "Ignore me, I'm in a strange mood and slightly hungover. I did not mean to bring your spirits down."

He shot her a charming smile, which did not touch his eyes at all. "It's very clever," he said. "Damnably clever. Just…it's a little uncanny, how you do it. Caught me off guard. That's all."

Uncanny? Theo watched him uncertainly, biting her lip. He remained strangely distant and polite throughout their meal, scaring her a little. Almost as though he was treating her like someone he did not really know. Then at last, he seemed to notice her unease and made the effort to rouse himself, keeping up a flow of easy conversation that somehow did not entirely dispel Theo's disquiet.

By the time they returned home, things seemed a lot nearer normal, and Theo told herself she was likely imagining things. Besides, she had a matinee performance to put on, so she did not have time to dwell anymore on Clem's strange manner.

24

"Lil," Theo asked determinedly on Sunday evening as they readied themselves for their fifth performance. More flowers had arrived at The Eagle that morning. She had received a large bouquet from Clem's fight promoter friend Nat Jones that, along with Clem's tributes, took up a whole corner of their poky dressing room. Lil had also received her fair share of posies, which stood about the room in various jam jars filled with water.

"Yes, darlin?" Lil responded, not looking up from where she was straightening her stockings.

"What *was* the joke Friday night, when the curtain came back up and you were knelt at my feet?"

Lil glanced up. "Dunno wot you mean, sweetheart," she answered, but Theo could tell at once her friend had a shifty look in her eye. Theo had duly repeated Clem's warning on the afternoon of their Saturday performance, and Lil had rolled her eyes but dropped the pose from subsequent shows.

"I thought you were wiping off your smudged lip stain until Clem said that about the Moral Decency Board. Even they could not be as puritanical as all that."

Lil gave a gurgle of laughter. "Fancy 'im getting his knickers in a twist over a thing like that," she said, sounding amused.

"If you don't tell me, then I'll be forced to ask someone else," Theo warned, turning over her shirt collar. "As my closest friend, I think it is rather unfair of you to withhold such knowledge from me, especially now we are partners."

Lil sighed. "It was just a visual gag, love. An oral joke if you will." At Theo's blank response, Lil was forced to elucidate.

"Oh, I *see*," Theo breathed. "I wonder why he would not simply tell me outright."

"Maybe he's trying to act the gent around you," Lil pondered, adjusting the drawstrings on her hooped petticoat. "Sometimes men can be funny when it comes to women what they actually respect."

Theo frowned. "But he has no objection to performing orally on a lady, so why should he find the reference so distasteful the other way around?"

Lil went off in a coughing fit. "Lord, Theo!" she gasped at last when she managed to swallow down half a glass of water. "The things you come out with! Gawd bless you, darlin', you'd have to ask 'im that question yourself. For the time being, I'll just straddle your lap and 'ope that don't affect his delicate sensibilities."

"I suppose to be fair, it would be just as bad if I was kneeling between your legs when the curtain came up," Theo mused, drawing on her silk waistcoat. "To a Purity Committee, or whatever they are called."

Lil wiped her eyes. "Very likely," she agreed in a choked voice.

"Only I have not heard of such a regulating body before. Is it something that occurs often to music hall acts?"

"It does 'appen occasionally," Lil admitted cagily. "If you gain a certain level of notoriety, but mostly they just leaves the great unwashed to it." She shrugged. "Fame often comes with a cost, but I don't think we've reached them dizzy heights just yet, love."

Theo pinned her tie pin into place and shrugged on her jacket. "What do you think?" she said, turning to Lil.

"Pure Percy has become a man," Lil said with a wink. "I quite fancies you meself!"

Five minutes before they were due on stage, a knock on the door turned out to be the biggest and ugliest of the doormen called Eddie, who had come along to carry their props.

"My, aren't we honored?" Lil said sotto voce after he had collected their bits and pieces. And that was not the only sign of high favor. When they exited their room, Lil inhaled sharply and pointed at the door Theo was shutting behind them. "Look!"

Theo turned and found a painted sign on the door now proudly proclaimed, "Dora Dabney and Lillian Longdon." A grin spread over her face. "Lil," she said, turning to her friend. "We are no longer miscellaneous."

"We've bloody done it!" Lil said, plunking her hands on her hips. "We've arrived. Now, where's that lovelorn pianist of yours? We've got a show to put on!" They linked arms and started along the corridor.

"Lovelorn?" Theo echoed in surprise.

"You should of seen the way Allsop was staring at you with his mouth open at rehearsal," Lil observed, squeezing her arm. "I told him flat, it's too late for that, lad; that ship has sailed."

"Oh, Lil! It was the risqué lyrics that put that look on Harold's face," Theo replied roundly. "And he was such a dear about it too and has not uttered so much as a single reproach though his face was scarlet at the run-through." She dwelt a moment fondly on Harold. "You know, lately I've begun to think he might have had a thing for Henrietta all these years."

"Oh Henrietta!" Lil said irritably. "You think everyone's sweet on that sister of yours. She's yesterday's news."

Theo frowned. "I wish she would hurry up and write. I can't be quite easy in my mind about her until she does."

Lil made no reply, as at this point a gaggle of dancing girls came down the corridor toward them and they had to separate and walk single file to make room. Theo smiled and nodded but received only surreptitious glances in reply. As soon as they had passed them, the dancers burst into giggles and whispers.

"Silly tarts," Lil observed.

"Lil…"

"Listen, I'm allowed to say such things, cos I was one meself and it takes one to know one!"

"I hope the other acts warm up to us soon," Theo sighed, casting a glance over her shoulder. One of the dancers who was staring back at her looked hurriedly away.

"Fat chance!" Lil snorted. "We're too popular with the paying public, my dear. Everyone else will be jealous as hell." Lil sounded vastly smug about the fact, and really, Theo thought as they emerged into the auditorium and took their place at the shadowy side of the stage, she could not be *too* cut up about the fact they weren't popular with their fellow entertainers. Not when they were already the audience's darlings.

Larry the compere was running through a few gags, but he had lost the crowd as soon as they took their place beside the stage steps. The murmuring started, and though she tried to ignore it, Theo could see people pointing and jostling each other. "*Lil and Perce!*" were the names she heard repeated over and over again, increasing in volume.

"These are the ones I was tellin' you about, Mother!" Theo heard one woman hiss excitedly in the front row. "You'll love this!"

Theo felt her chest swell with pride. She glanced across and saw Harold already seated dutifully at the piano. This was what she had longed for all those years. All her practice, all her wishing had finally come to fruition. She was a male impersonator at last. And she was *appreciated*.

"That one!" someone announced nearby. "Ooh, 'e's my favorite. Ain't 'e lovely?"

"That's a woman, you fool!" her companion pointed out.

"I know that, you great berk! No man could be that pretty, more's the pity!"

319

"And now, I'll stop denying them the stage, for I know full well you're all clamoring to see them once again," Larry said with his oily charm, gesturing toward them. "Without more ado, I give you the Lovely Lily Longdon and Piccadilly Percy himself!"

Theo first handed up Lil and then ran up the stairs behind her as Harold launched into a spirited rendition of their signature chorus and all was right with her world for the next golden half hour. Performing at The Eagle made her ecstatically and blissfully happy. She drifted back off stage and afterward could barely remember what she and Lil had chattered about as they changed out of their costumes.

A knock on the door revealed Eddie's blunt features again. "There's some urchin out here," he said doubtfully. "Says as he's a friend of yours, Miss Dabney."

"Albert?" Theo called out. "Is that you?" To her surprise, Albert did not elbow Eddie out of the way and immediately appear in the doorway but instead loitered bashfully in the corridor until he was ushered inside. "Never fear, we're all decent," Theo assured him with a smile.

Dragging his cap off his head, the boy cast a fleeting glance at her face before coloring hotly. "I seen your act," he muttered hoarsely.

"You came to see me?" Theo was both startled and delighted. "Who did you come with? Your brother or some of your fellow paper boys?"

"Me bruvver," Albert answered. "Only he don't believe we're friends," he started hotly. "Says I'm tellin' tales and not to pull his leg!"

Theo looked at his flushed, indignant face. "Well, that is a good deal too bad of him!" she pronounced. "Where is he? Have him brought here at once and I shall put him straight on our friendship of long standing!"

Albert's expression brightened. "Would you tell him, miss?"

"Gladly!"

Albert broke out all smiles. "'E's round the corner at The Dog and Duck," he said eagerly. "'Im and 'is friends. 'E said to bring you along and he'll stand you to a mug of rum punch. Only 'e said it as a jest like," Albert added bitterly. "And they all laughed like 'e's a proper wag!"

"Well, we shall go there forthwith, and I shall set them to rights," Theo pronounced. Albert instantly perked, up and Theo drew down her paletot from its peg.

Lil crossed the room and opened the door. "Eddie!" she shouted up the corridor. "Come back 'ere, luv. Only Miss Dabney requires an escort for 'alf an hour."

Theo was surprised, for it was only four o'clock and still light out. Seeing her raised brows, Lil said quietly, "Don't want to get on the wrong side of that 'usband of yours again, do I?"

"Clem's not even here," Theo pointed out. "He has business this afternoon in Clapham."

"I don't care if he's at Buckingham Palace," Lil responded dryly. "He has a disquieting habit of finding things out. He also would not like you consorting with unknown men in rowdy drinking places. You take my word for it."

"I been out wiv Miss Theodora an 'undred times wivout no chaperone!" Albert muttered resentfully.

"She wasn't married then though, was she?" Lil retorted smartly. "I mean to make sure she avoids the pitfalls I fell into." A wistful look passed over her face which Theo knew meant she was thinking of the husband who had left her.

Theo, having pulled on her gloves, reached for Albert's hand and gave it a consoling squeeze. "Never mind, Albert. We both know you are all the chaperone I require, but we had better respect Clem's feelings on the subject."

She had been expecting the boy to put up a spirited argument, but to her surprise, he acquiesced at once, mumbling in agreement, and she rather wondered if he was not a little under the weather for he was very red in the face.

Eddie pronounced himself agreeable, and the three of them set off for The Dog and Duck where Theo spent an agreeable hour being regaled by Albert's older brother and his friends. It was true, at first, they had been disbelieving, then frankly stunned, then rather cowed by Eddie's looming presence. But after a couple of rum punches, they had lapsed into enthusiastic admiration of her performance, and they had been quite the merriest table in the place.

Albert, when not fetching her lemonade, for she turned down the rum punch as she still had an evening performance to deliver, had spent the whole time perched at her side, holding her handbag, and reminding her of the many offices he had performed on her behalf over the years. "Why, it was even me wot bore her love notes to Dabney and his to her, ain't that right, Miss Theodora? 'Twas me wot brought your courtship off so to speak."

"It is true," she gravely told the table at large. "Albert is one of my oldest and most trusted friends. If it were not for him, I would not be the performer that sits before you now."

"Here's to Albert!" cried one of the young men, raising his mug aloft. "Love's messenger and Miss Dabney's champion of hearts!"

Albert had been highly gratified, and the episode a huge success. She told Clem of it on their way to the evening performance and he was remarkably quiet in response. "Eddie accompanied you, you say?" was his only comment. "Next time take Sam along with you too."

"Both of them?" Theo was startled.

"This isn't The Parthenon," he replied. "I have twelve doormen, not just Vincent. I can spare two of them to accompany my wife about town when I am not there."

Theo gave him a sidelong look and lapsed into silence. She could not quite put her finger on it, but something was still not right with Clem. Suddenly, she remembered something that had puzzled her from the Friday night when they had been out with his boxing friends. Could that be the reason he was so off-color? "What was that thing that Nat Jones wanted from you on Friday night?" she asked curiously. "He sent me some beautiful flowers to the concert rooms, you know, almost as nice as yours."

Clem turned his head to look at her. "Noticed that, did you? Old Nat's trying to butter me up, but it won't do any good. I'm too out of condition for a fight. I haven't trained in…let me see, it must be eight or nine months."

"He wanted to sign you up for a boxing match?"

Clem nodded. "They want a money match for the next challenger."

"Challenger?"

"The Diamond they call him. He's an American, and he'll be the next to face Ben for the championship. Once he's got through this next match. They want to drum up a bit more interest in this country first and make a little money off his back."

"And Nat Jones wants you to fight this Diamond?" Theo asked. "What a strange name. I thought that was what they call beautiful women, diamonds. Is he so very attractive?"

"Not to me. Diamonds are also the hardest natural material known to man," Clem pointed out. "I think that might be the reason for his moniker."

Theo was impressed by this fact. "Why does Nat want you to fight him?" she asked. "Are you the next best in England after your friend Ben?"

Clem gave a short laugh. "No, but folks here know my name, and I've always been able to draw a crowd." He shot her a sly look and stroked a finger lightly down his jaw. "Maybe on account of this handsome face people want to see me get punched in."

"It seems a lifetime ago that I said that," Theo said defensively, shifting in her seat. "I scarcely knew you back then!" He smiled but shook his head, refusing to be drawn on the subject. She was strangely disappointed, for she could not help but suspect that in the past he would have teased her further, whereas tonight he let the subject drop. Why was Clem being so, so…*cool* with her?

"Clem," she said impulsively.

"Hmmm?"

"Did it…feel strange to see me dressed as a man, I mean?" she asked, suddenly prey to the strangest fears. Had he finally noticed her distinct lack of feminine charm?

"Strange?"

The hackney cab came to a lurching halt, and turning her head, Theo saw they had arrived at The Eagle. "Never mind," she mumbled and made a grab for her reticule and umbrella. "I'm just being silly. Forget I said anything."

25

"Clem?" Dora's voice startled him out of his thoughts as he sat opposite her two weeks later on the new couches in their sitting room. He looked up enquiringly. "I want to get my hair trimmed again tomorrow but"—she hesitated—"will you be honest with me? Does its short length give you a repulsion of me?"

He stared at her a moment, her words not making any immediate sense. "What did you say?"

"I said—"

"Of course not!" he thundered. "Where the hell would you pick up an idea like that?"

She swallowed and averted her eyes. "I couldn't really say," she responded unconvincingly. Then when he narrowed his eyes at her, she added, "Albert said I would catch it if I let the barber take the clippers to the back of my neck."

"Catch it?"

"From you. Because you would be annoyed, presumably."

"Albert being the expert on husbandly reactions," Clem could not help himself from retorting. Albert was an annoying little fucker as far as Clem was concerned. He was tempted to give him a thick ear next time he saw him.

He was starting to feel that way about a few people lately, he realized tetchily. Larry, that smarmy bastard, had started referring to her theatrically as "our Dora" in a way that made Clem want to punch him square in the face. He had a feeling Jim had taken the announcer aside and had a word as he had not done it the past couple of days, something Clem was profoundly grateful for.

It was odd, as Clem had always been so unruffled in the face of provocation before now. It had always been so well known in the fighting fraternity that he could not be baited or tricked into losing his temper by a smart mouth. In the past, he had been more inclined to laugh at ring antics than snap. Well, he did not feel like laughing now, and the likes of Harold Allsop and Larry Burgess were frankly undeserving of his mettle.

It wasn't even as though they were trying to rile him up. Allsop was a nervy, artistic type, and Larry was just a fucking fool. Clem did not really know what had gotten into him, but he guessed it was partly due to his guilty conscience. Now he was no longer dreading Dora flopping, he was starting to sweat about her learning of his shares instead. A permanent knot in his stomach was starting to feel familiar to him.

Dora had given over a dozen sellout performances as Piccadilly Percy. Each and every one of them had brought the house down. Clem had been forced to concede that her initial triumph had been no fluke. With each performance, she had seemed to grow before his eyes in stature and strength. This was not a blind spot or an obsession to her, he realized belatedly. Front of stage was her rightful fucking place, and she *excelled* at it.

Each successful showing seemed to embolden her further, and she varied her performance each time, trying out different gestures, laying a different stress on her words, revealing a different expression. As such, no two performances were ever the same, so he was scarcely surprised that the same people came to see her over and over, sometimes to both matinee and evening performances on the same day.

So many bunches of flowers, from humble nosegays to great big arrangements, had found their way to Dora's dressing room that Clem had been forced to tell Jim to swap them to a larger room to house them all. Some were for Lil, it was true, but not the majority, not by a long shot. Clem was under no illusion about that.

People had started hanging around the exit to call out to Dora when he escorted her from the building after her evening performances. She would smile and wave and they would run alongside the cab, shouting greetings or throwing flowers to her. Some of the most ardent were female admirers, who called her "Dora darlin'" and showered her with lavish compliments. He had to instruct Eddie and Sam to take her to and from the house whenever he could not accompany her.

Thank God she was sensible enough to turn down all the invitations to lunch and dinner that flooded in and seemingly turned a blind eye to the rolled-up and concealed missives that were tucked amid the posy stems, propositioning her to God only knew what. Clem didn't want to know. He was seriously in danger of losing it if directly confronted with such information.

The audience had started joining in on the choruses now, and Clem frequently heard his bar staff whistling both of her catchy songs. Dora was already working on adapting another of Allsop's musical numbers for her purpose. As for Allsop, he had nervously confessed at dinner the night before that he had started writing a brand-new composition for her, "Though," he had added painstakingly, "you will need to add in the lyrics yourself."

Allsop had then turned to Fields and told him with apparent sincerity that he should really come along and watch his sister's performance as it was "Terribly good, you know." Clem had snidely asked him when he was going to tell his great-aunt that he was now a music hall performer. Poor old Allsop had turned quite pale and almost dropped the salt cellar into his gravy.

"He's joking," Dora had assured the anxious musician, and Clem had flashed him his teeth in a mirthless smile. If anything, that seemed to alarm Allsop even more.

"Maybe I should pop along," Fields had harrumphed, casting an uncertain look about the table. "One of the, er, newspaper reviewers gave you a mention this morning, by the way. Did you happen to see it?" He glanced enquiringly first at Dora and then at Clem. "In the *Standard*."

"No, really?" Dora was wide-eyed, and to give him his due, her brother promptly abandoned his dinner to go and fetch the paper in question. He had folded it to the correct page and outlined it in green ink by the time he passed it to her. "'The incomparable Miss Dora Dabney,'" Felix quoted humorously. "Is that what you are going by now?"

"It is," Dora agreed, taking the newspaper from him and casting her eyes over the print. Clem watched her flush as she read the review. "Well," she said calmly, "that is quite the ringing endorsement, though I think the reviewer is being needlessly snobby about music hall."

Clem held out his hand and she passed it to him. "'Mistress Dora Dabney outshines the rest like a beacon of light poised atop a dunghill,'" he read tonelessly.

"Mixing their metaphors there a bit," Fields said dryly, "but there is a compliment in there somewhere."

"Not to The Eagle," Clem remarked, and Dora bit her lip.

In truth, he could not even resent it, for he knew the *Standard*'s critic spoke no more than the truth. Even Clem could not prevent himself from stealing into the auditorium night after night to stand at the back and watch this dazzling performer who commanded the stage with such assurance and sheer bloody talent.

She took his breath away.

He could scarcely believe this was the same actress he had watched all those weeks ago in that insipid bloody play. *Miss Fields…standing around in a pair of silk breeches does not a male impersonator make.* The words he had spoken back then now stung him like the lash of a whip. He had been unbelievably blind. He had not *seen* her. She had been right all along. She had not been given her chance.

328

Once she had, she had snatched that chance and spun it into pure bloody gold. All along, her blazing lamp had been hidden under a bushel. Slowly, missing puzzle pieces of Dora finally fitted into place. The avid people watching. It had always mystified him, but now it made perfect sense. She studied from life and drew characters from thin air. *She* was the magician, not Roberto Russo.

And she thought he had believed in her all along. His stupidity and his lack of trustworthiness made his own gorge rise. She must never, never find out what a faithless swine he was.

"So, you don't mind, then?" she persisted. "If I get it cut a little shorter into my neck? My hair I mean."

Clem gazed at her a moment, then on impulse, he reached for his notebook and threw it across to her. She caught it and looked at him enquiringly. "Take a look," he recommended.

"What is this?" Dora asked, starting to flip the pages. "It looks like reminders for your daily tasks. How organized you are—" she started only to stop abruptly and stare at the page. "Why Clem," she breathed.

"Keep turning," he said grimly.

She flipped a few more pages and then halted again, her throat working. "Clem," she repeated, sounding choked. "You're an artist! And you never said!"

He gave a short laugh. "An artist? Hardly that."

"But you *must* have studied," she said wonderingly, lifting the book closer to her face.

"A little," he admitted cautiously. "There was a drawing master at my school, but I never took it seriously."

"You were at that school a long time though," she reminded him quietly.

He shrugged. "Drawing and mathematics were the only lessons I liked."

"You said your mathematics teacher was an avid follower of boxing, I think," she said, screwing up her eyes.

Once again, Clem braced himself against the memory. Yes, he had told her that, another time when he was being a condescending prick. "Yes," he murmured, shoving down his uncomfortable recollections. "It was he who gave me my first boxing lessons. Mr. Mapperly. Not that he was an expert, far from it, but he was one of the few decent teachers at that godforsaken place."

"Was it so very bad a time?" she asked sympathetically.

"My accent at that age set me apart from the other boys, and I had bitten off half of another boy's ear before they realized I was no victim. Mr. Mapperly decided it would be beneficial to teach me 'the gentlemanly art' of boxing. Eventually he managed to convince the headmaster that pugilism would be more useful to the boys they taught than fencing and we got a new sports master."

"What was he like?"

"Old Rigby?" Clem answered with a grin. "Well, he had none of Mr. Mapperly's illusions about it being a gentleman's sport. He was more of a realist, was Rigby. I could already throw a solid punch, could use my fists far better than any of my fellow pupils, but I learned the rudiments of the science from him, after a fashion.

"Rigby told me Mapperly's accounts of 'Gentleman Jim' and the pamphlets and clippings he collected were mostly horseshit," Clem admitted. "Not that cared. I read all Mapperly's scrapbooks cover to cover. He had printed accounts of all the famous fights of the period, and they were better by far than anything else they were trying to force us to read."

Dora was listening intently. "Did Mr. Mapperly or Mr. Rigby never come to watch you fight after you became a prizefighter?"

He was surprised she had guessed such a thing. "They did," he admitted. "Rigby was an alcoholic and died a couple of years back, but old Mapperly still writes to me from time to time. He didn't approve of me buying a concert hall," he said with a smirk. "Those aren't gentlemanlike in his book."

Her eyes met his for a moment before they fell away and returned to his sketches. "You know, you've almost made me look…" She broke off to turn another page. "Do I *really* look like that to you?"

"My poor skills can scarcely do you, or anyone, justice."

"You're wrong. You've flattered me to an uncommon degree. I daresay you would be vastly popular for society portraits with such a generous interpretation."

He shook his head. "I don't see everyone in a generous light, Dora," he admitted.

She swallowed. "Only me?" she suggested uncertainly, then flushed. "Forget I said that!" she added quickly with an awkward laugh. "Felix would say I was fishing for a compliment!"

Clem could feel his own eyes burning into her. "Dora," he whispered achingly. He had not touched her the past few days. Well, he had *touched*, the merest brush of an arm, the whisper of a polite kiss to her cheek. Such touches were not enough. They never had been, where she was concerned. Even when he had thought her a dotty old maid, he had wanted to bed her. And why was that?

"Clem?" She rose from her seat and came across to join him on his couch, dropping down beside him. She shook her head slightly, still holding his notebook clasped in her arms. "When I think," she marveled, "that all this time I worried you did not even like my short hair."

"I didn't at first," he admitted, "until I became completely obsessed with it." He reached across and brushed his fingers across the back of her neck. "It's the shape here"—he

331

hesitated—"at the base of your neck. The line of your neck and shoulder is…" He swallowed, his words roughening. "It's just exquisite, Dora." Jesus, was he blushing? He sounded ridiculous. Like some idiot who did not know how to talk to women.

"You really *must* view me through the eyes of an artist," Dora continued wonderingly. "My uncle always said I was all arms and legs."

"I see you with the eyes of a man," he contradicted her flatly. "A man who likes your body. A lot."

"Would you draw me from life?" she asked excitedly.

"What?"

"Would you? I have some charcoal somewhere and plenty of cartridge paper." She started up impetuously and Clem reached out to catch her wrist.

"Dora…"

"*Please*, Clem?"

She looked so hopeful he did not have it in him to refuse her. Besides, he was in a strange mood, had been in one for days. "I'm rusty," he warned, releasing her.

"You can just do some rough sketches," she wheedled. "I promise you I will be thrilled with whatever you produce." Well, he could believe that. He sighed and shrugged, and Dora's eyes lit up. "Give me just one minute," she said, dashing out of the room. He heard their bedroom door bang and picked up his glass, swirling his drink. He should have just pounced on her, he realized belatedly. Sex would have been a far easier way to feel closer to her.

When Dora reappeared, she was carrying a box of crayons, a sheaf of papers, and a drawing board and looking very businesslike. She had also changed into one of the strange theatrical robes she favored so much when she was just at home. After plunking the supplies down in front of him, she turned about surveying the room.

"How should I arrange myself?" she asked, sitting rather formally on the couch opposite.

"Not like that," Clem said, eyeing her as he spilled the crayons out onto the table. He did not know how he wanted her precisely. More relaxed somehow. "A more informal pose."

She propped her elbow on the arm. "Like this?"

Clem frowned. "No," he said, picking up a red crayon.

"Tell me someone to do an impression of," she said, eyes gleaming.

"No," Clem repeated swiftly. He did not know what he wanted precisely, but he knew he didn't want that. "Do something else for a while," he suggested instead. "Something that will occupy you and take your mind off posing altogether."

He saw her frown and then get an idea, for she stood up again and walked to the cabinet, opening the drawer. When she returned, she held a pack of cards up to show it to him. "I used to play clock patience a lot as a child."

Clem nodded and watched as she sat back down again and started placing the cards in the shape of a clock face. He leaned back in his chair, propping the drawing board against his leg, just watching as her actions became more fluid and natural.

"We used to play cards all the time when we were younger," she confided. "Felix, Hetty, and I."

"What games did you play?" Clem asked automatically as he started to stroke the crayon over the page.

"All kinds."

"Poker?"

"Oh yes," she said. "That one was Felix's favorite for a while."

After discarding the first sketch, Clem rolled up his shirtsleeves and leaned forward in his seat. Dora, it seemed, had grown tired of patience, for she was now shuffling the cards, fanning and cutting the deck, her actions swift and deliberate. Each time she reassembled the pack, she paused to hold her

333

hands out before her in a curious gesture he suddenly recognized.

"Who taught you to shuffle a deck?" he asked, a suspicion forming in his mind.

"A doorman we had years ago when I was a girl. Long before Vincent started. His name was Thomas."

"Hmmm. Do you know why Thomas showed his wrists like that each time before he touched the deck?"

She looked up, startled. "No. I just liked the way he did it, slowing his quick hands for a moment." She looked suddenly intrigued. "Why *did* he do it?"

He was amused in spite of himself. "He was showing you there was no card hidden up his cuffs."

"Ohhhh."

"Show me what else you learned from him," he prompted her.

She spread out the cards again, her clever fingers dancing over the pack, touching one card before selecting another. *Distraction.* He doubted she had even been aware she was imitating a card sharp all these years.

"Best of all, I liked the way he took snuff," she confided. "But when I tried it in the privacy of my own room, it made me sneeze for five whole minutes. Then when I blew my nose that evening, the color of my handkerchief alarmed me."

A reluctant smile curved his lips. "Show me how he did it."

She dropped her cards at once and pretended to flick open a small lidded box before peppering the contents along the back of her hand with a studied nonchalance. Then she lowered her nose, sniffing with first one nostril and then the other, and then tugging at her nose with thumb and forefinger. "Uncle used to say Thomas thought himself quite the dandy."

Clem laughed. "Ever seen anyone chew tobacco?" he asked.

334

"Yes," she admitted. "But my uncle caught me spitting once and it was the closest I ever came to getting a hiding. In any case, I doubt they would ever let me do that on stage, even at a music hall." He saw her peer across. "How is the sketching going?" she asked. He gave a short shrug. "Should I put my ringlets in?"

He frowned, shaking his head. "No. It's the shape of your head that I like." He hesitated before confessing, "I'd like to draw the nape of your neck next." His voice thickened strangely over the words. Instead of asking what the hell was wrong with him, Dora stood up abruptly and went to grab one of the chairs next to the window, dragging it into the middle of the room. She turned it about, so she was facing away from him. Then she plunked it down and dropped back into it.

Clem cleared his throat, discarded the page he had been using, and started a fresh sketch, this time focused on the back view of her bent neck and shoulders. He had no idea why he found the sight of her exposed neck so erotic; he just knew that he did. "When you get it cut this time, you could maybe go a little shorter at the back," he suggested, wondering why that made his pulse race. "And really give Albert something to think about it.

She chuckled. "I think I could go shorter too," she agreed, sounding pleased, "as really, it's quite long at the front. If I pull it straight, it practically touches my chin." She was quiet a moment, then mused, "I wonder if the reason you like my nape so much has anything to do with how much you like to be touched there."

Fuck. "I don't know," he admitted raggedly. "Maybe?"

"Can I get up and grab a book?" she asked.

"Of course." She retrieved one from a side table. "What are you reading?" he asked to distract himself as his fingers worked the crayon over the page, his pencil strokes slowly forming a semblance of her lovely, lovely neck.

335

"I found a copy of a sanitized version of *Romeo and Juliet* in the parlor," she told him guiltily. "I think it must be Harold's as Felix and Hetty both feel the same as I do about leaving the Bard intact. I was curious and took it, but I will be sure to put it back once I am done."

"How are you finding it?" Clem asked lazily, but really only because he wanted to hear her voice.

"An awful lot of the original text has been expunged," Dora said disapprovingly. "The character of Juliet's nurse has disappeared *altogether*, and I just cannot imagine what the ending will be. I mean, if the ending has been rewritten then…well, it's not even a tragedy anymore, is it?"

"What was the original ending?" Clem asked without much interest.

"Mmmm? Oh, the lovers both die," Dora said absently.

Clem snorted. "Sounds nearly as bad as that play we saw the other week."

"But through their death, their family's feud is ended," she explained. "So, it was not as bleak as *The Duchess of Malfi*. But now that Romeo has *not* killed his wife's cousin, then…well, a lot of the motivation does not make sense." He could practically hear the frown in her voice.

"Killing his wife's cousin sounds a stupid thing to do, in any case," Clem remarked dispassionately.

"Yes, but people are always doing ridiculous things in tragedies…" She trailed off, turning the page.

Sometimes in real life too, Clem thought as the room fell into silence save for the scrape of the crayon against the page and the crackle of the fireplace. He was fully absorbed now in his task and let her concentrate on her book. He was just wondering if she had finally nodded off when she snapped the book shut almost an hour later.

"Well?" he asked.

Dora turned her head to look at him over her shoulder. "Have you finished your sketch?" She looked surprised to see he was now sat at the other end of the sofa.

"I wanted to see your profile," he explained. "I've done a few scribbles, but they're nothing to get excited over."

Dora stretched, then walked over to the table where most of the drawings lay. He heard her sharply indrawn breath. "Oh, Clem," she quavered and kept a reverent silence as she sifted slowly through the pages, darting the odd incredulous glance his way. "You're really talented."

He made a dismissive noise in his throat. "How did the revised play end?"

"Hmmm?"

"*Romeo and Juliet*, was it?

"Oh, well, it was all a bit…anticlimactic to be honest," she said, still examining his sketches. "I mean, they're not star-crossed lovers anymore, are they? They just run off together to Mantua at the end." She chewed the side of her mouth. "It always broke my heart when Juliet awakes from her drugged slumber just that fraction too late to prevent Romeo from taking his life, but…"

"But what?"

"Well, the revised play simply does not have the impact at the end that it does with their deaths."

Clem grunted. It sounded fucking stupid to him, but what did he know? He was an uncultured lout, even if he had been to school.

"Clem, could I have one of these?" she asked, clasping her hands together. "*Please?*"

He snorted. "You can have all of them. Except these two," he said, glancing down at the drawings he had spent the longest over, the ones that still rested on the drawing board in his lap.

She moved across curiously. "May I take a look?"

337

He nodded but made no move to hand them over. Instead, she sat down beside him and leaned across, resting her shoulder against his as she stared at the uppermost picture he had drawn which showed her side in profile as she sat reading her book. She reached up to trace her finger over her nose. "I always thought I had a rather long, bony nose," she murmured. "But you make it look perfectly in proportion to my jawline."

"It is," he said dismissively. "Your face is perfectly balanced."

She breathed in sharply. "Perfectly balanced?" she echoed lightly. Then she drew the top picture aside to see the one that lay beneath. The one depicting her bent neck and the back of her head. For some reason, Clem felt himself squirming inside as though he had been caught indulging in something frowned on. He felt like his soul had been slightly exposed, a notion he realized was both fanciful and absurd.

"You make me look beautiful," she said at last with a queer little laugh. "I can hardly believe it."

"You are beautiful," Clem said, and the wonder of it was he fucking meant it. He meant it, though the beauty he was speaking of was an entirely different beauty to that which he had always measured women by before, and by which he knew society measured them. His eyes roamed over her face. "Every time I look at you—" He broke off, shaking his head in disbelief. "It seems like I notice more and more things about you that I like."

Dora breathed out. "Clem," she murmured, sounding shaken.

Suddenly, he felt his spine tingle a warning that he was poised on some dangerous ledge and about to fall off it. If he did not rein things in at this point, he and Dora would go plunging right off the edge, and he could never pull back.

This was a momentary infatuation after all. He just wasn't himself lately. He always bored of women. Some lasted longer than others, but all his liaisons burned out into indifference in the end. More importantly, he did not want her to be hurt when this inevitably happened. Dora was different. She was incredible and he needed to protect her, even if it was against his fickle self.

He needed to lighten the tone. Leaning in closer, he murmured flirtatiously, "You have the loveliest nape in all the world, Dorabelle. *That* is why you cut your hair, you sly thing."

She gave a startled laugh. "To show it off?"

He nodded and leaned in again. "To seduce me. I never even knew that area of the body was erotic," he said wonderingly. "What an innocent I was."

"Hah!" Dora regarded him sidelong and shook her head. "Probably hundreds of ladies have napes far lovelier than mine, they just hide them under great swaths of hair."

"Impossible. I won't hear of such blasphemy." Her eyes danced, and he had to kiss her, lingeringly and with far too much tenderness. He wanted to *worship* her body with his, and even the thought of it had him groaning into her mouth. "Dora," he whispered.

"Yes?" she asked breathlessly.

"Kiss me like you did the other night," he responded huskily.

"Which night?"

"That night where I was in a bad mood, and you took control," he admitted. What the fuck was he even saying?

Dora's mouth formed a silent *oh* of comprehension. With deliberation, she slid her hand up his muscular upper arm and across his shoulder. When she finally reached the back of his neck, he bit back a groan. Dora rubbed her hand there a moment, running her thumb over and over a spot he seemed to like. "You *are* sensitive here, Clem," she murmured. He gave a noncommittal rumble, which almost had her smiling. Who was he trying to fool? It must be blatantly obvious to her by this point.

Then she slid her hand up into his hair and tugged him there, so he lowered his head to receive her kiss. Then she let him have it, kissing him without any reserve at all, holding nothing back. Christ, who had taught her to kiss like that? Was it him? He groaned into her mouth, his hands first gripping her hips and then wrapping around her back to pull her in tighter against him.

She kissed her way over to his ear. "Let's go to bed," she suggested, setting his heart racing.

"Seduce me here instead" was his counteroffer.

"Here?" She sounded startled.

"That was what I wanted the other day," he admitted, "but I didn't quite have the nerve to ask for it."

"*You* lacked nerve, Clem?"

"It's true; you make me feel *almost* bashful sometimes," he murmured.

"I do not believe that for an instant!"

"It's true," he insisted, stroking his fingers through the short hair at the back of her neck. "I'm also a little jealous that Albert gets to take you to his barber tomorrow," he confessed, not quite meeting her gaze.

She pulled back to look at him quizzically. "You are not serious?"

"Oh, but I am. I'm in a bad way." He leaned forward to kiss the skeptical look off her face.

Thoughtfully, she dropped her other hand back to his hard shaft and started fondling him there.

His groans started up again, and she pushed against his chest until he sank back on the sofa.

"Remember how you toyed with me at the theater, Clem?" she asked lightly, beginning a little experimentation of her own. When his hips began to strain, she dropped her fingertips down

340

to lightly trace his balls, gently caressing, squeezing, and rolling them when he made no effort to stop her.

"Uhhhh, Dora," he moaned, tearing his mouth from hers. "What the hell are you doing to me?"

"It's pleasurable to delay sometimes, was what you said at the time," she reminded him. He gave her a tortured look, and she began to stroke his shaft again in earnest, before slackening off when he grew too eager.

Clem breathed in a ragged breath. "Dora, sweetheart…"

"I remember it specifically," she said sweetly, her hand slowing down to the most delicate of flutters.

His eyes narrowed. "You, madam, are becoming quite the tease."

Dora could not quite hide her smile. "Shall I put you out of your misery, then?"

"Yes, please," he answered frankly, and she gave a breathless laugh as she reached down to palm him.

"Clem," she murmured. "You will have to tutor me on this next part, as I have not done it before."

"What do you mean?" Small wonder but he could scarcely think straight by this point.

"Well, my contraceptive veil is in the bedroom, so…we need to use an alternate method."

Clem's brows snapped together, and he tried to sit up. *Jesus*, he'd nearly forgotten all about the damn preventative! She pressed back down on his shoulder. "I think you should just stay where you are and let me take you in my mouth," she said, making him blink.

"Take me…?"

"I want to try it."

"Dora…" he groaned again.

"Why should I not? You do it for me."

341

Clem's brain whirred furiously as he struggled with this. "There's no reason why not," he admitted after a moment's pause. "Except I don't know if you would enjoy it."

"Well, neither will I, until I've tried it."

"I suppose that is true enough," he conceded.

"Lil thought you might be prudish about your wife doing it."

Clem almost choked on his own tongue. "She—er—she did?"

She nodded her head. "Apparently some men would only ask their mistress for such a thing."

Clem beheld her with a feeling he was starting to feel familiar with. A sort of mingled horror and awe. "Just *why* was it that you and Lil were even discussing my attitude to such a thing?" he asked in a strangled tone.

"Well, you see, I had to ask her to explain the joke. After the kneeling thing when the curtain went up."

Clem closed his eyes. "I should have explained that to you," he said ruefully.

"Yes, you really should have," she agreed. "Then again, Lil and I are very close, so it was not so very awkward."

Clem found himself wondering for the first time about the topics of private discussion among the fairer sex. Apparently, it was not all embroidery and recipes after all. Making a swift decision, he sat up, tucked himself back in, and gathered her into his arms at the same time.

"Clem?"

"We're taking it to the bedroom," he explained, swiftly standing. Seeing her expression, he promised, "We will definitely get around to that…other matter." He wondered what the hell the polite term was for that particular act. He could think of several vulgar ones but none appropriate for this occasion. His vocabulary was failing him now as well as his judgment. "But not tonight," he stated firmly. "Tonight, I want…other things."

*

They took a leisurely bath together afterward, and Theo whispered the whole time, lest her brother should hear them splashing about in the tub. Clem seemed to find her attitude amusing, tickling her feet, and teasing her about the likelihood of possible discovery. "Is it so very scandalous to share bathwater, then?" he asked, arching a brow and passing her the soap.

"I don't know about scandalous," she mused, "but it is certainly unconventional. The last time I shared a bathtub would have been with my siblings, in infancy," she added hastily. Clem grinned and ran a flannel over his shoulders.

"I think you should draw me naked next time," Theo said, soaping her arms.

Clem made a muffled noise. "Now this is what I am talking about," he complained. "Your sense of propriety makes no sense to me. You turn prim over a practical time and money-saving practice such as sharing a bath. Then in the next breath, you suggest something truly outrageous without so much as a blush upon your lovely cheeks."

Theo snorted but looked thoughtful all the same. "Perhaps because my family is artistic?" she suggested.

"Perhaps."

"Nudes in paintings and sculptures are practically respectable after all. My uncle let us run amok in museums and art galleries growing up, and we were allowed full run of his library."

"You were fond of your uncle," he observed.

"Oh yes," she enthused. "Life with him was chaotic and wonderful. It was never dull." Clem nodded.

343

"You still have not yet introduced me to your uncle," she observed lightly and noticed the way his expression turned evasive.

"I only visit him every four weeks," he admitted after a moment. "The second Saturday of the month."

"Are you fond of him? I think you said he was good to you when you came to London."

He leaned the back of his head against the edge of the tub. "He was," he agreed, closing his eyes.

"Yet you are not close?"

"Not really," Clem admitted. "He's a quiet type. My aunt Nancy did all the talking. He was sort of in the background. Then, too, I only lived with them for twelve months before I took lodgings of my own."

"It does not sound like you take much after your mother's side."

Clem's eyes sprang open. "I'm *nothing* like my father," he said abruptly. Theo jumped at the vehemence of his words. The soap slipped through her fingers, and she groped about the bottom of the tub to retrieve it.

"My mother's brothers were all big and burly like me," Clem added after a moment in a more reasonable tone. "Honestly, Uncle Danny was the quietest of the bunch. My uncle Miles was rowdy and loved a drink. My uncle Mickey had a quick temper and got killed in a bar fight when he was only twenty."

"Do you remember your mother at all?" she asked gently.

"Just occasional flashes. I remember her singing on washing day."

Theo nodded, carefully balancing the soap on the edge. "It's nice to have something to remember them by. I don't remember my parents much, but I recall my mother's scent and how my father looked up when she walked into a room."

344

Clem was silent at her wistful tone, then he said suddenly, "My father was a clerk and always wanted to better himself. That's why he sent me off to school. He thought to give me a better start than he had in life."

Theo was surprised. "Well, that sounds pretty admirable," she said hesitantly. For some reason, she had not formed the best impression of his father before now. She cudgeled her brains to remember what Clem had said about him.

"He always thought he'd married beneath himself by all accounts," Clem said, as though she had spoken her thoughts aloud. "He was always in and out of work, and they had crippling debts. My mother was a laundress," Clem said, stretching out his legs on either side of her. "I remember she was always cheerful and full of life. Until she fell sick, that is, but that happened fast, and I don't remember much. My uncles came to our lodgings and wanted to take me away to stay with my aunt Nancy. My father refused though."

"Why did he refuse?"

Clem's smile twisted. "At the time, he thought I was bound for better things than a stevedore." At her puzzled frown, he added, "To work the docks, as they did."

"Oh."

"I don't remember much of that time. Except that there was a punch-up at the funeral. My uncle Danny laid my father out." He shrugged. "Which is not that unusual at an Irish funeral."

"Laid him out?"

"Punched him. Knocked him out cold."

"Why did your quietest uncle punch your father?" Theo asked in surprise.

"Uncle Dan was slow to anger, but none of them were saints. Turns out my father was fixing to marry again," Clem answered, "before my mother was cold in the grave. If he had married beneath him the first time, he did not repeat that mistake. This time he'd caught the eye of the boss's daughter."

Theo considered this. "So, he married for love the first time and for money the second time, *I* see."

Clem gave a short laugh. "You could put it that way. By all accounts, poverty did not suit him." His lip curled. "My uncles always said he preferred an easy life."

"Is he good-looking like you?"

Clem was silent a moment. "Yes," he said shortly. "At least, he was the last time I saw him. I don't know how he's aged. I only take after him in features, mind. My father's height was only average."

"When was the last time that you saw him?" Theo asked curiously.

"When I was fifteen."

She turned her head sharply to look at him. "That was the last time you saw him?" A vague suspicion entered her head. "On the occasion you finished school?" she guessed.

"Aye, they had me pack my trunk and told me I was now a man," Clem agreed flippantly. "I knew the direction of my father's office, for I had seen it on a letter once when he sent in my school fees. It only took me two hours to walk into Winchester. He had a big office," he reminisced, "likely the best in the building, for his father-in-law had retired by this point, so he had taken over the running of things." He fell to silent contemplation.

"You told him your schooling was done?" she prompted him.

"Yes," Clem agreed absently. "I remember being surprised by how small he looked. Or maybe it was just his big desk dwarfing him. He looked nervous, ill at ease; he told me I should not have come. I had to remind him that Drummond Hall would not board boys after they reached fifteen years. He must have forgotten that fact. Either that or my existence. One or the other."

"Drummond Hall was your boys' school?" Clem nodded. "I expect he was astonished to see you had grown to manhood. Likely you reminded him of your uncle who had punched him to the ground."

Clem laughed grimly. "I certainly hope so."

"Then what happened?"

"He told me I had best make my way to my family in London, for he had no use for me there. I'd had all the money I was going to get out of him."

Theo breathed in sharply. "He said that?" she asked indignantly. "Why did he not let you go to your mother's people in the first place? Why stick you in a boarding school in Hampshire for ten years?"

Clem shrugged. "I don't know. Maybe at first, he had meant to take a fatherly interest, but then that wore off. He gave me a lot of bluster about how he'd done his duty and seen to my education, and I was on my own now. I just looked at him." He fell into silence, seemingly lost in that memory. "I remember feeling glad," he said suddenly, "that he had not visited me at the school like the other boys' fathers did."

"I hope he saw that in your face," Theo said fervently. "I expect he did. I expect he saw your disgust and he could not get you out of his office fast enough. Doubtless it made him vastly uncomfortable to see his handsome grown son, beautiful like his mother."

"I don't know about that," Clem snorted. "I was fifteen, and there was nothing handsome about my behavior. I had plenty about me even then. I told him to thank his rich wife for my second-rate schooling and told him he could go to the devil. Said the next time I saw him I'd give him the hiding he deserved. Then I tipped a plaster bust off his shelf, knocked a portrait off his wall, and walked out of the office and his life forever."

Theo lay still, contemplating this in the rapidly cooling water. "Whose was the portrait?" she asked quietly.

"Can't you guess?"

"His second wife?"

Clem made a noise of agreement in his throat. "And two dear little boys in sailor suits."

"Your half brothers?"

"My replacements."

"He sounds awful. I expect he's grown bitter and corpulent in later years," Theo decided. "Unhappy men often do. Either that or look for solace in a whiskey decanter."

"You think he's grown into a fat drunkard?" Clem asked, sounding amused. "Why do you think he's unhappy?"

"Of *course* he's unhappy." Theo sat up in the tub indignantly. "How could he be otherwise? He let the best thing in the world slip through his fingers."

"The best thing?" Clem echoed. "An oldest son, you mean?"

"I mean you, Clem Dabney."

His gaze clashed with her own, and Theo could not breathe for a moment at the blazing expression his eyes held. He swallowed and scrubbed a hand over his face. "Ah, Dorabelle," he sighed, and when he lowered his arm, he looked suddenly sad. "What am I going to do with you? You've got it all wrong. I'm not the special one."

"And *I* say you are," she said stubbornly.

When he would only shake his head, she shivered, realizing the mood had soured and the water turned quite cold. "Let's get out," Clem said, drawing up his knees. "We'll both catch our deaths."

26

The next morning, Clem woke early and lay gazing up at the ceiling as memories of the previous evening flooded his brain. He was horrified by all that he'd shared. That was what came of getting carried away with this pretense of a partnership. It was not just Dora anymore, tricked into thinking they were confidantes and best of friends. Now he had fooled even himself. He'd fallen into the trap of his own making and needed to claw his way back out.

There would be no more baths together, he decided. And next time she offered to suck his cock, he wouldn't carry her off to the bedroom and make love to her like some…what? *Lovestruck idiot?* Instead, he would toss a cushion down for her knees.

He would still be considerate of her, but he wouldn't get carried away.

There would also be no more of this…*intimate* talking. It messed around with your head. He'd never had that problem before. He could talk alright, liked to talk, could talk the hind leg off a donkey. He could charm the birds down from the trees, could Clem Dabney.

He never talked of things like his past and his bloody family though. Just why *had* he volunteered all that information for Theodora's perusal and judgment? It wasn't even as if she'd poked or prodded him into it, not really. He had just bared his soul to her like a regular fucking sapskull.

There would also be no more talk of babies. Yet another thing he could not actually blame on Dora. That was all on him. *Well, no more!* She wanted a career, and he wanted to be rich, damn it, not a bloody father!

He slipped out of bed as soon as it turned six and crept out of the house to start his day as a free agent. The cold morning air cleared his head as he walked briskly through London, and by the time he had reached Shoreditch, he had formulated a working plan.

Okay, so he would not be denying himself when it came to the bedroom; he wasn't fucking stupid, but he *was* going to keep things on a more basic level. There would be no more of this tender stuff he kept slipping into. He liked Dora. What wasn't to like? She was sweet and funny, and good in bed, but that was it. When it came the time, he would set her aside and get on with his own life.

Of course, now she had revealed herself as a star of the stage, tucking her away in some obscure cottage to await his pleasure and eventual retirement was not really an option. Maybe they could have one of those wealthy people marriages where they barely saw each other, and when they did, they were freezingly polite to one another?

None of that fucking other people though, he thought uneasily. He could not countenance that. Clem cracked his knuckles. Maybe they could have fancy apartments in the same building, somewhere like Mayfair. Then when he wanted to fuck his wife, he could just nip up two flights of stairs. Simple.

Now he just had to convince everyone else as well as himself.

Clem's newfound resolve was shaken a few hours hence when Jim rapped upon his door then flung it open. "One of your boxing brethren has shown up," he announced darkly.

"Oh, yes?" Clem barely glanced up from his list. "Well, I'm not free right now, Jim, you can deal with it. Comp them some free tickets or drinks or whatever you think appropriate." When Jim hesitated, Clem sat up in his seat. "Unless it's Ben or Nat Jones," he said, seeing Jim's uncertainty. "I'll always see them."

"No, no, it's not either of them," Jim said, looking uneasy. "He's not come to see you specifically neither, boss." Jim cleared his throat. "He's come to see Miss Dora as it 'appens."

Clem's hand froze in the act of reaching for a pencil. He struggled to get his feelings under control after a moment. "Who?" he asked in what he hoped passed as a calm enough voice, though there was a definite edge to the barked word.

350

"Young Ewell," Jim said grimly.

Clem relaxed at once. Barty Ewell had an eye for the pretty ones. "It's one of the dancing girls he comes to see, Jim," he said dryly. Evie or Katy, or something like that, he couldn't remember which specifically.

"Nope," Jim responded. "It was Dora's room he asked the direction for." Jim cast his eyes up to the ceiling. "Him and that Ruby have cooled off considerably of late." *Ruby, that was it.* "After pointing out it was none of my business, he said, seein' as I was so curious, he was gonna ask her out to lunch," Jim continued.

Clem's pencil snapped. He stared at the two halves in bewilderment for a second then threw them down on his desk. "Lots of people ask her out to lunch these days, Jim," he pointed out, striving for a bored tone. Striving and missing. His teeth sounded clenched. "The only invitations she takes up are with that impudent guttersnipe of hers."

"Albert," Jim supplied. He hesitated. "Why don't you let her know you're taking her out?" Jim recommended. "That way there won't be any misunderstandings or hurt feelings about it."

Clem shot him a sharp look, but Jim's expression was blank as ever. *What the hell?* And why did he have a horrible suspicion Jim was talking about *his* feelings being hurt? It was definitely time he set such talk to rest.

"Dora is perfectly at liberty to consort with whoever she chooses, Jim," he said coldly. "Our arrangement is far from a traditional one, as you are no doubt aware." Returning to his lists, he ignored Jim's disapproving presence until he heard his footsteps stomp to the door, banging it shut behind him.

Hurt fucking feelings.

Twenty minutes later, he heard a knock on his door and flung down his pen. "Come in!"

It was Dora, smiling at him and looking wholly unaware of the fact that he felt like he'd swallowed a bitter lemon for

351

breakfast. "I was wondering if you would care to accompany me to luncheon today, Clem," she suggested brightly. "Only one of your friends has called by and made a charming suggestion we visit that new place that has opened on Villon Square, next to the gin palace," she said, naming a place ten minutes away.

She wanted to go to lunch with Barty Ewell. His spirits plummeted so hard he wasn't sure they didn't sink through the floorboards. *Careful, Clem*, he admonished himself before answering. "I had no idea you were interested in widening your acquaintance with the boxing world," he managed to utter with something approaching indifference.

Dora hesitated, then turned and shut the door behind her before crossing his office to stand before his desk. "To be perfectly candid, I have an ulterior motive when it comes to Mr. Ewell," she confided. Clem forgot to breathe, and by the time the pounding in his head stopped, she was in full flow.

"—so you see, I feel like he would be an *excellent* study for me," she enthused, her eyes sparkling. "Only imagine if I was to secure a future role, playing a sporting young gent or even a suitor from a less than salubrious background! Just think of all the *material* I could glean from an hour spent in his company!"

By the greatest of efforts, Clem managed to dispel the red fog that was crowding his brain. "You want to study his mannerisms," he ground out with dawning realization and relief.

She nodded, bright-eyed and practically clasping her hands with enthusiasm by this point. "Then by all means," Clem said urbanely, or as close to it as he could manage, present circumstances considered. "You may go with my blessing."

"You really won't come?" she sounded gratifyingly disappointed. He shook his head, and she looked resigned. "And should I take just Eddie with me or him and Sam both?" she enquired.

352

"Neither," Clem replied shortly. "You won't need protection from the masses if you're with Ewell."

Still, after she had left the office, he had the strangest feeling of light-headedness. Almost like you experienced after shutting your finger in a door. Stupid really, for Dora was not Barty's type at all. Far from it. He was a handsome devil and had his pick of the girls. He liked them short and curvy, not tall and gangly. Dora probably equaled him in height. Likely Barty was hoping for an introduction to some other act, not realizing they all held Dora at arm's length.

Maybe it was Florrie Foss who had caught Barty's roving eye. She was more his type than Dora, Clem kept telling himself as he glanced repeatedly at the clock, though in truth, Florrie was likely too long in the tooth and not pretty enough either, strictly speaking.

They would not even have finished their predinner drinks by now, he told himself grimly after another half an hour passed. Dora would be watching Barty's every move and filing away each gesture to practice later. No doubt Ewell would think her manner bizarre and her way of dressing ugly. Afterward, he would laugh later to the likes of Claude Pfeiffer and Jeb Morris that Clem's wife was a peculiar sort of female.

Clem's mouth flattened into a thin line as he imagined it. Dora would be frank and artless as always, and a cocky prick like Barty would write her off long before her natural charm started to shine through. At least Clem hoped to God he would, for the alternative was unthinkable.

At two o'clock, Clem's composure finally gave way. He strode out of his office and made his way resolutely toward Dora's dressing room. Hearing Dora's voice high with distress, he burst the door open without hesitation and found her sat kneeling on the floor examining a newspaper with her young friend Albert.

"Clem!" she burst out, scrambling to her feet at once. "Look at this!" She thrust a page toward his face. "I don't understand it at all."

Clem gazed blankly at the newsprint and then back at her troubled expression. "What exactly am I looking at?"

Instead of gesturing to a critic's review, she pointed her finger instead at a prominent society column. "Here!"

"Read it out to me," Clem ordered, feeling quite thrown off course.

Dora rustled the page agitatedly and then read out, "'A little bird tells me that Sir Matthew H has been seen around town squiring a new favorite, an actress bearing the initials R.B. after his Dresden shepherdess fell from grace and quite shattered her reputation.'"

"What does all that mean?" Clem asked, his eyes roaming over Dora's pale face. "I don't read those kinds of columns."

"Well, their stock in trade is usually vague hints and innuendo," she replied, "but I very much fear that 'Sir Matthew H' refers to Sir Matthew Hillingdon and that the 'Dresden shepherdess' they mention is none other than my sister! Her last role was as the titular Faithful Shepherdess in Fletcher's play."

"How can that be?" Clem asked, frowning. "I thought you said they'd eloped to France."

"Well, so Hetty's telegram led us to believe, but Albert here brings other news." She turned back to gesture toward the lad who was sat cross-legged, eating an iced bun. "Tell him, Albert."

"Thas' right, guv," he said, sticking his hands in his braces. "I 'eard it from my friend Arfur. 'E said as 'Illingdon's back in the city and taken up wiv some new piece of skirt by the name of Rhonda Bettinew. She's playin' in some melodrama at The Royal George. She's caused quite a stir on account of 'ow she dances in a see-fru petticoat in the second act."

354

"You see," said Dora eagerly. "R.B." She stabbed a finger at the newspaper page. "The initials. It *all* fits."

Clem was bursting to ask where Ewell was but realized this was not the time. He cleared his throat. "This all sounds like idle gossip to me," he said damningly. "If your sister was back in London, surely you would be the first to know about it."

Dora's cheeks turned a little pink. "But what if he's abandoned her in France, friendless and without a penny to her name?" she demanded.

"Sounds unlikely to me." Clem shrugged. He could not admit that the last time he had seen her, Henrietta Fields had walked away with a tidy sum of money from his own bank account. "This is just hearsay, Dora. I would not worry about it if I were you."

She stared at him a moment. "But I *am* worried, Clem," she said frankly. "She is my only sister."

That evening, however, over dinner, her brother also pooh-poohed the idea of their sister languishing stranded over the channel. "Henrietta?" Fields had repeated, lowering his book. "Dear me, Theo, have your wits gone a-begging? Is it possible you have forgotten just how capable Hetty is? She is quite ten times as resourceful as you or I. No, no, the idea is *quite* preposterous."

"But Albert's friend swears he sold a newspaper to Sir Matthew in the street where his father's townhouse lies," Dora responded with forced calm. She turned impetuously to Allsop, making Clem bristle. "What do you think, Harold?"

Allsop considered a moment, then said with quiet dignity, "I cannot imagine Henrietta ever doing anything to bring her reputation into any disrepute as that column implies. She is too much a lady."

"Hear, hear!" Fields echoed. "A snot-nosed ragamuffin is hardly a credible source."

355

Conversely, their dismissal of Dora's fears immediately put Clem on the defensive. "We could always make some discreet enquiry," he suggested once he and Dora had retired to their sitting room for an after-dinner drink. He did not think it a bad suggestion, despite the fact he had never done anything discreet in his life.

"I was thinking of sending Vincent around to Sir Matthew's father's," Dora confessed, biting her thumbnail.

It seemed Dora lacked subtlety even more than he. "The banker's house? By all means, if you want to get Vincent arrested," Clem responded wryly.

"No, of course not! Do you really think—?" Leaving her sentence unfinished, she jumped out of her seat to move to the window and gazed moodily out of it for a while. "Have I lost all sense of perspective about this?" she asked slowly. "Only, it seems to me that—" She broke off again, stiffening.

"What is it?" Clem asked, lowering the bottle he was pouring.

"Hetty!" Dora cried, rushing for the door at once. Clem moved to the window, scanning the view, but though there were several shadowy figures in the street below, none of the women struck him as remotely resembling Henrietta Fields.

Following Dora swiftly down the stairs and out of the open door, he found her standing by the front gate, shivering in the night air. "Come back inside," he urged her.

"Clem, I know no one believes me, but—"

"I believe you are very worried about your sister," he said smoothly, slipping an arm about her shoulder. "And I don't want you to take a chill. Come on."

"Clem," she sobbed, sounding in such distress that he forgot his resolve to drop the tender stuff, and enfolded her in his arms, murmuring nonsense comfort phrases in her ear.

"Come on," he said at last. "The sooner I get you back inside, the sooner we can get our hats and coats on and get to The Parthenon."

"The Parthenon?"

"I think we need to speak to Vincent."

"Vincent?" The dawning hope in her eyes did funny things to his chest. "But you said—?"

"Not to send him to Hillingdons' London residence," he clarified, "but to set him on a patrol in his free time."

"A patrol. You mean of the vicinity?"

He nodded. "In case she is haunting the locality." She looked instantly stricken, and Clem pinched her chin. "I meant in the sense she is skulking around. Nothing else. Come on. The sooner we set our watchdog on guard, the sooner we can find out if there is any truth to these rumors."

"Yes," she agreed tearfully, seizing his hand. "Oh yes. Thank you, Clem."

It was a fool's errand, but it was almost worth it when she raised his hand to her cheek and pressed it there. He did not even care that it was wet with tears.

27

Theo spent the next three days on edge. Of course, Clem had meant nothing by that "haunting" remark, but it had struck a discordant note with her. Theater folk tended to be superstitious, and she felt jumpy and uneasy despite the fact Vincent pledged his every free hour to the cause.

It had been fortunate that both she and Clem had jointly recruited Vincent, for only their combined efforts prevented him from flinging off for an immediate and violent confrontation with Sir Matthew. Theo had been forced to point out he would be of no earthly use to Henrietta in a jail cell, and he had finally seemed to quiet down at that.

Even less than Clem did he seem to understand the implications of what the gossip column had printed, but the solitary account of a paper boy was good enough for Vincent. Theo realized that she could not have hit upon anyone more devoted to her sister's cause and she slept easier that night for it, though she could not dispel her fears altogether.

Work was a welcome distraction, and she threw herself into it. Midweek, she finally got her long-awaited introduction to Florrie Foss. That lady looked her up and down with a jaundiced eye before sniffing and saying, "Oh yes?" in a decidedly cool manner. "The boss's wife, is it? Better mind me p's and q's then, hadn't I?" she said, digging her companion in the ribs. That gentleman gave a roar of laughter, and the two of them had sauntered away without giving Theo a backward glance.

Jim, who had performed the introductions, directed a sheepish look in Theo's direction. "She don't mean anything by it, Miss Dora," he said awkwardly.

"Oh, I'm sure," Theo agreed quickly. "I know sometimes that performers can be territorial." Jim looked confused by this, so she did not elaborate. Later on, though, she spoke to Lil about it at length.

"Forget 'em," Lil recommended. "If they come around, they come around. If they don't"—she shrugged—"well, it's no skin off our nose, is it? You're the boss's wife and I'm far too tough an old boot to give a damn for anyone's opinion. I don't give a snap of me fingers these days."

Theo knew deep down that her old friend was right, but even so, she felt encouraged when their change of dressing room meant they were next to a large communal room where the temporary acts tended to congregate. A few of these made tentative overtures, and within a couple of days, they had struck up friendlier relations with folk who were happy to exchange a bit of friendly chitchat in the corridors or between stage appearances.

Theo's particular favorite was a rubber-faced comedian called Robert Spence, known to his friends and intimates simply as "Spence," who appeared as part of a double act with a much better-looking and smoother individual called Lawrence Dukes. Sadly, Theo did not like Lawrence, who, despite being suave and witty on stage, had a cutting and abrasive manner off it. She frequently overheard him being downright mean to poor Spence, berating him for all manner of petty things.

When she mentioned this to Lil, her friend pointed out that Lawrence was the straight man and Spence the butt of all his jokes. "Sometimes on-stage personas spill off stage." She shrugged. "You have to admit, poor old Spence would be nothing without Lawrence. He's got all the charm and the looks."

"I disagree," said Theo staunchly. "I find Lawrence dull and predictable in his stage craft. He relies on his looks and brings very little else to the table. I think Spence should dump him and find someone else."

"Let's not get too carried away," Lil said on a gurgle of laughter. "Lord, when you like someone, Theo, you don't half take their cause to your heart."

Theo ignored this. "I also think Lawrence is only pleasant to our faces because he imagines I hold some sway on who gets to stay and who falls by the wayside," she persisted.

"Lord, as to that, Theo, that's the only reason any of 'em speak to us!" Lil responded with feeling.

"Not Spence," Theo argued, though she knew Lil had a point about most of the temporary turns. "He's sweet."

"Who's sweet?" Clem interrupted them, coming suddenly into the room. Something about his tone made Theo look up quickly.

Lil let out a tinkling laugh. "That little urchin what sells the newspapers," she said, fluffing her hair and gazing at her reflection. "Little devil's sweet on her. Starstruck, I should say." She sighed. "It's a difficult age for boys, is twelve."

Swiftly, Theo masked her surprise at Lil's lie. Clem's shoulders relaxed and he told her that, unfortunately, he would not have time to meet her that day for lunch or indeed any of the remaining days that week. Theo nodded. "I understand, do not worry," she told him, ignoring the pang in her chest. Clem beheld her frowningly a moment and then left just as abruptly.

When the door shut behind him, Lil turned to look at her gravely. "You need to watch yourself, Theo love, that man of yours has a touch of the green-eyed monster. You want Spence to have a shot at a permanent slot on the bill, for gawd's sake don't go calling him sweet in front of Clem. He'll show him the door soon as look at him."

Theo blinked. "Clem?" she asked in startled accents. "Jealous?" Suddenly, she recalled his words about being jealous of Albert the other day, but that had plainly been a joke.

"I know the look," Lil said, pressing her lips together. "Take it from one who knows. My Johnny couldn't hack my being surrounded on all sides by admirers. That's why he took up and left me."

Theo drew in a quick breath. "I can't see it somehow," she said with an uneasy laugh. "After all, he just breezed in here to cancel our plans for lunch! Our marriage was, well, first and foremost a business arrangement…" Her words trailed off at the skepticism in Lil's face. It was the first time Theo had admitted as much aloud to anyone, and her heart sank a little at the confession.

Lil simply gave her a disbelieving look. "Was it?" she said dryly, and Theo felt rather at a loss in the face of Lil's blatant skepticism.

She looked down at her hands in her lap. "Well, that was how it started, in any event," Theo mumbled.

Lil sniffed. "Maybe for you."

Theo was so astonished by this retort that she could think of no other response before they were interrupted by a stagehand telling them they had ten minutes before they needed to make their way to the stage for their practice session and that Mr. Allsop was already set up there waiting for them.

"He's keen," Lil observed. "Never thought he'd take to it like he has, but he hasn't tried to make any excuses even once!"

"I think he feels he's coming out of his shell and seeing a bit of life," Theo answered. "He was saying as much the other night at dinner, but Clem made an unfortunate remark about how he should tell his great aunt Emma and Harold clammed up."

"Oh, so Clem didn't like the idea of Allsop being joined at the hip to you these days, fancy that!" Lil said, poking her tongue in her cheek.

"Now, Lil!" Theo retorted, but she could not help her answering smile. She knew it was stupid, but she could not help but feel a little flattered that Lil could think Clem might nurture feelings for her, let alone suffer pangs of jealousy over her now. The notion was patently ridiculous. *Wasn't it?*

Strange to say, Theo found herself remaining silent to her oldest friend over the recent business about Henrietta. In recent years, relations between Lil and Hetty had been strained, and both had viewed the other askance. As such, Theo decided against confiding in her or mentioning the gossip column to her at all.

Instead, she asked after Peggy's health, and Lil went into raptures over a new tonic that really seemed to be picking the old girl up. "In a few weeks she'll be well enough to come along and watch the show! Such a relief, I can't tell you," Lil sighed. "I really don't know what Mother Longdon and I would do without her. The three of us have come to rely on one another to such an extent. I can't even imagine ever living with a man again, much less anything else!"

"Your many admirers would, no doubt, be quite cast down to hear that," Theo teased, and Lil chortled.

"Get away with you!" she said. "I'm far too old and wise for any of those shenanigans!"

When Sidney sidled up moments later for his usual chat, Theo greeted him cheerfully enough. "You got more floral tributes than Florrie Foss this week," he told her, eyes twinkling. "Wot u fink about that, eh?"

"Oh, well…there's two of us, isn't there, and only one Miss Foss," she pointed out, hoping Sidney had not highlighted this fact to any of the other performers.

"I weren't including Miss Longdon's tributes in the count, as it 'appens," Sidney sniffed, adjusting the fit of his cap. "Everyone's whispering the boss will give Foss the old heave-ho sooner or later'n you'll be top of the trees then."

Theo glanced about uncomfortably. She and Lil had only just managed to make a few friends among the other acts. She did not want any further setbacks at this point. "I am sure gossip

362

is rife," she murmured. "That aspect of theatrical life remains the same, it seems, no matter the venue."

"I just thought you'd like to know," Sidney responded, clearly disappointed he did not get a more excited reaction from her. He shuffled off bearing his broom with an injured air. Theo sighed and walked over to Lil, who was sat studying the new song lyrics. "Ready for a run-through of the new number?" she asked.

"We'll have to wait for Casanova," Lil remarked dryly, nodding toward Harold, who was talking to two dancing girls. One reached out to smooth his lapel.

Theo's eyebrows shot up. "Now just why is Harold proving more popular with our fellow artists than us?" she asked archly.

Lil snorted. "They're hoping he can write them a couple of numbers so they can go solo and snatch the spotlight, that's why."

"Well, I suppose I can't really blame them for envying our maestro."

"Pity he can't write a racy lyric to save his life!" Lil remarked. "Come along, Harold," she called in a louder voice. "You've plenty of time for flirtation in your own time." Poor Harold almost dropped his sheet music as the dancing girls giggled and made themselves scarce. "Daft mares," Lil observed mildly.

That night, Mrs. Cherwell interrupted them at the dinner table, barreling in with a look of self-importance on her face. "There's some hulking great ruffian at the door asking for you, Miss Theodora," she huffed.

Theo lowered her soup spoon. "Did he give a name?" she asked, dragging back her chair and ignoring Clem's frown.

"Said as to tell you Vincent needed to speak with you," Mrs. Cherwell said disapprovingly. "I told him you was at dinner—"

363

"Vincent the doorman?" Felix echoed in surprise. "What the deuce does that fellow mean by showing up here at this hour?"

Theo was already out of her seat. "Did you show him into the parlor?" she asked, tossing down her napkin.

"No, I did not!" Mrs. Cherwell huffed, clearly outraged at the notion. "The very idea!"

Seeing Clem had come to his feet, Theo turned to him impulsively. "Clem, could I receive him in our sitting room?" she asked beseechingly. "He would probably be terribly ill at ease in the formal parlor."

He paused a moment before making a reply. "By all means." His tone was cool, and Theo could see he was not entirely happy about having an outsider in the space they had made their own. She could even understand his sentiments.

"Thank you, Clem," Theo said placatingly. "And will you let me speak with him alone first? She lay her hand on his sleeve in quiet appeal. She thought she saw some strong emotion flash across his face, but it was gone before she could register what it was.

For an instant he did not speak, but then he inclined his head. "If that's what you want."

"Thank you," she said gratefully and hurried out to the hall in Mrs. Cherwell's wake. "Vincent!" she hailed, spotting him stood on the hall rug with his hat in his hands, looking uncomfortable and strained. "Please come up to the private sitting room with me."

He started forward at her words, and she hurried up the stairs, hearing the steady thud of his feet behind her. Mrs. Cherwell's outraged gaze followed their progress through the banister, but Theo did not care a rush for convention. She needed to speak frankly with Vincent and learn the truth.

As soon as they crossed the sitting room threshold, Vincent walked over to the fireplace and turned to face her. He looked

364

rather as though he was about to face a firing squad. It suddenly hit her that the now sumptuous sitting room was likely even more alien to Vincent than the stuffy parlor would have been.

"Please take a seat, Vincent; you look fit to drop." He had a grayish hue to his skin, and she wondered how many hours this week he had spent trudging about the area.

"I found 'er, Miss Theodora," Vincent said quietly, ignoring her words.

Theo's heart leaped into her mouth. "You did?" Her legs suddenly shaky, she dropped onto the nearest couch. "Where? Please tell me, she is well?"

Vincent's face tightened. "I can't tell you that, miss," he said hoarsely.

"Oh God." She covered her mouth with her hand. "She is sick?" Her voice rose with concern.

If anything, Vincent turned an even more sickly shade. Seeing his acute discomfort helped Theo get her own fears under control. If it was a straightforward fever or decline, he would not be acting thus. She took a deep breath. "Has he ruined her?" she asked quietly.

Vincent's whole face flinched. "Please don't speak of her like that," he said, his throat closing on his words.

Theo contemplated him gravely. "You know what I am speaking of, Vincent."

"It ain't a subject ladies like you should ever be addressing," he said, avoiding her eye.

"Very well, then," Theo said, getting swiftly to her feet. "Take me to her. I will speak to her myself."

"You don't understand!" Vincent burst out rawly. "You'll break her if you do that!"

Theo sat back down in alarm. Her cool and collected sister? "What do you mean?" she asked carefully.

"She—she just needs to come 'ome, and for none of you to ask questions," he said gruffly. At her wide eyes, he added, impassioned, "If anyone can swing it, it's you, Miss Theodora." He looked rather like a dog in that moment, his trust in her implicit.

"Me?"

"It's like what I told her," Vincent answered simply. "She could have no greater champion than her sister. You'll stand strong and true, and you'll browbeat that brother of hers into accepting her back into the fold," he said grimly.

Theo stared at him. "And what did Henrietta say to that?"

He shifted from one foot to the other. "She…she went off in a fit of weeping, miss," he confessed. "She seems to think she ain't treated you like what she ought to. Says she's ashamed to face you now." He swallowed. "I told her you wasn't one to bear past grudges," he said staunchly.

"Of course not," Theo replied quickly, though her heart sank. "And *of course* she needs to come home. The sooner, the better I should say." Vincent seemed to sag a little with relief. "Will she need help extricating herself from wherever she is currently?"

"No." He shook his head. "She's in lodgings. I can help her pack up her bags and bring her along as soon as it gets dark, and you've smoothed the way with Mr. Fields." He hesitated. "She…she don't want to talk about what's happened this past couple of months. Can you make that plain to 'im?"

Theo regarded him gravely a moment before she made a reply. "I can certainly explain to Felix that Hetty needs peace and quiet and no *immediate* requests for information," she stressed, "but I don't know that I can work miracles, Vincent."

Vincent shook his head. "That's not what I've 'eard," he said simply.

"Pardon?"

He stood silent a moment before relenting. "My neighbor Mrs. Warrender's goes to see you every Saturday afternoon at The Eagle," he said. "She's 'ad a lot to contend wiv this past year. Lost 'er 'usband, then 'er son. She says she'd see you twice a day, if she could. Says you're a regular tonic, a ray of sunshine in a dark world. Says you're what gets her through the week."

Theo stared. It was the most eloquent speech Vincent had ever made in her presence. "You lodge in Whitechapel, I think?" He nodded. "You must give me your neighbor's address so that I can send her some complimentary tickets," she managed at last.

"That would make 'er day," he acknowledged.

Theo's mind was a whirl. "I—I suppose I could say that Hetty has been ill, the channel crossing adversely affected her health. That all her plans were overset by this," she continued slowly, "and she was forced to return home."

Vincent's eyes flickered. "That could work," he acknowledged cautiously. "I could tell 'er what you're going to say, and she ain't quite 'erself yet, truth be told."

Theo nodded. If she said Hetty was delicate and needed to be handled with kid gloves, the gentlemen in Felix and Harold would understand. They would back right off at the notion of mystery feminine illnesses.

"Let me go down now and speak to…to everyone," she said, standing up and squaring her shoulders. This was not going to be easy. She would have to have a care she did not bristle Felix's feathers and turn him indignant. She needed to consider how best to handle him.

Vincent nodded. "I'll wait in the 'allway," he said gruffly. "Till you give me the nod. Then I'll go and fetch 'er 'ere."

Theo agreed and made her way downstairs to face the rest of her family. It was only halfway down the stairs that she realized she *did* think of Harold and Clem now as part of the family.

Harold *was*, in truth, something like a cousin. Dear to her, but the idea of her ever holding a candle for him felt truly

367

bizarre now somehow. Maybe all along, she had really only considered him in the light of a close relative, but her limited experience around men made her think it something more.

She shut the dining room door behind her and came into the room wearing a tight smile. Immediately, three pairs of eyes were trained on her. Four. She noticed Mrs. Cherwell lurking by the sideboard ostentatiously refilling the mustard pot.

"Well, we must all be thankful," she announced briskly. "Hetty is once more safely back on our shores and can return home to the bosom of her family where she belongs. She has been *most* unwell, poor thing. The traveling, the double crossing of the channel was all too much and overset her health completely."

When no one spoke immediately, Theo clasped her hands together at her waist and forged forward. "It has all been a great ordeal for her and her doctor thinks it's best she returns to normality as soon as possible. In his medical opinion, it is thought it would be beneficial if she is made comfortable with the minimum of fuss. We need to give her time and space for her recovery and have faith that she will tell us what occurred when she is ready."

A blank silence met her words, and though she could meet Felix's and Harold's startled gazes squarely enough, she could not quite bring herself to stare down Clem, who was leaning back in his seat, observing her.

Felix glanced about the rest of them, plunking down his glass of dessert wine. "But this is all preposterous!" he said hotly. "Why does our doorman know more about our sister's whereabouts than us? What of her husband? What does Hillingdon have to say about all this?" Felix demanded. "Seems a queer sort of business to me."

"As I said, Felix," Theo said calmly, "our sister's failing health was a major factor in proceedings. It seems likely it interfered greatly with their plans for the trip. I am afraid their intentions were probably overset and I, myself, cannot be clear on those points. I think we need to be patient for the time when Hetty feels sufficiently well enough to satisfy our curiosity."

Felix blew out his cheeks. "Well, your feelings are not the only ones on the matter, Theodora!" he thundered. "I, for one, would like to hear what others present at this table have to say about this!" To Theo's surprise, the first person he turned to was her husband. "What say you, Dabney?" he said gruffly.

Clem's eyebrows rose. "It seems a reasonable enough request to me," he answered blandly with a shrug of his shoulders.

Felix paused heavily, opened his mouth, shut it again, and then turned to Harold. "And you, Allsop?" he barked.

Harold looked a little shaken, but he nodded. "I, er—agree with the Dabneys," he said. "Henrietta should recuperate and share her story only when she is ready."

Theo almost breathed out a sigh of relief but managed to nod and smile instead. "I am *so* glad we are all of one accord," she said, ignoring Felix's baleful glare and the cynical gleam in Mrs. Cherwell's eye.

Turning to the housekeeper, she thought she had better seize that bull by the horns at once. "Do let me know, Mrs. Cherwell, should you require any help in the matter of catering to the invalid. Sourcing recipes, or anything of that sort."

The lady bridled at once. "I should say not, Miss Theodora! Why, I got a book in the kitchen what deals with five different ways to make a strong beef tea! I shall consult it now," she said, sailing out of the room in a high dudgeon at any implication she was not equal to such a task.

"I will go up and see that Hetty's room is aired out and ready for her," Theo announced to the room at large before turning on her heel and leaving also.

She spent the next hour making her sister's room ready, opening the windows for fresh air, and closing them again when the cold March winds plunged the temperature too low.

She lit the fire in Hetty's grate and laid clean bedsheets upon her bed. Then she gathered up two of her own bouquets from the sitting room to freshen up her sister's room. Luckily, she had plenty to spare these days. Poor Eddie and Sam were forced to carry great armfuls back from The Eagle every time they escorted her home from the weekend matinee performances.

The large arrangements of roses and lilies made the neglected room look much more cheerful, and Theo placed them on the dressing and bedside table before returning to her own. There she found Clem removing his jacket. "Was that someone arriving?" she asked, hurrying to the window, but the cab had drawn up to a house on the other side of the street. "Oh, it's not for us."

A quick glance at her husband showed her he was now removing his cuff links. Feeling strangely in need of something to occupy her hands, Theo fussed about, moving one of her small posy jars to her desk and another to the chest of drawers.

In truth, she received enough flowers these days to fill all the vases throughout the house. Her own preference was for the humbler nosegays, as she liked to imagine they were from the likes of Vincent's neighbor, Mrs. Warrender. These she kept in her bedroom.

Theo found herself dwelling for a moment on the Mrs. Warrenders of this world. She had been vastly touched by Vincent's account and his apparently high opinion of Theo's capabilities, a thing she had never so much as suspected he held before.

"Dora?" She turned about to find Clem watching her with a guarded expression on his face.

370

"Yes?" For a minute she thought he would ask her for an account of what Vincent had really said, and she could unburden herself of her hopes and fears, but this was not forthcoming.

After a moment, he just said, "A cab's just pulled up outside."

"Oh." Theo hurried from the room and leaned over the banister to watch as Mrs. Cherwell opened the door for Vincent and Henrietta's arrival.

28

Over the next couple of days, Henrietta kept herself mostly to her own room, taking her meals there and frequently pleading a bad head when anyone poked a head around her door to check on her. She was quiet and withdrawn, and at first, Theo could see no signs of the possible breakdown that Vincent had been so much afraid of. In front of Felix and Harold, she was polite and composed, but then, she had always been the most reserved member of their family.

Then, Theo noticed that when it was just the two of them, her sister's shoulders would slump, and she would look weary and drawn and admit to being terribly tired. Mrs. Cherwell rallied around bringing up trays of nourishing food and drink, and to everyone's surprise, Hetty sent for Vincent to come and sit with her most afternoons when he was free and even one evening.

"Fellow spends more time in our house than I do," Felix complained hoarsely when they heard Vincent's heavy tread on the stair, but he made sure to keep his voice low as he said it. Even Theo was a little scandalized that Hetty received the great hulking doorman in her own room on a daily basis. Hetty, who had always been so proper and correct!

She would never have behaved thus two short months ago. Indeed, if anyone, Theo had thought Hetty would appreciate having a nonthreatening male like Harold around, but no, Vincent was the one she wanted and no one else would do.

Whenever she tried to broach the subject with Clem, he made it clear that he considered it none of his business. "I barely know your sister," he would repeat, and she was forced to make do with that.

At the end of the first week, Hetty appeared in her doorway as Theo, returning from a matinee at The Eagle, had reached the top of the stairs.

"Theo!" her sister called out to her, and Theo paused with her hand on the banister. Hetty was fully dressed for the first time that week, instead of swathed in frilly wrappers and dressing gowns. Today she wore a dove gray gown with white lace at her throat and cuffs. She looked like a very pretty governess.

"You have some color in your cheeks today, Hetty," she said approvingly. "How are you feeling?"

Hetty gazed back at her steadily. "I am improving daily," she said in a low voice. "Will you—will you come and sit with me awhile?"

Theo was surprised. Her attempts to bustle around her sister had been politely but firmly kept to the bare minimum thus far. "Of course. Just let me go wash and brush up first. I won't be long."

Hetty nodded and disappeared into her dressing room as Theo hurried to tidy herself. "Come in," she responded to Theo's gentle knock.

"I have more flowers for you here," Theo said, setting down a bouquet on her sister's side table.

"Thank you, they're very pretty," Hetty said. "Do these ones contain love notes wound among the stems?" At Theo's stunned expression, a faint smile touched her sister's lips. "I am aware they originate from your admirers, sister. Will you come and sit beside the fire with me?"

Both sisters moved toward the hearth and arranged themselves into the seats there. "I have a tray of tea which Mrs. Cherwell kindly brought up," Hetty said, gesturing to the small table and sounding almost nervous. "It's been brewing awhile, so it should be ready."

Theo frowned as she took her seat. Why would her composed sister look so tense at the prospect of taking a cup of tea with her? Finally, she detected Henrietta's brittleness that Vincent had seen all along beneath the charming veneer.

373

It put her in mind of that odious gossip column that had compared Henrietta to a Dresden shepherdess. She looked like one even now with her pink and white complexion and her abundant chestnut hair. Under her beauty, she was fragile. Terribly fragile. Accepting the cup and saucer with thanks, Theo took a tentative sip. "Nice and strong," she said approvingly.

"How was your performance today?" Hetty asked. "Did it go well?" At Theo's nod, her sister tipped her head to one side. "Vincent tells me you are wildly successful at music hall."

"It has all worked out beautifully," Theo admitted with a smile, then instantly wondered if that was tactless. Hetty did not seem to take it amiss though, merely nodding and looking thoughtful.

"I should like to see you perform," she said, quite knocking Theo for six.

"You would?"

"Oh yes. I mean to ask Vincent to take me. Maybe in a week or so."

"Felix did mention the other day that he might come along."

"Perhaps we could make up a party," Hetty suggested, quite winding her sister.

"Er yes…" Theo agreed weakly, before rallying. "Harold is currently playing accompaniment for Lil and me," she said, feeling she ought to mention Lil, in case her sister was blissfully unaware of her new partner, but again Hetty only nodded.

"What a strange turn of events," Henrietta murmured, turning her head to stare into the fire. When she looked back, she seemed more substantial somehow. "I'd like to apologize now if you would let me, Theodora."

"Apologize?"

Hetty's cheeks grew a little warmer in tone. "I am mortified when I recollect the things I said to you the day before I left. Simply mortified. I was so…*smug*, so pompous, so secure in my certainty that I alone knew best." She lapsed into silence a moment before continuing.

"I really had no notion I was about to get my comeuppance, and that my whole world was about to come crashing down about my ears." She gave a bitter little laugh. "When I remember the words I said to you most of all, sister, I *die* a little on the inside." She fell silent again.

"*That* was why I could not approach you even on my return. I took lodgings instead and kept trying to work up the nerve to beg your forgiveness, but I was too much of a coward. I cannot tell you the number of times I walked up to this house and then turned about again, my heart failing me." She covered her eyes. "I am so sorry for everything, Theodora. Will you accept my apology? I offer it with my whole heart."

Theo made a quick gesture with her hands. Part of her was tempted to say "Don't think of it, put it out of your mind" or to just deny how much her sister's words had impacted her. Instead, she decided honesty was the best policy.

"I shall not lie; it hurt a lot at the time," she said instead. "I felt like a part of me died also in that moment." She blinked back the tears which surprised her by springing into her eyes. "Fortunately, the part that died turned out to be a part that had been holding me back all along."

Hetty bowed her head, remaining silent. Theo sighed and continued, "Shortly after your departure, I endured a most humiliating ride in a hackney with Felix, where he finally let me in on the plan for my future."

Hetty winced. "That must have added insult to injury," she murmured.

"I think I lost my head a little," Theo admitted, "for it was at that point that I started plotting and scheming for myself."

She met her sister's eye full on. "I do forgive you, Hetty," she said, holding out her hand. Henrietta clasped it in a surprisingly firm grip. "You are my sister and I love you," Theo continued calmly. "Let us put that whole business behind us now."

Hetty nodded and Theodora returned her smile, starting to feel optimistic that, after all, everything was going to turn out for the best.

*

If Clem had been struggling before, with keeping his marriage on an acceptable footing, then the arrival of a third Fields sibling at the premises made everything ten times worse. The first thing he realized was that the sisters were closer than he had appreciated. He had liked being Dora's closest person, and he did not appreciate that her sister was now muscling into that territory.

It was also a cursed nuisance having her in the room next door. Dora was a married woman now, and the sitting room was *their* private sitting room. He did not want Henrietta Fields waltzing in there whenever she saw fit. As it happened, Dora's sister seemed to appreciate this fact more than his wife and was highly discreet. He caught only a few fleeting glimpses of her over the next few days, for which he was profoundly grateful.

Still, it did not alleviate the first and foremost concern he had which was that Henrietta could let slip at any time the fact he had purchased her shares in The Parthenon. Indeed, she might impart this fact without any mischievous intent at all. She might genuinely imagine that Theo had been apprised of the fact her husband now owned fifty percent.

At the end of the day, Clem knew he should have found a way to broach this subject already. He should have, but he had not. He still did not want to admit as much, where his wife was concerned. His marriage had not really operated on the lines he had imagined it would from the very beginning.

As such, he retreated fast from any disastrous detail his wife wanted to confide in him about her sister's return. She was *aching* to lay it all out before him and get his opinion on the matter. That much was blatantly obvious, and he just did not want that. Indeed, he would go to great lengths to avoid it.

Not wanting to encourage her confidences, Clem resolved to pull back hard, withdrawing from Dora in every which way he possibly could. To his astonishment, he found this extraordinarily difficult. He started taking brandy after dinner with Fields and Allsop in the front parlor and lingering there for as long as he could stand it.

To his annoyance, Fields's only topic of conversation proved to be The Parthenon, which Clem found himself surprisingly uninterested in, or his sisters, which was Clem's current sore spot. Allsop seemed similarly disinclined to discuss The Parthenon, which surprised Clem, for did he not also own a quarter share? Yet it was music hall that Allsop spoke of, when he spoke of anything at all.

He talked of it with a stammering enthusiasm you could not mistake. "It's f-fascinating to get a glimpse into the splendor and the squalor of working-class entertainment," he had said one evening and then blushed very red. "I can't tell you how much it means to a chap, when you hear your own tune whistled by a working man going about his day."

Fields had exchanged raised brows with Clem. "You met a woman there or something?" he asked outright, and Allsop had been reduced to almost stammering incoherence.

"N-nothing of the s-sort! Though there are several ladies there who I admire very m-much," he protested.

"Perhaps he feels about music hall as you do about the theater," Clem had suggested when Felix opened his mouth and looked about to utter something scathing.

He could see his brother-in-law wanted to scoff at this but did not quite dare. "Thought Henrietta looked a little better when I caught sight of her this morning," Fields said, changing the subject.

"Yes," agreed Allsop quickly. "Clearly coming home has done her much good."

Clem made his escape not long after as the two men discussed Henrietta's improved health. He could not listen to it. Ever since Henrietta had returned to the bosom of her family, Clem's feeling of impending disaster had been almost overwhelming. Even a chance remark falling from Dora's sister's lips could betray the role he had played in pulling the wool over his wife's eyes.

He just did not know what to do for the best. Should he confront Henrietta and cajole or bribe her into holding her peace? What would be the point when it would all come to light eventually? Whenever that happened, whether it was sooner or later, he would appear as the villain of the piece. The vile deceiver who had been stringing Dora along from the very beginning.

Fuck, he should have told her from the very start. But if he had done that, she would never have married him in the first fucking place. He wished to God that Henrietta had never come back from the Continent. If only that bastard Hillingdon had married her as he had promised, then he, Clem, would not be in this position.

No, that was not true. Even if she had stayed in France for five years, at some point she would have written to her siblings and disclosed that she had sold her shares. He could not have gotten away with his perfidy forever. Still, it was a bitter pill to swallow. He struggled to look sympathetic when Dora gave him updates on how Henrietta was doing.

Luckily, Dora had not noticed his attitude for she was so busy of late, distracted by her preoccupation with her sister and the increasing demand for her at work. Already her stage time had been officially increased from thirty to forty minutes and he was starting to think he should just give her and Lil a full hour. Once they had performed their encores they were on the stage for that amount of time in any case. *Give the punters what they want* had always been his philosophy, and it was clear they wanted her.

Dora had already penned two more sketches and a whole bunch of adapted song lyrics. The amount of time she spent scribbling in her notebook, he would not be surprised if she had enough material already for a new sketch every week. He knew she would leap at the chance of more stage time. She seemed to blossom in front of an audience. She thrived there.

Dora Dabney, the performer, was not the one keeping him awake at night with strange anxieties. No, that was Dora Dabney, his wife. His wife who might not be able to find it in her heart to forgive him when she found out what a scheming swine he was. What a viper she had nurtured in her bosom.

He paused a moment outside the sitting room, bracing himself before he opened the door and walked in. He found Dora sat bolt upright and frowning heavily over a pile of fabric scraps. "What are you doing?" he asked, crossing to the cabinet and reaching for a fresh box of sweets.

When at her leisure, he liked to see his wife curled up on a velvet couch, enthusiastically scribbling away and eating luxurious bonbons, not plying a needle and thread over some murky-colored garment.

"Trying to put this gown together," she admitted, sounding defeated. "I could almost cry with frustration! It's my own fault, of course, for I started it over two months ago and then abandoned it. Now I can scarcely fathom how it is supposed to even fit together."

Clem removed the lid and set a box of marzipan fruits before her. "Why should you?" he asked coolly. "You have better ways of employing your time these days. Let me hire a professional seamstress to work up your patterns. There are hundreds of them about this city."

Dora's eyes flashed with surprise, and Clem returned to the cabinet to fix some drinks. "I suppose that is an option," she said slowly. "I confess I never considered such a thing before, because, well, the expense involved, but now I am earning such a high wage…"

Dora had been overjoyed and incredulous on receiving her first pay packet. Clem had been forced to point out that he currently paid Florrie Foss ten percent more before she would accept the payment could be correct.

"You should let me buy you some new bolts of fabrics too, while you're at it," Clem commented, replacing the stopper on a bottle of blackcurrant liqueur. "I've never understood why you always wear such dull shades, the browns and greens. They don't suit your personality at all."

He carried one of the delicate glasses and set it down before her. "You should be clothed in bold, dazzling color, Dora…emerald greens, ruby reds, and sapphire blues." He had no idea where all this was coming from, but as he uttered the words, he realized every single one was true.

Dora's lips parted. "Clem…" she breathed.

"Why don't you let me? You can keep your patterns and your principles, just bring some color into the picture."

"But that's just it," Dora answered, looking sincere. "There *is* a reason I only wear those kinds of colors. Vegetable dyes just do not come in those bold shades."

Clem braced himself. "And just why is it that you limit yourself to fabrics dyed with vegetables?" he asked, preparing himself for whatever involved reason Dora undoubtedly had.

"Well, I have heard there are health benefits for wearing only naturally dyed fibers against your skin," she said earnestly, "but mostly because I am not sure that all these factories and

380

new manufacturing methods are better than the traditional ways."

Clem's eyebrows shot up. "This is the way the world is headed, Dora. A few woolly-headed idealists won't halt the progress of industrialization."

She caught her breath and regarded him with an oddly frozen look in her expressive eyes. "Do you think me woolly-headed, then?" she asked abruptly.

To his annoyance, Clem felt uncomfortable answering her straight. He knew damn well she wasn't supposed to call him out like that. Ladies were hampered by all kinds of unspoken social rules. They were supposed to tiptoe around conversational subjects when it came to engaging in them with men, using words like *perhaps* and *might* and *would you mind terribly*.

Theo might be unconventional, but she was still gently reared at the end of the day. She knew social convention better than the likes of him. He cleared his throat. "Perhaps a little naive," he admitted and saw her grow very still. She didn't like that, but damn it all, what was he supposed to do, lie about it?

"I see," she said quietly and, to his discomfort, just *withdrew* into herself in front of him. He didn't know how else to describe it. He watched her covertly as she gathered up her cut outs and folded them into a neat pile. Carrying his own drink to the opposite couch, he sat down and tried to ignore her.

She had turned her face toward the fire and was gazing into it now in perfect abstraction. It was the damnedest thing. Her expression was not stony in the least; she did not harangue him or argue or protest her cause. He almost wished she would, for he would know how to react to that. Instead, she simply retired from the field with a vague air of…yes, disappointment. *For fuck's sake.*

It should not bother him, he told himself, frowning as he took a swig of whiskey. It did *not* bother him, he corrected

381

himself testily. What kind of fool would prefer his wife to fly into a temper then clam up whenever they had a difference of opinion?

Suddenly he could stand it no longer. "I suppose Allsop shares your outlandish views?" he remarked and almost winced at the undeniable edge to his words. What had got into him? As a rule, he was easygoing to a fault. *Everyone* said so.

Dora turned her head on the chairback to glance at him in surprise. "What makes you think that?" she asked, a pucker appearing between her brows. "Harold's manner of dress is probably the most conventional in this house, apart from Hetty." She seemed to consider. "I don't think he holds any decided views on the matter."

For some reason, this did calm him a little. "He doesn't? Not even a view on his late cousin's attire?" he asked. He was dismayed to hear his question sounded more like a jibe.

Dora's eyebrows rose even further. "I do not recall him ever mentioning her manner of dress once," she said slowly. "I have seen her photograph, for he keeps it in a leather-bound frame. In it she was dressed very simply in a sort of sprigged muslin." She shrugged, shooting him a puzzled look, and Clem felt suddenly a fool.

Why had he reacted like that? He was supposed to be putting distance between them, not strife! Every word she had said about Allsop made sense. He was the most strait-laced person in the household. He might be a musician, but he was no forward thinker or revolutionary.

Allsop wasn't even a bohemian like Felix and Theo, not really. He was mild-mannered and rather dull. The most interesting thing about him was that he liked playing piano at The Eagle. Clem could not think for the life of him why such a man should have caught Dora's fancy.

Perhaps it was being raised in a house by an eccentric uncle? She craved a little mediocrity in her life. No, that was not fair. He had to admit Allsop could write a catchy tune. Just because he did not like him did not mean he was without talent. Maybe it was just sheer proximity. There had been no other males within her sphere after all.

It was only five minutes later when Dora said his name in a small voice. "Clem?"

"Yes?" His reply was far too keen.

"I would very much appreciate it if you would engage a seamstress on my behalf," she said quietly. "In fact, I would love it. As for the fabrics…" Her gaze was steady. "I would dearly love that too."

Unable to think of a reply, Clem gave her a nod. "Eat your sweets," he said gruffly and tried to keep his eyes off her for the next couple of hours before they turned in. He failed, of course, miserably. Just as he failed to keep to his side of the bed once the candles were blown out. If she could only see his face in shadow, then maybe he could fool himself he was keeping to his resolve.

"Clem?" Dora whispered in his ear as he kissed down her neck. He made a discouraging noise in his throat. He didn't *want* to talk to her. That way problems lay. He kept incriminating himself. "I've put my preventative in."

He drew in a sharp breath. "You have?"

"Just on the off chance you might want to…"

He breathed noisily against her collarbone. "I do want to," he admitted raspily.

"That's good, then." Feeling her wrap her arms about his back, Clem gave up all thought of resistance and gave in to his body's needs to join with Dora's. As the room was only dimly lit at this point by the glow of the fireplace, he felt free to indulge in his baser promptings. He was a little cruder, a little brusquer than he had let himself be with her before.

She did not seem to mind when he dragged her knee up high, opening her up to him so he could pet her there. "You're nice and wet, Dora," he said huskily after a couple of minutes. "How do you feel about trying a nice, fast fuck to take the edge off?"

"I'd like to try it, certainly."

Something about her solemn reply made Clem's lips twitch, but instead of laughing, he lowered his head and kissed her again, slow and unhurried, which did not really fit with his mood at all. Then he reached down and caught her other knee, dragging it up so she was fully open to him. "Tell me at any point if you want to slow things down," he said before grabbing his cock and positioning himself to push inside her. Dora gave a little sob of pleasure when he started the slide inside, which had him instantly wanting more. "Is it good?" he asked. "Tell me."

"Yes, yes, it's good," she assured him breathlessly, and it was at this point that Dora did *the thing*. The thing that Clem liked so much. Clem could never rationally explain why it had the effect on him that it did. She was likely only echoing his own preoccupation with her nape, but when she reached up and squeezed the back of his neck, Clem *lost* it, thrusting into her without restraint until he was buried up to the hilt in Dora's sweet, tight pussy.

"Fuck," he wheezed. He had meant to be less tender with her, it was true, but not fucking brutal. "Are you—?"

Dora moaned. "Clem," she breathed. "Oh *yes*."

He was lost. Dora arched her back and took his thrusts—more than took, she met them, her own hips moving fretfully, emitting breathy sighs and gasps that somehow set his own chest burning. Feeling her hand not only touch him there, but apply pressure? God alone knew why but it gave him a full-body shiver and drew a groan out of him so loud it startled even him. "*Yes, Dora,*" he had panted.

She had gazed up at him with glazed eyes, but she did not remove her hand. Instead, she had tugged on him there, drawing his face down to hers. "Kiss me," she had murmured simply,

and Clem's pulse had kicked in like she had asked for
something far more exciting.

When she had tangled her tongue with his, he had groaned
again. Jesus, what was wrong with him? His heart was
pounding, and he felt almost breathless when the kiss ended. He
even chased her lips for more, though his chest felt like it was
bursting at this point, and he was panting from the effort.

"Do it again," he wheezed as soon as he could bring his
lips to leave hers. "Again," he all but begged, though it brought
him perilously close to the brink. She likely didn't know what
the hell he was talking about, he realized, but even as he opened
his mouth to explain, he felt her fingers squeeze his neck, and
he had to grit his teeth against the pleasure.

Holy hell, the squeeze there, the squeeze on his cock, was
she deliberately making them simultaneous? He was going to
come. He wasn't ready, he realized, not by a long shot. "Stop."
He had to force the words through his lips, and they weren't
convincing at all. "Jesus, Dora, I'll spill."

"Stop?" she asked. In the dim light he could just about
make out her looking at him through her eyelashes. "Are you
sure?"

Christ, the quirk of her lips—they looked swollen and
kissable. He wanted to kiss her, he wanted to come, he
wanted...*her*? The thought had him blinking. She was his
anyway, what did it matter? His thoughts were stuttering,
disjointed. He couldn't focus, not when she had him bound so
tight in pleasure.

"Because," she interrupted, drawing the word out teasingly,
"you really don't look sure..." He saw she was going to do it
the instant before she did it.

"Don't you dare," he ground out, but his lust must have
been written all over his fucking face. She squeezed, and Clem
uttered a whimper. There was no other word for it. He was
hanging on by a fucking thread.

385

"Don't come," she said, and his head snapped up to look at her in an agony of desire, shock, and sheer fucking awe.

Speech was beyond him. His cock was already pulsing inside her. "Dora," he gasped. "I can't…"

"You can," she insisted, her hips moving fitfully. "I'm so close."

He felt the sweat standing out on his brow. "I—*fuck*—" Clem shattered and, mercifully, for the sake of his pride, so did Dora. In the aftermath, he lay flat on his back, feeling utterly undone. He was a heaving, panting mess. What the hell just happened? So much for him taking a more detached approach.

Fuck it, he had already messed up this encounter. He would try again on the next. Rolling into her, he dragged her body back against his own. "Allsop would not have done for you, Dorabelle," he heard himself tell her. "He was not man enough for you."

Shut the hell up, Clem, he told himself when Dora's head turned slightly to look back at him. Even in the failing light of the room he could see the surprised bewilderment in her expression. She had no idea why he wanted to talk about Harold Allsop in this moment and neither the fuck did he!

29

When Theo woke the next morning, Clem had already made himself scarce. She frowned and made her way down to fetch hot water for a good wash. Today was a Thursday so she did not have an afternoon performance, only an evening one. As such she could have the morning off. Maybe that was why Clem had taken off for The Eagle without her? Then again maybe not.

He had been doing that more and more lately, she reflected as she washed and dressed. Telling her to simply catch a cab in for rehearsals whenever she saw fit. Foolishly, she wished they could just travel in together as they had in the early days, but Clem clearly did not feel the same way. He was busy, of course, and that was why Eddie and Sam so frequently escorted her.

His being busy, she also hoped, was the reason she and Clem did not take luncheon together so often anymore, even when their schedules did coincide. She missed those shared meals more than she could say, though, of course, they now lived together which was a whole new level of intimacy. She should not begrudge the fact they no longer ate alone together, that would be ridiculous.

She did not mind sharing him, in fact she took great pride in the fact she had brought someone into their family. It still seemed astonishing that she could lay claim to such a man as her husband. She fancied that even Felix had already started to notice some of Clem's better qualities. Impulsively that morning, she had shown both her brother and Mrs. Cherwell the sketches Clem had done of her.

Felix had been considerably taken aback and had looked them over several times in baffled surprise.

"He has flattered me, of course," she said when her brother remained speechless. "But you must admit they contain some artistic merit."

Felix cleared his throat. "You never said he was an artist," he said, sounding vaguely accusatory.

"He is a man of many hidden talents," Theo had not been able to stop herself from bragging.

Mrs. Cherwell was a lot more straightforward. "Guess it's like wot they says. Beauty lies in the eye of the beholder. He's made you look like one of them wotsits."

"Wotsits?" Theo had echoed, feeling mystified.

"Fast women wot 'angs in portrait galleries," she said forebodingly. "Lives their lives steeped in sin and then comes to nasty endin's."

Theo could only suppose she meant artist's models and felt highly gratified. "Do you really think so?" she asked, sneaking another look at herself through Clem's eyes.

"'E could have at least drawn you on some hair for decency's sake!"

"He rather likes my short hair now," Theo said, trying not to sound smug and failing in the endeavor.

"I can see that, miss!" The housekeeper retreated to her kitchen muttering what sounded suspiciously like "Indecent, I calls it!" under her breath.

Theo had shrugged and returned the drawings upstairs. Mrs. Cherwell's words had strangely bolstered her spirits after her recent misgivings. Sometimes lately, she would catch Clem silently observing her with a troubled expression on his face, but if she ever questioned him, he immediately snapped out of it and denied anything was amiss.

She hoped to goodness that everything *was* fine as he repeatedly insisted. Only sometimes she could not help but worry that he might have grown tired of her companionship already. It would not be so very surprising, she reflected. She had lived a rather narrow life experience so far, though she was eager to broaden her horizons. Clem had always lived such a full and colorful life.

Before she got too anxious, she reminded herself that he had finally shared more of his beginnings with her which was highly gratifying. Maybe it would just take Clem longer to view her in the light of family, she considered. His own experience of family life had been so disjointed after all. That boarding school of his had not sounded a pleasant place, even if he had come across a sympathetic schoolmaster or two.

After his mother's death he had no female presence in his life at all until he moved in with his aunt Nancy and uncle Dan at fifteen. Then it had not been long before he had struck out on his own. Though she was sure he must have never lacked for female company as a young man, he had probably not seen much by way of working marriages, she thought and marveled anew that his father had treated him so shabbily.

At the top of the stairs, she paused before crossing the landing to knock lightly on Henrietta's door. "Come in," her sister called, and Theo entered, still carrying Clem's sketches.

"How are you feeling this morning?" she asked. Once again, Henrietta was fully dressed, this time in a sober gown of navy blue. She wore a coral-colored cameo at her throat that had been their mother's. "You are looking better by the day," she added approvingly.

Henrietta smiled wanly. She was unpacking her trunk. "What have you there?" she asked with a flicker of curiosity.

"Oh these? Just some sketches Clem did of me last night." Theo suddenly felt a little self-conscious to show them to her sister, who was a lot more perceptive than their brother. "I was just showing them to Felix in an attempt to prove Clem is not an out-and-out philistine."

"Let me see," Henrietta said, straightening up.

Theo crossed the room to stand beside her, holding up the drawings, the one of her profile uppermost. Henrietta was very quiet and stood very still, regarding it in silence for a long time.

389

So long in fact that Theo went to move to the next sketch, but Henrietta shook her head.

"No," she said with a quick gesture. "I am not finished."

Theo turned her face to look at her sister. "You think it good, then?" she asked, flushing before adding jokingly, "Only Mrs. Cherwell thought it slightly indecent."

Henrietta nodded slowly. "It *is* rather revealing," she said solemnly.

Theo was startled. "Revealing?" Clem had drawn in her high collar and pintucked bodice.

"Of how he sees you, I mean."

"Because he flatters me?" Theo asked, after a pause, thinking of Mrs. Cherwell's other response. *Beauty lies in the eye of the beholder.* Could Clem think that *she*…?

Henrietta gave a quick shake of her head. "Do you remember Mr. Dirkson's portrait of Katie Grigg?" she asked, naming a famous actress of a few years back.

Theo pulled a face. "I never liked that painting. He somehow took a beautiful woman and made her look entirely supercilious and smug. Like a sleek, pampered cat sat upon a silk cushion."

"Precisely, because Dirkson saw more than just her pretty features. He saw the woman behind the fleshy façade."

"Fleshy façade?" Theo repeated. "What a horrid way of putting it!"

That brought a reluctant smile to her sister's lips. "You know full well what I mean," Henrietta said, nudging Theo's shoulder with her own. "I do not have the same way with words that you do."

Theo wound an arm about her sister's waist, and they stood in companionable silence as Henrietta looked through the rest of them with a sigh. "I should like to have one for my side table," she said, surprising Theo, "but I don't expect he could be brought to part with them."

"Well, that is where you are wrong," she told her roundly. "These two, he will not part with, but the rest belong to me now. Which one would you like?"

After great deliberation, Henrietta selected one, and Theo handed it over. No sooner had she done so than Henrietta made for the table under her window and picked up a large vacant silver frame there. It must have had a picture in it previously. It dawned on Theo that it most probably had been a photograph of Henrietta's erstwhile suitor.

"Is Vincent visiting with you today?" she asked casually. Was it her imagination or did Hetty flush slightly?

"He is coming by this evening, before dinner," her sister responded in the same offhand manner as she slid the back off the frame.

"Why do you not ask him to join us?" Theo suggested impulsively. She waited for Henrietta to dismiss such an idea out of hand, but instead her sister seemed to consider the matter before replying.

"It would not be fair," Hetty said finally, "to subject him to Felix's outraged glares while he tried to eat."

Theo pulled a face. "I think Felix is finally warming up to Clem," she said, hoping more than believing this to be the case.

"And what about you?" Henrietta asked, apparently absorbed in her task of fitting Clem's sketch to her frame. "Are you warming to him?"

"Me?" Theo stared at her sister in surprise.

Hetty stood the frame upright and took three steps back to survey the end result. "Yes, you," she said lightly, her eyes still on the frame rather than her sister. "You no longer thirst to see him bloodied and bruised in the ring?"

For a moment Theo could not think what her sister was referring to. Then she remembered her words from that first encounter with Clem and blushed hotly. "I was never in earnest

391

about that," she said quickly. "Those were just hasty words. We get along extremely well, I assure you."

"I hope so," Hetty said slowly. "I did tell you to have a care around him, but it was plain even at the time that you did not take me seriously."

To have a care around him? Theo puzzled and her thoughts must have shown in her face, for her sister sighed. "Men like that always ruthlessly pursue what they want," she said fatalistically. "I daresay, even if I had warned you outright, it would not have put you sufficiently on your guard against him."

Theo felt tongue-tied and strangely reluctant to explain that it was *she* who had pursued Clem, not the other way around. How funny that first Lil and now Hetty should think differently.

"Are you going to the concert rooms today?" Hetty asked, generously giving her an out from the awkward turn of their conversation.

"Yes," Theo responded at once. "But not until this afternoon. Lil and I have a practice session booked to run through a new routine." Hetty opened her mouth then closed it again. Theo eyed her curiously, wondering what she wanted to say, but after a couple of minutes, it seemed nothing else was forthcoming.

"What do you think?" Hetty said finally, gesturing to the framed sketch.

Theo turned to look at it. "I love it," she said and smiled.

The sisters took lunch together, and then Hetty announced her intention of pressing some clothes which had been sadly crumpled from her trunk and Theo readied herself to set off to The Eagle.

"Guess who's in the audience tonight?" Lil demanded as soon as Theo joined her in their dressing room.

"Peggy!" Theo guessed, naming Lil's old dresser and companion.

"That's right," Lil said. "And Mother Longdon too." She pulled a face. "Not sure what the old gal will make of the act, but I will say, she's mellowed a lot in recent years. When her son first wed me, she thought I was a scarlet woman."

"And now she is your greatest supporter," said Theo, dropping a kiss on Lil's rouged cheek.

"Well, I dunno about that," Lil extemporized, "but she does acknowledge I've done a sight more for her than her own flesh and blood daughter."

"Have you seen Marianne recently?" Theo asked after Lil's sister-in-law as she hung up her bonnet and scarf.

"Not for a couple of months at least. That woman she acts companion for had to take the spa waters, so they upped sticks for Tunbridge Wells." Lil sniffed. "S'alright for some."

"I've always thought it must be rather awful to be someone's paid companion," Theo reflected. "And forced to be always agreeable and cheerful no matter what."

Lil snorted. "Marianne's never been agreeable in her life, the sour-faced cow! You should hear the way she lords it over her mother that she lives in a Georgian townhouse with four servants while we live in two tiny rooms over a hat shop. 'Mrs. Montague-Smythe wouldn't dream of sleeping in a room that faces south,' she mimicked in a pretentious voice.

"With a bit of luck, you'll be able to start looking for new rooms soon," Theo pointed out. Their pay packet had already increased three times, each time they had been bumped up the bill. Now they were second only to Florrie Foss.

Lil nodded, her eyes softening. "I know, but my two old dears are anxious lest I overstretch meself. They want us to save up a bit of a nest egg first."

Theo cleared her throat as she sat down at her own dressing room table. "Henrietta's home," she said. "Her plans with Hillingdon didn't work out."

Lil turned in her seat to stare blankly at her. "What d'you mean, things didn't work out?" she asked.

"I'm not entirely sure to be honest. She's asked us to give her some time before she's ready to explain. I think she's had a rough time of it." She avoided Lil's piercing gaze. "The only one she's really confided in is Vincent."

"Vincent?" Lil repeated, sounding flabbergasted.

"Yes."

"Vincent, your brother's doorman?"

"Yes." Theo took a deep breath. "I would not be surprised if, well, if Henrietta has finally started to think of him differently. In the light of a suitor, I mean."

Lil dropped her powder puff. "What?" she squawked. "That great hulking brute? With your beautiful sister?" She laughed derisively. "I wouldn't get your hopes up, Theo love. Henrietta knows her own worth, and there's no way she'd throw herself away on Vincent with his ugly mug."

"She's different with him now," Theo insisted. "She was always kind to him, but...sort of distant. And she isn't now." Theo screwed up her eyes. "She's, well...I don't know how to describe it. And you know Vincent was always slavishly devoted to her."

"Gawd, anyone with eyes in their head knew that!" Lil responded with spirit. "But if you're trying to tell me Haughty Henrietta is giving him the come hither... Well, I just can't picture it, darlin'. Sorry to say."

"I don't know that anyone could accuse Hetty of that," Theo admitted, thinking of her sister's rigid sense of propriety, "but when I walked into the hall the other night, she was holding his hand in hers."

Lil squinted at her. "That's all?" she uttered derisively. "Lord, that could just be in friendship."

394

"N-no." Theo shook her head. "No, not with Hetty's reserve. She would *never* have done that before. She would not have wanted to give him false hope."

Lil snorted. "I still say as you're reading too much into it. I told you she'd find Hillingdon a slippery customer to get up the aisle. She's likely just seeking comfort in a familiar friend after her letdown. Unless…" A suddenly suspicious expression passed over Lil's face.

"Unless what?" Theo asked.

Lil gave her a sharp look. "Lord, you're an innocent, Theodora love."

"What do you mean?"

"You're telling me, Henrietta spent all those weeks finding her way home from Paris? And still not married the whole time? He grew bored of her, love, once she'd succumbed. She didn't have the arts to keep him once he'd had his way. Stands out a mile."

"Lil!"

"Maybe there'll be some consequences she don't fancy facing on her own in nine months' time," Lil continued. "Vinnie might do, then, at a pinch."

"Lil!" Theo was shocked. "Hetty would never… You think that Hillingdon lied to her? That he gave her false promises and then when she was away from the protection of her family—" She choked on the words.

"Lied to, or your sister thought she could persuade him to do the right thing by her. She wouldn't be the first, Theo."

"No," Theo said decidedly. "Hetty would never have eloped with anything less than a promise of marriage."

"Maybe so," Lil agreed. "But Hillingdon's name's been linked with a lot of actresses, Theo, and he ain't never married a single one of 'em."

Theo swallowed, thinking of Rhonda Bettinew, who danced in her petticoat at The Royal George. At the look on her face, Lil jumped up from her seat, bustling about her. "Now, don't go looking like that, Theo. You're right, of course. You know your sister better than anyone. Don't mind me, love. I'm a jealous old cow with a suspicious, nasty mind. I'll get used to sharing you again. Eventually. Now come on, look lively. We've got an audience to prepare for."

With some effort, Theo managed to put such alarming thoughts from her head. It turned out that Lil's family were not the only family members in the audience that night. Though she did not know it at the time, Felix also attended the same performance. He appeared in the parlor doorway in his velvet smoking jacket as Theo and Clem arrived home.

"Saw the show," he said, clearing his throat.

Theo's footsteps halted so fast, Clem nearly walked into the back of her. "You did? What did you think?"

A strange expression passed over Felix's face. "Never knew you had it in you," he admitted, casting a fleeting look at Clem.

"Well, now you do know," Clem responded coolly.

Felix coughed. "I daresay you know what you're about." He scratched his ear. "You pack the place to the rafters like that every Wednesday night?"

"Every Thursday, Friday, Saturday, and Sunday night," Clem confirmed.

"And afternoons, too, on a weekend," Theo added proudly.

"That headline act is really something," Felix said with an odd tone to his voice. "Florence Foss, I think her name was."

Theo regarded her brother with interest. "Isn't she just," she agreed.

"We'd better go up," Clem said, taking her elbow. "Dora has to do it all again tomorrow night."

As if on cue, Theo found herself yawning. "Good night, Felix."

"Neither of you fancies a nightcap, then?" Felix asked, looking disappointed.

Glancing past his shoulder, she could see he had set out the decanter and glasses including a small sherry glass for herself. She was touched in spite of herself. "I'd love one," she said quickly, seeing a refusal trembling on Clem's lips, and sailed past her brother into the parlor. "You should have brought Hetty along with you," she said brightly as she flung herself into a chair. "She was only saying earlier today that she wanted to come and see my act."

Felix, she thought, looked rather horrified at the notion, though he swiftly tried to rearrange his expression. "Er, I thought—her health considered—better not," he mumbled as he bent over the drinks.

"She's looking a good deal better, I think," Theo said as Clem lowered himself to sit on the arm of her chair. He looked resigned to exchanging chitchat with her brother for a few minutes, though clearly not ecstatic at the prospect.

Felix passed her a glass of sherry and Clem a whiskey and soda. "Saw your drawings earlier, Dabney," Felix said abruptly to Clem. "Rather good, I thought."

Theo purposely did not meet the accusing glance Clem threw her way. "You're too kind," he said without expression, tossing back his whiskey.

"Not at all," Felix responded. "We're—er—a creative family. Always have been."

Theo took a hard look at him. Was her brother nervous about something?

"I—er—used to fancy myself as a bit of a playwright, in younger years," Felix said with a mirthless smile. "Another Sheridan in the making. Hahaha." At Clem's blank look he added, "Richard Brinsley Sheridan. *The Rivals? School For Scandal?*"

Clem spread his hands wide. "It's an uncultured swine, I am," he said in his blandest manner.

"Oh, er, well, it's comedy of manners," Felix explained, taking a hasty sip of his own drink. "That type of thing."

"I never knew you were interested in writing comedies, Felix," Theo broke in. "How did I never hear of this?"

"Oh, well." Her brother gave another nervous laugh. "I was always far too self-conscious to let others read them," he said wistfully. Theo nearly dropped her glass. When had Felix ever been wistful?

"What about Uncle?" she asked, slightly incredulous. "Did you never let Uncle see them?"

"Always promised myself I would," Felix admitted with an awkward laugh. "Had this grand idea that I could get them produced one day on our own stage. I even tied one of them up in green ribbon once and put it on his desk with a note. Then twenty minutes later I reclaimed it and locked it back in my own drawer." He took another swig of whiskey. "Hadn't the nerve, in case he told me it was so much dross."

"Why don't you let Theodora read one of them?" Clem suggested. Theo swiveled in her seat to look at him. "What?" he asked. "You know the business as well as anyone. Comedy, I mean, and what the public likes."

Theo spluttered. "I hardly think—"

"Would you, Theo?" Felix broke in, in strangled tones.

Good grief! She stared at Felix. "If you would value my opinion on the matter," she said slowly, and her brother nodded, looking rather choked.

"Why don't you run up and fetch it now?" Clem suggested. "In case you get a case of cold feet in the morning."

"Already thought of that," Felix admitted and, to Theo's surprise, crossed to the bureau, unlocked it, and lifted out a sheaf of pages done up in faded ribbon. He could not quite meet Theo's eye as he solemnly handed it over.

"I will start reading it tomorrow," she promised, giving her brother a reassuring smile. It felt wrong seeing Felix uncertain of himself. "Has something happened, Felix?" she asked impulsively. "Something you have not told us, I mean."

Felix's guilty start told her all she needed to know. "Oh, just theater concerns," he said with an attempt at breeziness he could not quite pull off. Theo guessed things were not improving at The Parthenon. Far from it.

"What kind of concerns?" Theo heard Clem ask harshly and was surprised he'd bothered to ask. He was always rather dismissive of The Parthenon these days. Even more surprising, Felix did not immediately bristle up and get defensive over the question.

Her brother swirled his drink a moment in his glass. "Been having a few problems with some of our sponsors," he admitted hoarsely. "Most of them, in fact. Either threatening or actively pulling their support altogether."

Theo drew in a sharp breath. This was not good. "Why, all of a sudden?" she asked slowly. Things had been going downhill at The Parthenon for months if not years. Why would their financers all of a sudden start defecting en masse?

Realization only came when she saw the covert look that passed between her brother and her husband. *The scandal over Henrietta*. Oh God. She supposed it was the final nail in the coffin.

*

"We need to talk," Clem said as soon as the bedroom door shut behind them. Something about the way he said it had her instantly on her guard.

"Clem? What is it?" she asked, feeling close to alarm seeing the look on his face.

He made no move to remove his jacket. "I need to tell you something, Dora. Something I should have told you from the outset."

Theo gazed at him as a hundred unformed fears immediately flashed into her mind. He was bankrupt. He was a bigamist. He had killed a man. "What?" she croaked, feeling panicked.

"That day you came to my office," he said, completely throwing her with his opening, "it was the second offer I'd received that day pertaining to The Parthenon."

The Parthenon? Her mind had immediately leaped to it being his second offer of marriage that day! She gave her head a little shake. "The second?" she asked tentatively. He made a gruff sound of assent in his throat. "Who made the first?"

"Your sister."

"Henrietta?" Theo's voice rose. "I don't... What do you mean?"

"When I came to see you in that play," he said carefully, "I'd already identified your sister as the easiest way in. The weakest link in the chain."

"Way in?" Theo sat on the edge of the bed and gripped the coverlet for dear life so she did not slide off. She felt strangely weak and shaky.

"Into becoming a shareholder," he explained. "I told her at once I was interested." *Interested in The Parthenon or in her person?* a little voice inside Theo's head whispered, and she felt a little sick. "I did not have to wait long," he continued. "She called on me at my office the same day as you did. A couple of hours prior in fact. Vincent brought her along," he added. "Her terms were less involved than yours. She wanted money. Nothing else."

Theo nodded, feeling rather like a marionette whose strings had been cut. Once she started nodding her head, she wasn't sure she could stop. "I see..." she whispered.

"I kept this to myself when you showed up, of course," he carried on brutally. "I knew you would not dream of giving me a controlling interest in your family business."

400

Theo swallowed. She felt such a *godawful* fool. All this while she had been telling everyone how well she and Clem had been dealing together and he had been deceiving her. Had he been laughing up his sleeve at her the whole time? It seemed Felix was right after all. She *had* been a naïve little idiot. She had been completely taken in by him. She was mortified.

"Say something, Dora," he said, and she almost jumped at his harsh tone.

"I don't know what to say," she admitted, staring down at her hands which were twisted in her lap. She felt numb, like she had fallen down a well and was still falling. *As soon as you walked out that door, I felt it… Regret.* That was what he'd said, and it had *all* been a lie. "I thought we were partners," she uttered painfully, "but it turns out I am one of your dupes too."

He was silent for a few heartbeats and then he simply said, "I'll clear out of your sight for a while. It's the least I can do."

Theo heard the door close behind him and let the tears roll silently down her cheeks. Just like a card sharp, Clem had concealed something up his sleeve all along.

30

Clem's day started badly and went rapidly went downhill after that. The couch in his office was just as uncomfortable as he remembered it, but this time he felt he deserved his rotten night's sleep. His wife loathed him, and really, who could blame her? She had trusted him implicitly and he had deceived her. Did marriages recover from such deceit?

He had been expecting this very disaster ever since Henrietta had returned to the fold. In truth, it should almost feel like a relief to have it all out in the open, especially as he had finally told her himself. It *should*, but somehow it did not. Now he wished he *had* approached his sister-in-law about keeping the whole thing under wraps. When had he ever had a problem with lying? At least that way, Dora would not have hated his guts.

It was not so much the lying, he finally realized after a couple of hours of wrestling with his conscience. No, it was the idea of going behind his wife's back that had stuck in his craw. Having a secret between himself and Henrietta would have been a real betrayal of Dora in his book. He rubbed his brow and tried to ignore Sidney noisily sweeping his office and eyeing him askance.

Probably by noon, the whole place would know he had spent the night away from home and was in disgrace with his wife. Clem remained tight-lipped, staring down at his page of numbers. Today, he could not even get the column on the left to balance with the column on the right, a task he usually excelled at. He refused to look up and give an opening for the lecture Sidney so clearly wanted to give him.

No sooner had Sidney exited his office, with one last reproachful look over his shoulder, than Jim was back, with a list of trivial questions that could clearly wait for another time.

In the end, Clem threw down his pen. "Out with it," he said bluntly. "What is it you really want to say?"

Jim cleared his throat. "Want me to have a word with young Master Ewell?" he asked, keeping his gaze fixed on the wall behind Clem's head.

"Barty?" Clem was startled; he had not been expecting that. "About what?" Clem asked, though he had a strong suspicion.

He had given Dora leave to carry on with her study of the wiry prizefighter for as long as Ewell would indulge her. Clem had reckoned at most that the lightweight would come to The Eagle once or twice, fast losing patience with it, but to his surprise, Barty's visits to the concert rooms had been thick and fast for the past two weeks now.

Any tentative query Clem voiced on how it was going was met with Dora's enthusiastic reply. She had rattled on about it to Clem one evening the week before, seemingly unaware of his inner turmoil. He had managed to hear her out without an explosion of jealous wrath, but it had tested him sorely.

According to Dora, even the way Barty walked was different, "As though his physicality underlined his every move and gesture" was how she put it. When pressed to explain further, she had said the only comparison she could make was to trained dancers who had a sort of sinuous grace to them even when they were not performing.

When Clem had scowled and asked her why she did not find *his* every move fascinating, she had laughed so heartily that he had been forced to drag her into his lap and tickle her. Later, much later, she had lain in his arms and assured him that she found him just as fascinating, but the difference in their build made it well-nigh impossible for her to replicate the way he moved his body.

She had sounded so regretful about that fact that Clem's jealousy had melted clean away. Then she had rewarded him with a dizzying array of small gestures she *had* already stolen

403

from him for her repertoire, including the way he looped part of his neckcloth when he shaved, the way he stroked his thumb down his jaw when deep in thought, and the way he lifted one lazy brow in enquiry. Clem had been entranced.

"Now show me Ewell," he had said softly, bracing himself for another blast of resentment.

Dora had not even hesitated. Instead, she walked to the door, still clad in her nightgown, and when she had spun around again, there was a total change in the way she carried herself. She *prowled* into the room, all wiry grace and arrogance. There was an unconscious challenge in the way she bore herself and nothing remotely feminine about it.

It was almost shocking how she seemed to disappear before his eyes. Clem sat up to watch her, feeling startled and impressed in spite of himself. "Do it again," he said gruffly.

She did it again, this time adding even more brash flourish, shooting imaginary cuffs and dropping him a wink at the end. That was all Ewell. Shit, had Barty been winking at Dora like that? Clem had flopped back onto the pillows feeling winded. It would not matter if he had, for Dora was no flirt. Clem knew that right enough. Still, it smarted. *Cocky little bastard.*

Jim shrugged. "Just wondered if he might be making a nuisance of himself, that's all."

Clem tensed. "Not that I'm aware."

Jim nodded. "So long as you're sure."

"What the devil do you mean by that?" Clem's tone was sharper than he'd intended.

Jim's expression was carefully blank. "Only he's called round to see her again this afternoon. He also sent her a huge bunch of flowers last weekend so big it could barely fit through the door."

Suddenly, it occurred to Clem that Jim thought the young boxer had played some role in stealing his wife's affections from him. "Are you trying to imply that Dora has acted somehow improperly with Ewell?" he asked softly.

"'Course not!" Jim said roundly, "but he's a charming little fucker and you don't seem to be trying to stay on her right side at all!"

Clem took a deep breath in and out. "I gave Dora full permission to associate with Ewell whenever she sees fit," he said coldly. Jim looked at him doubtfully. "Something else to say?" Clem asked, narrowing his eyes.

"Yes," Jim replied scathingly. "What did you want to do a bleedin' stupid thing like that for?"

The worst thing was that Clem couldn't give him a satisfactory reply.

*

"What the 'ell's going on between you and Clem?" Lil hissed as the curtain dropped that evening. "'E's been glarin' daggers at you all night."

"Nothing that I am aware," Theo lied. "Look out, the curtain's coming back up."

They had three curtain calls before they managed to totter off stage, still drunk from the applause. Lil turned impulsively to her in the corridor outside their dressing room, tears in her eyes.

"Theo darlin'," she said, grabbing her hand. "I don't know's I've outright said this, but you do realize you've turned me life around, don't you?" Theo opened her mouth to respond, but Lil cut her off. "You don't know what it means to me, returning to the top of the bill at this time of life, after all these years of shifting for meself with nuffink to look forward to but a pauper's grave!"

"Lil." The last couple of days had been emotionally exhausting, and Theo felt quite overcome.

"Oh, come 'ere," Lil said, throwing her arms about her neck. They embraced. "Don't you let 'im browbeat you, that's all!" her friend scolded.

They both jumped when an angry voice broke out nearby. "I might have known this was how I'd find you, Lillian Longdon! A leopardess does not change her spots!"

Theo turned her head in surprise, feeling Lil stiffen in her arms.

"Johnny!" a white-faced Lil gasped, her arms falling away. "Is that really you, darlin? I thought for sure you was long dead!"

"I just bet you did!" came the bitter reply. The speaker was a tanned man of rangy build with graying hair at the temples. The cut of his suit was at least a decade out of style, and he looked out of place somehow to his surroundings, as though ill at ease to find himself here. There was a strange inflection to his words. A faintly American accent, Theo thought, though not one she was familiar with.

Johnny, thought Theo belatedly, *as in Johnny Longdon, Lil's absent husband?*

"He's a bit young for you, ain't he?" continued the man snidely, looking Theo up and down. "You want to stay away from this one. Didn't she tell you? She's a married woman, albeit not a respectable one." His expression twisted as he took in Theo's dapper evening wear. "Or maybe the likes of you don't much care."

"The likes of me?" Theo repeated loudly before turning back to her friend. "Don't tell me this is the husband you've held a torch for all these years, Lil?" she said. "Only he seems a bit of a prick to me."

Lil went off in a choked fit of laughter as Longdon seethed. "Oh, you'll be laughing on the other side of your face soon," he promised Lil through gritted teeth. "I've made my fortune now and I'll be setting my mother and sister up for life, while you'll

406

see never a penny from me! You can get by on your immoral earnings!'"

Theo snorted. "Well, I think you'll be interested to find just who Lil has been supporting all these years with her so-called 'immoral earnings,'" she mocked. Just then, they heard a roar from down the corridor, and all three turned to see Eddie charging toward them.

"Oi! I told you to sling your 'ook, mate!" The burly doorman was clearly furious a stranger had managed to slip backstage.

"This isn't the last you've heard from me, Lil," the irate Longdon vowed, quite white about the mouth. "You're still my wife, but that ends now. All these years I wondered if it was *me* at fault. Guess those doubts end here and now, yes sir!"

A growling Eddie seized hold of the interloper and started hauling him bodily away. "As for you, my young sprig," Longdon yelled, his eyes darting angrily toward Theo. "You'll be hearing from my solicitor."

Theo rolled her eyes and raised her voice to follow his retreating form. "You'll find that difficult without my name!"

"I'll find it out, never you fear!" John Longdon spat.

"It's Dora, Dora Dabney," Lil called after him. "The best male impersonator in London's fair city!" Theo looked at her friend's flushed face and sparkling eyes. "Fancy 'is bein' so mad at finding me in your arms," Lil chuckled. "Daft sod!"

Lil maintained a steady flow of chatter as the two of them changed out of their clothes, and Theo could only be glad of the fact it distracted her friend from any further questions about Clem. Theo had felt desolated to a ridiculous degree to wake in their bed alone that morning. It had been the first time since they had been married that they had slept apart.

"Did you hear 'is accent?" Lil marveled. "Sounded like a proper American born and raised, didn't he? I wonder if he's sought out his old mum, or if he popped along to see me first…"

Fortunately, Lil was far too caught up in her own ruminations to notice that off stage, Theo's spirits were decidedly lackluster. "I had better nip 'ome sharpish tonight, I reckon," Lil said, offering her cheek to Theo to kiss. "In case he turns up all hot-headed and spoiling for a fight." She sounded more cheered than daunted by this prospect.

"Do you think you might need Eddie's or Sam's services," Theo asked, frowning. "I'm sure if I offered a good tip—"

"Oh Lord no!" Lil said, waving a lacy mitten. "Mother Longdon would soon put 'im in his place and remind him of his manners." She smirked, then gripped Theo's hand again. "Fancy 'im turnin' up now I'm at the top of me game again!" she said, eyes shining with excitement.

"Like a bad penny," Theo said darkly. "Do not forget his abandonment these past ten years, Lil!"

"He didn't look like he was on his uppers, though, did he?" Lil asked eagerly, and Theo considered this a moment before deciding that, no, Johnny Longdon did not look like he was penniless despite his old-fashioned suit. "I wonder if he spoke the truth about makin' his fortune."

Before she could reply, Lil said with satisfaction, "We proper put him in his place, didn't we, girl?"

"That we did, Lil. That we did." A knock on the door heralded Eddie's arrival to take her home, and Lil pinched Theo's chin and whisked out of the door.

Theo turned back to look herself over in the mirror without enthusiasm. "I'm ready, Eddie," she announced, walking to her peg to fetch her bonnet, but to her surprise, it was not Eddie stood in the doorway, but Clem.

"What's this I hear about you getting in a brawl with some intruder?" Clem asked tightly.

"A simple misunderstanding," Theo managed to say, pleased to hear her voice sounded calm and even.

When she went to walk past him, he reached and caught her arm. Clem's eyes were hard and suspicious. "He threatened you?"

"Not really. It was Lil's husband, as a matter of fact, returned from his years of prospecting in America." She gave a short laugh at Clem's disbelieving look. "It may even turn out he discovered gold, or diamonds, or whatever it is they dig for in those places," she said, shrugging out of his grip. "Stranger things have happened."

"Get your coat on."

Her breath quickened, and their eyes met. "Are you coming back with me?"

"I'm seeing you home safely," he responded shortly before glancing away. "Your brother met with your family solicitor today."

"How do you know that?"

"Before I left last night, I told him I was a shareholder. He said he would seek confirmation today."

"Oh." She gave a short laugh. "A shareholder, you say," she murmured. "More like the *majority* shareholder." She slipped her arms into her paletot and pulled on her bonnet as Clem stood silently watching her.

They took a hackney cab to Juniper Row but found the parlor and dining room empty of occupants. Running upstairs, Theo glanced in on Hetty for her own peace of mind and found her sitting before the hearth with her head resting on Vincent's shoulder.

Quietly closing the door, lest she disturbed them, she turned and discovered Clem behind her. "Felix was in his room," he said quietly and sent a glance of warning back over his shoulder. "I told him to come to the sitting room."

409

From his conspiratorial manner, Theo deduced he did not intend for her siblings to know they had fallen out with one another. She nodded and preceded him into the sitting room which, without its fire lit, did not seem its usual welcoming self. After the stage, it was probably her favorite place in the world, but today its charms seemed diminished somehow, as though Clem's recent revelation had tarnished it.

31

Clem felt his stomach muscles tighten when Dora made for the window seat instead of her usual spot next to him on the couch, but he made no comment. Had it really only been twenty-four hours since he had confessed his part ownership of The Parthenon? It seemed far, far longer, at least for him.

Suddenly he wished Fields was a thousand miles away. He wanted to peel off Dora's socks and demand she rest her feet in his lap as she usually did when they relaxed here together. That he could miss such mundane domesticity boggled his mind. What the hell was he going to do about this mess?

His brother-in-law closed the door behind them and turned with a frown to face his sister. "Not sure if this should be man-to-man, Theo, no offense."

"None taken," she replied promptly, "as I have absolutely no intention of making myself scarce. What's it all about? Come and sit down, Felix."

Clem made for the drinks cabinet and poured three whiskey and sodas. He passed one to his brother-in-law and one to Dora, who looked appreciative of the gesture, though he knew she was not overly fond of whiskey.

Not that Felix noticed, for he was too agitated to be scandalized by his sister imbibing spirits. He fiddled with his collar and then stared evasively around the room. Christ, was he about to call him out or something? Clem wondered. Had their uncle Barnabus left him a couple of dueling pistols in the attic? He would not put it past Theo's drama-loving brother.

Fields cleared his throat. "I—er—asked Henrietta outright," he said, "if Hillingdon was formally seeking a legal separation."

Clem darted a glance at Dora. She widened her eyes at him in response. Was Fields still hopeful that a marriage had taken place? It seemed Dora was not the only naïve member of the family.

Dora gave a small cough. "And?" she asked, leaning forward in her seat.

"She said there was no existing marriage to dissolve," Fields answered hollowly. He took a gulp of whiskey. Dora sat back in her seat. Clem remained silent. After all, it was not his place to comment. "So, to all intents and purposes," Fields continued doggedly, "our unmarried sister traveled to Paris for over a month in the company of a man entirely unchaperoned."

Clem looked once more to Dora. "Well," she said briskly, "I for one am heartily glad that Hetty came to her senses before taking such a disastrous step as tying her lot in life to a man like Sir Matthew Hillingdon. A man *clearly* beneath her," she added, lifting her chin.

Fields's head snapped up, and he stared first at Dora and then fleetingly at Clem. "That's the line you mean to take, is it?" he asked.

"Pray, what other line is there?" Dora asked pointedly. Felix puffed out his cheeks, but Clem guessed he did not have the heart to point out that most so-called respectable families would throw Henrietta out on the street for such a thing. "Once people see her family standing behind her then others will follow suit," she said firmly.

"She's an actress," Clem pointed out, "not a debutante. Luckily."

Fields bristled a bit at that, but then the starch seemed to go out of him, and he slumped back in his seat, scrubbing a hand over his face. "People are already saying things," he grumbled. "Gossip is rife. We could lose *all* our backers over this," he warned, "and we've lost most of them already this past week. Jameson has already written me a damn haughty letter. Man's nothing but a damn jumped-up sawbones at the end of the day! Infernal cheek of the fellow!"

412

"If we lose them, we lose them," Dora said grimly.

Clem held his tongue. Losing every last sponsor would be a blow, a sizeable blow. Willing financers were much harder to come by than pretty actresses. Still, one glance at Dora told him now was not the time to point this out.

"I seem to have a done a damn poor job protecting either of m'sisters," Fields commented morosely.

"That is hardly flattering to present company!" Dora pointed out.

"Your pardon, Dabney," Felix said absently and drained his glass.

"Another drink?" Clem found himself offering.

Fields perked up. "Ah yes, good of you," he said, handing over his glass.

Clem glanced at Dora's glass, but she had done no more than wet her lips, so he did not refresh hers. Once seated again, he eyed Fields curiously. He'd accepted his drink and now sat staring down at it in brooding contemplation. This was not the conversation Clem had anticipated having at all.

Fields suddenly straightened. "I've been thinking," he said resolutely. "How much would it cost to hire a couple of thugs to rough Hillingdon up good and proper?" He addressed his words at Clem, and Clem waited a moment before responding.

He regarded his brother-in-law steadily over the rim of his glass. "It depends what you mean by good and proper," he answered coolly.

"Enough to make him feel very sorry for himself for a week or two, but no broken limbs," Dora interrupted promptly. She threw an approving glance at her brother. "I was thinking along the same lines myself," she admitted. "Only I was going to ask Eddie."

"Eddie?" Clem said sharply, turning his head. "Why the hell were you going ask Eddie and not me? At least your brother had the sense to keep it among family!"

413

"That was precisely why," she replied. "I did not want there to be any direct link to any of us."

"Well, I wasn't considering assaulting him in person," Clem responded with asperity. "And did it never occur to you that Eddie might be traced back to The Eagle and Sun and, consequently, us?"

"Perhaps so," Dora conceded, "but Eddie does not have a motive or a direct link to our family should the reprehensible business come to light." Clem opened his mouth to argue, but she forestalled him. "I also wanted to get it organized before Vincent does anything rash, and you have rather a lot on your plate right now."

"Vincent?" Fields repeated, sounding vexed. "Now why did I never think of asking that fellow?"

"Because he would be the principal suspect should anything happen to Hillingdon," Dora responded with exasperation. "Everyone knows he would lay down his life for Hetty just to earn her smile."

She turned back to Clem. "No, I have thought it through," she said sincerely. "Whomsoever performs the deed should also divest the victim of his wallet and watch. That way it will simply look like common theft, and the authorities will conclude no personal grudge is involved. Afterward the perpetrator can"—she waved a hand vaguely—"throw Hillingdon's personal effects into the Thames or something."

Clem thought of Curly Watkins, who had been the first candidate to come to mind for the job. Curly would not need telling to help himself to Hillingdon's possessions. He would be lucky to keep his shoes and the coat off his back. "He would be more likely to head for the nearest fence," he admitted. The lack of broken limbs, however, would need to be stressed several times over. Curly was not gentle.

414

"How much would it cost to arrange such a thing?" Felix repeated for all the world as though he was ordering his shirtfronts starched.

Clem shrugged. "This one's on me."

"That's damned good of you, Dabney," Felix enthused.

"Think nothing of it."

"You must let me know when it will take place, so we can ensure Vincent has an alibi," Dora said in all seriousness.

Clem lowered his glass. "*I* will speak to Vincent, Dora," he said with a frown. "*You* are not to utter another word about the business."

"Yes, Theo," her brother concurred sternly. "It's hardly a fitting matter for you to be involved. You should leave this to your menfolk." Dora rolled her eyes but thankfully made no argument.

"And the other matter?" Clem asked, giving Felix a level look. "What of that?"

"Eh?" Fields actually looked bewildered. "What other matter?"

"The Parthenon," Clem said through gritted teeth. "The meeting you had today with your solicitor."

"Oh, that." Felix shrugged. "A straightforward business apparently. I took Hetty with me, and she freely admitted she had sold her interest outright. Tolley confirmed Hetty no longer holds any shares; you do. What more is there to be said? Unless…" He paused heavily. "You have some stratagem to suggest for dealing with our deserting sponsors?"

"None," Clem admitted shortly. "We will have to play that by ear."

"Only, I've been thinking"—Felix swallowed—"that we might have to abandon the current production and lay off the cast. Ticket sales…" His words trailed off hopelessly.

"As bad as all that?" Dora asked, sounding dismayed.

415

Clem hesitated. "Why don't you let me look over the books?" he offered. To his surprise, Fields didn't instantly bristle.

"Would you?" he mumbled. "Who knows, a fresh pair of eyes…?"

Things must be even more dire than they had appeared.

"Bring them home with you this week," Clem said, "and I'll take a look at them."

Fields nodded and rose from his seat, taking this as a cue to leave, and did so promptly after wishing them a good night.

All along, Clem had been intending to leave after Fields had said his piece, but instead of doing that, he remained seated where he was, watching his wife.

Dora was absorbed in her own thoughts for a moment after her brother left, and when she refocused on Clem, she seemed almost surprised to find him still there. "What do you think are the odds of Hetty taking a role at The Eagle?" she asked, instantly going on the attack.

For a moment, Clem could not even speak. He gave an incredulous laugh. "Your sister? In music hall?"

"Yes, a minor role could work," she insisted. "Maybe as the straight role with a comedian," she suggested with, he thought, more than just a hint of desperation.

"Oh, really? A barmaid seems more realistic."

Dora flushed. "If the sponsors will no longer tolerate her presence at The Parthenon, then obviously it behooves us to find something else for her to do."

"She won't find anything at The Eagle," he answered bluntly.

"Why not?"

He hesitated, trying to answer her truthfully without causing offence. "She doesn't have your warmth, or your wit, Dora. She doesn't possess your appeal."

She looked utterly stunned by his words. "Clem," she spluttered. "For years she was the main draw at The Parthenon!"

"The main draw at a failing box office," he answered with a curled lip. "Your sister's pretty, I'll give you that, but it's not enough. Pretty actresses are two a penny. She got main billing as she owned a quarter of the theater," he added coolly. "No other reason."

Dora shook her head. "Pretty? You're doing her a disservice, Clem, and you know it."

"What do I know?" he demanded, arching a brow at her.

"You *know* she has appeal, that she's beautiful," she insisted. "When you first came to the Parthenon—" She broke off.

"What?"

Dora inhaled a shaky breath. "She was the one you were interested in, not me," she started calmly.

He cut her off contemptuously. "That's bullshit, Dora."

"No, it's not, Clem!" Dora's voice was rising now with indignation. "You approached her with an offer to join your outfit. When I came over, she was telling you that she was not interested in signing up to another repertoire. I remember it well, I tell you!"

Her breasts rose and fell, and though she did not point out he had turned *her* down directly after this, he knew she was thinking of it. "You're misremembering what happened," Clem said flatly. He did not like the scarlet flaming in her cheeks or the fact she would not meet his eye. He did not like it one bit.

"I *don't* think so," she answered bitterly, turning away from him.

"I only approached your sister as I realized she was the least invested in your family business," he reminded her coolly. "I have already explained this to you. I never had the remotest

417

interest in your sister performing at my concert rooms. I was only ever interested in her share in The Parthenon."

Clem watched her expressive face and cursed himself for casting salt into the wound. Still, making her angry at his sly cunning was better than her mistakenly thinking he had admired her sister.

Finally, she looked up at him. "You're such a conniving *bastard*, Clem Dabney!" she burst out with feeling. And Clem knew there must be something wrong with him because he felt hugely relieved that she was venting her feelings at last. "You *tricked* me!"

He shook his head. "Nay, Dora love—" he started calmly, but she stood abruptly, thrusting a finger in his face.

"I can accept the 'Dora' under sufferance, but pray do not address me as love again, I beg you. It is…inappropriate."

He stayed seated where he was. "Come on then," he prompted. "Let me have it."

She blinked at that, but then drew in a deep breath. "Oh, I will," she said hotly. "Never you fear!" She backed up a couple of steps as though making room for her blast of anger and pushed up her sleeves. Clem felt his lips twitch and had to rein in a wholly inappropriate impulse to smile. He wondered at it, for he had not smiled all day, and listening to hysterics or impassioned speeches usually bored him rather than not.

He found himself wondering idly what he would do if she launched herself physically at him. Her slight bosom heaved under her ugly dress, and Clem felt an entirely different emotion. God, he wanted her. It had only been a day, but it felt like a lifetime since she had been open and affectionate with him.

Luckily, Dora was now in full sail, and too far gone to notice his abrupt mood change. Her cheeks flushed and her eyes flashing, she looked…fucking beautiful. She was almost fizzing with ferocity, and it suited her, he realized. Her face might not

418

be considered classically beautiful, but it was so expressive, and he found he could not tear his gaze away.

"I thought we laid our cards on the table fair and square," Dora said indignantly, "but you still had an ace up your sleeve! You held out on me!" The last sounded almost bewilderedly hurt, and Clem sucked in his breath as though she'd punched him. He would rather have her angry with him than hurt by his words or actions.

"Now, Dora," he said reasonably. "If I'd told you I already had a quarter stake in your family business we both know you would never have married me, and I *really* wanted you to marry me, sweetheart; we both know how much."

"We were *supposed* to be in cahoots," she pointed out with dignity and swung away from him, pacing along the length of the room before turning back to glare at him again. "You crafty, *duplicitous* thing!"

Her tone surprised him, for a new note had joined the stiff outrage. Now there was a grudging admiration mingled in with her anger, and the fact warmed Clem strangely in the cockles of his heart. "Dora," he whispered raggedly.

The incredulous gaze she was sweeping him with, too, somehow held a hint of dazed admiration. He liked it. Liked that she appreciated his underhandedness. "I do believe you are almost as Machiavellian as Mrs. Cherwell," she added wonderingly.

Well, that was like a bucket of icy water down his back. He did not want to talk about the Fieldses' housekeeper right now, but he had to know why Dora's thoughts had strayed there. "What about her?" he asked. "Explain."

"She once suggested that I gain the upper hand by marrying Harold and securing a fifty percent majority stake—" Dora started to explain, but Clem had bound out of his seat and closed the distance between them, dragging her into his arms.

"Over my dead body," he growled.

419

"This was *before* we were married," she pointed out huffily, but Clem did not care.

"Just tell me what it will take, Dora mine," he growled at her.

"I don't know what you mean," she said haughtily.

"Yes, you damn well do. For you to let me off the hook. For deceiving you."

"You can give Hetty a job at The Eagle," she responded so quickly that Clem was blindsided.

He blinked down at her. Absolutely not. *Absolutely* fucking not. "And that's all it would take?" he heard himself ask cautiously. "You would forgive me? Just like that."

"Well, according to you, it's a *huge* ask," she pointed out sarcastically. *Little wretch.*

"She isn't cut out for it."

"Like nine people out of ten would say I was not?" she retorted tartly.

"Fine," he heard himself answer. What the *fuck* was he saying right now?

She squinted up at him doubtfully. "Really?"

"Whatever you want. Let's not talk about it anymore."

Her expression wavered. "But you…you will stick to your word, right, Clem?"

"Have I ever given you reason to doubt I would?"

"No," she admitted.

"And I never will," he said coolly, shocking himself more than her. "Let's seal the bargain."

"Very well," she said, taking a step back and thrusting out her hand.

Christ, her handshakes… He felt weak with the realization that there could be so many things he loved about his woman. "Dora…" he groaned. "I don't want to shake your hand. I want to be…inappropriate with you."

Dora blinked. "What?"

"Wildly inappropriate."

"But I'm your wife," she pointed out. "How can it be inappropriate?"

"I don't know," he admitted. "Why don't we find out?" He held his hand out to her, and she grasped it immediately and he towed her out of the room, across the landing, and into their bedroom.

They both immediately began to strip as soon as the door closed behind them.

"By the way, you need to learn some new insults," he said, slinging his shirt over a chairback. "You started out strong, but then ran out of steam. For a minute I thought you were going to call me a blackguard or accuse me of 'not playing the game.'"

Dora looked instantly so thoughtful that Clem felt the hairs on the back of his neck rise in warning. "I don't know about that…" she admitted. "I called Lil's husband a prick today."

Clem straightened up. "You called him a *what*?" Did she just fucking say what he thought she did?

"You look very shocked," she said, stepping out of her petticoat. "Is it worse than that time I mentioned pregnancy corsets in Wards?"

"Honestly? That shocked the hell out of me too." Her face fell. "Turns out I'm a lot more narrow-minded than I realized," he admitted with a frown. "Marriage to an actress has been rather an education." She smiled at this but shook her head. "Did anyone else hear you?"

"Hear me swear?" she asked, taking a hold of the hem of her chemise. He gave her a tight-lipped nod. "Possibly Eddie," she admitted, "though he was some distance away and might not have caught it."

Clem was not happy about Eddie the doorman hearing such utterances from his wife's lips and it must have shown in his face.

"That displeases you," she commented, climbing into the bed.

"It does," he said, though he could not precisely say why. In truth, Clem was not entirely sure why he felt so strongly about it. He was not usually censorious about bad language or how women employed it. Dot, Nat Jones's business partner, and Jeb's partner, Effie, swore in front of him all the time and he never batted an eyelid. Maybe it was because they were not his wife.

"It's funny," she said slowly. "I know my brother would probably suffer an apoplexy to hear me say such things, but I would not have thought that you—"

"It's the part where you say it in front of other people that bothers me," he admitted. His voice thickened. "In fact, I'd prefer it if you kept that sort of thing between us and for the bedroom."

She sucked in a breath. "Ohhhh, I *see!*" she said, looking relieved. "You do not want me to betray myself in front of others." She seemed satisfied with this. "I was so angry, it just sort of slipped out. I'm sorry, Clem. I did not mean to show you up in front of your friends or employees."

Clem had stripped by this point and joined her in the bed. He pulled her abruptly toward him. "Why don't you practice some of your new vocabulary on me now," he whispered against her jaw.

"New vocabulary?"

"Tell me what other bad words you've learned," Clem suggested. "I'm all ears."

Dora stilled. "Bad words?" She seemed, at last, to have picked up that his reaction was not entirely innocent. "It was just—Albert sometimes—"

"Don't tell me who originally said it," he interrupted her swiftly. "I don't want to know. I just want to hear the words on your lips."

Dora pulled back to gaze at him. "Um…fucking?" she faltered.

He caught his breath, his eyes lingering on her lips. "Yes?" he said smoothly. "And what else?"

"Prick," Dora repeated succinctly.

Clem's gazed down at her. "And do you know what those words mean, Dora?" he asked.

"Er…yes?" she admitted in a strangled whisper.

"Tell me."

Her face was practically glowing. "Clem," she began pleadingly.

"Well, you saw fit to use them, Dora, and in mixed company too," he pointed out coolly. "So, you should not be embarrassed to explain them to your husband now, should you?"

She took a deep breath. "*Fucking* is a crude term for the act of sexual congress," she said haltingly.

"Is that so? And the other?"

Dora cringed. "It is a profane word for…for male genitalia."

"What is?" he asked silkily.

Her eyes flew to meet his. She swallowed. "Prick," she repeated faintly.

He breathed noisily in and out. "It sounds almost pretty on your lips," he said, running his thumb over her mouth. "Say it again."

"Prick," she repeated, louder this time.

He nodded slowly. "Now take my prick in your hand," he instructed softly.

Dora gasped. "Clem!"

He raised an eyebrow at her. "What?" he asked, his eyes still on her mouth. "Don't want to?"

"No, I—it's not that—just—"

"Don't want me to fuck you?" he asked, and Dora held her breath for a little too long.

"Clem—you should not—" she started in shocked accents and could get no further for she had to drag some air into her lungs.

His arms were around her in an instant, his brow pressed to hers. "Shh, it's alright," he murmured, soothing her. "I was just teasing. If you don't like it, we'll stop, Dora. It's fine. I pushed you too hard, too fast."

"No," she gasped. "I just...you took me by surprise, that's all." She hid her face in his neck as he stroked her back. "And of course, I do want you to fuck me," she added in a muffled voice. "Though I need to put my preventative in first."

"Why, Dora," he breathed. "You shameless thing."

He felt her smile against his neck. "You say that rather as though it were a compliment, Mr. Dabney."

He reached up to cup her face with his hands and draw it against his own. "I should have told you about the shares," he said harshly, wondering why he was fucking up the mood. For some godforsaken reason, he wanted this out of the way before he got between her thighs again. "I wish I had told you," he said hoarsely. "Not telling you was a mistake," he added for good measure so there could be absolutely no mistake about the matter.

She swallowed and nodded her head. "Yes," she agreed. "Next time, don't be such a prick to your wife."

32

Afterward, they lay together catching their breath, and Clem passed an arm about her until she relaxed against him. "When you said to keep my use of strong language in the bedroom, I thought you didn't want me using such language in public," Theo confided.

"Oh, I don't," he agreed, his hand shifting up and down her side. "Not if you can help it. I realize that is somewhat hypocritical of me, but I can't find it in me to care much."

"No, I mean, I thought you found profanity shocking on a woman's lips, not—well—*stimulating*."

He laughed softly. "I know what you meant, Dora."

"Well, I didn't," she admitted forthrightly. "Not at all!" She tipped her head to one side consideringly. "It must be vastly inconvenient for you," she said with a frown.

"How so?"

"Well…some ladies do swear, just as a matter of routine I mean," she admitted. "Mrs. Cherwell says 'bleedin' Nora' quite often under her breath."

Clem gave a short laugh. "I would not find that remotely—er—*stimulating*," he assured her, though she was not sure that had been the word he had been going to use. "So, you need not worry about my getting hot under the collar if she drops the potatoes."

"It seems an odd thing to get—um—disordered about," Theo persisted, one hand straying absently to Clem's hairy chest.

Clem glanced down at her fingers toying with his hair and slipped his other hand behind his head on the pillow. "Does it?" he asked lightly. "It's quite common, I assure you."

She drew back her head to regard him with astonishment. "It is?" He nodded, looking down at her with a slightly wary look in his eye. "Oh." She digested this a moment then tucked a hand under her chin. "Why do you suppose that is?" she asked quickly before he could change the subject, for she could see that was what he was about to do.

It was a strange thing, for she did not believe her husband was remotely shy, but he did seem oddly reticent to discuss certain topics with her at times. Could this be part of the conventionality he had mentioned suffering from? He cleared his throat. "I don't really know." He shrugged. "I've never really given much thought to it."

She narrowed her eyes. "Tell me, Clem Dabney. Why does my saying naughty words excite you so much?"

He laughed, but she saw him redden all the same. "I don't know, Dora," he admitted with a strangled groan, "but even you saying the word *naughty* in bed with me gets me going and that's the truth."

"Even Shakespeare uses that particular word," Theo pointed out. "Mercutio says, 'The bawdy hand of the dial is now upon the prick of noon.'"

"That does sound rather rude," Clem conceded.

"Shakespeare was rather rude on occasion," Theo agreed. "Uncle said he had to appeal to the cheap seats as well as his noble patrons."

Clem's eyes had drifted shut despite slightly stirring against her thigh. He was likely tired. She had no idea where he had spent last night after leaving her. She ought to let the poor man sleep. "Clem?" she asked.

"Yes?" he replied without opening his eyes.

"Where did you sleep last night?"

"At my office," he answered promptly.

"I thought you said the sofa there was uncomfortable."

"It is."

"Oh. Maybe you should get a new one."

He opened his eyes to frown at her. "Is that your way of informing me we will be fighting a lot from now on?" he asked.

"Not unless you have any more dark secrets hidden from me," she answered lightly, and to her dismay saw something flicker momentarily in his eyes. "Clem?"

"Yes?" He sounded wary.

"*Do* you have any more secrets you are hiding from me?"

"No," he answered. Then before she could follow this up, he asked in an odd-sounding voice, "Do you really hate me calling you 'my love'?"

"No," she admitted in a whisper. "I don't hate it at all."

33

Theodora woke the next morning as Clem was dressing, but instead of asking if she could accompany him to the concert rooms like she might have done in the past, she remained silent and still. She wasn't precisely sure why, only that she did not want to hear him tell her to come along later under her own steam.

She would *not* think about that look in his eye last night when she asked him if he had any more secrets from her. She would not. She would not. She would not.

The bedroom door shut gently behind him, and Theo's eyes sprang open. It was stupid how shaken she felt by the events of the past two days. Like a rug had been pulled out from under her feet. *You would forgive me? Just like that?* he had asked. And she had answered impulsively, thinking only of her sister's plight.

When she had fallen asleep, Theo had felt soothed and reassured by Clem's presence and his passion for her which still burned unmistakably bright. In the cold light of day, however, she no longer felt so secure.

Lil had told her not to take Clem lightly. Even Hetty had warned her to have a care around him. And like a fool she had plunged recklessly forward and fallen headlong in love with him anyway. Theo covered her face with her hands.

That was why it had hurt so badly, she realized dully. For Clem was not in love with her. Oh, he doubtless liked her well enough, and he had *not* liked falling out with her or sleeping in his office. That much was true. But it was not love.

She let her hands drop. She had no one to blame for this, save herself. Clem had never claimed that any finer feelings were involved in their marriage. He had married her to obtain a majority share in The Parthenon, and he had done so without a moment's unkindness to his new wife. Indeed, he had been very considerate toward her at all times. So much so, that she had forgotten altogether that their marriage was a business transaction only.

She had mistakenly felt that Clem was a foundation rock in her new life. Then she had discovered he saw her more as a steppingstone.

The burden of responsibility for that was all on her shoulders. Doubtless, Clem had been no more charming to her than he was to anyone else. Moreover, he had upheld his side of the bargain. He had launched her career at The Eagle and now he had even agreed to Hetty working there in some capacity.

She dragged herself from the bed and took her sweet time over washing and dressing. She had no appetite for breakfast but supposed she had better make her way down there anyway. To her surprise, she found both Henrietta and Harold at the breakfast table.

"Good morning," they greeted her with enthusiasm, and Theo struggled to match their tone, though she hoped she made a good attempt. "Why, this is quite like old times," she said with determined cheerfulness as she reached for the jam.

"I was just telling Hetty of how they queue up on weekends all the way down the street to get admission for the show," Harold said.

"Did you know that Felix finally caved and came to see us two nights ago?" Theo asked.

The other two nodded. "He was strangely quiet when he spoke of it to me," Hetty said with a spark of her old dryness. "*Most* unlike Felix." She turned to Harold. "Did he tell you that you were casting your pearls before swine?"

Harold choked on his piece of toast. "No, no," he hastened to assure them. "He would not, he knows how much I... How much I enjoy it," he said, flushing to his roots.

429

"If you ask me," Theo said, rallying her spirits, "I think our star turn Miss Florrie Foss made rather a conquest of him. He was quite dazzled by her ebullience and badinage."

Henrietta's eyebrows rose. "Is Miss Foss really so awe-inspiring?" she asked curiously, turning to Harold.

"She is quite the most terrifying woman I have ever met," he confessed, making both sisters laugh.

"I cannot wait to see her perform," Henrietta confessed, "but alas, it turns out Vincent does not care for music hall so I must pester someone else to take me."

Theo almost dropped her butter knife. How could she have forgotten that Vincent did not care for music hall? This cast a spoke in the wheel, she thought, for he would not be happy for Henrietta to pursue such a career.

"What is it, sister?" Hetty asked, seeing her consternation. "Why do you look like that?"

"Oh—er—no reason," Theo said quickly. "I just recalled something I had overlooked." *Bother!*

"Well, Hetty," Harold said, clearing his throat. "Could you not simply accompany myself or Theodora one evening?" he suggested shyly. "You need not attend as a paying guest surely when you have so many connections at The Eagle?"

Henrietta seemed to like this idea, and so it was fixed on that she would come along to the next evening's performance. Mrs. Cherwell interrupted them at this point about some caller at the door asking for Theodora.

On investigation it turned out to be a seamstress Clem had engaged for her called Miss Clegg. Theo showed her upstairs to the sewing room and let her rifle through the many patterns she had accumulated. She examined the patterns without comment or any ostensible judgment that Theo could see.

"This was the one I got myself into difficulties over," Theo said, passing the pattern to the efficient Miss Clegg. She cast a doubtful look toward the fabrics she knew Clem thought were drab and unappealing. "Did Mr. Dabney make any mention of the fabric you were to use?" she asked.

Miss Clegg nodded. "Oh yes, I have had my instructions," she said brightly. "Now if I might be permitted to take your measurements?" Miss Clegg turned out to be almost as thorough with her tape measure as Charlie Finch. It was at least an hour later that Theo led her back downstairs and saw her out.

"I will be back at the same time tomorrow," she promised, brandishing the two patterns she had selected, including the one which had defeated Theo. "I am now going shopping for materials," Miss Clegg informed her. "My hours will be ten till three as negotiated with Mr. Dabney. I assume your housekeeper can let me in if you are not home? Good day!" Theo made for the kitchen at once to inform Mrs. Cherwell of the new arrangement.

"Fancy!" the lady sniffed. "What next? Your own personal cobbler?" Ignoring this jibe, as Mrs. Cherwell was clearly in a bad mood, Theo climbed the stairs once more. Her sister called out to her as she passed her door, and poking her head around it, she found Hetty employed in trimming a bonnet.

"Come in," her sister said, motioning with her hand, "and shut the door." Theo did as she was told and advanced into the room with an enquiring look.

"Would you sit here beside me a moment?" her sister asked, gesturing to an empty seat next to her own. Once Theo had complied, she began, "I did not like to mention it in front of Harold, but I suppose all is well between you and Mr. Dabney?" She hesitated before continuing. "Only Felix took me along to see Mr. Tolley's office yesterday and…well, not to put too fine a point on it, he seemed to think that he was not the only one who had no prior knowledge of the fact I had sold my shares."

Theo paused a moment before answering. "Felix was right," she admitted at last. "I did not know. Clem never told me."

431

"Oh," Henrietta said with obvious dismay. "Selfish creature that I am, such a consideration did not even enter my head. I was so wholly taken up with my own woes. Is there—is there any question you wanted to put to me about the business?" she asked, looking pale but resolute.

"How could you do such a thing to me and Felix?" Theo asked before she could stop herself.

Henrietta flinched. "Because all I cared about was getting what I wanted," she answered, lifting her chin. "And it seemed obvious to me, at least, that The Parthenon will not last another twelve months. Not under current management."

Theo sighed and slumped in her chair. "How funny," she said softly. "Did you know both of us made deals with him on the same day?"

Henrietta lifted a hand to her throat. "Do you mean to tell me he no sooner had my deeds in his hand than he approached you for yours?" She looked slightly appalled at the notion. "I suppose you would have been ripe for any mischief after being so vilely betrayed by your own brother and sister."

Theo said nothing. "One has to admire his single-minded determination if nothing else."

Hetty pulled a wry face. "He offered me money and you marriage. I wonder how he will divest Felix and Harold of their shares!"

Theo managed a smile, though the effort cost her dearly.

"Theo?" her sister said, her smile fading fast. "That was an ill-judged attempt at humor. I did not mean anything by—"

"No, no," Theo said, rising to her feet. "You have said naught amiss. I am just a little tired today."

Hetty cast down her bonnet, but Theo was already heading toward the door. "Theo?" she called after her.

"Pray do not give it another thought!" Theo flung over her shoulder and then shut herself in her room for a hearty bout of tears.

The tears, funnily enough, had given her some relief for an hour or so. Theo indulged in a nice soak in the tub and felt a good deal better. She and Harold then shared a cab ride to The Eagle, for Theo was meant to meet with Lil to practice a new routine and Harold, it turned out, had promised to play accompaniment for a female singing duo who had joined the temporary acts a week before.

"They are much further down the billing than yourself and Miss Longdon," he assured her hastily, "so there will be no conflict in my performance schedule."

"That is very kind of you, Harold," Theo assured him. She was secretly impressed by how Harold was branching out in his music hall connections. "Though you should address Lil as *Mrs.* Longdon by rights." She then distracted herself for the rest of the cab ride by telling him of the reappearance of Mr. Longdon from foreign parts.

On arrival at the theater, Theo was not entirely surprised to find Lil was a no-show. She wondered if Johnny Longdon had indeed turned up at Lil's rooms and been confronted by his mother. If so, perhaps Lil had a good deal more on her plate than another routine rehearsal.

She had just opened Felix's manuscript to delve back into his play for an hour or so when a rap on the door surprised her. "Come in," she called out, thinking Lil must have turned up after all.

To her surprise, the door opened to reveal Barty Ewell stood lounging on the threshold. "Barty!" she exclaimed on seeing the wiry boxer. "Did we arrange to meet today…?" She did not think they had, but perhaps it had slipped her mind with all the goings-on lately.

"No," he admitted, sauntering into the room. "Just thought I'd look in on you, as it happens. I was in the vicinity. Did you get my flowers?"

"Oh, I did, thank you, they were beautiful," Theo replied promptly. "You shouldn't have, really. I should be sending *you* flowers after all the time you have kindly given me. I'm so grateful."

He swiveled Lil's chair about and sat astride it. "Fancy getting a bit of lunch?"

Theo hesitated. In all honesty, she did not want to go to lunch with Barty, however entertaining he could be. She had his mannerisms pretty much down pat now, and besides, she wanted to read more of Felix's play which had turned out to be an unexpectedly frothy delight.

"To be perfectly honest, Barty," she said sincerely, "I do not think I would be very good company today. I am feeling a little out of sorts."

He gave her a shrewd look. "Oh, yes? Trouble in paradise. Had a falling out with your hubby?"

Theo could not help but give a start at his words, though aloud she said, "Of course not!"

Barty smirked. "Only I heard a rumor," he said, casting his eyes up to the ceiling before dropping them down to meet her own.

"What rumor?"

"That Clem's been banished from the marital roof."

"What nonsense!" Theo scoffed. "Really!"

"Only, if you're not getting any at home…I could always oblige," he suggested, looking up at her through his lashes.

Getting any? Theo gazed at him blankly. Then he reached across and turned her hand over, his fingers lightly tracing her palm. "Barty!" she blurted, snatching back her hand and cradling it to her chest. "What are you doing?"

He gazed at her half rueful, half something else. "I like you, Dora," he said forthrightly. "If you ever fancy a bit." He shrugged. "I'd be happy to—er—supply it."

"A bit of what?" she asked, and his face broke out into a grin.

"A bit of male attention, that's what."

"Oh!" *Good grief!* "Well, that's very kind of you," she said politely, "but I manage just fine, thank you. Albert squires me as does Harold, Eddie, and even Sam sometimes too. I do not lack for an escort."

Barty gave a huff of laughter. "You and Clem have an arrangement or…?" He looked at her expectantly, and it dawned on Theo that she had not been paying close enough to his words.

"An arrangement?" she repeated slowly.

"About lovers," he answered coolly.

Oh. *Oh!* "What about Ruby?" she demanded, scandalized. She had definitely heard that Barty was courting one of the dancing girls.

Barty snorted. "What about her? We're not exclusive. She went out to dinner last night with a justice of the peace."

The truth dawned on Theo, and she shot him a knowing look. "Oh, so *this* is your manner of revenge on pretty Ruby, I see."

Barty shook his head. "Oh no, don't go running away with that idea. I've had my eye on you for a while now, Dora Dabney," he admitted without shame.

"Barty!"

"It's the God's own truth," he assured her, quite unabashed. "I could properly go for you in a big way," he said, his eyes flickering over her with an unashamed appreciation that made her feel quite stunned. "Why don't you let me? I'd make it good between us, Dora."

Theo's face suddenly felt hot. He was talking about physical intimacy. She gave a strangled cough. Astonishing as it was, Barty was…well, *making a play* for her it seemed. However surprised and faintly gratified she felt, she needed to

435

nip this in the bud. Also, to somehow make it so things were not eternally awkward between them in the future.

"Actually, we don't," she said apologetically. "There's no arrangement in place, I mean." This was not strictly true as she *had* once promised Clem that he could continue with his womanizing. He, however, had not responded in kind. At the time, neither of them had considered the remote possibility that she would want to take a lover.

Impulsively she turned fully toward him. "Barty, I like you very much, but I like Clem most of all of anyone I ever met." She felt her face flood with color at this confession. "He's my very best friend, you see." This was true, even though she assuredly was not his. She bit her lip. "I could never do anything to jeopardize our marr—I mean relationship," she corrected herself hastily. "We're partners. I trust him implicitly and he trusts me." She was not entirely sure this was true after the past two days, but she said it anyway.

Barty looked at her hard a moment. "Christ, Dora. Don't look like that when you talk about a bastard like Dabney."

Theo blinked. "Like what?"

"Starry-eyed," he said with a twist of his lips. "He don't deserve it, love. Not one bit."

Theo bridled slightly. "Do you imagine *your* conduct around the ladies is any better than his, Barty Ewell?"

He sighed. "You're in for one hell of an awakening, Dora. Never told you I loved you, did I?" he said. "I was open and aboveboard about what *I* wanted."

Theo could not speak for a moment, and when she tried, her lips wobbled. To her horror, a tear spilled over and rolled down her cheek.

"Dora, *fuck*, I'm sorry—" Barty started as she sprang up from the chair and blundered toward the window. "I never meant—"

"No, no, it's fine," she lied, feeling angrier at herself than him. He was right; she was wearing her heart on her sleeve over Clem. Her skin felt hot and itchy. It hurt that someone she had come to see as a sort of friend pitied her like this and thought her a lovesick idiot.

She fumbled in her cuffs for a handkerchief before giving up and wiping her cheeks with the back of her hand. She drew in a shaky breath. "But as a matter of fact, you wrong him. Clem never spoke a word of love to me either. He was honest to a fault."

"Well, then he should have, damn him!" Barty said angrily. "It was the least he could have done!"

She threw up her hands in exasperation. "Can we please just drop this subject?" she asked. "You told me, without varnish, what you wanted. I explained that I could not accommodate you. Can we be friends again now and pretend this *never* happened?"

There was an embarrassing tremor in her voice that made her feel awash with fresh embarrassment. Any other actress in this establishment would know how to turn Barty down without making a complete exhibition of herself. Why was she so woefully inept at everything off stage? When Barty just sat there staring, she added a breathless, "Please, Barty."

He swore under his breath, then raked a hand over his face. "I made a right mess of this," he said ruefully, then stood up. "You still want to be my friend, Dora?"

She gave a wobbly smile. "Yes, please."

He drew in a sharp breath. "Even though I'm a clumsy fucking idiot?"

She gave a short, grateful laugh. "No, you're not, Barty. I'm the idiot, and we both know it." She swallowed. "I would just appreciate it if you did not mention it to me again."

Barty opened his mouth, then closed it again before breathing out slowly. "I wish I'd put a bit of varnish on it now, truth be told," he said so frankly that he brought a tremulous smile to her lips.

"It would not have made any difference, I assure you," she replied.

He snorted, then looked thoughtful. "Let's not be too hasty. Who knows? It might be that you can *accommodate me* at some future point," he mused, clearly deriving amusement from the way she had phrased it. "After you've had your heart well and truly broken, I mean."

Theo's spirits abruptly plummeted into her boots. Now he was just being rude. "And my standards have fallen to a more realistic level? I collect you think it an impossibility for someone to form a genuine attachment to me?" she asked in a brittle voice. Before he could answer she continued swiftly, "I believe you're right, Barty Ewell, you *should* apply a coating of varnish in future. Your own particular brand of honesty has a rather nasty sting in its tail."

"That was not my meaning—" he started with a frown, but she thrust out an abrupt hand for him to shake.

"So, we're in agreement?" she said briskly. "No more talk of love affairs between us, Mr. Ewell?" Barty cocked an eyebrow at her, but he took her hand and let her pump it. "Thank you *so* much," she said politely then turned her head. "Eddie?" she yelled over her shoulder. "Sam?" She had certainly heard one of their heavy tread in the corridor outside only a few moments prior.

"You don't need to get me escorted off the premises," Barty objected wryly, reaching for the hat he'd discarded on Lil's dressing table.

The door opened and Eddie's curly head popped around it. "Mr. Ewell is just leaving us," she said brightly. Eddie's look of surprise quickly transformed to one of narrowed suspicion. Theo bustled about the room busying herself putting garments on hangers as Barty's footsteps halted at the door a moment.

438

When she kept her attention firmly fixed on the waistcoat she was buttoning, the door closed. Theo let the waistcoat slip from her fingers and burst into her second bout of tears that day. She had only just wiped them away when there was a short, sharp knock and Eddie loomed in the doorway with a grim expression on his face

"What 'appened?" he asked vengefully, shutting the door behind him. "He get handsy wiv you, Miss Dora?"

Theo gulped. "N-no, of *course* not, Eddie."

"Don't come that wiv me, Miss Dora," he replied, surprising her greatly. "I can see you been crying."

She hesitated, then realizing she had come to trust this man-mountain, she took a steadying breath. "He was very polite," she said with quiet firmness. "I've just never…never been propositioned before, you see. It caught me off guard." Eddie's eyes blazed and he reached for the door handle. "Eddie!" she squeaked in dismay. "Where are you going?"

He hesitated. "'E needs teaching a proper lesson," he growled. "I'll tear 'im limb from fucking limb!"

"Oh, *please* do not, Eddie!" she shrilled, sounding even to her own ears like some wronged damsel from a melodrama, but his wrathful expression was somehow alarming. "Besides." She eyed the hulking brute doubtfully. "Mr. Ewell is a trained pugilist—"

Eddie gave a nasty laugh. "Oh yeah? Well, I fight by London rules, not the Marquess of fuckin' Queensbury."

Theo did not precisely know what this meant, but it sounded ominous. "I promise you; it wasn't the way you think," she persisted doggedly. "The only reason I'm crying is because…"

"Because what?" he asked suspiciously.

"Because I am selfishly sorry that I have now lost him as a friend," she sighed, realizing it was true. She sank down wearily into a chair. "Now everything's spoiled between us, and I can never again treat him with the casual camaraderie that I do with you or Albert, Sidney, or Jim."

She did not mention Sam, who was extremely monosyllabic and could barely be brought to give more than one-word answers or grunts to any of her attempts at conversation.

"You never could," he said harshly. "He ain't like me nor Albert. Albert's just a lad and I'm—well, I'm a different story." His Adam's apple bobbed. "You got to have your wits about you, Miss Dora. When it comes to men. I dunno why Mr. Dabney allows it. For you to go about the way you do—to associate wiv all them rough types. They're not fit company for you, and so I shall tell him next chance I get."

Theo spluttered. "Eddie, I'm an actress, not some delicate creature who needs shielding from the world."

"You're a lady," he said grimly. "No matter that you prance around in trousers on the stage." He shifted uncomfortably from one foot to the other. "You can tell you was raised a lady and you *are* one through and through. I know all about it, me and 'Arold Allsop talk about you often. He couldn't 'old an 'igher opinion about you and that's the truth."

Theo's mouth fell open to hear that Eddie and Harold were on such familiar terms. She had not realized they were even friendly. "Mr. Dabney should never permit the likes of that Ewell to be calling on you casual like that," Eddie continued in an ominous rumble. "He should be keeping a better eye on you."

Theo gazed at him fondly. "Eddie, I am truly flattered that you think so highly of me, but the truth of the matter is that I *love* the freedom Clem affords me, the freedom that being a married lady brings me. You cannot comprehend how hemmed in by life I was, how *restricted*, how stifled. My life now is…so much richer. Can you understand?"

440

He looked at her with troubled eyes. "It was probably safer," he said at last.

"Perhaps," she concurred, "but it was also a good deal narrower, and…I was lonely. Even this experience"—she shrugged—"I can benefit from. I can learn and grow." She fell silent a moment, reflecting on this. "Mr. Ewell was not rough with me in any way, I promise. He was respectful in his word and manner." She ignored Eddie's snort.

"It was not his fault that I had no notion how to respond and…rather fumbled it. We have promised to remain friendly." At Eddie's dire expression, she added quickly, "Though of course not as we were before. But friendly acquaintances, in any case."

He breathed out noisily through his nostrils. "You sure I can't plant him a facer for his impudence?" he asked gruffly.

She shook her head. "I would be most distressed if you did."

He straightened up, looking regretful. "Well, if you're sure."

She smiled at him. "It is so nice to know I can count on your friendship, Eddie."

He gave her a smile at that which served to transform his heavy, brutal features into something kind and rather sweet. Eddie's idea of "being a lady" was rather vague and a good deal more flexible than either Clem's or Vincent's. He swore before her without compunction, and once he had told her a very rude joke about a bishop and a barmaid.

She liked him ever so much, she realized. He had achieved almost the impossible that day and managed to cheer her up.

34

Clem made it till just after twelve and then he broke. Ignoring Jim's gaze, which followed after him, he headed toward the auditorium in search of his wife. He found Allsop there with a pair of vivacious redheads practicing a song and dance routine. "Theodora is here somewhere," Allsop said, abandoning the piano keys and fumbling with his eyeglasses, "but Lil did not turn up for practice so I think she must be in her dressing room."

Clem nodded and made his way back there without more ado. After a short knock on the door, he opened it and found Dora perched on a hard wooden chair, reading her brother's play in total absorption.

"That seat does not look comfortable," he said, shutting the door behind him and catching sight of her red-rimmed eyes. "What's happened?"

"Nothing," she replied quickly. Too quickly.

Clem regarded her a long moment before advancing further into the room and leaning against a side table. "Is Felix's play a tragedy?" he asked carefully.

"Far from it. It is a vastly diverting comedy. Charming in fact." She pulled a face, echoing her brother's own words. "I never knew he had it in him."

Clem ignored her diversionary tactics and focused on her pink eyes. Something had clearly happened between this morning and now. "I hear Lil did not turn up for practice," he said slowly. "How have you spent your time this morning?"

"Mostly reading," she said, stretching and wincing at her lower back. She needed an armchair in here, Clem realized belatedly. If she had her own dressing room, then that would make room for more furniture.

"I saw Allsop is practicing with a new act," Clem said casually, keeping a keen eye on her reaction. Was that why she was upset?

"Ah yes, the Misses Stepson," Dora answered, drawing her shawl closer around her. It was a ratty old thing she only used backstage. She needed a new shawl too, perhaps in cashmere. "They are sisters apparently. He was telling me all about it."

"No callers?" Clem asked, deciding the vivacious Misses Stepson were not to blame. Was it only his imagination or did she pause slightly before answering?

"Barty Ewell called by," she said, avoiding his eyes. "He—er—invited me to lunch, but I did not feel like it."

"You weren't hungry?" Clem probed.

"Er—no," Dora said brightly. She closed the manuscript and set it carefully down. "In any case, I do not think I will be going to lunch with him again in the foreseeable future." At Clem's narrowed gaze, she added, "I have completed my study of him now so close association is no longer necessary."

Jesus. "He made a pass at you, didn't he?" he stated flatly.

Theo nearly jumped out of her skin, her frightened, guilt-stricken eyes meeting his. "No! I mean, yes, but probably not how you are thinking! Oh, *please* do not knock his block off, Clem!"

Her impassioned plea should have been funny, but he wanted to fucking *strangle* Barty. "Tell me how it was then," he said, his fingers tightening on the edge of the table.

"I won't be close friends with him anymore. I told him as such," she gabbled, "and he accepted it fair and square."

"I'm still waiting."

"He just asked if we had an arrangement about such things," she blurted, "and that was it, honestly. He was *very* respectful and did not try to force his attentions in any way, I assure you. He…well, he just sort of intimated that if I was ever agreeable—" She choked on the words and directed an agonized look of appeal at him.

"That if you ever wanted any extramarital, he would be available, is that it?" he asked dryly. She nodded. *That little shit.*

"Please, Clem," she said timidly, rising from her chair and approaching him. "Don't be angry."

"I'm not," he lied and caught hold of her hand, raising it to his lips. "Not with you." That part was true in any event.

"I will be more guarded in the future," she promised. "It's just that—well—I never needed to before, and it never even occurred to me that I should watch my step."

"Mmm." *Naïve*, he thought again, but did not voice.

"I have been over my every interaction with Mr. Ewell a thousand times in my head since. I promise you it was *never* my intention to…to…"

"Lead him on?" he suggested. Her face was scarlet by this point. She nodded. "You would not need to, Dora mine. Ewell is not some tame, neutered tabby like Allsop."

He saw her lips half start to frame a defense of Harold Allsop before she decided against it. "I suppose not," she groaned, dropping her face into her hands. "I just feel terrible about the whole thing." The last was muffled, for it was spoken behind her fingers.

"Well, don't. It wasn't your fault. You turned him down, and he took it like a man, you said. That's right, isn't it?" He could not quite keep the thread of tension out of his words. "Because if he did not…"

"No, no, I promise, Clem. I would tell you if he did not," she said, meeting his eyes fair and square.

He felt his shoulders relax. "Good," he said gruffly. "Then, that's that. Still not hungry or can I take you to lunch?"

She gave him a faint smile. "Still not hungry," she said, surprising him slightly. "I have a bag of apples Albert bought

444

me somewhere." She glanced about, and they both saw a crumpled brown bag of apples resting on her vanity.

"You're sure?" he hesitated. Strange to say, he did not think she had ever turned him down before. "How about coming back to my office and curling up on my couch to finish your play?"

"Your uncomfortable couch, you mean," she answered, the corners of her lips turning up, though the smile was not echoed in her eyes which still looked a little swollen.

Next time he saw Barty… he thought, while stating aloud, "It can't be any worse than that chair. Thing looks like it's on its last legs."

She shook her head. "No, I'm fine where I am. In fact"— she straightened up—"I've changed my mind. I'm going home. There's no point in my being here this afternoon. I'll be back at quarter to seven for this evening's performance. Henrietta is accompanying me," she added, casting a look of challenge his way. "Though I am not entirely sure anymore that a music hall career will suit her after all."

Clem was surprised by her turnabout after her resounding victory over him. "What changed your mind?"

"I had forgotten that Vincent has rather old-fashioned notions of feminine propriety. He does not care for music hall."

"What do Vincent's feelings have to do with it?" Clem asked with a snort.

"Well, I think, that is, I'm practically certain that Hetty has finally accepted his love," she answered.

Clem paused. He very much doubted that. "She could just have a temporary dependence on him, you ever think about that? He would gladly offer himself up. I do not think he would begrudge her using him for a while."

"She would not do that, Clem," Dora said, instantly firing up. "You do not really know her at all!"

Clem shrugged. "She'll have to do a lot more than hold his hand if she means for him to view her as anything but an item of worship."

"What do you mean?"

Clem sighed. "She's not inviting like you, Dora. She hasn't got your charm." She stared at him seemingly in disbelief over his words. Clem lifted an eyebrow at her. "I have mentioned this before," he said with slight impatience. "Or do you still insist on believing it was her I wanted to sign all along for The Eagle?"

"No," she answered, flushing. "I believe you now. I understand that you don't think she can do it at all, but I wish you would have a little faith in her, Clem. That same faith you gave me when you agreed to let me on your stage. You were the *only* one who believed in me, even Lil had her doubts, but you..." Overcome with emotion, she broke off her words, and just as well, for Clem felt them like a punch to the gut.

He had not believed in her. Not for a single moment.

Dora took a deep, shaky breath. "I think I will be better off at home this afternoon," she reiterated. "Perhaps I could take a nap after finishing my reading."

"Get your things," he said. "I'll come out with you and make sure you get a hackney."

Clem felt strangely disquieted as he secured the cab door behind her and waved her off. He felt annoyed with himself. He had never been a worrier, yet these days he could never seem to shake off some nagging unease from dogging his every step. Usually about the state of his marriage.

It seemed to him that ever since he had married, he had been plagued with a newly awakened conscience. His days of a callous, self-serving existence seemed to be well and truly over. It wasn't even as though he could decently mourn the fact. He no longer desired them, not really. His desires all seemed to be focused around one source these days. Dora.

446

If anyone had told him in the beginning that *this* would be the outcome of his purely business decision to wed, he would never have believed them. As it was, he could barely muster any interest whatsoever in The Parthenon, the thing that had motivated him to take the plunge. He almost felt as though he would go out of his way to avoid the damn place. The very thought of it made him feel wretched and…guilty, he supposed. He almost wished he had never heard of it, but then, of course, his path would never have crossed with Dora's.

What was he going to do to divert this latest disaster looming, he wondered, banging his office door shut behind him. No sooner had one worry been dispelled than he was beset with another! He needed to get over this inconvenient guilt he had developed over Dora's misplaced trust in him. None of the things he had tied himself in knots over had worked out the way he thought they would.

First, there had been his steadfast belief she was going to disastrously implode on stage. That had not happened. Then there had been the worry over her finding out his underhand dealings with the theater shares.

Okay, so that had not gone well. He was still feeling the aftereffects from that discovery, even though he had promptly acquiesced to her demands. He had apologized, he reminded himself. He was not to blame now for this *distance* he felt it had created between them.

Unless you have any more dark secrets hidden from me, that was what she had said.

Clem tried to consider this impartially. At the end of the day, there was no earthly reason why Dora need ever find out that he had lacked faith in her abilities. He had every motivation to keep the knowledge to himself. Jim was probably the only other person aware of it, and Jim would never knowingly betray him. Whichever way you looked at it, he was on safe ground.

Why then, did he feel like a huge great chasm was about to open up under his feet?

In vain, he reminded himself that making a clean breast of it about the shares had not relieved his feelings in any way. It had made him feel worse, if anything. Dora had been shaken by it, and she had not fully recovered from it, however much she tried to hide the fact. Sleeping with her had only been a temporary reprieve. It had solved nothing.

The knock on the door made him jump. "There's a Maurice Howard waiting out here to speak to you, Clem."

Clem stared blankly at Jim. "Who?" he said.

Jim scratched the back of his neck. "Says as it's about your wife," he added awkwardly.

Clem stiffened. "Who the hell is he?"

Jim squinted at a small white rectangle. "Well, his calling card says as he's the owner of The Princess Royal Theatre in The Strand."

Well, that gave Clem pause for thought alright. *The Princess Royal?* Even Clem knew that was a class act. An establishment of pedigree. Why the fuck would its owner be here, wanting to discuss Dora? He nodded and gestured for Jim to show him in, and seconds later, an affluent-looking gent with luxuriant whiskers was ushered in wearing a dark gray frock coat and a glossy top hat.

They made their introductions and shook hands as Clem gestured for Howard to take a seat. "I understand you wanted to speak to me about my wife?" he said without preamble. Maurice Howard looked a little pained at Clem cutting through the conventionalities, but he took a seat and leaned forward in his chair.

"I was wondering what sort of contract you had Miss Dabney under," he confessed and, seeing Clem's quick frown, continued swiftly. "Principally, my interest lies in your terms for breaking it." He paused to let Clem absorb this fact before

448

continuing. "I have a new production which we start rehearsing for in three short weeks. Unforeseen circumstances have meant a principal role has become available at the last minute. A principal role which we have come to believe Miss Dabney would suit admirably."

Clem leaned back in his seat, unable to speak for a moment. "What play?" he asked. "What role?"

"Shakespeare's *Twelfth Night*," Mr. Howard responded promptly. "She would be playing opposite the great Orlando Kirby. I am sure I do not need to tell you which role, for it almost seems made for her."

Clem gazed back at him steadfastly. "You perhaps forget I run a music hall, Mr. Howard."

The other man flushed. "The role is that of Viola, a maiden forced to don men's habit."

Shakespeare, thought Clem bleakly, *it would be Shakespeare*. "Might I ask how you have come to this conclusion, Mr. Howard?" he asked blandly. "You have seen my wife perform at The Parthenon, perhaps sometime over the past ten years?"

Mr. Howard met his steady gaze ruefully before shaking his head. "Alas, I have not had that pleasure," he confessed. "It was my nephew and my godson that originally put her name forward. They were most insistent that I could not dismiss their suggestion out of hand." Mr. Howard coughed, and Clem guessed he had probably done his best to do just that.

"They were most enthusiastic proponents and have seen her several times over the past month here at The Eagle and Sun," Howard continued. "Such was the conviction of their arguments that myself and a few others involved finally acquiesced to come and see her perform." He was silent a moment. "I am sure you understand my sentiments when I say that once we saw her, we were convinced one and all that she could play Viola as no one before her has ever done."

449

Fuck, thought Clem. This was it, Dora's dream laid out before him on a platter. She had a shot at appearing in a principal role at one of the most prestigious theaters in London, performing Shakespeare, no less. It was simultaneously the end of Dora's music hall career and the end of the illusion that she needed him in any way.

35

On the top of the stairs, Theo was surprised to be accosted by her sister running straight into her arms. So off guard was she that she dropped Felix's play in an untidy heap of pages. "Hetty! What on earth—"

"It came!" her sister said, covering her trembling mouth. "My...courses," she gulped, "and I was so afraid they would not." She burst into tears, and Theo ushered Hetty back into her room with her arm about her shoulders.

"You have been worried about this the whole time," she murmured. "I did not realize."

Hetty nodded. "I have given you and Felix enough concerns without that on top of everything else," she said wryly. She collapsed into her armchair and pressed a hand to her breast. "I am so, so relieved. This means I need not scruple about Vincent."

Theo felt a sudden pang. "What do you mean, dear?" she asked, remembering Lil's words. Would this mean that Hetty no longer had any need of Vincent?

"Well, that I need not feel guilty about pursuing him," Hetty said so frankly that Theo sat down with a thud in the seat opposite her.

"Pursuing him?" she said faintly. It seemed funny to think of her sister in the role of ardent pursuer somehow.

Her sister nodded. "Yes. I told him everything, of course, everything that transpired with Matthew." Her expression hardened a moment. "Vincent insists he does not care and that it did not make him look at me any differently." She shook her head. "He has the most faithful and truest heart in all of England," she said stoutly. "No one could make me think differently. I know I did not always appreciate his finer qualities," she said, reddening, "but now when I look at him, they are *all* I see. I am quite mad at myself for not realizing

451

earlier that he is quite the finest man to have ever looked my way. I cannot fathom how I overlooked him all that time."

Theo smiled. "I am glad," she said with relief.

Her sister regarded her gravely. "You have never asked me what happened, Theo," she said gratefully. "I hope you know that I would never have gone to France if I had not believed his initial promise of marriage."

Theo nodded. "I have always known that," she said simply.

"Sadly, once we reached our destination, he made it plain that the only role he saw for me was that of his mistress."

"Hateful beast," Theo muttered, glad that Sir Matthew had a nasty surprise heading his way.

Hetty nodded. "He had even engaged a luxurious Parisian apartment for me and was most offended when I declined his generous offer. Things went rather sour after that. I was forced to find my own way back to England, without his company, a thing I might add, I was heartily glad to dispense with by that point."

"He did not…" Theo could not bring herself to utter the words.

"Force me?" Hetty asked, then shook her head. "No. And now it seems I am to escape my folly entirely without consequences." She sighed. "Though your and Felix's livelihoods may well suffer due to my actions." She shot a look at Theo. "You have all tried to shield me, but I am aware my actions have had certain repercussions when it comes to The Parthenon."

"We are better off without the support of such a stuffy lot of hypocrites," Theo said roundly. "Really, I have no patience with any of them and never have!"

Henrietta shook her head. "Tell me the truth," she said softly. "Is the theater staring ruin in the face?"

"No such thing!" Theo assured her. "Absolutely not. Clem and Felix are already putting their heads together to think of a plan. If you only knew the wage I command now, sister! Really, I think you should consider a career in music hall, for it is most lucrative," she rattled on, ignoring Henrietta's expression.

"And even if you do not think The Eagle is for you, there is still Felix's play!" she said determinedly. "You must read it after me. There is a wonderful part for you, the fair Dorinda, who is wooed by three suitors and cannot fathom which is the worthiest. I can see it playing to a full house, I promise you!"

By the time they left the house four hours later, Henrietta was once again her usual composed self and sat sandwiched between Theo and Harold in the hackney cab. She seemed agog at the hustle and bustle of the concert rooms and gazed about her in wonderment as they moved through the rabbit warren that was the back rooms.

"Oi! You, Dora Dabney!" shouted a woman's voice as they turned the final corner to the performers' rooms. Theo turned in surprise to find Florrie Foss accosting her in full stage costume. The curvy brunette pointed a frilly parasol in Dora's direction. "A word with you, young lady, if you please!" her voice rang out.

Theo obligingly turned and waited until the other woman caught them up. "I'm not so sure 'young' applies," she remarked humorously. "I'm fully six and twenty."

"Not sure 'lady' does either," the other responded promptly. "Not after the way you carry on on stage."

Theo smiled but refused to take the bait. "Perhaps not," she admitted, turning to Henrietta, who was observing their exchange with interest. "Miss Foss, this is my sister, Henrietta Fields, who has come along to spectate tonight. Henrietta, this is the star turn of The Eagle and Sun and top of its bill, Miss Florrie Foss."

Hetty assured Miss Foss she was pleased to meet her. Florrie looked Henrietta up and down. "Well now, aren't you a pretty one," she said dismissively, then turned back to Theo.

453

"Turns out, I had you all wrong," she said brisk and businesslike, extending her hand. "My friends call me Florrie, you can be one of 'em, if you like."

"I would love it!" Theo said, feeling a gratified smile break out across her face. They shook hands, a firm exchange on both sides.

"Let's go to lunch next week," Florrie said. "My treat. I want to 'ear all about it, your beginnin's and such like."

"That sounds wonderful," Theo agreed. "I, too, would like to hear about yours."

Florrie nodded. "Wednesday," she said. "I'll meet you out front. One o'clock sharp." Rather like royalty, she sailed past them, her wide skirts skimming the walls on either side of the corridor.

"I see what Harold meant," Henrietta murmured. "She is rather terrifying, is she not?"

"You haven't seen anything yet," Theo replied. "Just wait until you see her perform 'Mr. Mellar's Prized Marrow.' Then you will truly understand Harold's terror."

When they reached her dressing room, Theo found its way blocked with a huge bouquet of white tulips and purple hyacinths. Scooping them up, she opened the door and found Lil already in residence.

"There you are!" Lil exclaimed, wheeling around. "*So* sorry for not showing up this afternoon, sweetheart. I'll make it up to you, I promise." She stopped abruptly, catching sight of Henrietta.

"Do not give it another thought," Theo assured her. "I felt tired in any case and went home early."

"There she is," Lil said, stepping forward to awkwardly embrace Hetty. "Ain't seen you in an age, darlin."

"It's good to see you, Lil," Hetty managed to respond, though she looked a little self-conscious.

454

"Take this seat here, Hetty," Theo urged her sister as she looked around for a jar or vase big enough to accommodate her bouquet.

"Clem begging your pardon, is he?" Lil asked, eyeing the large bunch of flowers meaningfully.

Theo was reading the short accompanying note.

Sorry and I really mean that. You deserve to get everything you ever wanted. I never meant the sting in the tail, Dora. I was just disappointed. Friends it is. BE.

"Not at all," Theo insisted, though Lil's question seemed an odd one, as Clem sent her flowers to almost every performance. "These are from a friend."

"A friend what's done you wrong," Lil commented, exchanging a significant look with Henrietta.

Theo glanced up, startled. "Why do you say that?"

"Purple hyacinths mean regret and white tulips signify sorrow. It's the language of flowers," her sister explained.

"I doubt Mr. Ewell knows the language of flowers," Theo responded dryly. Though perhaps his florist did.

"Oh ho! From that young scamp, are they?" Lil looked diverted. "What did he do? Forget himself?" To her embarrassment, Theo felt herself turn very red. Lil whistled. "I thought the wind was in that quarter," she said sotto voce. "You tell him it's early days and Clem ain't got bored of you yet."

Theo opened her mouth, but Henrietta got there first. "I'm sure he never will grow bored of Theodora," she said quickly.

"Hah!" Lil huffed. "That's what we poor women always think, but—"

Mercifully a knock on the door interrupted them, for Theo could see Hetty's face was growing tense at the direction the conversation was taking. It turned out to be another bunch of flowers arriving, this time for Lil, who preened and cooed over them.

"Anyway," Theo said, reaching for her evening suit, "stop trying to distract us. We want to know what has happened with your husband. I was telling Hetty all about his astonishing return on the way here." She turned to her sister. "Hetty, would you mind putting all these flowers in water?" Her sister stood up at once and started filling up the jars. "Now, Lil, as we dress you must tell us all about it."

Lil laughed. "Just wait till you hear what's happened now, girls," she said with a wink, and as they got ready, Lil filled them in on the fact Johnny Longdon had been utterly stupefied to find that his mother had been supported by Lil all these years. "For it turns out, he's been corresponding with his sister all this time and she's been spinning him some right yarns! According to her, Mother Longdon had been living with *her* these past ten years. He's even sent them money, not a penny of which reached his poor old mother! Lord knows what Marianne's been spending it on, bonnets most likely," Lil sniffed. "Johnny's reeling."

"Surely his sister will be held accountable for her lies?" Hetty asked, pausing in the act of topping up the jars from the water pitcher.

"Huh! If she is, it'll be the first time, mind you. Their mother's spittin' mad. You should have heard her," Lil cackled. "There he was, on my doorstep, breathin' righteous indignation and holding forth about how I'd reap what I'd sowed in the hereafter and Mother Longdon bolts past me through the doorway and delivers him a great ringing blow to his ear! 'I know you ain't talkin' about my Lillian!' she says. 'The daughter what's treated me like her own. The daughter what's kept me off the streets this past ten years!' He didn't know where to put himself! Looked like he'd seen a ghost, he did!"

"Good!" said Theo. "I am vastly glad to hear it!" She frowned over her neckcloth. "I wonder how he found out your address."

456

"Most likely paid one of those hired thugs of Clem's," Lil said disparagingly.

"Not Eddie," Theo said quickly.

Lil clicked her tongue. "You and your favorites."

"And did Mr. Longdon seek out his sister yet?" Hetty asked. "It seems to me an odd thing that he started with you, Lil, considering he was so determined to reward the virtuous. Yet the first person he seeks out on reaching these shores is none other than his estranged wife."

Theo turned to look at her sister. "That, Hetty," she said, "is a very good point." She looked back at Lil. "He seems rather fixated on you, Lil, for someone who supposedly no longer cares."

Lil snorted. "He probably wanted to rub my nose in it. A surly, resentful creature is Johnny Longdon. Besides, the Montague-Smythe mansion is empty right now. Marianne's in Tunbridge Wells, so he can't even get a hold of her even if he wanted to."

Theo buttoned up her shirt. "Where's he staying? At a hotel?"

"Too right he is! He's plump enough in the pocket and there's sod all room for him round ours! Fasten me up, would you, love?" Lil said, turning her back to Henrietta, who was quick to oblige. "You should have seen his face, Theo. *Thunderstruck* is the only word for it." Lil chuckled again. "It was just as good as when he realized you was a woman."

*

That evening's performance went off without a hitch. As always, Theo soared like a bird before her audience. She tottered off stage, feeling her customary euphoria, her sister joining them in the dressing room afterward, full of congratulations.

"I don't know how you do it though," Henrietta confessed with a faint shudder. "It's so…raucous in there." She fanned herself with her hand. "I don't know that I could even look Miss Foss fully in the face after seeing her turn!"

Lil laughed, and Theo belatedly remembered to tell Lil of the thawing of relations with Florrie. "She's probably realized she's better off having you as a friend than a foe," Lil commented dryly. "You're not going anywhere and she's not getting any younger. You need to pick your battles once you're the wrong side of thirty." She turned to Hetty thoughtfully. "As for you, dear, don't write music hall off yet. You never know."

Hetty shook her head. "The only capacity I could see myself working here would be to serve as dresser to you two," she said, looking about the room which now appeared a good deal tidier after her ministrations. "You need one, you know. Even if it's only to deal with all these floral tributes!"

Theo was a little disappointed by this, but in truth, seeing Hetty in this setting felt wrong somehow. It was just not her sister's milieu, and she realized that now. "Did anyone spot Clem in there?" she asked lightly. Usually, she caught sight of him lurking at the back of the hall, but tonight she had not seen him once.

The others shook their heads and Theo wondered at the vague unease she felt. Everything had been fine between them that morning, she told herself, ignoring the way she had feigned sleep and not spoken a word. Unbidden, the words popped into her head. *Do you have any more secrets you are hiding from me?* And Clem's response—Clem's *guilty* response.

Then on top of everything else, there had been that disastrous business with Barty this afternoon. Theo's heart sank. She had been willfully turning a blind eye to the truth. Everything was *not* fine between her and Clem.

When she climbed into bed that night, alone and without word from him, and woke the next morning to an empty bed, she was even more convinced of that fact.

With a grim expression on her face, she dressed and made her way to The Eagle without more ado.

"Where's Clem?"

Jim looked up quickly at Theo's question and exchanged an uneasy look with Sidney. "He's—er—not here," he said awkwardly.

"I can see that," Theo responded patiently. "I've just been in his office and the fire's not lit." She braced herself. "Did he not sleep here last night, then?"

Jim darted his eyes meaningfully toward Sidney, who had now settled in for the duration and was now leaning comfortably against his broom.

"'E was dead drunk, darlin'," Sidney supplied. "Couldn't let him come 'ome like that to you like that now, could we?"

"Sid!" Jim burst out, sounding annoyed.

"What? What's the point in 'oldin' out on Dora? She's his wife, ain't she?"

"What's the point in taking him somewhere else to sober up if you're going to spill the beans in any case?" Jim retorted.

Theo leaned against Jim's desk. Winkling the truth out of a stoic type like Jim would take work. "Why was he drinking so heavily?" she ventured. "Some sort of celebration?"

Sidney made an explosive sound of disagreement. "More like the bleedin' opposite!"

Jim turned on him angrily. "If you can't keep your mouth shut, Sid…!"

Theo straightened up. "Sid, perhaps you and I should go for cup of nice hot cocoa."

"No, wait!" Jim said, looking alarmed. "Don't do that, Miss Dora."

She propped herself back on the desk. "Just why was Clem commiserating himself in a bottle, then?" she asked shrewdly.

"On account of—" Sidney started, only to be interrupted by Jim.

459

"Because he'd decided to fire you," Jim said heavily.

Theo gasped; she could not stop herself. "*Fire me?*"

"The silly sod," Sidney interjected.

Jim nodded. "He felt like he had no choice. For your own good, like."

"But *why* in the name of all that's holy?" Theo demanded.

Jim hesitated. "You should probably hear it from him," he said, looking troubled.

"How about you prepare me for whatever I'm about to walk into," Theo replied, steeling herself for a confrontation. "I would consider it a great kindness if you would."

36

Clem was not prepared for the sharp knock on the door. "Come in," he responded gruffly, guessing it was the razor he had requested and glancing at his unshaven face in the looking glass. He felt like hell, despite having washed. His suit was crumpled, and his pride dented.

Then he realized he could feel a lot worse.

Dora came into his room at The Prince Rupert Arms looking neat and pale and very serious. She shut the door behind her and sat herself down into the chair opposite him. "What's all this I hear about you having the cheek to fire me, Clem Dabney?" she asked with perfect composure.

He reared back like she had slapped him. "How did you—? *Bloody Jim!* Did he tell you the rest?"

"It wasn't really Jim's fault. Sidney was the one that blabbed."

"I can't rely on any of them when it comes to you!" he said wrathfully.

"Well, that's neither here nor there." Theo shrugged. "I want to hear it from your lips."

"Did he tell you about Howard's offer?" Clem persisted. "About *Twelfth Night* and The Princess Royal? And starring opposite that actor, the one that plays all the big roles." She nodded her head. "They reckon they'll tour with it to Europe. Paris, Rome…" he listed before trailing off. "All those places."

"Paris?" she echoed.

"You've always wanted to go there; you once told me." He had to drag the words out. Each one was an effort, and he had to swallow down the bitterness rising in his throat.

"It sounds like a wonderful opportunity," Theo said quietly.

The feeling in Clem's gut soured. "You should do it," he said abruptly.

"Do you really think so?"

461

"Of course. Your talent deserves more than being reduced to a smutty joke."

She stiffened a moment at that, a red flush mounting her cheeks. Then she seemed to force herself to relax. "Can you imagine us in Paris?" she continued lightly. Even looking at her somehow hurt. "On the Avenue des Champs-Élysées, perhaps." She tipped her head to one side. "Since I met you, Clem Dabney, all my dreams have come true."

He gave a harsh laugh. "Nothing to do with me this time. Maurice Howard is your man."

"And whose stage brought me to Maurice Howard's attention? Yours. No one else's. No one else ever afforded me the slightest chance. No one ever looked at me twice before you, Clem." Her utter conviction defeated him. *Christ.* He closed his eyes a moment. He could not do this anymore.

"Dorabelle…" he started, then dropped the affectation. That was bullshit too. He had only called her that in jest. He had not thought her beautiful at the time. Far from it. "Theodora," he started again. "Let's just drop the act for once, love."

Her enquiring gaze flew to meet his. "We've reached the end of the road, and I think we both know that. I've got what I wanted out of this marriage and so have you. I've got my theater and you've got your glittering career." He swallowed. "The time has come for us to go our separate ways now. You to the left, me to the right."

"Me to the left and you to the right," she repeated, folding her hands in her lap. "Just what do you mean by that, Clem?"

"This is where you start your real adventure," he said coolly. "This is where you start down the path you should always have taken. Take a lover, hell, take two. You need to make up for all that time you lost." Her pretty color drained away, then flamed back in her face livid and red.

Good, she should be angry. He was a liar and a cheat, and the blinkers needed to drop from those eyes for once. "You say no one ever looked at you twice before me," he carried on conversationally, snatching up the half-empty bottle of liquor from the table and pouring himself a measure with hands that weren't entirely steady. "Well, truth is, I never looked at you twice either, Dora."

He knocked back the drink, then poured himself another, steeling himself for the task ahead. He knew exactly where to hit her. He knew all her weak spots. She had laid them bare to him over the past three months, holding nothing back. She was brave like that. Brave and…fucking foolish, laying herself open to a bastard like him.

"I know you think I took one look at you and saw your untapped potential, but the fact is, Dora, that I thought you were as useless as everyone else." He swallowed down the second shot glass of fiery liquor. It burned in his throat and numbed the self-disgust he felt clawing at his gut. "When I sent you out on the stage that first night, I fully expected you to fall flat on your arse. No one was more surprised than me when you turned that crowd."

Carefully, he replaced the shot glass on the table before he mustered the strength to look at her again. She was sat very still and expressionless, breathing fast. Her fingers clutched at her skirts and her eyes darted here and there about the room, focusing intently first on a chair, then on a picture frame, anywhere but at him.

"There's nothing special about our connection," he continued brutally. "You're just—" His words broke off as his throat closed. *You're just the latest in a long line of women who have warmed my bed* was what he had intended to say, but his traitorous lips would not form the words. His throat closed on them. Great, now even his ready tongue had abandoned him. He was forced to finish instead with an eloquent shrug.

"Nothing special," Dora supplied.

Her words made him suck in his breath. "Don't be fucking stupid," he snarled. "They want you in The Princess Royal. They'll want you in Paris. You're something special alright."

"Just not to you."

His gut twisted. "You knew what I was when you married me," he said coldly.

She nodded and stood up, walking toward the table. He let himself stare at the back of her lovely neck one last time before he let a cold numbness take over.

"I think I'll take Barty Ewell as my first lover," she said conversationally, picking up the bottle he had abandoned. He stiffened and took a ragged breath. She sniffed at the bottle. "What is this?" He did not even know. He had drunk two glasses of it and not tasted a drop.

When he did not answer, she poured herself a splash in the same glass he had used. Her hand didn't even tremble, damn her. "Harold doesn't really appeal to me anymore," she mused. "It turns out I like something a bit...rougher."

Clem felt his gorge rise. "You will not touch that bastard while I'm still living," he seethed.

"Who?" she asked, lifting a brow. "Barty?" She tipped her head to one side and considered him a moment impartially. "No, perhaps you're right. Ruby would likely scratch my eyes out too. I should probably wait for Paris before I embark on my trail of debauchery." She tipped her head back, then slammed the glass down on the table, wiping the back of her hand across her mouth. "My, my," she choked out, her eyes watering. "That stuff is...quite something."

"Pour me another," he said tightly. He would take a pull from the bottle, but he wanted his lips to touch the glass the same spot hers had. It would be the last time he got to taste her. The thought caused him a blast of almost physical pain. What the fuck was wrong with him?

464

Dora obliged at once and handed him a brimming glass. He took it and turned the glass before tipping it into his mouth. She watched him without comment. "Mr. Pfeiffer is French, is he not?" she asked brightly, and Clem saw red.

Flinging the glass to the floor, he crushed it under his heel as he yanked her into his arms. "Don't fucking push me, Dora," he growled, seconds before his mouth slammed into hers. She accepted his tongue, and he shoved her backward toward the wall.

She did not even try to resist, wrapping an arm around his neck and molding her body to his. "*You're* the one doing all the pushing," she pointed out breathlessly. "Trying to push me away."

He ignored the words, which were as annoyingly perceptive as ever, and concentrated instead on the tremor of emotion in her voice. He closed his eyes and rested his brow against hers. "You deserve better than me, Dora."

"Clem," she said, "I refuse to let you be tiresome about this. And it's not just me that's cross with you. Jim is spitting mad."

He gave a short laugh. "Did you listen to a damn word I said to you?"

"Very little of it," she said briskly, "was worth listening to." He huffed, turning his tired face aside. Dora reached out and caught his chin, turning his face back to her own. "What do you want me to do? Fly into a temper that you had no faith in me? Challenge you to a duel? Weep into a cushion, maybe? Hmmm?"

"Not weep," he said quickly. "But—"

She reached out a hand and struck him sharply on the right cheek. "*That* is for not believing in me, Clem Dabney!" He caught his breath and stared at her. She leaned slowly forward and kissed a spot on his stubbly chin. "And *that* is for giving me my big break anyway. What now?"

465

He held her challenging gaze for a moment before he swallowed. "Do it again," he muttered, turning his face to present his other cheek.

Theo hesitated only a moment before delivering a stinging slap to his left cheek. "That is for grossly deceiving me," she said briskly. Then she leaned forward and kissed the tip of his nose. "And that is for having my back in any case."

His breathing quickened. "You can't just forgive me like that," he muttered, his gaze falling away.

"Who says I cannot? You have a checkered history and a shady reputation, but I don't worry about either of those. What's another transgression between friends?"

"We're not friends!" he said through clenched teeth.

"Lovers, then," she suggested lightly and watched his expression turn furious.

"You're my *wife*, Theodora!" he exploded, his chest heaving. "Make no mistake about that."

"Yes," she agreed blithely, "but since you don't deserve me at all, I think we should start again from scratch."

"What the fuck are you talking about?" he fumed, releasing her and striding across the room to put some needed space between them. He stared moodily out of the window at a gray, cheerless day outside.

"Does your head hurt?" she asked sympathetically.

"No, it does not!" It was pounding, but what did another lie matter?

"Good, then if you are feeling up to it, we can get back to the business at hand. Here's the thing, Clem, even if you had no belief in my talent at the time, you still launched me to the public and championed my cause. Won't you take some credit for that, at least?" He pressed his lips together.

"The entire reason you wanted to get into the theater business was for another source of income now your boxing career is winding down. A thing which was highly sensible of

466

you," Dora continued stoutly. Clem rubbed his eyes which felt now like they were burning in his head like hot coals. "And for that you needed me," she continued calmly.

"You?" he repeated in a raspy voice.

"I'm your man," she corrected him swiftly. "Well, woman."

"You're my woman?" She didn't miss the catch in his voice.

"Yes. And I don't mean that you won't be a vital part of getting The Parthenon back on its feet, for I think you will have some very valuable input. I just mean that, well, your first responsibility is toward me."

"As my star turn?"

"As your wife," she corrected him, and he fell silent. "You see, I need you here with me, Clem. By my side. It is not that I cannot, but that I will not do without you. Not when we should be *together*."

*

Theo was not at all sure she was getting through to him now. He had responded so nicely when she had prodded his jealousy. Now that she was appealing to him reasonably, he seemed to have gone all stubborn again.

She took a deep breath. "You hurt me very much when you said that we should go our separate ways—"

He made a noise in his throat and twisted his torso. "You don't understand," he said, breathing hard. "It's—well—better all-round if we part altogether, just make a clean break of it."

The words cut through her like a cruel blade. "Better?" she echoed, staring at him. "For us to part?" She felt a heaviness overwhelm her chest that had not been there before. It pressed down so hard she found it suddenly difficult to draw in a breath.

"Yes, damn it!"

"How could that be?" she faltered, feeling utterly lost.

"Better than me ruining your whole entire career, everything you've worked so hard for and dreamed of all your life!" he answered angrily. "Do you know how tempted I was to tell Howard that no, he could not have you for his damn production? That on top of that, I forbade you leave London? To tell him you were not permitted to leave my side? I nearly did it, Dora. I nearly destroyed your dream to appease my own damn feelings!" He closed his eyes. "The worst thing is, I would have done it without reproach," he said bitterly. "I could have sabotaged your whole life as though it were my perfect right."

"You wouldn't do that," she said with conviction.

He gave a harsh laugh. "Oh, believe me, it was a close-run thing. Ultimately, I decided I would be the better man and cut you loose."

"Is that what you are doing?" Theo felt a spark of anger. "Being the better man, by *breaking my heart*?"

"Better I broke your heart than your dream," he said stubbornly.

"Why could you not simply join me in my dream?" she practically yelled. "Is that so hard? To be my manager first and foremost."

His expression grew rigid. "And be a kept man like my father?" he asked tensely.

"What are you talking about? You're a successful businessman and entrepreneur in your own right. You discovered me!"

"Discovered you?" he scoffed. "You presented yourself to me on a platter. I did nothing."

"Believe me, no one else would have accepted that platter. Why can you not see it?" she despaired, walking across to the opposite side of the room and facing away from him as terrible doubts began to assail her.

"Where are you going?" he asked sharply.

"Nowhere," she whispered, wiping her sleeve across her eyes. "Home." Her stomach lurched with sudden sick conviction. "If you—" She broke off her words and sucked in a painful breath, stumbling to look out of the nearest window. "Clem, will you be honest with me? Did I misread everything between us?" she asked, her voice wobbling. "I thought…but perhaps you do not. Perhaps I'm making an utter fool of myself and you're just trying to…to be gallant about it."

"Turn around!" His voice was harsh. "Dora, let me see your face."

She shook her head as tears coursed down her cheeks. *Oh God.* She had felt so sure that this was just some stupid misunderstanding, but what if the simple fact was, he did *not* love her? What if he was tired of her? Tired of it all? After all, The Parthenon was sinking fast, and for all his scheming, Clem had shown precious little interest in it. What if he wanted to be free of her *and* his bad investment and she had stupidly failed to read the signs?

When she really looked at it, this was the only solution that made sense. She barely heard him cross the room. The next thing she knew, Clem's arms were around her.

"Don't, sweetheart, don't cry," he said gruffly. "I'm not worth these tears."

She shook her head. "You didn't mean to hurt me," she said blankly. If only she could stop trembling. She must look such a pathetic creature, and she wanted to be brave and bold and—well, Dora Dabney. But underneath it all, she was still the same woeful creature she had always been. "It is just one of those things," she said numbly. "We haven't ruined each other's lives or anything of that nature. We can just—"

"What the hell are you talking about?"

"You should have just told me you did not love me!" she burst out in a sob. "You should have been honest with me." She struggled like a mad thing. "Then I would not have been so

469

foolish and…and so blind! I wouldn't have made such an exhibition of myself!"

"Of *course* I fucking love you!"

"No, Clem." She shook her head wildly. "I know now that you do not—beyond a shadow of a doubt!"

He growled low and tightened his grip on her so hard that she was forced to stand still. "I love you so much I've lost my damn reason!"

"No," she whispered, screwing up her eyes. "No, stop it, stop this, please. We can put it right with no harm done! Just—please—not another word. I can't bear it! *Please*, Clem."

He scooped her up in his arms and carried her over to the unmade bed, flinging her down and then following her so he landed heavily on top of her. Theo lay winded, blinking up at him. "I love you!" he said shakily, smoothing her hair back from her brow and framing her face with his hands. "Whatever doubts are rolling through that clever head of yours are my fault, and mine alone. You're right. Nothing I said made a damned bit of sense. I've been acting like a bloody fool. My place is here, beside you, always. Till death us do part. That was what I signed up for."

"No, Clem, you did not," she whispered.

"Yes, I did," he insisted.

"It was just a business arrangement," she reminded him painfully. "I lost sight of that fact and—"

"*I* lost sight of that fact long before you did!" he interrupted her loudly. "I started wanting you way, way before you even noticed me as a man." Two more tears leaked out of her eyes and ran down the sides of her face. "God, *please* don't cry, Dora," he appealed desperately. "I love you so much. Please tell me I haven't fucked this up beyond repair." He lowered his brow until it rested against hers.

"I watched you on that stage, night after night," he said in a low, insistent voice. "I could not take my eyes off you, and I finally realized I had married a fucking *genius*. A genius, Dora, a one-of-a-kind, bona fide genius. And you had been overlooked, ignored, and neglected for *years*. No one had noticed what a jewel you were, what a fucking gem of a woman, a masterpiece." He lowered his mouth to hers and kissed her hungrily, desperately.

He tore his mouth away frustratedly. "Then, suddenly, *every* fucker noticed it. I just felt—God, I felt so unworthy of you," he admitted rawly. "Even Harold Allsop is more deserving of you than me," he pronounced with loathing. "At least he can make himself useful and write songs for you." He ground his teeth as though admitting that had cost him. "I won't stand aside for him though," he vowed with ill-concealed resentment. "Don't expect me to be noble about it, because I won't!"

Dora blinked. "Clem—" she began, but he cut her off.

"*Please*, Dora," he begged. "I swear to God, I will never act so fucking stupid again if you'll just give me this one last chance." She swallowed and nodded, and his face lit up. "*Sweetheart!*" he groaned. "You will?" As though unable to stop himself he started dropping kisses indiscriminately over her face. "I swear I'll try and be the man you deserve," he promised.

"Just don't be a blithering idiot again," she said with a spurt of spirit. "How about I settle for that?" He gave a choked laugh. "You *scared* me, Clem!" she admitted, growing serious again. "So badly. For a horrible moment, I thought you didn't care. I thought it was just me."

"*No*, never, never, never," he vowed, his hand sliding down to cover her heart. "I was scared too," he admitted, pulling back to let her see his sincerity. "I've never lost my heart to anyone before, and it was bloody terrifying. I was so fucking scared, Dora. I thought you would notice that I wasn't fit for you to wipe your shoes on."

471

"Clem!" she protested.

"It's true, my darling, but if you love me, then…it doesn't matter if I'm unworthy," he said simply. "I'll just make it work." He looked at her searchingly. "Tell me you love me, Dora."

"I love you."

"*God*, I've been such a fool. How can you possibly put up with me?"

Theo smiled at him again, with more conviction this time, and he lowered his face to hers, groaning into their kiss.

"I love you," he rasped. "I've been so fucking miserable. We've only been apart two nights our whole marriage and I can't tell you how much I regret both of them."

She lifted her arms to circle his shoulders. "I love you too," she whispered. "I missed you badly too. It feels like it was longer than two nights."

He stroked her face, gazing down at her for a full minute without words. "I'm a fortunate man. How did I get so lucky?" After a moment, he grimaced. "I expect your family wants my blood."

"No," she admitted. "I don't think they've even noticed we've been fighting. Lil was the only one who picked up on it."

His arms tightened around her. "What did you tell Lil?" he asked gruffly.

"Well, she sort of found out about Barty, and she thinks you're a jealous type so she drew her own conclusions."

"Turns out she's right," he murmured.

She gave a gurgle of laughter. "You can't be as bad as her husband. *Ten years* they were estranged. We've only been apart two nights and they weren't even consecutive nights."

He grunted but did not look interested in pursuing this subject. "There's something else I should tell you. I do really want a baby with you, Dora," he said gruffly. She glanced down. "You shouldn't agree to it, not for a long time," he added, his gaze sliding away from hers.

"Why shouldn't I?"

"Because you're the toast of London," he pointed out. "And career highs do not last in this profession. You should make the most of it while yours shines bright."

"My career will last," she said with such confidence that he turned his head to look at her. She nodded slowly, propping a hand under her head. "I mean what I say. I'm a character actress, Clem, not a beauty. My ability to portray sporting vicars won't fade."

He seemed to consider this. "You won't be able to portray young bucks when you're big with child," he pointed out.

She shrugged. "So then I'll play fat old bishops."

He laughed at that, but it quickly faded as his eyes roamed over her face. "You're really not worried, are you?" His tone was slightly awed.

"No. Besides, my husband's a successful businessman. Even if my work does dry up eventually, he can afford to keep me in relative comfort. And any children that come along," she added as an afterthought. "If all else fails, you can always take up that match with The Diamond," she joked.

Clem smiled briefly, but he was breathing hard. "You mean it?"

She nodded. "Every word. Though we should probably delay having a baby until we've got The Parthenon back on an even keel."

He swallowed. "When I was feeling really insecure, I worried I'd unconsciously tried to sabotage you that time I almost forgot," he admitted, looking guilty as hell.

Theo laughed softly. "You've reminded me of my preventative more times than I can say," she pointed out gently. "You would never jeopardize my career."

"No, I know."

She jabbed him suddenly in the ribs.

"Ow, what was that for?"

"That," she said tartly, "is for suggesting I take a lover! Two lovers," she added belligerently.

"God, don't," he groaned. "You punished me for that already. As soon as I said it, I wanted to rip my own throat out. Then you brought up that fucker Ewell…"

"Yes, that *was* a low blow," she admitted, running a hand over his shirtfront, "but you hurt my feelings, so I wanted to strike back where it hurt."

"A low blow?" he repeated. "It was damn near fatal!" She gave a gurgle of laughter and dropped her face onto his chest. "Are you laughing?" he asked incredulously.

"It's just…you're being so dramatic, Clem. And *I'm* supposed to be the theatrical one!"

He rolled her onto her back. "You think I'm exaggerating?" he demanded.

She gazed at him, shook her head, and then reached up to cup his face with her hands. "You make me so happy, Clem Dabney," she said with feeling.

"God," he groaned. "I'm so in love with you, it's embarrassing." Theo spluttered. "No, it's true," he insisted. "I think everyone at The Eagle knows it too. In fact, I *know* they do, looking back on the cryptic comments I've received these past couple of months. I thought I was so bloody clever, tricking you into marriage. Then you wrapped me right around your little finger, right from the very beginning."

Theo peeped up at him. "Whereas I think I fell in love with you when you bought me my first suit." He laughed. "Clem," she said, running a hand down his shirtfront. "If I tell you something now, something that is very important to me and which you may find hard to believe, will you hear me out?"

He drew back at her serious tone. "Of course. Tell me."

"Viola's role may not precisely be a breeches role," she said, "but it is in the same kind of spirit."

"A what?"

"A breeches role. You remember I told you once, it is a role written for a woman to be masquerading as a man."

"Yes. That is why Howard said it would be the perfect role for you," he answered with a frown.

"But playing those kinds of roles is not my dream, Clem. The Princess Royal is a beautiful theater, with a wonderful history. It has put on some truly wonderful productions. And Orlando Kirby is a fantastic actor. But I don't *want* to appear opposite him as his leading lady; I never have. I want *his* roles! Don't you understand, Clem?

"*Twelfth Night* is a wonderful play, but my dream role in it would not be Viola but Feste the jester. Or even Sir Andrew Aguecheek! I know exactly how I would play him, Clem." She could hear the enthusiasm in her own voice. Clem was staring at her hard. He was actually listening and hearing what she was saying. Her heart sang. "Oh, he would be such a pitiful creature, Clem. I'd play him with *such* pathos. I'll have all the ladies weeping into their handkerchiefs and wanting to mother him.

"And Clem, I just *know* you're going to make this dream come true for me too," she said with utter conviction. "Just like you made *all* my other dreams come true." She nodded her head. "We're going to put Shakespeare on the stage at The Parthenon, and people are going to come and see it. People from *all* walks of life, not just the titled or the monied but *everyone*.

"I don't *want* a life performing just for the privileged few," she continued passionately, "and let me tell you, that would be *truly* throwing away my talent because being born with a silver spoon in your mouth does not make you *any* cleverer or more compassionate or more *worthy* of being entertained and transported away from the constraints of the role you were born

475

to in life. If anything, someone born to less privilege deserves my talent more, for they have more they need to escape from!"

Clem blinked and made a sound of cautious agreement in his throat. She nodded her head, seemingly satisfied that he was still on board, and wrapped her arms about his neck. "Believe me, I'm going to play the roles I want in life, Clem. And you are going to help make it so. Shakespeare *will* play at The Parthenon, but first," she said briskly, "we are going to produce Felix's play."

"Felix's play?" he repeated blankly.

"Yes, *The Maiden's Dilemma*."

"So, you're telling me your brother's a better playwright than William Shakespeare?" he asked. That silenced her. "Here's the thing, Dora. We both know if I march into that house and tell your brother and sister you've been offered a chance to star in a first-class production of Shakespeare at The Princess Royal, they will both say you would be crazy to turn it down. *Even* against their own best interests. Because they know it's true."

She took a moment before answering this. "Maybe Felix and Hetty *would* agree with you that I should take Mr. Howard up on his offer," she admitted judiciously, "but that is because they are both a little bit snobbish at the end of the day and hanker for acceptance in certain circles. Let me tell you they will also be *vastly* relieved that I have no intention of taking him up on it, for though they both love me, they do not love me with one-tenth of the unselfish devotion that you do, and they most assuredly do *not* put me first and foremost in their lives as you do."

Clem swallowed at this. "Dora," he said raspily, but she interrupted him, keen to make her point.

"First you try to tell me music hall isn't good enough for me, and then you tell me that light entertainment pieces aren't worthy of me, and I just don't believe in that way of thinking,

476

Clem. I tell you, I get the same rush, the same satisfaction for performing for the crowd at The Eagle and Sun as I ever would at The Parthenon, and that's nothing but the truth. Do you really think I mean to abandon the likes of Mrs. Warrender when they need me to bring a little bit of joy into their lives?"

"Mrs. Warrender?" he repeated blankly.

"Vincent's neighbor," Theo explained. "And let me tell you, I honestly believe that Felix has written something that has the potential to run and run," she continued earnestly. "Particularly if we could persuade Harold to write a few numbers to intersperse throughout. We can produce it in-house at little expense. Hetty can play the beauty and I"—she drew in a deep breath—"I want to play one of the male roles, Clem." She felt the excited flush climbing her neck. "Felix may take a little persuading," she admitted with a wince, "but—"

"We'll persuade him," Clem interrupted her grimly. "After all, you'll be the one bringing in the crowds, Dora. No one else."

"I just know we can do it," she enthused. "I can feel it in my bones! There's even a role in it that would be perfect for Florrie Foss," she admitted, biting her lip. "If she can only be persuaded to take it!"

Clem's eyebrows rose. "What role?"

"A vulgar, social climbing widow," Theo admitted. "She would be fantastic in the part. I bet Felix would love that too. She made quite a conquest of him the other night." Clem snorted. "In any case, I have no intention of abandoning The Eagle," she told him squarely. "Even when we are performing *The Maiden's Dilemma*, I can still appear there a couple of times a month at the very least. Do you think I am going to let them forget me?"

"You would not manage that in a hurry," he said with a brief smile that faded fast. "Did I really make your dreams come true, Dora? Even though my motives were far from noble when I put you on that stage?"

"Yes, you did, you wicked man," she said fondly, laying her hand against his stubbly cheek. "And not just my dreams of stardom either. I also mean your falling madly in love with me. I never expected anyone to do that, Clem. I dreamed of the successful career I wanted all the time. My life was one long daydream before I met you. But I never dared to dream of falling in love with a husband of my own who wanted a family and a future with me."

"Dora," he breathed.

"Yes, my love?"

"I don't think I ever dreamed before I met you. Not my entire life."

"And now?"

He nodded. "I want a place in your dream," he said softly. "At your side."

EPILOGUE

Six Months Later
The Parthenon

It was the opening night of *The Maiden's Dilemma* and Clem's attention was glued to the stage. To his surprise, Dora had not demanded the part of the romantic lead in the play. No, that role had gone to Lionel Greenfinch, an actor who was a favorite of his brother-in-law's. Neither, to Felix's relief, had she requested the part of the debonair second suitor; that role had gone to another actor friend of Felix's, James Fitton.

Instead, the role that Dora had requested and ultimately won had been that of the youngest and third of the suitors. Clem had secretly read the play and had been baffled by her choice. He could not see what had attracted her to the role of Ralph Bixby, who had arguably the least dialogue out of the three principal male parts.

In rehearsals, Dora kept her performance low-key. She recited her lines, marked her spots, and listened with grave attention to everything her brother and Symes, the assistant stage manager, said. But Clem had not been fooled; Dora had a vision, and he could not wait to find out what she was going to do with it.

Night after night he had watched her scribbling on her copy of the script, underlining things, circling things, and jotting notes in the margins. He had tried his level best not to give in to his rampant curiosity, but finally, the night before, as they had lain on their bed together side by side, he had snapped. "Alright, that's it," he had said, flinging down his own notebook and turning toward her.

Dora lowered her pencil. "What is?" she had asked, clearly bewildered.

479

"I can't stand it anymore," he'd admitted. "Just put me out of my misery and tell me."

"Tell you what?" Dora had asked, lowering her script.

"Tell me what you mean to do with this role, of course!"

Dora had caught her breath and stared at him before discarding her pencil and shifting around to face him head on. "You really want to know?" she'd asked with a faint catch in her voice.

"I'm *dying* to know."

A smile had slowly lit up her face, and she had shuffled closer to him, staring intently into his face. "You do, don't you?" she had breathed wonderingly. He'd nodded slowly. Then she had done one of her astonishing things and swung one of her legs over his lap until she sat fully astride him.

It had been Clem's turn to catch his breath, his hands immediately closing over her hips in a loose clasp.

"You really want to know, Clem?" she'd asked close to his ear.

Clem had swallowed. "Yes," he'd muttered huskily.

"Well," she whispered. "You'll. Just. Have. To. Wait. And. See."

Clem had turned his head to snag her gaze. He had felt faintly outraged and very aroused. "You're not going to tell me?" he'd asked, wanting for some goddamned reason to prolong the moment with Dora, confident and teasing. He loved it when she was like this. "Why?" he'd persisted. "Why won't you tell me?"

Her eyes had flickered as she'd considered this, a funny look spreading over her face. "It's almost…like a wish," she'd said hesitantly. "As if speaking it aloud puts it into jeopardy somehow and I want it to come true, so badly." Clem had watched her then, his gaze riveted to her face. "It almost feels like when we were engaged," she'd admitted self-consciously, and Clem's heart had flipped right over in his chest.

"What about our engagement?" he had asked hoarsely.

"That month when we were meeting every Sunday. I kept it so close to my chest, and it made me feel so…excited and terrified all at once. It was the biggest and most wonderful secret I had ever kept in my life, and it was all mine. I didn't even really understand what I was feeling at the time. That came later. I just knew if anyone found out it would all come to nothing, all come tumbling down like a house of cards so I had to cherish it and guard it and hope and pray it came off like I hoped it would."

Clem had stared at her, breathing so hard she had finally noticed just how much her words had affected him. Realizing she had cherished their engagement so much, he had resolved at that very moment to buy her an engagement ring for their first anniversary.

On stage, the three suitors had sauntered into view for their first scene, and Clem sat up, brought back into the present moment. The audience shifted excitedly; it was a full house and almost all the seats were taken up with fans of Piccadilly Percy.

Lil and her husband, Mother Longdon, and Peggy were all sat in the same box as Clem along with Vincent, Vincent's special guest, Mrs. Warrender, and their own housekeeper, Mrs. Cherwell, with her husband, Herbert, in attendance. "Here she is!" Lil whispered excitedly, jostling the people on either side of her.

Clem barely registered the dialogue spouted by the first and second suitors in their clipped, well-bred accents, wearing their immaculate day suits. For some reason, instead of having a new outfit made up, Theo had elected to save the money and wear the second suit Charlie Finch had made all those months previously. The day suit of yellow and brown tweed.

On stage, stood next to Greenfinch and Fitton, Clem could see the suit was all wrong somehow. It looked…too loud and brash, he realized suddenly, and Clem cursed under his breath that he had not insisted she had a new one made up. Due to budgetary constraints, they had cut corners on the production in every way that they could, but he seethed inwardly that Dora should have been the one stinted on wardrobe.

He did not even think she had any good lines in this scene, he thought, trying to remember the swaths of Felix's "witty" dialogue, most of which had gone over his head. On stage, the Stepson sisters drifted past the actors, tricked out in their finest matching gowns. Most of the smaller roles were taken up by performers from The Eagle.

On stage, Theo pursed her lips and began to whistle loudly a popular vulgar tune mostly known by its chorus "You wouldn't know she was a natural redhead by her temperament alooooone." She aimed a sly, conspiring glance toward the cheap seats, who convulsed instantly with delighted laughter. A few male guffaws were also heard in the balconies before.

Christ. She was so bright, so clever, Clem marveled. So quick with her wits. In that one moment, and an unscripted moment at that, she had captured the audience in the palm of her hand. Instantly Clem knew who Ralph Bixby was. He was not cut from the same cloth as suitors one and two. He was from the wrong side of the tracks. He was a bit brash, a bit knowing, and a bit of a lad.

Clem wanted to know Ralph Bixby's story, and from the reaction of the audience, he knew he was not the only one. He trusted Dora to show them just who Ralph was and why he was there, throwing his hat into the ring for the fair Dorinda's hand.

Over the course of the next hour, he watched entranced as Dora played Ralph to the hilt. She played him with the aggressive stance of a prizefighter, not the languorous grace of Greenfinch's hero or Fitton's practiced polish of the young man about town. Clem recognized a few touches of Ewell at times and even himself, but it was not a direct impression of either of them. Instead, it was a masterful and composite sketch of a character she had assembled from many different parts, all making one unique sum.

And it was glorious. When Ralph strode across the stage, he inadvertently scattered what was clearly betting slips from his pockets. When the young men awaited their lady love's appearance in the parlor, Ralph shuffled cards with the unmistakably flair of a card sharp.

When he flirted with the heroine, though, Clem thought his lines no less insipid than the ones the other two uttered, but somehow, by a quirk of his eyebrows, the way his gaze dwelt on her mouth, just *something* about her delivery showed he was not a suitor who could be trusted to behave if no chaperone was present.

Then, too, Ralph would unconsciously tug at his collar or touch his knuckle to his nose in a casually ill-bred gesture that brought a ripple of amusement to the audience. A quick self-conscious glance about him to see if anyone had noticed his slip would make them titter even louder.

At the dining scene, Ralph would down the drink the butler poured him in one gulp, then watch the retreat of the bottle with plain regret written across his face. The audience guffawed again. When Dora's bored young man fidgeted with his empty glass, the actor who played Paton the butler, in a move of genius as far as Clem was concerned, retrieved the bottle and glided to Dora's side, refilling her glass.

The audience broke out into appreciative laughter. Dora's character gave the butler an approving nod which seemed to promise a tip later, and the butler trickled back to the ice bucket, his expression benign, but somehow his eyes seemed to twinkle even from twelve feet away.

When the actor playing Dorinda's father had finished his monologue and demanded the glasses be refilled, the butler returned and paused meaningfully next to Dora, who flourished her glass, apparently in need of replenishing once more. The audience once more broke out in mirth.

At one point, when Dora and the butler stood stage left and the main stage stood empty awaiting the heroine's entrance, Dora deftly slipped the butler a tip. The fluid way that Paton took the money, in a blink and you'd miss it, drew another gale of laughter.

His wife was so bold and creative, Clem acknowledged all over again. She read the audience and played off the other cast members so well. She was just a delight to watch. He was fascinated, fucking fascinated, there was no other word for it. He stared just as avidly as the rest of them. He'd bet Dora could even make Shakespeare watchable.

When in the third and final act, she delivered Ralph's lines on being refused by the heroine, she looked more wryly regretful than anything. Something about the way she delivered "Couldn't you, Dorinda?" managed to convey Ralph was more disappointed by Dorinda than by the rejection itself. As though he had hoped she would see past his lack of polish to his underlying heart of gold. It was as though you got to watch Ralph fall out of love with the heroine in that instant before your very eyes.

The discontented murmur in the cheap seats drew a half smile from Clem. It was obvious where their sympathies lay. "You daft cow!" burst out one vocal female to a rumble of agreement. "'E's worth ten of that twerp you've taken up wiv!"

The gallery shushed noisily, and finally Henrietta was able to speak her tearful lines of regret on breaking her youthful admirer's heart. Hisses and suppressed boos greeted her words, and Clem felt Vincent stir with annoyance at this hostile reception to his fiancée's performance. To add insult to injury, Vincent's own guest, Mrs. Warrender, was huffing and puffing with indignation. "What's she want to go and do a thing like that for?" she asked loudly and discontentedly.

Too bad, thought Clem, his smile fast becoming a broad grin. Dora was the crowd favorite here, even Florrie Foss's cameo as a frolicsome young widow could not charm them away for long from Ralph's corner. At the conclusion, her bow drew the biggest cheers and a standing ovation. Whistles and cries of "Dora!" and even "Good for Percy!" rang out about the auditorium.

Felix would have to write Ralph some more lines, Clem decided, swiftly standing and excusing himself from the rest of the box to make his way to her dressing room. They were meeting the others in an hour's time for a celebratory meal at Wards Hotel in any case.

Right now, though, Clem needed to see her flushed with success, wearing breeches with her shirt open at her neck. He wanted to put his lips there, right at the base of her throat and to taste her sweat. And she would be sweaty after her stage performance. It was strange to think that before Dora, Clem had always liked women perfumed and powdered and dressed up to the nines. That seemed a long time ago now. A long, long time ago.

Thank God she had her own dressing room these days.

Two Years Later
Paris

So, this was Paris, Theo thought with a contented sigh as she and Clem strolled along hand in hand. She was wearing one of her newest and favorite dresses in a flaming burnt-orange satin. It was bold and it drew the eye and Theo adored it.

No pattern was too complicated or concept too outlandish for Miss Clegg to tackle. Miss Clegg had in fact become Mrs. Grigson nine months ago, but she still made all of Theo's gowns, and over the past two years, she had introduced a dazzling array of colors and fabrics to her wardrobe. No more

485

did Theo espouse the cause of naturally dyed fabrics. She flaunted like a peacock these days in her finery, though she still adhered to the principles of artistic dress.

Theo also did not trouble to wear her false ringlets much anymore, except for Albert's benefit when he took her out to lunch. Albert was still sadly conventional in his outlook, but she forgave him as he was an unending source of amusement.

Only last month she had bought him a pocket watch for his fifteenth birthday, something he had longed for ever since his brother had bought himself a fine one. Theo had Albert's engraved *With dearest love from Dora* which had both highly gratified Albert and caused Clem to narrow his eyes at her.

"You are determined to keep me on my toes, Mrs. Dabney," he had complained. "You just wait till Jim hears about this."

Theo had laughed. "Jim will say it is quite your own fault," she had told him roundly, "for like Sidney, he is always on my side."

"Don't I know it," Clem had complained, but she knew he didn't really mind at all.

"I must send a telegram to Lil after lunch, do not let me forget," she said, pausing to consult her travel guide. "I think we need to turn left down here. Lil said that she and Johnny found a wonderful café on their second honeymoon that we simply must visit."

Lil had kept her husband dangling for six months before she had agreed officially to their reconcilement. She had blown hot one day and cold the next, allowing his attentions one minute and refusing them the next. Theo had almost felt sorry for him, but both she and Mother Longdon had agreed that Lil deserved to call the tune when it came to his second attempt at wooing.

Indeed, Johnny Longdon had been on the brink of despair before he hit on the happy notion of buying pretty silk shawls

not only for his mother and Lil but also for Peggy, which had
finally touched Lil's heart. Shrewdly, realizing this one gesture
had won him more favor than anything else, Johnny started
making up to Peggy, sitting with her and reading aloud to her
and including her on all the outings and treats he showered
upon Lil and his mother.

Peggy consequently became Johnny's greatest advocate,
and when he eventually bought a smart townhouse in Belgravia,
he made it clear that his dearest wish, after achieving his wife's
forgiveness, was for Peggy and his mother to make their home
with him also. He insisted on their input in even the smallest
detail, soliciting Lil's taste in carpets and furnishings, even
when she was adamant she still had no intention of ever living
with him again.

Despite the fact Theo and Lil appeared only twice a month
now at The Eagle and Sun, she had claimed her career came
first and foremost and her love life a poor second. Johnny had
solemnly sworn that he would never stand in the way of her
acting ever again. Finally, after the amount of pleading that Lil
deemed appropriate, she relented, and the Longdons moved into
their new plush residence along with Peggy. In fact, the only
member of the family who was not allowed to darken their
doorstep was Marianne Longdon, who was outraged to find her
brother had no intention of forgiving her.

From time to time, her mother would still meet with her for
tea and cakes, and on those occasions, she made sure to speak at
great length about dear Lillian's new diamond bracelets or the
portrait Johnny had commissioned of his wife which now hung
above their fireplace in pride of place. Marianne gnashed her
teeth with envy whenever she heard of her brother's
extravagance, but she could not stop herself from making
enquiries, presumably to report back to her employer, Mrs.
Montague-Smythe.

"We also have to find that music hall Allsop told us of," Clem reminded her mildly. "The one with the cancan girls."

Theo laughed. "Mrs. Cherwell was quite scandalized that he admitted to visiting it on his European tour last year."

Despite everyone's whispered conjecture about which of the Misses Stepson Harold might be sweet on, the person he actually ended up spending most of his time with these days was Eddie. In fact, the burly doorman had ended up moving into Harold's attic rooms with him after some falling out with his own landlord.

This was initially meant to be a temporary arrangement, but somehow twelve months later, Eddie had become so firm a fixture at number six Juniper Row, that no one even dreamed of asking when he would leave. Eddie was extremely useful when it came to fixing loose skirting boards and tidying the unkempt garden. He had many skills which the rest of Theo's impractical family lacked. It made him invaluable about the place.

Eddie and Harold had not only toured Europe together, but they traveled to and from The Eagle and The Parthenon as required in each other's company. Clem, when organizing the rotas, made sure their schedules coincided. "It has all worked out so well," Henrietta had remarked before Clem and Theo's sendoff dinner. "One could almost wish the two of them remain our unmarried lodgers forever. Is that so very selfish of me?" she had asked, turning to her husband.

Vincent had cleared his throat, but Felix had interrupted at this point. "I don't think we need to worry about that, old girl," he had said firmly. "Confirmed bachelors the both of them. I daresay they'll be rattling around in our attics till they're old and gray."

"Hear, hear!" Theo had said enthusiastically.

As Eddie had come lumbering into the dining room by this point, with Harold close on his heels, the conversation was swiftly changed to that of Vincent and Henrietta's firstborn

488

child which was due that summer and much anticipated. Names and possible godparents were floated and discussed at every meal with much enthusiasm.

Following the wild success of *A Maiden's Dilemma* which had run for a full nine months, Felix had dusted off another of his literary efforts, *The Erstwhile Suitor*, and this one had run for thirteen. Felix had been firm from the start that Theo should take the male lead in the next play. "If the character's not interesting enough for you, then tell me how to adapt him so he is," he had insisted, and after only a little demurring, Theo had done so. To her surprise, her brother had thrown himself wholeheartedly into the rewrites and she had been delighted with the result.

On the back of the huge success of both plays, the third floor of the house was converted for Clem and Theo's exclusive use and the second floor was shared between Felix, Vincent and Henrietta. They each now had their own bathroom and sitting rooms and Hetty was taking great pains converting the old sewing room into her nursery. Luckily Mrs. Grigson now worked from her own establishment in Battersea and did not require the space.

"Clem and I mean to keep our spare room for a nursery," Theo had confided in her sister the previous month.

Hetty had almost dropped the teapot. "Are you—?"

"No, not yet," Theo laughed, "but I think I need to set some time aside soon. I will be twenty-eight next month after all, and we have finally agreed that next winter will be when we bring Shakespeare to The Parthenon. I think I need to fit in having the baby before that."

Henrietta had looked a little taken aback, but Theo was taking the endeavor seriously. She had put a lot of time and effort into convincing Felix that a comedy and not a tragedy was what they needed to bring to the masses. *Much Ado About*

Nothing was the play they had finally agreed upon, with Theo playing Benedick to Florrie Foss's Beatrice.

Theo was of the private opinion that her brother had been in the throes of a full-blown love affair with Florrie the previous year. Their relations now seemed to have cooled off, but both were still frequently found in each other's company. It seemed they had formed a mutual fondness and respect for one another which promised a long-standing collaboration, now Florrie was looking to expand her range.

"I think it is nice that Hetty means to ask Lil to be a godmother to her baby," Theo mused. "They have grown so much closer. Indeed, I think they are quite as close as I always wished they would be."

"Mmm," Clem rumbled, glancing at the buildings on either side of the street. "I'm not sure we've turned down the right street," he commented, not sounding too concerned at the idea of a detour. "I can't see any cafés."

"If we have a son, I should like Eddie, Harold, and Vincent for godfathers," Theo continued.

Clem crooked an eyebrow at her. "Don't I get any say? I want Ben, Nye, and Nat," he said, promptly naming three of his prizefighter friends.

"Oh." Theo considered this. "Perhaps it might be a good idea if we have twins. Then they can have three each."

Clem laughed at this. "We do keep delaying this baby. Maybe twins would be a good idea after all."

"Well, they must run in the family," Theo pointed out. "Your half brothers are twins, are they not?"

Clem admitted this was so without pulling a face. For some time, Theo had tiptoed around the issue of Clem's family as though it was a sore spot, but he had opened up a good deal over the past twelve months. Now, no topic of conversation was off-limits to his wife. He even took her along with him to visit his uncle Dan where they ate grilled cheese on toast which his uncle called "rarebit" and fried sprats and drank beer, much to Clem's cousin Grace's displeasure.

"Can you believe we have been married for over two years by this point?" Theo mused, tugging Clem's arm toward a shop window. "Look at these sketches. They're not as good as yours."

Clem snorted. "Maybe I should get some supplies," he suggested after a moment. "I could draw you later on tonight, Mrs. Dabney." He waggled his eyebrows. "In the buff."

"What, again?" Theo asked archly.

Clem laughed. "You are shameless. I suppose that is what comes of marrying an actress."

"Hmmm, remember how you thought I was a terrible actress when you first married me?" she teased, glancing up at him. "Incidentally, what *were* you going to do if I had fallen flat on my face that first night? It never occurred to me to ask. Expected me to keep house for you?" she hazarded.

He snorted. "Christ no! Have you forgotten how I found you that day, covered in flour and burns from the stove?"

"Oh yes," she gurgled. "If not your housekeeper, then what?" she asked curiously.

"I had not really thought that far ahead," he admitted, a pucker between his brows. After a moment, he reached up and scratched the back of his neck. "I toyed with the idea of buying you into some business or other. Either that or retaining you in some advisory role for the theater. I wasn't worried; I would have found something for you to do about the place."

Theo nodded. "I expect you would have been very charming about it all, picked me up off the floor, and seen to my hurts, and very likely seduced me out of my mopes."

Clem glanced around to check no one was listening to their conversation. "Dora," he said in a strangled voice.

"Yes, Clem?" She bit back her smile. "You would have, you know. You would not have been able to help yourself.

Imagine how crushed I would have been. How helpless, lost, and needy—"

"I don't find helpless women particularly attractive," he put in dryly.

"No, but you had already started flirting with me, even when you thought I was a batty eccentric."

"When did I—?"

"'I believe I will call you Dora,'" she quoted. "And that was on our first meeting too. My sister was very shocked."

A lazy smile curled Clem's lips. "You had your legs out," he reminded her. "Even when you seemed a lost cause, you had fantastic legs."

Theo laughed. "You're the hopeless one."

"Besides, you got saucy with me first."

"Me?" She was startled by that. "I don't believe I ever did!"

"'Why Mr. Dabney, I would just love to see you punched repeatedly in the face,'" he mocked.

"That wasn't what I said at all!" Theo flushed and regarded him sidelong. "Anyway, how is that remotely saucy?"

"It was a great piece of cheek," he said firmly. "I considered putting you over my knee. As you were wearing breeches at the time, it gave my thoughts a peculiar bent. I took a good look at your backside as you walked away and thought your words were not the only pert thing about you."

"Clem!"

He laughed. "What? It's true."

"Incorrigible!"

"Anyway"—he screwed up his eyes—"it's hard for me to really remember with any degree of accuracy how I felt about you back then." He squeezed her hand. "How I feel about you now colors even my memories."

"That's rather a lovely way of putting it," Theo said, throwing him an appreciative look. "You do have quite a way

492

with words sometimes, Mr. Dabney," she sighed. "A way with words and a way with women."

He shook his head and swung her around to face him. "I'm strictly a one-woman man now, Mrs. Dabney." He leaned in and stole a kiss.

"Clem," Theo whispered and crooked her finger. "Come closer. I'm about to say something very shocking."

His eyes widened but he narrowed the gap between them. "What is it?"

"I have not brought my preventative to the hotel." He looked alarmed, but before he could say anything, she added, "Deliberately."

"Dora," he breathed. "Are you sure?"

She nodded, looking earnest. "I think we should start trying in any case. Otherwise, I'm not sure when we will fit a baby in. We are rather busy."

Clem cleared his throat and cast a quick look around them. "Shall we forget this café and head back to the hotel?" he suggested.

Theo's smile widened. "Yes, I think so," she agreed. "After all we can always order room service."

THE END

If you enjoyed this book, please consider leaving me a rating on Goodreads, Amazon, Bookbub or wherever else you leave your reviews. I would be very grateful.

You can find my website at: www.alicecoldbreath.com where you can sign up for my monthly newsletter and find out what I am up to.

Also, please do check out some of my other stories! Many thanks, Alice.

The Vawdrey Brothers Series:
Book 1: Her Baseborn Bridegroom
Book 2: His Forsaken Bride
Book 3: An Ill-Made Match

The Brides of Karadok Series:
Book 1: Wed By Proxy
Book 2: The Unlovely Bride
Book 3: The Consolation Prize
Book 4: Her Bridegroom, Bought and Paid For
Book 5: An Inconvenient Vow
Book 6: The Favourite

The Victorian Prizefighter Series:
Book 1: A Bride for the Prizefighter
Book 2: A Substitute Wife for the Prizefighter
Book 3: A Contracted Spouse for the Prizefighter

THE VAWDREY BROTHERS SERIES

Book 1 – Her Baseborn Bridegroom

Lady Linnet Cadwallader has been raised a helpless invalid in her own castle. Brought up to believe she will "never make old bones," she lives a quiet and lonely existence, hiding away her excessive freckles and red hair from a world that believes her to be hideously misshapen and ugly.

Until one day her uncle arranges a marriage of convenience for her, a marriage in name only with a young puppet groom…but Sir Roland does not show up. In his place turns up his baseborn brother Mason Vawdrey. And dark, forceful Mason is no one's puppet.

Things are about to get interesting at Cadwallader Castle. And Linnet is about to discover that maybe a golden leopardess does not need to change her glorious spots.

THE BRIDES OF KARADOK SERIES

Book 1 – Wed by Proxy

Thrice wedded, but never bedded, Mathilde Martindale has long lived in the shadow of her indomitable mother, and meekly done as she was told. Until one day she decides to become mistress of her own destiny and leave the royal court to find her own path.

Married by proxy, Lord Martindale has never even met his bride of three years. Wed as part of a peace treaty, he bitterly resents the mercenary wife who cares only for wealth and prestige. And then he meets her…

www.ingramcontent.com/pod-product-compliance
Lightning Source LLC
Chambersburg PA
CBHW020917020726
47495CB00002B/223